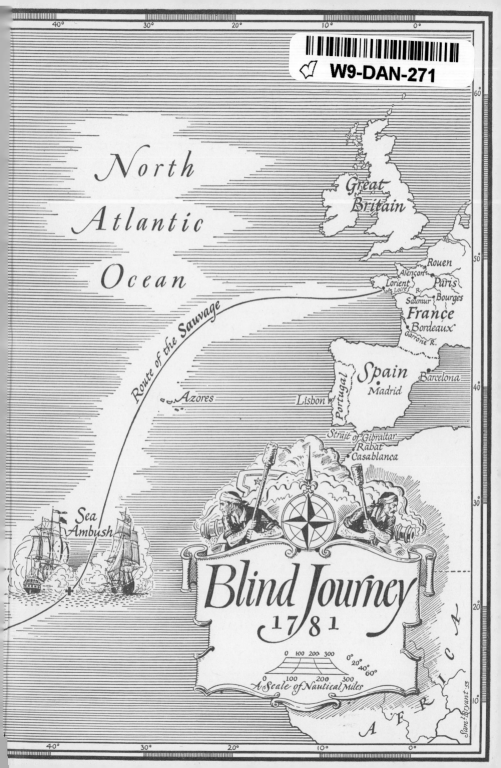

WHEN a ship is caught in a heavy storm at sea, life and hope depend upon the skill of the captain. He is singled out of the mass for his experience and ability.

The Library of
**STEVEN
KULDANEK**
Dedicated to
My Wife

BLIND JOURNEY

BLIND JOURNEY

BY BRUCE LANCASTER

AN ATLANTIC MONTHLY PRESS BOOK

LITTLE, BROWN AND COMPANY · BOSTON

ATLANTIC—LITTLE, BROWN BOOKS
ARE PUBLISHED BY
LITTLE, BROWN AND COMPANY
IN ASSOCIATION WITH
THE ATLANTIC MONTHLY PRESS

*Published simultaneously
in Canada by McClelland and Stewart Limited*

PRINTED IN THE UNITED STATES OF AMERICA

To

Jeannette *and* Dudley Cloud

Foreword

THE WANDERINGS and vicissitudes of Lieutenant Ward Gratwick in the year 1781 are, of course, fictitious. They are, however, shaped by a framework of known fact. They could have happened to an American who found himself on the river-peninsula of Passy during the days when Doctor Benjamin Franklin wholeheartedly devoted his amazing mind and talents to the service of the United States of America. A journey such as Ward's could have taken place. There were leaks in Franklin's entourage and many of his plans were thwarted. On the Doctor's known habits, methods and precautions, Ward Gratwick's movements were plotted.

Once at sea, the fictitious *Le Sauvage Royal,* with its imaginary captain, passengers and crew, followed a course based on what could have happened to such a ship in times like those. In all matters connected with the *Sauvage* I have been guided by the counsel of Mr. Charles H. P. Copeland, Curator of Maritime History, and of Colonel G. L. Smith, United States Army (Ret.), Curator of Maps and Charts, both of the Peabody Museum, Salem, Massachusetts. If in things maritime I have erred, it is because I have wandered from the course they so carefully and cheerfully charted for me. My thanks are due, too, to Mr. Ernest S. Dodge, director of the Peabody Museum, for many kindnesses and much assistance.

In the interests of clarity, I have referred to the estate in Passy where Franklin lived as the Château de Chaumont and to his house as the Petit Manoir. The more customary designations are the Hôtel Valentinois and the Petit Hôtel. The phrase *"men greatly in earnest"* which I attribute to Franklin is really out of its century, but it seemed so to fit his character and mode of thought and speech that I felt no hesitation in using it. It may be found in a letter from Governor Oliver Perry Morton of Indiana to Abraham Lincoln early in the Civil War, and is quoted by Bruce Catton in his memorable *Glory Road*.

In the Virginia scenes I have purposely done some telescoping of time. For example, the arrival of Washington at Williamsburg did not coincide with the appearance of the Duc de St. Simon's troops. The cavalry action between the Duc de Lauzun and Colonel Banastre Tarleton is moved ahead in time and altered in some details, but it is based on a brush that did occur between them. None of these small liberties, to the best of my belief, distorts the major currents and events of what actually did happen in the fall of 1781.

The public libraries of Beverly and Salem have been most helpful to me in this work, as have the Boston Athenaeum and the library of Harvard College. Beyond all else, I wish to record my deep appreciation of the always helpful and always constructive assistance of my wife, Jessie Payne Lancaster, throughout the research and writing of this book. She has been "greatly in earnest."

Bruce Lancaster

Beverly, Massachusetts

Contents

BLIND JOURNEY

I

The Hollow Tree

ON A HILLTOP crossroads just east of Marly-le-Roi, Ward Gratwick halted and looked somberly about him. The westering sun of that May afternoon in 1781 flooded golden along the valley of the Seine where fields and vineyards already lay faintly emerald with their promise of the harvest to come. His eyes played over the panorama spread before him, over the sweeping bends of the Seine, the distant Bois de Boulogne, and, far away, the sun-touched hill villages of Auteuil and Passy that masked the city of Paris off there in the east. But Ward found little pleasure in the soft gold-green landscape. He did not belong here.

Healthy, in his mid-twenties, a trained soldier — an American soldier — he should still be with the rumbling batteries of six-pounders that mounted guard with the rest of Washington's army along the Hudson. The memory of his capture by that British patrol in the fall of 1780 jabbed at his mind. That he, who had served as a gunner officer since 1776, should have been taken in by such a ruse! The jibes of his captors still rang in his ears.

His luck seemed to have quite run out when a few days after his capture he was packed aboard a swift brig for passage across to England. Then a French privateer had captured the brig and taken it in triumph to Bordeaux. Ward had hoped in vain for a transfer to another ship, America-bound, and a quick return to his cannoneers. Had he landed a week earlier he might have been able to take passage on the French frigate *Concord,* bound

3

for Newport and Rochambeau's French troops. Then the British blockade had tightened and French ships, unless in heavy convoy, were reluctant to set out across the Atlantic with its dotting of British sails. So Ward had been sent up to Paris — or rather to the suburb of Passy — to become part of the household of Dr. Benjamin Franklin.

This little household on the grounds of the Château de Chaumont had turned out to be stimulating and more than a little bewildering. And nothing in it was more stimulating, more bewildering than Franklin himself, that seventy-five-year-old philosopher-inventor-scholar-romanticist, the Boston-born Philadelphian, now first Minister of the Republic of the United States to the Kingdom of France. Franklin had begun by assigning Ward to routine clerical work under the eye of the Doctor's grandson, Temple Franklin. But Temple enjoyed the gay social life of Paris and became more and more absorbed in his flirtations with various French beauties, some of title, more of none. Gradually the Doctor had turned many details over to Ward. Now much of his work was of an importance and secrecy that made Ward catch his breath when he thought about it. There was the prodding of Spain to take a more active part in the alliance against England. There were matters that dated back to 1776 when the Doctor had first arrived in France, matters that dealt with dummy firms which shipped the stores of royal arsenals across to Washington. The Doctor watched closely the British agents as well as the many foot-loose Americans in France. Some of these Americans Ward thought stanch patriots until he saw the Doctor's files on them. Others, including a few supposed Tories, were really secretly working for the new American republic. Lately Franklin had even sent Ward on confidential errands, sometimes to the French court, sometimes to wineshops along the river below the pumping-works, on slow-gliding Seine barges, or to bright salons in the heart of the city.

The Doctor would say, "Go and see so-and-so. He's a pleasant fellow and you'll enjoy listening to him." Later Franklin would ponder long over Ward's reports of what he had heard. And lately the Doctor had opened his most secret journals to Ward, tracing the progress of this negotiation, of that, showing how some had failed, how and why others had been successful.

Ward scratched irritably in the dirt with his heavy knobbed stick. The work was probably well worth doing. And yet — as he gravely greeted a marquis at court or bowed over a white hand extended from a sedan-chair or when he listened to a cloaked man in a dim *auberge* who muttered that a hitherto unimpeachable American had been secretly to England and was now tossing gold pieces about, Ward's thoughts kept slipping back to America, to the rutted roads of Westchester County where the gun-teams labored on through the rain and cannoneers pushed desperately at mired cannon. That had been his life since 1776, that was where he really belonged. Trained gunner officers were at a premium, never more so than now, with the army, so far as he knew, melting away along the Hudson and tragic failure looming in the Carolinas. He ought to be back there with all those men to whom he was welded by a shared conviction. And there was another reason —

He looked sharply west toward Marly-le-Roi. Up the hill that led to the crossroads came shrill cries of *"Hue! Allez!"*, a slow pound of hooves and a rumble of wheels. A low, heavy tumbril was laboring upwards, the driver trotting along beside a massive gray draft-horse whose high collar was bright with brass and clamorous with little bells. He moved out onto the road with an easy, gliding step and held up his hand. As the tumbril came nearer, Ward saw that its wheels and slatted sides were brown with dried mud and its interior heaped high with turnips.

The driver, a short, swarthy man in a gray smock and red stocking-cap, checked his horse. *"Monsieur désire?"* he asked

5

grudgingly. His dark eyes were suspicious as they took in Ward's shabby clothes.

"You go near Passy, perhaps?" Ward's French was slow and halting.

The man edged away.

Ward went on. "I am American. I lodge with the Doctor Franklin, Doctor Benjamin Franklin, at Passy. Will you take me there?"

The driver flung up both arms and erupted into a torrent of French. *"De la maison du Docteur Franklin?"* He bowed, whipped off his red cap, bowed again. "But with pleasure. I, Nicodème Blanc, will take Monsieur to a little hamlet just across the Seine from the lower edge of the Bois de Boulogne. And there he will find a ferry of the most reliable. A few strokes of the pole and Monsieur will be but a short stride from Passy."

Ward settled himself among the turnips as the tumbril started off. The driver's sudden change of temper at the mention of the Doctor was one more proof of Franklin's popularity. It was amazing how Franklin had captured the hearts of the French people. Ward remembered the day the French privateer had landed him at St. Nazaire nearly three months before. He had seen engravings, drawings, paintings of Franklin in all the shop windows and decorating many of the inns. Snuffboxes, buttons, heads of canes, rings, printed handkerchiefs — all bore his likeness. Later in Paris he had noticed that the very mention of the Doctor's name melted the haughtiest of nobles, the most choleric of officials. Truculent gendarmes became affable, innkeepers exacted the barest minimum of payment. Nicodème, the carter, was only acting like most Frenchmen whom Ward had met.

As the sunlit countryside flowed slowly past, Ward thought of his latest disappointment. He had been assured, by a chance-met

6

nondescript American, who had wanted money for his information, that at Marly-le-Roi he would find a French skipper willing to risk the blockade and a swift run to America. Here, he had thought, was his chance to get home. But there had been no French skipper at Marly-le-Roi. Glumly Ward recalled the Doctor's comment that people who clutched at straws should first make sure the straw would float.

Why had he believed in a rumor from such a shabby source? Ward sighed resignedly. The answer lay as close at hand as the nearest turnip. He had wanted to believe. God, how he wanted to go home. It was not only the war. The war was an expression of his life and his convictions. Instead of the green-gold glow of the rich French countryside he saw in his mind's eye the rolling ridges that swept west from Marlboro toward Worcester and, at last, toward the high bastions of the Berkshire Hills. He saw his slender mother, silvery hair bright in an autumn morning, standing in the fanlighted doorway of the Gratwick house. There would be a cat or two purring about her ankles as she called to his big, ruddy father as he left for the family sawmills or the gristmills or the great forest stretches that the family owned, reaching right on to the shores of Lake Quinsigamond.

Those sawmills. He could smell the sharp, clean tang of fresh-cut lumber, the resinous scent of stacked pine boards that would someday be paneling in someone's drawing room. Was it the sight of all this raw material for homes and schools and churches that had first turned his mind, as far back as he could remember, toward architecture? He could remember playing on unsteady legs about the sawmill, stacking blocks and shavings into miniature houses. The urge to build had stayed with him through boyhood, through adolescence, into maturity, had led him to decline his father's offer to send him through Harvard. Instead he had bought books on architecture, many of them from the

7

bookshop of Henry Knox, now chief of Washington's artillery, many from the Tory Rivington in New York.

Jolting along among the French turnips, his early dreams came vividly into his mind. He had conceived a new type of architecture, one that would break free of the British and French types so universally favored in America. He had nothing against those types, save that they sprang from a different climatic, geographic and social environment. He had struggled toward a form of shelter that would spring from American soil, that would express American life and thought, as well as the unpredictable American seasons. Perhaps if the war had not come, he would by now have laid out a few tentative drawings on fine white paper.

To build, to create — that was what he wanted to do when the war was over, when America had won her rightful place among nations. He thought longingly of his home in Marlboro where his books and instruments waited for him, waited for an end of destruction and a beginning of creating.

Then there was Faith.

Always she was part of his dreams of the future. Even the genial afternoon sun of the Ile de France could not dispel his vivid memory of that raw night along the Schuylkill. Instead of the homely, comfortable scent of the turnips, he smelt the harsh reek of fog and melting snow that clung to the rough hutments on the hills by Valley Forge in far-off Pennsylvania. Ward had been overseeing the siting of two field-pieces beyond the camp of John Glover's Twenty-first Massachusetts Infantry, slush slopping through his broken boots. He would report on the guns to Henry Knox, and then retire to the drafty, leaking hut he shared with his friend, Caleb Blair, a gunner-ensign from Waltham.

The windows of the stone headquarters house shone gold in the dusk. He had hunched his ragged cloak about him, glancing casually into the room at the right of the entrance. The scene inside was far from the tempo of the Valley Forge camp, from the slightest hint of war.

He had seen Lady Washington seated in a deep chair, her calm, serene face bent over a length of linen through which her needle played in swift, darting motions. Beyond her, Kitty Greene, wife of General Greene, was slashing through a bolt of homespun with long gleaming shears. Lucy Knox stood with her back to the window, talking to someone who sat just beyond Martha Washington. Like Kitty Greene, Mrs. Knox was holding a length of homespun.

The scene was somehow unsettling to Ward. Here at Valley Forge, in the midst of the sick, starving American army, was a friendly group of women busy with womanly tasks in the hour before supper.

Ward had turned abruptly away and tramped into the office, clanking his sabre as though to recall himself sternly to the world in which he lived. He made his report quickly to a red-eyed adjutant and took his leave.

As he stood in the drafty hall he was startled to hear Lady Washington's low, pleasant voice call through the half-open door, "Is that you, Mr. Gratwick?"

Whipping off his dripping hat, Ward bowed before the Commander's wife. Martha Washington had a way with junior officers, and with non-coms and privates, too. She seemed to remember them all, somehow made them feel important, appreciated, individual, not merely minute clots that massed together to form a company or battery.

Of course Mr. Gratwick knew Mrs. Greene and Mrs. Knox, Lady Washington was saying. And she knew he'd be glad to know that she and her friends had managed to lay hands on quite a lot of cloth to be made up into shirts. The hospitals first, then the more ragged regiments. Oh, and hadn't Mr. Gratwick

9

yet met her newest ally? Then she must present him to Miss Faith Kortright, the daughter of Dr. Kortright who lived up there on the Fatland road beyond the camp.

Faith was tall and slim, with soft masses of golden hair above arched brows and steady hazel eyes. As Ward bowed in acknowledgment he caught himself thinking that those eyes were a little too serious, that the expression of the full lips and rounded chin was grave, almost severe. Then she spoke, in a low voice. "From Massachusetts, Mr. Gratwick, so Lady Washington tells me. You've come a long way for our country. I do not need say that we're grateful to you and all like you." When she smiled, a new warmth filled the little room. It was a smile from the heart and was answered by little wrinkles of humor about her eyes. It left an afterglow, as though eager to break out again.

Ward could not remember just what he had said in reply. Probably something formal and stilted. But that had been his first sight of Faith Kortright. Somehow he must have known at that very moment that no other girl would exist for him, just as he had known long ago that he could have no other calling than that of architect. He had seen her again and again throughout that winter and spring till the breakup of the camp.

She had listened thoughtfully while he told her about his family, about what he would have done save for the war, what he planned to do when the war was over. Of herself, she had little to say, but Ward managed to build up a picture of a comfortable life in the rich lands to the south of the Schuylkill, of a beloved mother lost in earlier years, of a doctor-father lamed in the French Wars, of a brother who had been at the College of New Jersey planning to follow in the father's footsteps. The war had come, and her brother had been lost trying to rally the broken troops at Kip's Bay in '76. Hessians had burned out the fieldstone house and wantonly slaughtered the cattle. Now she and her father still lived in that stone and timber house out on the road beyond Fatland Ford, and Lady Washington had virtually taken her into her official family, while Dr. Kortright, a civilian, limped among the huts where typhus and dysentery raged, laboring long hours to help out the younger doctors.

And now Ward remembered keenly that day when he and Faith had reached an understanding, when he learned that she could only visualize the years ahead with him, as he with her.

A violent exclamation below him broke in on his thoughts. Perched on the nigh shaft of the tumbril, Nicodème was gesticulating furiously with his whip, pointing ahead and shouting, "It is now that we see it, Monsieur! A sight that always eases my journey to the Seine." He flourished his whip. "Behold! Our Notre Dame de Paris!"

A twist in the road, the dip of a hill had brought into view a low saddle in the high ground of the right bank of the Seine. Through the gap, just lifting above the green, the two square towers and the delicate steeple of Notre Dame caught the nearly level rays of the sun and seemed to hang, glimmering, in midair. It was eerily beautiful and Ward tried to answer Nicodème's enthusiasm, but in vain. He would trade a score of such towers for the view of a white steeple, pure and aspiring, seen on the far shoulder of a New England hill, or a solid red barn with golden pumpkins stacked against it and the glory of an autumn maple grove behind.

A clamor and clatter filled his ears and the turnips rattled under him. The tumbril was jarring over the cobblestones of a village and at the end of the street he saw a quay, the glitter of the Seine and beyond it that green of the great peninsula formed by a long loop of the river where lay the Bois de Boulogne, Auteuil and Passy.

Ward dropped lightly from the tumbril, offering his thanks and a few coppers to Nicodème, who accepted the thanks but waved the money away with a repeated *"Mais avec plaisir, avec plaisir!"* Ward left him and the tumbril and ran toward the quay where stone steps led down to the water. His luck was out again. The narrow ferry, poled languidly by a lean old man, was just pushing off, fully laden with two nuns in gray, who sat with folded hands and downcast eyes, a carter or two, a corporal of the Swiss Guards and a fat woman in black who balanced an immense basket on each arm.

Ward fanned himself with his hat. After all, there was no hurry. His only remaining task was to see the Doctor's wine-merchant, old Vedi, in Auteuil. The last bill had not tallied with the careful inventory of the Franklin cellar which Ward had made, and Vedi must toe the line. The wrangle would take a long time, but it would have its amusing features. No hurry at all.

Elbows resting on the parapet, he looked about sharply as he heard his name called. A thin, spare man with neat, iron-gray hair was coming toward him along the quay. Ward looked appraisingly at him. "Not a Frenchman, clothes are too drab," he thought. "Not an Englishman, or he wouldn't be speaking to me. American, sure as fish."

The man came on, taking off his hat as he neared Ward. Then he spoke in a creaky voice. "Have I the pleasure of addressing Captain Gratwick? I am Jabish Frost, of the State of New Hampshire. Captain Gratwick, your servant, sir."

Ward lifted his own worn hat. "Yours, sir. But it's Lieutenant, not Captain. Thanks for the promotion, though," he answered noncommittally, running a cool eye over Frost.

"You'll pardon the intrusion, I hope," Frost went on. "Naturally, I'd heard your name. Not long ago you were pointed out to me in the company of Dr. Franklin and the physicist, Lavoisier. Seeing you here by the ferry, I took advantage of the opportunity to pay my respects as one American to another. You're a very well-known young man, Lieutenant."

Ward, now facing Frost, leaned against the parapet, elbows hooked over the stonework and one foot drawn back. The pose looked easy and relaxed, yet from it Ward could have shot himself forward. The position had been taken unconsciously as though from long habit of being always alert. He still studied Frost carefully, though he answered pleasantly enough, "Anyone with the Doctor is well known in Paris, Mr. Frost."

"He's a great man," said Frost gravely. "One of the very greatest. But I didn't mean that, sir. You're well known in your own right."

Ward stirred uncomfortably. "The Doctor makes too much of the fact that I've served four years and managed to survive."

Frost looked approvingly at him. "That, sir, is just the attitude I'd expect to find in you. But more people than the Doctor have talked. The captain of the French privateer who took you from the British barque that was ferrying you to England was much impressed by you. He talked at the Ministry of Marine, where I have friends, on his return. More than that, your military dossier was among the papers seized in the British captain's cabin. Monsieur de Sartine, Minister of Marine, showed it to me."

Ward gave a short laugh. "If the dossier came from the British, it was probably forged."

Frost looked keenly at him, then chuckled. "I'd be inclined to agree with you, except that some of us here have had oral confirmation. The Comte de Fleury came back from the American wars last year. A few days ago he told me that you and he and Christopher Greene alone kept the guns going at Red Bank. He also spoke of what you did at Stony Point." He held up a thin hand as Ward started to protest. "I shan't push the point any further. I know that it embarrasses you. I merely mention these matters to explain why I, as a fellow American, wished to speak to you."

"Always a pleasure to meet a compatriot," said Ward. "You've been here long? You seem very well acquainted."

"Since '77," answered Frost. "You know of the firm of Hortalez et Compagnie?" Ward nodded. Far off in New Jersey he had heard of the dummy firm set up by Caron de Beaumarchais in the early years of the war to cover shipments of French arms to the struggling States. Frost went on. "There's been no need of the company since the French declared war on England, but the old channels, which few knew better than I, were found to be useful."

Ward stiffened. "The old channels? From here to the States? Mr. Frost, you may be just the man I've been looking for! Sir, I've got to get back. I've *got* to. Tell me how!"

Frost shook his head sadly. "For the moment, in fact for the predictable future, the British blockade is too tight. A whole French *corps d'armée* is cooped up in Brest, waiting for a chance to join Rochambeau's contingent in Rhode Island. Short of a paralyzing storm or a most improbable French naval victory, that blockade will hold."

Ward rapped his stick on the ground impatiently. "Damn it, there must be fast, single ships that slip out of the French ports."

"No doubt," agreed Frost. "I could name several that have attempted it. Most of them were nobbled up by British brigs or frigates."

"I'd take a chance on that," said Ward shortly.

"No doubt. But in all kindness I could not, would not help you to that chance. Your fate, sir, would not be pleasant if the British took you again. You know that as well as I." Ward's face set in the hard lines of disappointment, and Frost went on hurriedly. "But I'll keep my ear to the ground. If I know of a fair chance of your getting through, you'll hear from me. Ha! Here's that ferry at last. I take it that we may cross together."

Following a trickle of townspeople down the slippery steps, Ward boarded the ferry, seating himself beside Frost amidships. The old ferryman gave a weird, quavering cry and pushed off. Frost, tucking his coattails over the seat, looked quizzically at Ward. "You know, sir, I'm rather surprised, in view of what I've heard about you, that you have advanced no higher than lieutenant."

Ward shrugged. "I've had a bad habit of getting wounded. When you're in the hospital, you're out of mind. Besides, I'm artillery. We don't have regimental organization, so we have a lot of ensigns, and lieutenants, fewer captains and an occasional major. Why, Henry Knox, Washington's Chief of Artillery, is only a brigadier. The rank simply isn't there."

"Just the same," said Frost musingly, "it seems to me that something should have been done. There was your work at Barren Hill, at Germantown and — well, to a civilian it seems a pity." He glanced sidewise at Ward. "And you're not bitter about lack of rank?"

Ward said sharply, "I told you there simply wasn't rank among the gunners. Anyway, I've done nothing except survive and get wounded. If you gave out shoulder knots on that basis, you'd have nothing but an army of generals. If I know that I can handle men and horses and guns well enough to get them where they're needed when they're needed, that's enough for me — or any gunner."

Frost laid a bony hand on Ward's sleeve. "Sir, that's the spirit that has kept our army in the field. May an older man who's been some time in this odd world of Paris give you a warning." He looked along the narrow boat cautiously, then dropped his voice. "There are still a good many Englishmen about Paris, despite the declaration of war. Some of them would be glad of a talk with you."

Ward smiled sardonically. "To slip a length of hemp about my neck."

"Not at all." Frost's voice was still lower. "They know your record. They'd love to be able to announce in their Gazettes — and in the French press, too — that you'd undergone a change of heart." He was whispering now. "That you'd taken His Majesty's service."

"What's that?" Ward cried. The ferry rocked and the old ferryman shrieked a warning while a crateful of hens in the bow squawked madly.

"Gently, gently," urged Frost. "I said this was a *warning*. You'd be surely offered a major's commission, a sinecure post and a pension."

"And precisely why are you warning me, Mr. Frost?" Ward said coldly.

Frost ignored Ward's tone. "I can see readily how you'd act were such an offer made to you. You'd lash out, violently. We Americans are not too solidly planted here in France. Treaty or no treaty, there are plenty of people, including the Queen, who don't like us. They hold that it's outrageous for the most absolute monarchy in Europe to help a rebellion against a Crown, any Crown. A brawl between you and an Englishman would surely be used against us. A small affair, you say? But the small is often more effective than the large."

Ward recalled a maxim of Franklin's: "There is no small enemy." Nothing that an enemy used was small. He turned to Frost. "I see. Thanks for the warning. I'll be careful."

"I know you will be," said Frost heartily. He gathered his feet under him. "Here we are. You go first."

Ward handed a copper to the ferryman and leaped ashore reaching out a hand to aid the less nimble Frost. The latter shook hands with Ward. "I trust we shall meet again, Lieu-tenant, and be sure that I'll keep in mind the matter of a ship. May I say in parting that I'm glad, very glad indeed, to find that you're not bitter, even if many younger men do hold higher rank in our armies." He raised his hat, then walked away along the quay.

Ward watched him. "Seems well intentioned," he thought. He settled his shabby coat, took a firmer grip on his stick and started toward the long, flat-topped ridge where Auteuil and Passy lay. "Just the same, why did he make so much of my not being bit-ter? Almost as though he wanted the word to stick in my mind."

The wrangle with Vedi over the inventory took even longer than Ward had feared and a full moon was shining down on the Seine and its valley when he finally took his leave, duly receipted papers crackling in his pocket.

As he struck out for Passy the moon was turning the world into an unending pattern of silver and black. On either hand the loops of the Seine glittered peacefully. Here and there the pointed towers of a château seemed to hang suspended above the trees, tiles silver against the sky. In little, narrow streets the white walls of cottages were startlingly barred with the black shadows of elm and poplar. The beauty of the scene soothed him.

The park walls of the Château de Chaumont, on whose vast grounds the Doctor lived, loomed before him. He left the road and opened a little wicket gate that would lead him into a short cut across the park. He moved on with a soundlessness that years in the presence of the enemy had made instinctive. His steps barely crunched across a gravel path, were muted on smooth lawns. Through the trees he could see the façade of the château, its sweeping walls and clustering conical towers. Lights were dotted along the main part of the building, telling him that the owner, Donatien le Ray de Chaumont, and his family had returned from the soiree at Madame Brillon's.

Keeping by habit to the sound-killing grass, he passed close to a jutting turret where light sifted through curtains drawn across French windows on the ground level. One of the windows swung slowly open and two figures were outlined against soft candlelight. Ward halted mechanically in the shade of some yew trees. The figure nearer him was that of a young girl. Her slim bare arms were raised and she was settling a mantilla about her head. He could see her profile clearly against the inner light —a tip-tilted, impudent nose and a high-held chin.

Ward stifled an exclamation of mild surprise. "Damned if that isn't Deborah Dale," he thought. "I never knew that she was friendly with the de Chaumonts. Must be with Sophie, the de Chaumont daughter that Franklin likes to call his 'little wife.'"

Sophie's voice flowed out clearly. "No, but we speak in the English now, Deborah. Wait that I call Marie and Jacques who will escort you back."

Deborah Dale made a pretty gesture of dissent. "It's only a step. I'll go on past Doctor Franklin's and on to Madame's. Thanks for showing me the brocades, Sophie. I'd choose the old-gold one, and maybe the rose and white. Good night, Sophie." She slipped away from the French window, which closed gently.

Ward watched her pattering swiftly along the gravel path toward the Petit Manoir where the Doctor lived. "H'm," he thought. "A good five hundred yards through woods and open park and never a sign of light. She could be strangled for her rings a dozen times over and no one the wiser. Now if I call to her, she'll jump a mile. And she doesn't know me either."

He had never met Deborah Dale, but had caught glimpses of her twice at the Doctor's soirees. He knew that she was American, that she had come to Paris in her early teens, just at the outbreak of the Revolution, with her elder cousin, Mrs. Lathrop.

He had wondered about her, living softly, luxuriously in Paris while her countrymen bled and starved. Well, it was none of his business, any more than her lonely progress across the night-shrouded park.

At least he'd keep her in sight. An unexpected bend in the path that she followed suddenly swung her within a yard or so of him. He started to speak, then thought of a stratagem that would identify himself a little, lessen the shock of the sudden meeting. He began to whistle "Yankee Doodle."

The girl stopped in a whirl of rustling silk. "W-where did you come from?" she asked unsteadily.

"Across the park, Miss Dale," he answered.

Her head went back spiritedly, but her voice was still unsteady. "You were whistling an American tune. And how did you know my name?"

"From seeing you at Doctor Franklin's, Miss Dale. May I present myself, Lieutenant Ward Gratwick, of the Continental Line."

She pushed back the edge of the mantilla and moonlight fell on her face. He could see that her eyes were wide and her lips slightly parted. "You mean *the* Lieutenant Gratwick? The one who lives with Doctor Franklin and got taken prisoner by the British and saved by a French privateer? You're really the one?"

"So I am told — as the Doctor told me your name. He'll always remember it because Deborah was the name of his wife, whom he lost just before the war broke out."

The smile faded from her lips and her face grew severe. "But that doesn't explain why you whistled at me. And Yankee Doodle."

Ward bowed. "Yankee Doodle to show you that I was an American, like yourself. And I whistled because I thought you'd gone on alone long enough. My dear Miss Dale, you've been in Paris longer than I, but I must take the liberty of telling you that a great park at night is no place for a very pretty young girl alone, especially one who wears rings like yours and gems in her hair that show through the mantilla. In other words, I offer myself as escort at least as far as the Doctor's, where I have the honor to be billeted."

"You really think I need an escort? Just for this little distance?"

"The distance may seem short to you, but the park seems very dark to me. There are many charming people about Paris. There are also many desperate ones and still more unprincipled ones."

She looked gravely at him. "I suppose you're right. It is thoughtful of you to worry about me. I accept your escort. I don't know just why. You're only a name to me, but I've heard so much about you in the salons. Will you take me as far as Madame Brillon's? It's just across from the Doctor's and Cousin Sue — that's my cousin, Mrs. Lathrop — is waiting for me there."

He held out his arm and she laid her finger tips on it as he led her along the path, looking for a short cut that he knew. Deborah looked mischievously at him. "I'll tell you another thing about yourself. In the salons, people call you Pierre l'Ermite. Did you know that?"

"Peter the Hermit? Why?"

"Why you must know that dozens of people are simply dying to have you at their salons. They've heard about you from Monsieur de Sartine, the Minister of Marine, and Comte de Fleury who fought with your people in America."

"Your people, too," said Ward a little curtly.

"Of course, but it's all so far away. Anyhow, I know that all sorts of people send you cards and you don't even answer them."

The cards. Of course. They had begun to come in almost as soon as he had arrived at the Doctor's. At first he had accepted, but soon the novelty of being lionized had worn off as he had become more and more obsessed with the idea of getting back to America.

Deborah's pretty voice broke into his thoughts. "Cousin Sue used to go to the Doctor's a lot, but that was when I was too little to go out. Now she's suddenly started again. I love the Doctor."

"How long have you lived in Paris, Miss Dale?"

Deborah's manner suddenly changed and she began chattering away about herself as though to a friend of long standing. It was not self-absorption, Ward reflected. Rather, she was on familiar ground with a stranger with whom she was beginning to feel at ease. Her father, Ward gathered, had had extensive shipping and trading interests in New Jersey. When trouble broke out in '75, he took advantage of the Lathrops' offer to take her and her brother Paul to the safety of Europe where Mr. Lathrop maintained wide business connections, apparently in defiance of all British trade laws. Mr. Lathrop had died in '76. Since then the young Dales had stayed on with the widow, waiting out the war.

Ward smiled tolerantly to himself as she spoke of that conflict. She had been so young when it had started that it couldn't have meant much to her. Her life in Paris and in the obviously high circles where Mrs. Lathrop moved, had insulated her from the fevers and currents that broke over Ward and his contemporaries and elders at home. "Of course, New Jersey's where I belong," she said, looking up at him as though a new thought had struck her. "Father is alone. I wonder — do you think I should have been there all the time?"

He shook his head. "Your state hasn't been the most comfortable place in the world," he said. "It's been — well — " He tried to sketch out for her that winter retreat of 1776 where spent infantry and exhausted gunners and gun-teams toiled across the plains, while mounted Hessians and Tories and British hung on

21

the fringes of the fading American Army. Then there was the wanton pillage and burning of houses and downright murder of defenseless civilians by the enemy —

She sighed. "I've heard something about it. But it never seemed like the Jerseys to me. It's all so far away. And I've been in France so long that sometimes I almost forget that I am American."

"That," said Ward gravely, "is something you must *never* forget. It's your country. You're part of it and it of you. Here, pleasant as it is, you're just a visitor. You don't spring from this soil, but from the Jerseys."

"I suppose so," said Deborah slowly. "But Paul — that's my brother, you know, and he's older than I am and oh, so clever. Well, Paul says that he and I are citizens of the world. Doesn't that seem more sensible to you?"

"No!" said Ward shortly. "That's being a citizen of nowhere, with no ties and no beliefs, no convictions. It's — Lord, I'm talking like a schoolteacher or a member of the Congress, I'm afraid."

"Why I don't think so." There was a hint of wonder in Deborah's voice. "It's just — well, I've heard some of the old men at Doctor Franklin's talk that way — never anyone young like us. I'd like to hear you say all that to Paul and see how he answers. Oh — I didn't notice. We've quite left the path. Are you sure you're going the right way, Mr. Gratwick?"

"A short cut. It'll bring us out beyond the far wing of the Doctor's house and — " His voice changed suddenly. "Hold on! Don't move. Don't speak for a minute."

With a quick gesture he stepped ahead of Deborah, staring into the tree-cloaked darkness beyond. There was vague movement at the far edge of a moonlit stretch. Then he made out the head and shoulders of a man, showing eerily by a tree close to the great wall of the park.

22

Ward crouched lower, and Deborah peered over his shoulder. The man had moved a little nearer and in the clear moonlight on his face, Ward saw a bar of dense black that covered forehead, eyes and nose. "He's wearing a domino mask!" Ward whispered.

The stranger was fumbling along the trunk of a tree by the wall, his hands now clear in the moonlight, now lost in shadow. Something shone dully and one hand appeared holding a slim tube that looked like metal. Carefully he drew out a long, white cylinder and Ward caught the faint crackle of paper. The tube vanished, paper rustled again and the man was gone.

Still crouching, Ward waited, listening. From far off beyond the Seine came the voices of the bells of Paris tolling nine o'clock. The echoes died.

Ward was puzzled. He had expected the man to come along the path in which case he would have stopped him, demanded an explanation. "He must have gone some other way," he reasoned. "But there isn't any other. The wall's too high to climb and it's probably topped by broken glass." He turned, momentarily surprised to find Deborah still with him. Her bright shawl had fallen back showing high-piled masses of carefully powdered hair, whose whiteness was apparent even under the shadow of the oak. "What was it?" she whispered.

"It's all right to talk now. I don't know what it was. I don't know where or how he went," said Ward. "It looked odd enough, didn't it?"

She pulled up her shawl again. "What would have happened if we'd kept right on?"

"Nothing, probably. He would have seen us and hidden until we'd gone by."

"Oooh! Wait till I tell Paul about this. What do we do next?"

"Not much we can do. You saw the mask? It wasn't my fancy?"

23

"Indeed I saw it, and the silver tube or whatever it was."

"Right. Well, it's no concern of ours. Just the same, it did happen pretty close to the Doctor's house. I'll tell him about it later. Shall we go on? We swing off to the right here."

She started to take his arm, then paused, looking at him. "Did you see which tree he was at? Let's go look at it now."

"Well, I meant to, later." He started toward the shadow-flecked wall, Deborah following.

They stood in the clear space by the wall. "This is just where he was standing. His hands went like this — along the trunk and — ah!"

From a hollow in the trunk Ward drew out the same slim tube that had glimmered in the domino's hands. It was of some very light metal, capped at both ends. He handed it to Deborah who worked off one cap and ran a slender finger inside.

"Nothing," she said, disappointed.

"Of course. There were papers in it and he took them." He slid the tube back into the hollow. "I'm going to leave it right here. I'll slip down here from time to time and see if our domino repeats. Now if I could only figure out how he got away without coming past us. He didn't go on through the woods. The wall? No. And not this way." He moved a few steps off to the right.

Deborah picked up a long smooth stick and began prodding boldly among the rhododendrons that grew along the wall. Then she cried, "Look! Right here!"

She was bent low, one arm thrust deep among the bushes. "See? There's a gap in the wall."

Ward dropped on one knee beside her. Beyond the interlaced stems and branches moonlight flooded through a ragged rent in the stonework, not a high gap or a wide one, but ample for an agile man to wriggle through. Reaching far in, Ward patted the soft dirt carefully.

"You're right. I can feel a footprint right here, deep in the

24

mold. Now where does this lead? I know. Out to that little lane with the laborers' cottages and on to rue Bois-le-Vent."

"Do you think it was one of the laborers?"

"No. They don't wear high-heeled shoes like a courtier. Well, I'll take you back to Madame Brillon's. Come along. We'll go this way."

"Oh, what *do* you suppose the domino was up to?"

"Probably something rather bizarre and utterly harmless," Ward said easily. He refrained from mentioning that there had always been leaks about the most secret Franco-American transactions, that the terms of the alliance between France and America had been known in London before it was signed in Paris. Not that the domino really suggested any such leak; the performance looked too amateur for that. Just the same —

They were now passing the elaborate gardens, ghostly in the moonlight, that belonged to Franklin's house, the so-called Petit Manoir in the grounds of the Château de Chaumont. The two low wings and the connecting arch with its porte-cochere were dark, but lights glowed in the room that opened out onto the long terrace.

"Hello!" exclaimed Ward. "The Doctor's come home from Madame Brillon's reception already."

"Let's go in and tell him about what we saw."

"But Mrs. Lathrop — " began Ward.

"You let me worry about her," said Deborah firmly. "Anyway, even if the soiree has broken up, she'll be in a corner exchanging gossip with Madame Brillon and old Colonel LeNotre and that'll be good for another hour at least."

She ran lightly up the steps of the terrace and put a finger to her lips. "We'll surprise him."

As she spoke, a rich, pleasant voice called from inside the house, "Hello! Who's that?"

"Stuff!" exclaimed Deborah. "He must have ears like a field mouse."

Ward called, "Gratwick, Doctor, escorting a distressed American citizen."

There was a deep laugh. "Then bring her right in."

Ward pushed open the French windows. Seated back of a carved table, Doctor Benjamin Franklin, long white hair falling to his shoulders, looked up benignly over his small spectacles. He was wearing a dressing gown of fine, flowered silk, all blues and deep reds, that was at marked variance with his plain white shirt, open at the neck, his tobacco-brown breeches and gray wool stockings. A large Maltese cat was purring on his knees. By the Sèvres lamp on the table stood a pitcher, a glass of milk, a plate of fine sugar and a woven basket that spilled out big strawberries.

Ward stepped aside to let Deborah enter and Franklin rose, beaming, unceremoniously dumping the Maltese onto the thick red rug. Throwing out both hands, the Doctor cried, "My dear Deborah, this is most delightful."

He installed Deborah in a great, carved chair, waved Ward into another.

"This couldn't have been more opportune," the Doctor went on. "Madame d'Augesson brought me these strawberries this evening and you must help me eat them. There! A saucer of sugar for each of you. Milk? No? Then, Deborah, would you mind pouring some into that empty saucer for Minette?" He made a swooping motion, produced the cat from under the table and set her beside Deborah. "Thank you. Now, my young friends, dip a berry in the sugar and tell me if it isn't capital."

Ward set a dozen berries on a plate for Deborah and then he began to eat. Opposite him the Doctor was solemnly munching away. Nearer, Deborah's powdered head bent as she daintily dipped a berry then bit into it fastidiously. At her left, the cat Minette lapped at the saucer of milk with equal daintiness.

The Doctor caught Ward's eye and beamed. "Good berries, aren't they? Deborah, do take more sugar. These fellows need it. Grown under glass, of course." He sat back in his chair, eyes on the ceiling. "You know, this sets me wondering — this need for sugar now — mightn't it be possible by elements that go into the making of a cultivated strawberry, to alter the flavor, to grow berries so sweet that they wouldn't need sugar?" He gave a flick of his hand. "Tomorrow, Ward, I must see what Linnaeus has to say about strawberries. The volumes are on the table in the reception room. Remind me about it, will you?"

"I'll remember, sir," answered Ward. It took little to send the Doctor's agile mind off into the flights of fancy that often had amazingly practical results. He jotted a note onto a slip of paper. Then he saw that Deborah was trying to get his attention.

"Are you going to — or shall I?" she asked.

The Doctor looked quizzically at her. "What's this? A mystery? Some court secret?"

Deborah dipped her fingers into a bowl of water, then wiped them on a napkin that Franklin handed her. "It was down by the park wall, Doctor Franklin. I'd just run over from Madame Brillon's to see some new brocades that Sophie de Chaumont had. Then Mr. Gratwick said he knew a short cut across the park." Deborah plunged on with her story. "Then, you see, all of a sudden, we saw something — " She talked animatedly, small hands with jeweled rings glinting, darting gracefully.

"And then Mr. Gratwick found the hollow tree and the tube and *I* found the gap in the wall. It was just like a play by Monsieur de Beaumarchais!" Deborah concluded with a little bounce of excitement.

Franklin placed his fingers together judicially. "H'm! Papers in a metal tube. My young friends, I venture to say that I may read what was written on those papers without even seeing them."

Ward glanced keenly at the Doctor while Deborah said eagerly, "Not really!"

Franklin pushed his spectacles up on his forehead, looking benign and patriarchal. "The message would run something like this: 'My husband has gone to Tours and will not return for four days.' "

"Oh, Doctor Franklin!" cried Deborah with a shocked little laugh.

"Or, if you prefer," Franklin went on, "it could be this: 'My cruel father forbids that we meet. Be in front of the Cerf d'Or tomorrow after Mass. I shall drive by and wave to you.' "

"Pretty short messages for so much paper," observed Ward.

Franklin waved airily. "I was merely giving you the gist. Or the writer may have used remarkably large script." He turned to Deborah. "Thanks, my dear. I'm indebted to you for a most absorbing story, well told. However, I don't think it need concern us."

"But it was right on what amounts to your own property, sir," urged Ward.

"True," said Franklin, picking up the cat Minette. "But did it never occur to you young people that the writer of that letter or letters doesn't *have* to be a neighbor of mine or of the de Chaumonts? Said writer could have slipped onto the grounds just as easily as your domino."

Deborah looked at him in wonder. "Why, that's so. Wait till I tell all this to Cousin Sue."

The Doctor shook his head. "Deborah, my dear child, the story is amusing to us. But if it were noised about it might harm someone, might cast unjust suspicion on an innocent person. Let us, and Minette, keep it just among us four, at least until — or if — we know more about it."

Deborah's face fell. "You really think so, Doctor Franklin?" A tall clock in a carved oaken case boomed ten o'clock. Deborah gave a little squeak of dismay. "Now Cousin Sue *will* be wondering. I must fly."

Franklin sighed regretfully. "A pity that we must pay such heed to the worries of our elders. At least, Ward, you will have the pleasure of escorting our young lady to Madame Brillon's. I shall have retired when you return. Oh — and before I forget it. You were drawing plans of that smoke-consuming stove that I invented for Lavoisier. Could you make another copy for the Marquis de Condorcet and a set for d'Alembert? Good night, my dear Deborah, and come again soon."

An hour later Ward returned to his room. As he made ready for bed, he ran over in his mind the various matters to be taken up with the Doctor in the morning. He'd have to handle everything alone, since Temple Franklin seemed to have found a new focus of interest in the person of a diminutive lady from Les Baux, married to a cornet of dragoons, and was rarely at the Petit Manoir these days. There were the drawings for Lavoisier and the other Academicians; the letters in code to James Moylan, American agent at the port of Lorient; the dossier to be forwarded to John Adams, now in the Low Countries; the inventory of the cellar that old Vedi had signed; the secret appointment with the gaunt young secretary from the Prussian Embassy; the postponement of meetings with diplomats from Baden and Anhalt; the reference to strawberries to look up in Linnaeus.

Ward blew out his candle. It looked like a full day ahead of him. At noon he had promised to help little Benjamin Bache, the Doctor's grandson, to fly a kite in the open spaces this side of the Bois de Boulogne. After that — His mind went on to the strange scene in the park. He did not believe that the tube contained a billet-doux. Nor, he was sure, did the Doctor. A convenient way to exchange letters, that hollow tree. He sighed. If only all letters could be handled that way, and as speedily. He wondered if any of those which he had written to Faith, beginning with his first day ashore at Bordeaux, had been slipped out through the blockade. The frigate *Concord* had won through, why not a swifter privateer's brig? "Damn and blast!" he muttered. "If I only *knew*."

Men Greatly in Earnest

THE BRONZED PRIVATEER CAPTAIN with the scarred face leaned his elbows on the wall that shut in the moat surrounding the Bastille. He kept his beaky nose turned toward the flotillas of swans sailing over the scummed waters below, but his eyes kept seeking Ward's. "So this here Mason," he was saying, "out of Delaware, he's got his own ship now in the Mediterranean, under royal colors, and by God, if he ain't got a pension hanging over him, too."

Ward, his mouth compressed, tapped his stick against the parapet. "What's all this got to do with me?" he asked coldly.

The seaman hunched his big shoulders. "Did I say? I just been talking to you, one American to another."

Ward's eyes snapped. "Telling me about a string of rats who've sold their allegiance for British gold."

"Be I saying they done right? Look, Mister, I'm just warning you against them as spreads British gold about. The worst is a cross-eyed man named Bailey who's to be found most nights at a wineshop over yonder by the gendarmes' hut." He paused.

"Go on," said Ward coldly.

"Ain't nothing to go on with. If you want to seek out more, Bailey's over yonder most nights about eight."

Ward dropped his stick, as his hands clenched. Then he remembered Jabish Frost's warning. Retrieving his stick as though he had let it fall clumsily, Ward nodded. "Maybe I'll look in on him. Maybe I won't."

The seaman looked relieved. "Bailey's the name. Tell him the skipper from Stonington in Connecticut sent you." With a last furtive glance at Ward he shambled off.

Ward leaned against the parapet as the other had leaned. "Maybe I ought to have chucked him into the moat after all," he thought. "No. Frost was right. There'd have been a brawl. Hell, better this way. At least, I can tell the Doctor about Bailey."

Slowly Ward's anger passed, was replaced by a more somber mood. Across the moat, the sun was softening and gilding the old masonry, melting patches of deep shadow to show him a cunning trick of construction where some forgotten builder had transmitted a heavy thrust of stone down onto solid walls below and thence to the ground. He thought, rather morosely, that much he had seen in France and was seeing now would have fascinated him back, say, in '74. There would have been appeal to his mind, to his imagination, his sense of history and his instinctive feeling for mass and color. The façade of an age-old cathedral in the moonlight; a crumbling château whose ruins rested on foundations outdated in Charlemagne's time and which, in turn, incorporated the work of the Romans and before them, the Gauls; the Gardes Royales glittering at drill on the broad Champs de la Confédération just across from Passy; a levee at court where he, sponsored by Doctor Franklin, had bowed before the heavy-faced Louis of France, where he had seen pretty, petulant Marie Antoinette talking to the Doctor over her shoulder while she pushed stacks of gold pieces across the gaming-table. (Just one of those stacks would have gone far to pave the great road from Boston to Marlboro, or to build a chain of schools clear across the Commonwealth of Massachusetts. And how many barefoot patriot soldiers would they have shod and fed? How many bayonets would they have bought for lean infantrymen facing a British charge with empty muskets?) But all of France rose in his mind like a beautiful, shimmering wall that shut him off from the life and the land where he belonged and the work that he had to do in that life and in that land.

He pushed away from the parapet, eyes on the slow-sinking sun. There was nothing to call him back to Passy until evening and he must put in the hours somehow. The Doctor had hinted it would be useful if Ward were to follow up some of the cards that had been sent giving him entree to salons in the city. There were several doors at which he could at least leave his name. He could go to Mrs. Lathrop's house in the rue Neuve des Petits Champs not far away and take tea with her and Deborah. Or he might go to the barracks and take wine with the young officers of the Gardes who always seemed glad to hear of war as it was waged in the forests and deserts of America.

As he weighed these possibilities, his eye caught a patch in the lining of the flowing tails of his coat. At home he would never have thought to go calling in his enforced shabby-genteel state. But here in Paris—People seemed to look on his threadbare attire as they did on Benjamin Franklin's Quaker-like garb. The idea was fantastic, this worship of rustic simplicity in the most extravagant capital in the world. Yet that idea was one which Franklin deliberately fostered, to which he adapted his whole life in the interests of his country.

The Doctor's manner of living, his dress were shaped to create an impression on France, America's sole active ally. The French insisted that he was a Quaker. Very well, he would wear his hair brushed back to his shoulders, unclubbed and unpowdered. They cried that he was the embodiment of pure, republican virtues. To fall in with this mood the Doctor forgot his taste for fine clothes, wore sober browns, a round fur cap, wool stockings and carried a long, apple-wood staff. Good-humoredly and efficiently he was playing a part that a whole nation had written for him, playing it not as American citizen, but as American

33

minister. And from the Doctor's skill in this odd role, Ward benefited.

Shabby or not, Ward could go where he pleased. He could make up his mind later. He turned his back on the towering fortress-prison and walked to the entrance of the rue Amelot with its long, marching lines of trees. Far up the street he saw a green and gold sedan chair slowly approaching. A tall, slim man in sky-blue clothes walked by one window bending down as though talking with the occupant. As they drew nearer, Ward heard a cry of surprise from inside the chair, and the chairmen gratefully halted and lowered their poles. Ward whipped off his hat and bowed when he recognized Deborah Dale at the lowered window. The sky-blue man, dark and markedly handsome, was staring superciliously at Ward's shabby brown clothes. Ward returned the stare as coldly. Deborah said politely, "This is so nice. Paul, dear, this is Mr. Ward Gratwick, the American I was telling you about."

Paul raised his hat, then held out a sinewy hand. "A great pleasure, Mr. Gratwick. I've heard of you from Sis and Cousin Sue. They tell me you're in Paris for an indefinite time."

"That depends on the British blockade."

Paul smiled at his sister. "Then let's be selfish and hope that that blockade lasts a long time. So you're with Doctor Franklin. How is the old fellow? Do the nymphs of Paris still flock about him?"

Ward felt an instinctive liking for Deborah's brother. "As to the nymphs, they were still flocking until about ten this morning, when I left."

Paul laughed. "I know, I know. He does put us young chaps in the shade, doesn't he? I'm really looking forward to old age, if he's a sample. We're on our way home for a pot of chocolate. Won't you come along with us?"

* * *

34

It was pleasant, sitting in Mrs. Lathrop's rather mannered drawing room watching the graceful play of Deborah's hands about the Sèvres service, as she poured the chocolate. But he found himself more and more interested in tall, dark Paul with his American features and his clothes that suggested the French court. Paul was an unusually good talker. Effortlessly he led Deborah and Ward through the capitals of Europe, particularly Madrid where he had been spending several weeks. His grasp of commerce was so sure that at times Ward had difficulty in following the course of the talk. When he turned to matters political and diplomatic, Ward, because of his service with Franklin, was better able to appreciate the knowledge and power with which Deborah's brother spoke.

Many girls, Ward thought, would have resented a little such masculine domination of the conversation, but it was clear that Deborah idolized Paul. She tried, though it was hardly necessary, to draw him out, to toss out little hints that Paul would quickly expand into clever, sometimes brilliant thoughts. Ward smiled at her over the rim of his cup as Paul told a complicated story of smuggling across the Spanish border. Deborah met his glance, smiled back as though to say, "Didn't I tell you that Paul was wonderful?"

The talk veered to Paris, and Paul seemed suddenly obsessed with the doings of Benjamin Franklin. What did Ward really think of him? How was Franklin regarded in America? Of course, there was that matter of the — Paul coughed discreetly — the sub-rosa son, William Franklin, once Royal Governor of New Jersey and now an avowed and active Tory. And what would the sterner Americans think of the presence of Temple Franklin, William's illegitimate son, so close in the councils of the Doctor at Passy? For his part, Paul knew that frosty John Adams had cast an owlish eye at these points.

"But Temple's such fun!" broke in Deborah.

Paul smiled and said dryly. "A lot of girls think he's fun, Sis — for a while. Is it true, Gratwick, that you've taken over most of the confidential work that he used to do for the Doctor?"

"Ward!" cried Deborah. "You never told me that. I thought you were, well, just there. You really know all the weird things the Doctor does?"

"God forbid," said Ward solemnly. "Only the official ones."

"And what are they?"

"As your brother pointed out, confidential things."

"Oh poof!" said Deborah. "We're all friends here. You can tell us. Go on, Ward."

Paul said almost sharply, "Gratwick's right, Sis." His dark eyes, so like his sister's, rested approvingly on Ward.

After Ward had gone, Deborah stood in the oval window set deep in the thick wall and watched him make his way among the carriages, chairs and pedestrians. Paul crossed the white and gold salon, with its carved and gilded furniture, and joined her, dropping an arm about her shoulders. "There he goes," said Paul, looking down into the street. "He seems just to be flowing along without any effort. Like a fish swimming."

"Like an Indian," observed Deborah, rising on her toes to look farther down.

Paul pinched her shoulder gently. "Where did you ever see an Indian?"

"Well, I haven't really. But I've read a lot that people over here have written about them. Monsieur Rousseau wrote that savages are the only truly happy and virtuous people."

Paul laughed. "Rousseau never saw one either."

"But he could reason about them," said Deborah firmly. "And you ought to have heard the Princesse de Lamballe the other night. Pure air, forest glades, the clear sky overhead, the great clean rivers. She made it all sound very attractive."

36

"Come now. Would you trade your suite and your brocades and your maids for a smoky wigwam in a swamp? Of course you wouldn't. Neither would I. Paris was made for us."

She changed the subject abruptly. "Paul, what precisely were you doing in Spain?"

Paul gave a graceful wave. "Oh, a good many things. I even got to the court. If you think French manners are formal, you ought to see the Escorial! Amazingly pretty girls in Spain, too."

Deborah persisted. "Just the same, what were you doing there, aside from goggling at the girls?"

Paul settled the lace at his throat. "Business. I saw the Estavez people and old Miramon. Highly satisfactory. You know, I think I could turn into a pretty successful merchant-prince."

Deborah gave a happy laugh. "Your sister thinks you're a pretty successful brother. I do love those shawls and combs you brought me and that big leather screen. You could never find anything like that in America."

"And very few Americans, beyond yourself, who'd have the wit to appreciate them. I must say, though, that Gratwick did show an eye for that Sèvres chocolate service of yours. Do you like him?"

Deborah slowly drew the ivory sticks of her fan across her lips. "Like him? Of course I do. He's better looking than Temple and nowhere near so arrogant — the sort of man most girls would like. And he's a change from the people we've been meeting, people from the court and the upper merchants. Don't you think he's good-looking, even in those drab clothes of his? I'd like to see him in a uniform."

Paul looked quickly at her. "You're not getting serious about him, are you? He's got absolutely no prospects, even if his side does win over there. I could see that right away."

"Serious about Ward?" Deborah shook her head vigorously, pursing up her lips. "Nor anyone else. I do like him, but, heavens! I do wish he wouldn't talk so *much* about the war and the army and people I've barely heard of. He's too serious. And he never really seems to notice you. Temple has better manners."

Paul's fingers drummed on the curved sill. "Just the same, seeing Ward here and listening to him I confess I felt rather uncomfortable. A sort of uneasy feeling that I ought to have been doing what he's done. That I ought to have gone back to America. It would have been easy enough before the blockade. I really don't know which side I would have chosen, but he makes me feel as though I ought to have done something."

"You were just saying that Paris suits us both."

Paul laughed. "I'm only theorizing, like Rousseau and his noble savages. You know, he was quite right in not talking about his work, but just the same — "

Deborah patted his arm. "I know. Just the same. Don't you worry, Paul dear. He'll tell *me* all about it some day and then we'll both know. All these mysteries!"

"Sis, for a nice little girl, you've got very mature ideas," laughed Paul. "You let Gratwick alone if the Doctor needs him. Though it does seem to me that a man who's lived as Gratwick has would find being a confidential clerk confoundedly dull. Maybe — maybe — "

"Maybe what?" asked his sister.

"Maybe I'll buy you that pair of matched bays that Colonel de Kersaint wants to get rid of. Now run along and see if Sue's ready to go out with us. I'll join you in the main salon below."

When she had gone, Paul Dale turned back to the window and stared into the street below. A frown deepened between his eyes.

The following Friday Ward stood at the upper end of the Doctor's terrace, watching the bewildering swarm of guests who sat on folding chairs or milled about the tables, intent on sampling one of Franklin's famed collations. There were gaudy young officers of the French Guards, cornets and colonels of the Household Cavalry. He recognized painters who enjoyed court patronage, world-celebrated scientists, writers, rising young merchants, sleek attachés from a dozen legations. And everywhere, among the uniforms and bright civilians' coats, the colorful dresses and high powdered coiffures of the women showed. He looked beyond the terrace, across to the magnificent sun-bathed expanse of the Seine and the wooded heights of Issy and Meudon. The gathering, which had assembled at the call of a man who had begun life as a runaway printer-boy from Boston, was fascinating. The setting, from the intricate flower beds to the far scarps and bastions of the hills, was magnificent.

He caught a flutter of white at the left and waved, smiling. Later he would go over and pay his respects to Deborah and Mrs. Lathrop, the latter a handsome brown-haired woman in her thirties. Deborah seemed always glad to see him and her talk was apt to be amusing. Not quite so amusing, though, in Ward's mind, as Mrs. Lathrop's obvious wish to shoo him away from her young cousin — to her he was a well-enough young man but of course with no prospects. He waved again as he saw Paul, dark and handsome in hunter's green and white, beckoning to him. There was a rising young man! His mind was keen as the edge of a dragoon's saber and he made full use of it. Ward had had two other meetings with him, quite by chance, since the afternoon of the chocolate and was becoming convinced that somehow Paul Dale must be persuaded to come back to his own country. The new United States of America could use the marked talents of this expatriate son.

Ward felt a tug at his sleeve and looked down to see the round, solemn face of Benjamin Bache looking at him. Franklin's little grandson was wearing what seemed to Ward a sort of page's costume of red velvet, but the bedraggled lace at the boy's cuffs showed that he had forgotten decorum and etiquette enough to try to scoop out a goldfish or two from the pond below. A long grubby string which Ward knew belonged to the top he had carved for the boy, dangled from a pocket. Ward grinned at him. "Well, *Monsieur le Vicomte,* what may I do for you?"

"You were talking about pink cakes, Mr. Gratwick," said Benjamin. "It was while you were making me eat salad this noon."

"I remember."

"Well, I haven't had one yet. And I did eat the salad." Benjamin's brown eyes were fixed in gentle reproach.

"They're right down there at the big table where you see Hercule in his white apron," said Ward. "Come on. We'll go together." There was a sudden stir behind Ward and he saw the long windows at the end of the wing open slowly. "Sorry, Ben. Gramp is going to play on the armonica. We'll go later."

"Who? Oh, you mean *Gran'père?*"

"You're an American boy and I mean Gramp. Steady now. Here they come. Your Uncle Temple's helping."

Temple Franklin came out of the house, elegant in dark red, supervising two servants who carried a decidedly odd-looking instrument onto the flagstones. It was something like a harpsichord with broad treadles set at its base. Instead of strings and keyboard it was fitted with a slender spindle on which glasses were threaded, in a series that ranged from a very large glass at one end to a tiny one at the other. It was one of the Doctor's countless inventions, an idea that he had dreamed up and perfected back in the peaceful old days in Philadelphia. Now people played on similar instruments in Padua and Danzig and Rotterdam and Lille.

A rippling murmur spread along the terrace and Ward saw

40

a slow, respectful surge of powdered heads, court dresses, uniforms. Then the Doctor appeared from the house, patriarchal with his long white hair, his sober clothes and square-toed shoes, these last particularly noticeable among useless, red-heeled nothings that pressed lightly onto the lawns.

The Doctor beamed on his guests, gave a special nod and smile to Ward and Benjamin. At one elbow tall, cheerful Madame Helvetius swept along, her graying hair simply dressed as always, her eyes alert on the Doctor. On the other side, Madame Brillon, the neighbor across the street, glided gracefully, her Dresden prettiness set off by her powdered hair and her dress of sea-green silk. Her rounded chin was held high and her bright blue eyes darted this way and that, managing to find time in their watchfulness for a little wink at Ward. He chuckled as a tall, thin woman broke from the crowd, caught up a chair and tried to place it for the Doctor by the armonica. Madame Helvetius stretched out a firm hand, took the chair from the intruder and set it on the ground with a masterful thud. Madame Brillon nodded at her in understanding.

The Doctor looked blandly about, then seated himself before the instrument. He raised his hands and some of the women nearby sank to the turf, brocaded devotees of rustic simplicity. Then the square-toed shoes moved on the treadles, the spindle spun rapidly. His fingers touched the spinning glasses with surprising delicacy. Faint at first, then gaining in volume, rich tones flowed out.

"Will it take long?" Benjamin Bache's treble whisper barely reached Ward.

"Wait," Ward said, very low. "This is 'The March of the Insurgents,' that Madame Brillon wrote for him. You remember my telling you about it? It was in honor of Saratoga."

"I remember. Will there be any pink cakes left, Mr. Gratwick?"

"Plenty. What was Saratoga?"

"I know that! It was when the Americans beat Burgoyne in the forests."

"*Who* beat Burgoyne?" asked Ward softly.

"Oh — when *we* beat him."

"Good. Now I'm sure about the cakes." He laid a hand on the boy's shoulder. "Steady. This isn't over yet. He's going to play some of those Scottish ballads."

In the pause that followed the end of the march, Ward could hear a sudden chatter from the women. He wished that people at home could hear the buzz about their Minister to the Kingdom of France. There were Madame Helvetius's low hearty tones, calling the Doctor simply "Fronk-lan" without the suggestion of a title, Madame Brillon, gentler but equally possessive, addressing him as *"Cher Papa."* Both were devoted to him.

When the last of the Scottish ballads died away, there was a hush, then a rustle of applause. Ward guided Benjamin to Hercule's table, saw that the boy stuffed himself with such a weirdly chromatic assortment of pastry as to make his appearance at table during the next two days a matter of conjecture. Then he drifted out through the crowd. Old Marshal de Broglie cornered him to ask about the theory of gunnery current in the New World. An anxious-eyed woman in lilac begged him to speak to the Doctor about her husband. Really, ten years as a mere lieutenant of a regiment of foot-chasseurs was too much. If the Doctor when he next went to court would drop a word about a very deserving officer —

Ward finally made his way to Deborah, Paul and Mrs. Lathrop, who were the center of a knot of white and gold uniforms and civilian coats. Two girls in bright summery dresses were talking to Paul, and Ward was struck by the young man's command of French and the purity of his accent. Decidedly, he was someone to be watched.

Deborah greeted him warmly. "I was wondering when we'd see you. Paul's got a hundred things to ask you about America —"

"About home," Ward corrected firmly.

"About home. Come and sup with us tonight. Sue was talking about it on the way over."

"Delighted. About eight? It's very kind of you." Ward bowed his thanks. "Let me get you an ice. The Doctor's invented a new kind that combines pineapple and strawberries."

"Thanks, but I couldn't. Paul was saying that you might drive to Paris with us when this is over. Sue wants to stop at the d'Houdetots' in Passy on the way. You could meet us there."

"I'd like that," answered Ward.

"Till tonight," Deborah said. "Oh look! Here comes the Doctor. And just look at Minette."

Down the long flagged path the cat Minette marched with calm dignity, silver-gray tail hoisted high. After her came Docton Benjamin Franklin, fur cap on the back of his head, spectacles pushed up on his broad forehead and his patriarchal apple-wood staff tapping the stones rhythmically. Beside him walked a fellow Mason of the Lodge of Nine Sisters, la Rochefoucauld-d'Enville, hands behind his back and head thrust forward as though arguing some point with his host.

Like a most efficient rear guard, Madame Helvetius and Madame Brillon kept close formation, the older woman striding cheerfully on while Madame Brillon minced delicately. After them a cloud of women and girls straggled worshipfully.

Deborah giggled. "What a procession! All Minette needs is a drum-major's baton. Look, Ward, the Doctor's beckoning to you."

Ward crossed the grass quickly. "All in order at the Lodge, Doctor. I checked off all your points and those—" he inclined his head to Franklin's companion—"and those of Monsieur de Rochefoucauld-d'Enville."

"Famous," said Franklin while his friend nodded in silent approval. "Would you mind just looking into my study when this is over? I've a minor matter or two to talk over with you."

With a bow of acknowledgment, Ward stepped back and the cortege moved majestically on. He would have plenty of time to talk with the Doctor before stopping at the d'Houdetots' château. He made a mental note to ask Paul what he knew about a supposedly defunct firm which had once supplied powder to the States during the days of the fictitious Hortalez et Cie.

When the last guests had gone, Ward entered the far wing of the Petit Manoir and was surprised to see a few laced hats and light cloaks on the table in the porter's room. He glanced curiously at them. Then he stopped and picked a drying leaf from the collar of the farthest cloak before he went down the corridor to knock at the Doctor's door.

Franklin was again indulging in the secret luxury of his most un-Quakerlike flowered gown, against which Minette glowed softly silver-gray. He smiled blandly at Ward. "Come in, my young friend. Thank you for being prompt. Minette and I are planning on a little nap before we go over to Madame Helvetius's soiree. Sit down. Now for one thing—" he placed the tips of his fingers together and looked at Ward over the tops of his spectacles—"the most interesting, cross-eyed Mr. Bailey of whom your seafaring friend spoke need concern you no more."

"He's not dangerous, you think?"

"Not now. His sting, such as it was, is drawn and for good. That's one point. Now—" he leaned forward, peering at Ward's hand. "What have you there?"

"Something I found on the collar of one of your guests' cloaks

44

just now. A dark blue cloak, dove-gray lining and gold lace on a deep collar."

Franklin looked quizzically at him. "Now that's an odd place for it to grow. H'm, yes. The rhododendron Maximum. The blossom you know, has a campanulate corolla. I've often thought that it could be crossed with some climbing plant. The effect against a sunny wall would be magnificent."

"There's more about this leaf, sir," said Ward. "There's only one stand of this shrub in all the park. It covers that gap in the wall I told you about. Whoever wore the cloak came through that gap. Sir, I want to find the owner."

"It might be interesting. Now I have a small commission I wish you to undertake for me — "

"But sir," Ward broke in. "The gap — that metal tube. The owner of that cloak could tell us a lot about both of them."

"H'm," said the Doctor. "Now I must congratulate you on your powers of observation. There is but one stand of this shrub in the grounds. But — " he pointed a pencil at Ward — "but there are surely hundreds of them in this area. So I think we may relegate the cloak's owner to the same limbo that now holds — shall we say our cross-eyed Mr. Bailey?" His wise old face became less bland, and there were deeper wrinkles on his forehead. "My young friend, I want you to go to Rouen for me." His voice dropped lower. "Once in Rouen, you will seek out Monsieur Jules Ribault who lives on the rue des Chantiers. You will give him this." He drew out a heavily sealed letter. "What happens after that will depend on what he tells you. You will follow his directions as though they came from me. Further, you will take this with you." From a strongbox he drew a second, thicker packet, done up in oiled silk. Heavy seals dotted the surface and through the red wax ran a thin, strong chain. "You will fasten this about your waist," the Doctor

45

went on. "Next your skin, of course. Not the most comfortable underwear in the world, but necessary in this case."

"And what do I do with it?" asked Ward, frowning.

"If Ribault asks for it, give it to him. If not, you'll be guided by his instructions, always keeping it chained about you."

Ward pulled up his shirt, fastened the flat chain about him with a solid little padlock and slid the key into a tight inner pocket. He felt a controlled excitement as though the command, "Harness and hitch!" had been given in a gun-park.

"I can't tell how long you'll be gone," the Doctor went on. "You'll learn all that from Ribault. You'll leave in a half hour. If you meet anyone in the house or in the grounds, don't drop the least hint. And of course you'll write no notes canceling engagements that you may have."

Ward gave a last hitch to the chain. "Of course not."

"You'll go through the park and out through your famous gap, where a horse and a guide will meet you and take you to the west loop of the Seine. There you'll find a very ordinary sailing barge moored this side of the Ile de la Folie. It will have a blue lantern, bow and stern. Temple will go with you. He'll guide you there and introduce you to the master, Drouot."

"By barge!" exclaimed Ward. "I could reach Rouen far quicker on horseback."

Franklin looked gravely at him. "The horse will do from here to the barge. After that, you'd be most conspicuous riding the king's road by daylight. There is anonymity about a barge." He went on more gently. "This is a blind, mischancy errand. But it's no old philosopher's whim, Ward. You'll be in action, just as much as at Germantown or Monmouth."

"But are you sure I'm the man for the job?" objected Ward. "I've never been in Rouen. I don't speak very good French yet."

Franklin placed his finger tips together and looked searchingly at him. "My young friend, years ago, when our present

46

troubles were still in the realm of talk, before talk shifted to violence, I came to the conclusion that there was one thing which we needed beyond all else. Unity, money, munitions, supplies. We had to have them all. But most important, we had to have men who were greatly in earnest. I have watched you here, and I chose you."

Ward got up quickly. "I'm off. Here's the packet, here's Ribault's letter. Good night, sir." He hoped that Deborah and her family would not wait too long for him, but it couldn't be helped.

Franklin walked to the door with him. "Good luck and thank you, Ward. I trust I shall be welcoming you back to Passy soon."

III

Blind Journey

WARD FOUND IT HARD to maintain the role of a man greatly in earnest as the slow days dragged on in Rouen. He had located Ribault with no trouble, but the fat, dumpy man had merely assigned him to a small room in the house on the rue des Chantiers. He had made no demand for the oiled silk packet and made no comment on the Doctor's letter. Ribault put no restrictions on Ward's comings and goings, leaving him free to wander at will about Rouen. The whole affair was most puzzling.

Ward came to know the city well, feeling, even through his anxiety and restlessness, the medieval charm of the old river town. He discovered the little gem of St. Maclou with its Goujon carvings, explored the twelfth-century magnificence of the cathedral and was delighted with the south portal of St. Ouen and its grotesque little sculptured heads. He crossed to the Ile la Croix to stare up at the Château Baubet and rowed himself to the needlelike Ile Brouilly. As he studied the Flemish-looking Palais de Justice, Jeanne d'Arc's Tower or old Hôtel du Bourg-théroulde, he found some consolation for his enforced idleness in their antiquity, their richness. From Ribault he obtained heavy, leather-bound tomes, puzzling his way through the plates and the text, learning of the Cardinal d'Amboise who had erected the part of the west façade of the cathedral more than two hundred years ago, of the Butter Tower, built from the sale of indulgences to eat butter during Lent, of the meaning of the magnificent Cousin stained glass in St. Ouen.

On his eighth day in Rouen, the weather broke. Raw winds, from the Vosges or the Jura, swept along the valley of the Seine, bringing with them eternal, slanting rain. On the first rainy evening, Ward, irritable and jumpy, pushed aside Ribault's books, caught up a long cape, and went out into the night and the storm. Street by endless street he tramped, weaving down to the river, turning away from it, finding it again. The city was inky-dark, save for a few points of light where prosperous citizens kept great iron lanterns burning over their doors.

At an intersection, not far from the storm-shrouded cathedral, Ward stopped abruptly. A few yards down the street to his left, a lantern burned brightly throwing its rays on four men who, muffled against the drive of the rain, were talking animatedly. For a few moments, Ward stared fixedly at the group. Then he was sure. Two of the men were strangers. But the nearest cloaked figure was undoubtedly that of the New Hampshire-man, Jabish Frost, whom he had first met at the ferry below Mont Valtrien. The other, taller and slimmer, was surely Paul Dale.

Ward thought quickly. His own departure from Passy had been secret. From Rouen, he must not write to Paris. On the other hand, Ribault was unconcerned over Ward's comings and goings. Therefore, to reveal himself to anyone in Rouen must be entirely in order. He started toward the men.

As his footsteps rang on the pavement, the group broke up, Paul, Jabish Frost and one of the unknowns walking rapidly off in the opposite direction, losing themselves in the rainy night. The fourth headed straight for Ward.

Ward held up his hand. *"Monsieur, s'il vous plaît,"* he began haltingly.

The stranger, a squat, muscular man, brushed past him, shaking his head and muttering, *"Comprends pas!"*

Ward laid a restraining hand on the man's cloak. "I want only to inquire about those gentlemen with whom you were talking."

Unexpectedly the man began to flounder and thrash about like a hooked fish. Ward's grip tightened and his captive bawled, *"A moi! A moi! Ah, l'assassin! A moi, le guet!"*

Ward still clung to the man. "A simple question only. I mean no harm. *Pas de mal, hein?"*

But the man roared on. Heavy boots thumped on the pavement. A hand fell on Ward's shoulder, spun him about, and, panting, he faced two rough-looking gendarmes while two more hurried up shouting *"De par le roi!"*

Suddenly all the energy pent up in him through long months of inactivity flooded Ward with a quick, cold rage. He grappled the first two gendarmes, felling one with a quick twist of his hip and rolling the other across his stooped shoulder. A vicious blow from behind dropped him to one knee, but he rose quickly, driving a shoulder and his knee into a gendarme's midriff and sending him sprawling. The squat citizen danced about the outskirts of the melee still bawling, *"Ah, l'assassin!"*

Something loose and thin whistled through the air, coiled about Ward's head, about his neck. He reeled backwards, clawing at the hard cord that was cutting off his wind, strangling him. He felt his knees buckle, felt his arms pinned behind him. The noose about his neck loosened and he stood panting while more cords secured his arms at wrist and elbow. Then the gendarmes hustled him off, calling him a *"beau garçon"* and a *"solide gaillard"* with a sort of jocose ferocity.

After splashing on for a few blocks, Ward found himself shoved, not too roughly, into a dimly lit stone room where an officer of gendarmerie, elaborately braided, glowered at the group over a thick, open ledger. *"Eh, quoi?"* he growled.

The squat citizen plunged forward and burst into a torrent of French. Ward could only gather that the man was orating how he, a peaceful citizen who asked only to live peacefully under the benevolent protection of His Most Christian Majesty, had been set upon as he sought to return home. In his quality of good Rouenais, he had naturally called for the night-watch, protector of all virtuous citizens.

The officer turned to Ward. *"Et vous?"*

Ward had no sooner begun than the officer rose, fists planted on the ledger. *"Hein? Anglais?"* He made a sweeping gesture to the other gendarmes. *"A la cellule!* In solitary!"

Ward cried, *"Pas Anglais. Américain."* He was about to add the magic password, *"De la maison du Docteur Franklin,"* when something checked him. Laboriously he explained that he had seen two other Americans, talking with the squat man and another Frenchman. The Americans had gone before he could hail them and he had stopped the squat man to ask about them, to ascertain their whereabouts.

The officer sat down, still glowering suspiciously. "And these Americans, Monsieur Fournier?" he said to Ward's accuser. "You spoke with them, perhaps?"

Again Monsieur Fournier buried himself in a cloud of high-pitched French. Ah, but for himself, he knew no Americans. Yes, he had stopped to chat, outside the house of the cousin of the late Mayor of Rouen, Monsieur Mercadet. His companions? *Mais, quoi,* they were well known. Two of them, Messieurs Charny and Olivier, *marchands de vins en gros* like himself. The other, *quoi,* was *ce bon* Monsieur Pasquier who stood well in the sight of Monsieur the Bishop. Then he stamped up within two paces of Ward, pointed a thick, grimy finger at him and hissed, *"Assassin!"*

The officer shrugged and turned to his subordinate. *"Eh bien?"*

He emphatically backed up the statement of Fournier. *"Oui, mon capitaine.* It is as he says. Not only I, myself, saw these Messieurs of whom he speaks, but also did the Gendarme Nicèphore Loubet, who has an eye, *quoi!* We hear the cries of Monsieur Fournier and find him as he describes."

"But I only wished to question him," urged Ward.

"Sans doute," said the captain sourly. He picked up a pen. *"Vas-y.* Name and prename, address?"

"Ward Gratwick. American citizen. I lodge with Monsieur Jules Ribault, number twenty-seven-*bis,* rue des Chantiers."

The officer dropped his pen. "With Jules Ribault?" He snatched up another ledger, leafed through it, frowning. The frown deepened. "Monsieur Ribault has made no deposition with us, as required by law, concerning your *logement* with him."

"That may be because my stay was — and is — supposed to be brief," ventured Ward.

One of the gendarmes stepped forward, whispered at length to his superior. The latter tugged at his mustache and studied Ward. Then he said dubiously, "It is true, then, that you lodge yourself with Monsieur Ribault?"

"I have said so."

"En pension? You board with him?"

"No. As a guest."

The officer pushed back his vast cocked hat. "Ah, a guest of Monsieur Ribault. We shall summon him."

"What? Bring him out in this rain and at this hour?" protested Ward.

The gendarme looked shocked. "That would not be *convenable,* you conceive. In the morning. You will remain with us, Monsieur, reflecting the while on the fact that the gendarmes of Rouen do not hold their positions of honor in order to be knocked about like ten-pins. Cell number five, the second level."

The gendarmes moved toward him, blocking any chance of escape. Resignedly he let himself be led along a stone corridor.

To his disgust, the second level mentioned by the officer was below the street. He slithered down granite steps, along another corridor, down again, the air growing damper and damper. The building must have been very old, for even in the flickering lantern-light he made out worn carvings, strongly graceful vaultings above him.

At last one of the gendarmes produced a key, unlocked a thick door with a small barred opening and waved Ward in with a grand gesture. *"Voilà, Monsieur. Dormez bien."*

Ward entered reluctantly. The lantern shone on damp stone walls, a rude stool, a heap of straw in a corner. Ward sniffed disgustedly, stirred the straw with his foot. It was sodden and mouldy. He turned to the gendarme by the door. *"Ça pue,"* he said. "It stinks."

The gendarme raised surprised eyebrows. "And why not? I wish Monsieur a good night." The door slammed and Ward was left alone in the rank darkness. Restlessly he paced up and down, not daring to seat himself on the stool or use the foul straw.

Time slipped by, dragging and irksome. At some unmarked hour, light showed through the grating in the door, a key rasped. Blinking in the sudden flare of light, Ward saw the biggest of the gendarmes beckoning to him under a high-held lantern. *"Par ici, Monsieur,"* said the gendarme.

"Now what?" grumbled Ward as he stepped out under the ancient vaulting. He followed the gendarme along the corridor, finally coming to a halt in a lobby where an old iron lamp burned fitfully. From the depths of a battered wooden armchair Jules Ribault rose, handed the gendarme a coin. The latter bowed profoundly, saluted and vanished down the corridor. Ward drew a long breath. "I'm more than grateful to you, Monsieur Ribault."

Ribault hunched his wet cloak about him. *"Sans doute.* Now

you will follow me." He started down the long, stone lane that led off from the lobby, Ward close behind him.

"They sent word about this from the prison?" asked Ward.

"*Pas de tout.* You did not return. I became anxious. Where else to make inquiry if not at the various gendarmeries? Here we are." He pushed open a heavy door and his lantern glowed through the rain drops, showing a high stone wall a few yards ahead. "You will go with Chrysostome," continued Ribault. "He is a man you may trust. I have the honor, Monsieur, to wish you a good night." Gently pushing Ward into the open, Ribault closed the door.

By Ward's elbow a massive shape detached itself from the gloom. "Follow me, Monsieur," said a husky voice. "I am Chrysostome." He guided Ward through the long, drenched grass to the side of the long-abandoned moat.

The world was black in front of Ward, but his guide seemed to have a catlike gift of sight. Soon he felt stone under his feet, knew that he was climbing a long slope, a sort of narrow ramp cut in the wall of the moat. Then they were in a silent street with the smell of the Seine growing stronger every moment. Ward could vaguely make out the lines of the quays and the dull shimmer of the storm-whipped river. Ghostly in the gloom, tall masts pitched and tossed. Chrysostome hailed. *"Holà! Le Rossignol!"*

A lantern wavered into sight, shone on a narrow, slippery gangplank. Chrysostome turned to Ward. "It is here that I leave you. Monsieur Ribault instructed me to give you this." He drew a bundle out from under his cloak, forced it into Ward's hands and slipped off into the night.

Immediately a shape lurched toward him from the small ship. *"'Cré nom de Dieu,* do you wish to board or do you not wish to?"

Ward hesitated, then made his way cautiously up the swaying plank and onto the deck. His new guide led him down a steep companion way, threw open the door of a small cabin, sparsely furnished but immaculate. By the light of a lamp that hung in gimbals Ward saw a battered, swarthy man, his tangled black hair covered by a red stocking cap. The man pointed toward the bunk with its coarse, clean blankets. "Be comfortable. I am Georges Bovier, master of the *Rossignol,* Jules Ribault owner."

"You have perhaps a message for me from Monsieur Ribault?" asked Ward, tosssing his bundle onto the bunk.

"I, Monsieur? Only that I am to look to your comfort."

Ward sniffed curiously. "You carry wine?"

"But what else?" answered Bovier with a shrug.

"You know many who deal in wines — that is, wines in wholesale?"

"Who may know such, if I do not?"

"Then tell me if you know of a Monsieur Charny."

"Charny? No, the name does not recall itself," said Bovier.

"There was another name, Olivier."

Bovier's hands went out. "But certainly. Giles-Dominíque-Philibert Olivier, who only recently succeeded to the business on the death of his father. A man who is all that there is of the most respectable."

"Can you describe him?"

"Ah, he is young, that one. Say about the age of Monsieur. Tall and slim as a poplar. He carries his head *so.*" Bovier's chin tilted to a haughty angle. "And thus he walks, as I myself have often seen him." Ward watched Bovier's pantomime closely. Posture and gait actually did suggest a sort of caricature of Paul Dale.

When the skipper left, Ward sat on the edge of his bunk, chin in his hands. "So that damned Fourníer was right. It wasn't Paul."

55

Despite the lulling motion of the barge, sleep evaded him. He kept wondering where he was going, and why. Marching toward an unknown destination was no novelty to him. He had done that through the mists that hung over Germantown and over the killing roads that led down to Stony Point, far away on the Hudson. But this — The Doctor had, *must* have, something important on foot. For the time being, Ward was to know as little as possible about it. A phrase carelessly dropped, a word that might mean nothing to him, could be a whole encyclopedia to a British agent, an expatriate Tory, a Frenchman in British pay.

Ward turned uneasily in his berth. He recalled his conversation with Jabish Frost and his own reflection from *Poor Richard's Almanac* that "There is no such thing as a *small* enemy." A groom at an inn-stable, a potboy in an *auberge* who heard and reported a name or a destination could be damaging. For the moment, he could only wait and wonder.

One day the barge lay in a backwater that ran up into a circle of low blue hills. Again, the current took it between sunrise and sunset through a network of placid canals and back into the Seine again. Twice Ward questioned Bovier, only to be told he must wait and soon all would be clear.

Then in the black drum of a rainy night, Ward was roused from his berth, told to dress. When he jumped onto the soggy bank, a cloaked, dripping horseman was there, holding a spare mount. Down endless roads lined with ghostly poplars the two trotted on, halting once in each hour to rest the horses. Ward's guide did not give him any details, save that they were heading for the town of Alençon on the Sarthe. Two dawns found them sheltered in little white villages that lined the highways, two nights saw them on the road again. In another rainy blackness, Ward knew that there were houses about him, made out the shattered towers of a castle.

Slow hours stretched into days as Ward lived comfortably but furtively in a big stone house near the Sarthe, his host a dry-voiced youngish man who had something to do with the great lace industry that Colbert, Henry IV's great minister, had founded over a century ago.

Time went on uneventfully. Carriages and horsemen appeared at the porte-cochere but there was no word, that Ward could see, from Passy. He was not too surprised, at the end of a rather elaborate dinner, to have his host remark laconically that it was time to part. There was a small purse of gold pieces for Ward, another horse, another guide and once more the roads of France lay before him.

This time it was the city of Bourges, in the heart of France, and a triple-chinned abbé made Ward welcome in a Romanesque house close to the old mansion that Jacques Coeur had built about a Roman ruin. The abbé was genial, erudite and slightly disillusioned. Unusually well posted on what was going on across the Atlantic, he discussed anarchism, atheism and rebellion in general in the freest manner imaginable while remaining in fact a devout churchman and monarchist. Finding Ward's interest in architecture, he guided him through Bourges, from the Cathedral of St. Étienne to the Cujas mansion. For Franklin, he had a tremendous intellectual admiration and proudly brought out a copy of the French translation of *Poor Richard*, with Franklin's bold signature and a graceful inscription just below the title. But again, there was no news. Just a period of waiting.

In the abbé's guest-room, with its carved stone capitals supporting the fireplace, Ward again tried to reason out matters. At last a pattern began to form in his mind. "I was sent to Rouen," he told himself. "There I waited. Good. Now, under the Doctor's plan, if event 'A' happened, then I should follow course 'B.' If not, then I take course 'C,' which must have brought me to Alençon. At Alençon, I wait for event 'D.' 'D' may or may not have taken place, but anyway, here I am in Bourges and back there at Passy, the Doctor and his friends are watching this alphabet that I've dreamed up. Maybe in a few days 'M' or 'N' will have happened, someone will give me a letter and I'll head back to Passy. But what the devil is it all about?" He shrugged. "At least, I've been following instructions. But when is someone going to ask me for this packet of the Doctor's? I'd like to get rid of the damned chain, at least."

More days, and Bourges was far behind him. With still another silent guide he rode down the cave-lined banks of the Loire and into the town of Saumur with the ghostly ninth-century Tour de Tronc looming over it. There he was taken to the officers' quarters of the cavalry school founded a few years before and made welcome by a scarred major of hussars who had lost a leg at Rossbach.

Here there was no talk of the Rights of Man nor of intellectual revolt. The older instructors and the young officer-pupils were in no way concerned with the war across the ocean. War, to these lean, watchful men meant only the *next* invasion out of Germany which was sure to come — unless one struck first. War, it seemed to Ward, was an unwanted but too natural phenomenon to these horsemen. Peace was not a normal course of life; it was only an interval between two conflicts.

Glimpses of the cavalry school fascinated Ward. He kept wishing that real troopers like Harry Lee or Sheldon or Benjamin Tallmadge could be standing in his place on the level plains, watching troop after troop maneuver so skillfully. But there was always the question in his mind of what the future held for him.

At the end of a dusty afternoon, Major Debeney, his host, handed him a sealed packet and Ward's heart leaped as he recognized the familiar handwriting of the Doctor. This might send him back to Passy — and there he might even have news that at last passage to America had been found for him. Then his spirits dropped. The address was unmistakable — "To James Moylan, Esq., Agent for the United States of America, at Lorient, in Brittany. By the hand of my friend, Ward Gratwick, Lieutenant, Continental Artillery."

"What's at Lorient?" Ward asked. "It's a port I know little of. An important one?"

"*Quasiment comme ça,*" answered Debeney negligently, as though a mere naval base were beneath the notice of a hussar. "In the old days, one spoke much of it, among sailors, that is. But now — " he snapped his fingers — "it is as lifeless as the duck-pond of *le Père de Lustucru.*"

"But from there one could proceed easily to Passy?"

"Ah, I believe you, one could proceed to Passy or Warsaw or to the Bukhovina," announced Debeney. "So this bit of paper sends you on to that species of nowhere? I assure you, Monsieur, that it is we who are desolated. You have been *bon compagnon. Bon voyage et bonne chance.*"

All the way north and west toward the Breton coast, Debeney's words thudded in Ward's ears in rhythm with the trot of his horse. "Lifeless as the duck pond of *le Père de Lustucru.*" Why the devil was Franklin sending him on to a dying port where nothing could happen? He resigned himself to the fact that he had never known the bland philosopher to do anything uselessly or without reason. The answer might lie at Lorient or back at Passy. His horse trotted on, beating out the old nursery rhyme:

> *C'est le père de Lustucru*
> *Qui lui a repondu,*
> *"Allez, donc, la mère Michelle,*
> *Votre chat n'est pas perdu!"*

Ward hunched his shoulders. "Maybe Mother Michelle's cat isn't lost, but *this* one is!" Then through a rainy dawn he rode over the low ridges that shut in the knife-blade harbor of Lorient.

IV

Le Sauvage Royal

As HE RODE along the steep street that slanted toward the western side of the harbor, Ward studied the ships that idled at anchor, blunt little coasters and lean-flanked traders for longer ventures. A frigate floated near a great stone arsenal and beyond a ship of the line was being towed toward a graving dock. The street twisted, straightened out, showing Ward the far side of a building-crowned island that had been hidden before. Close under the island lay a long, low, graceful vessel, with extraordinary raked masts. Its bow was sharp and jutted boldly as though trying to hurl itself forward, even in repose.

The water front was slowly coming to life. Overhead, the clouds were lifting and a pale sun melted the last of the drizzle. He leaned from the saddle to ask directions, was told to make for a gray stone building farther down the street. He saw the white flag of France flying above the huge, cavelike door, then a deep-carved legend on the entablature: *"Compagnie de l'Orient,"* like an epitaph of French hopes for an Indian Empire. Farther along the façade, a bare pole jutted from a window.

As Ward watched, the window opened. A pair of hands were busy with halyards and bright bunting, as the harbor wind caught the folds, spreading them to the new day. Ward's vision blurred as he recognized the blue canton with its circle of stars, the thirteen red and white stripes. He reined in abruptly, raised his hand to his hat in salute. Then he dismounted and made his way to the smaller entrance under the new flag, his head high.

Through an open door on the second floor Ward could see a window and the brave tossing of the flag outside. He rapped on the doorpost, calling, "Mr. Moylan? I'm from Doctor Franklin."

A thickset man rose from behind a desk. He came forward, limping heavily. "Yes, I am James Moylan," he said. "Yes. The Doctor sent me your description. I'm glad to see you, Lieutenant Ward Gratwick, of the Continental Artillery." He limped over to his desk. "Here is something for you from our friend of Passy. You'd best read it right here."

Ward broke the seal and unfolded the letter. "My dear young friend," he read. "It has not been pleasant to me to send you running blindfold about France, but it was the wisest course. You have followed admirably, as I have been told from several sources, instructions that must have seemed galling and unnecessary. Your blindfold is now to be removed, though not by me since there is much that I do not wish to put in writing. It will be done by a man whom I greatly esteem, and to whom you will show this letter. Our friend James Moylan will guide you to him."

Ward glanced up from the letter. "You know about this, sir? I'm to meet someone through you, the Doctor says."

"That will be my pleasure, Mr. Gratwick," said Moylan. "You shall see him quite shortly."

"Then what? Am I supposed to start back to Passy?"

Moylan looked curiously at him. "As to that — well, I do not think that we need hurry about engaging post horses for you."

Ward returned to his letter. All was quiet in Passy. The cat Minette would have kittens soon. He himself had opened a most interesting correspondence with the naturalist Buffon on the feeding habits of the hippopotamus. De Chaumont had had his men cut down a hollow tree that Ward knew about. Mrs. Lathrop and the Dales had been again at the Petit Manoir and the two young people had shown a most unusual interest, for them, in things American. Madame Helvetius and Madame Brillon, who were sitting beside him as he wrote, sent their good wishes to Ward. "You have been missed by all," the Doctor concluded, "particularly by this writer who signs himself as the affectionate friend of — you recall the phrase? — of a young man greatly in earnest."

"You seem pleased," observed Moylan as Ward carefully folded the letter.

"The Doctor — well, I mean, he didn't need to say all this," said Ward slowly. "I thought I was just another American he was looking after."

Moylan smiled. "From the letter he wrote me I know you have earned his esteem, which is not lightly given." He pulled out his watch. "Now I suggest that you breakfast with me in the inn below. After that, you will go to the Quai Colbert, where you'll find a barge bearing the name *'Le Sauvage Royal.'*" He produced a slip of paper. "Show this to the bosun and he'll take you to the man you're to meet."

"You're not going with me?" asked Ward.

"It's not necessary," answered Moylan. "One last thing. I'm authorized to give you these few louis d'or. There may be expenses that you don't foresee before — well, before you see Passy again."

Two hours later, Ward sat in the stern sheets of an elaborate barge, rowed by sailors in blue and yellow uniforms. As the blunt prow moved out into the harbor, he stirred restlessly. Now the barge glided easily along, nosing past little coasting vessels, under the stern of a frigate, out into the open channel.

He shaded his eyes against the sun, looking ahead at the island he had noted before with its clustering stone buildings and the royal ensign above them. Then he saw the sharp bow of the ship that he had noted from the hillside road. As the barge drew nearer, Ward was struck again by the speedy lines of the vessel, the effect of swift power. The gun-ports along the near side were closed, but across the low deck he could see the breeches of a row of what he took to be nine-pounders lining the far bulwarks. Then he was under the stern, looking up in admiration at the maze of carved, gilded wood, the shining glass that enclosed a narrow gallery. His eye caught more gilded arabesques that curled and twisted into fantastic shapes to frame the name *Le Sauvage Royal*.

He turned quickly to the bosun. "Is this where we are going?"

"Where else, Monsieur?" answered the sailor politely. "The gangway — if it please Monsieur."

Ward swung from the barge onto a gangway of snow-white ropes and glistening boards. "Monsieur Gratveek?" the guard said. "This way." He pointed to an open door just under the break of the short quarter-deck.

Ward stood irresolute. The Doctor, Jules Ribault, James Moylan, the bosun and now the marine corporal — the world seemed full of people telling him to go here, go there — and to ask no questions. He squared his shoulders and strode toward the open door.

In the small cabin, a man sat at a paper-strewn table. He was a big, powerfully built man dressed in fine blue sea-cloth with white breeches and white silk stockings. The strong-featured face, tanned almost mahogany, was startling under carefully powdered and dressed hair. His eyes were dark and steady with humorous lines at the corners. Ward had a feeling that he was not only expected, but being coolly sized up.

Then the big man rose, bowed formally. "Enter, Monsieur

Gratwick. May I name myself? Yves Toutant Tremarec, captain of *Le Sauvage Royal*. Please seat yourself. Ah, that is good."

He turned to a second table, built to fold back against the wall, that held glasses and bottles. "Surely you will take a little wine with me. Burgundy? Bordeaux? The former? Your choice is good." He filled two glasses, raised his own. *"À votre santé. Ah, and the health of the most excellent Doctor Franklin. Tell me, does he still drink that fine Moselle that I tasted at Passy in the winter?"* The question seemed casual, but Ward was sure that Tremarec was watching him closely.

"I wasn't with the Doctor last winter, Captain. But I quite recently made an inventory of his cellar which is mostly Burgundy and Bordeaux, with some champagne. I did not see any Moselle."

Tremarec leaned back in his chair. "You, Monsieur, must be a greatly puzzled man, but there are always precautions that must be taken. Only yesterday did I know that I should have the pleasure of a call from you. I was given a description of you, and it was mentioned to me that you knew the Doctor's cellar. That is why I spoke of Moselle. A man might answer to your name, might resemble a written description of you. But it would be a chance of the most outrageous if he, too, knew each of the Doctor's bottles. But more than that, I was furnished a dossier of your services in the war in the Americas. I am used to judging men, Monsieur, and the man spoken of in that dossier can be only yourself. Shall I mention Brandywine Creek, Barren Hill, Stony Point? No, no, Monsieur, even without the Moselle I am satisfied."

Ward sipped his wine. "Then, Captain, you must know that by the Doctor's wishes, there is the matter of a blindfold to be removed by you."

Tremarec nodded. *"Parfaitement.* But not completely — at

least for the moment. You must have guessed that we are putting to sea. That much may be seen from the shore and cannot be kept hidden from the world. Now, since you must return to shore to lay in clothing and supplies — "

Ward shot to his feet. "I sail with you! My God — " his voice rose — "I'm — I'm going — "

Tremarec raised his hand quickly. "You go with me. For the moment, that must suffice. There are many on shore who would be glad to know whither we sail — and what our cargo is. I do not distrust your discretion, my friend, but those who undoubtedly watch you might read volumes in your least word." He smiled sympathetically. "Ah, that may be galling, still not to know. I have been told of your great anxiety to go home and I fully sympathize with it. The Doctor wrote me how uncomplaining you went quite in the dark to Rouen and thence to Alençon. Will not this small ray of light I now give you suffice — for a few little hours more?"

"Of course. You're right. But damn it, we may be just dropping down the coast to a Spanish port."

Tremarec spread out his hands. "To Spain or Morocco or — what will you? The seas are wide and there are many ports that a ship may touch. But I may give you this consolation at least. The Ministry of Marine does not send a brig like the *Sauvage* — nor, may I say in all modesty, a captain named Tremarec — to bring in a few haddock-heads and pilchards." He drew out a sheet of paper. "The barge still waits for you. The items marked on this list you will need in the days that you and I shall spend together. Make your purchases as quickly as you can and return here. The night will not be far advanced before you know at least our first port of call. Yes, by tonight you will know much more. *Diantre!* Tonight! My friend, I must find a few more men for my crew. I have applied to the navy authorities who seem willing to do nothing for a mere captain of the merchant marine. No matter. I'll manage somehow. In the meantime, a pleasant trip ashore."

By mid-afternoon Ward had finished with the ships' chandlers Tremarec had recommended. He strolled along the quay. Soon he was to sail somewhere in the *Sauvage,* but where? No French warships were making ready to form a convoy for Tremarec. A solitary *Sauvage,* if she ventured out into the sea-lanes, would, he thought, be quickly hemmed in and taken by British raiders. Well, the future lay in the Captain's hands.

He walked on, oblivious to the colorful throng. There were sailors from the fleet, fishermen, country people trundling low carts full of vegetables or crates of squawking hens. Nuns in gray, nuns in black, glided past, eyes on the ground. With a tramp and a clatter a detail of Marines swung past, followed by a few white-coated dragoons. Just as he was passing a row of low-doored hovels that gave out a reek of coarse sour wine, a tall man in rumpled clothes emerged from the nearest wineshop. Ward noted him out of the corner of his eye, his lip crinkling in unconscious disgust. The man looked at Ward, gave a sudden start, and then tried to duck back into the shop, cannoned off the solid door that had been slammed behind him.

Ward had a quick memory of a gold piece spent on false information, of a trip to Marly-le-Roi in search of a French privateer skipper who had never existed. That was the man, James Houston, American citizen, who had lied to him and taken his gold. Ward jumped forward, caught Houston by the collar, and spun him about. Houston struggled, but Ward only gripped tighter. Panting, Houston gave a last futile twist. "God damn you, let go of me!" he cried thickly.

"Stand steady," said Ward coldly. "I want to talk to you. There was no privateer skipper at Marly-le-Roi, *Mister* Houston."

"What are you talking about?" Houston's voice cracked. "I don't know anything about skippers. I'll —" He slipped sidewise, swung at Ward's chin, an unskillful, fumbling swing.

Ward evaded it easily. "You don't know anything about skippers?" he snapped. "Yes, so I found out, but it cost me nearly the last of my gold to learn it."

Houston whined, "Swear to God, I thought it was true." His reddened shifty eyes were darting left and right, but for the moment he stayed passive in Ward's grasp.

Ward shook him, still holding a fist close to his face. "Talk straight or I'll chuck you into the harbor."

"God damn you, quit badgering me. I'll call the gendarmes."

Ward gave a short laugh. "That's about the last thing *you*'d do."

"Is it? Is it?" Houston's thin mouth twisted into a sneer. "They know all about me. I got my papers. They'd never touch an American soldier, by God."

"A *what?*" cried Ward, easing his grip a little. A couple of sailors, a dragoon corporal, water-front idlers, fishwives carrying odorous baskets were stopping to listen. Then two gendarmes clumped up, sabers rattling. One of them growled, *"Qu'est-ce que c'est que s'agit, 'tit nom de Dieu?"*

Still holding Houston, Ward said crisply, *"Du maison du Docteur Franklin, Sergent."*

The sergeant stiffened, raised his hand to his big hat. *"Ah, parfaitement!* Does Monsieur require our assistance?" His companion stepped quietly, but menacingly, beside Houston, one hand raised.

Ward let go his hold. "You said they wouldn't touch you, Houston. Want to try it?"

Houston went pale. "No, no! My God, no," he said huskily.

Ward thanked the gendarmes and dismissed them with a small coin to the sergeant. Then he turned to Houston. "I'll listen to you. Get inside. We don't want a crowd. No, not that shop you came out of, the second one beyond." Alert against a sudden move, he followed him inside. There were a few rough tables in the dim interior, a stone floor where dirt crunched under his boots. Ward pointed to a table by the door and seated Houston on the inner side. As he himself sat down, the chain about his waist rasped him. He settled it quickly. What if the chain had broken in the scuffle and the Doctor's packet been lost!

Houston slumped sullenly over the table. "What do you want with me?"

What indeed did he want with Mr. James Houston? Even if there were the least chance of recovering the money, the sum was of little importance to him, thanks to the modest windfall provided by James Moylan. Then he remembered the sworn assurances that Houston had given him, remembered the demand for cash before giving information, and felt anger returning. "I don't like being butted around," he said coldly. "You dangled bait in front of me. You knew I only had a few sous over what I gave you. What were you up to?"

Houston looked up at him. "I'm weak. I can't talk unless I eat. Haven't since yesterday noon."

"And you expect me to feed you?"

"Why not? I'd do the same for you or any other American soldier."

"Yes?" asked Ward sarcastically. "And pay for it with money such as you took from me?"

"Got to eat," mumbled Houston.

Ward beckoned to a fat, one-eyed man in a greasy leather apron who was lurking in the shadowy depths of the room. "Bread, cheese and wine." He motioned toward Houston. "Nothing for me."

The food and wine were brought and Houston fell on them.

Ward watched him curiously. He wasn't a bad-looking man, save that all his features seemed somehow in need of tightening. He was big and broad, without being well-knit. He probably wouldn't last long on a march. Ward asked suddenly, "What service?"

"With Arnold," mumbled Houston through a mouthful of bread and cheese.

"West Point?" asked Ward with a hard smile.

Houston pushed away his plate. "God damn you, if you want to know, I was on the march to Quebec."

"You were? Whose command?"

"With Enos," said Houston, smearing thick crumbly cheese on a crust of bread.

"Then you never made Quebec. Enos and his men dropped out."

"Yes, and maybe you'd have dropped out with 'em," said Houston truculently. "You weren't at the discussions. I was. Rank of sergeant and an ensigncy to come. I was the only man of my platoon to vote against quitting. But I had to stay with my command, didn't I?"

"Technically, yes," admitted Ward.

"Then what happened?" cried Houston, waving his blunt knife. "When we get home, we'd better have been the Lost Ten Tribes of Israel and stayed lost." Everything had gone wrong after that, according to Houston. He had been in and out of half a dozen militia companies. In '77 his unit had reached the Hudson the day after Burgoyne's surrender. No pay, no glory. At last he had shipped aboard a privateer, hoping for prize-money. Treatment was so bad that when his ship touched at Le Havre, long before the blockade, he had deserted. Since then he had knocked about France, living, he stated frankly, on American popularity. Paris had brought him no luck, so he had drifted off into the country again. Until recently he had been taken in by a kindly widow south of Rennes. "She raised ducks," said Houston. "She was kind of ugly. So I came down here."

If the story were true, Houston was a weakish man who had certainly been dogged by bad luck. And at one time, he must have stood in a brighter light. To have been a sergeant under Enos, despite the decision taken on the road to Quebec, was an achievement in itself.

He asked abruptly, "Why didn't you go to Dr. Franklin?"

Houston made a disparaging gesture. "Not me. Up to his neck in duchesses and countesses. He's quit being an American. I'm too independent to trail around after him, bowing and scraping for every charity copper he doles out. He must be making money."

"You made a big mistake in not going to him," said Ward, controlling his irritation. "And he's losing money, not making it. Anyway, an independent man's the kind he likes."

Houston winked knowingly. "Do you think? But let me tell you, you weren't independent when you were with him. He had you. He knew you were straining like a moose in a mudhole to get home and he played on that, tied you right to him." He laughed harshly. "I could see. That's why I didn't have a qualm about lifting those louis from you. I needed the money bad, and I knew he'd open his strongbox a crack if you told him you wanted more. Tell him so from me when you get back to Passy," he concluded angrily.

There was an odd, warped conviction in the man's words. In addition to being a target for bad luck, in addition to seeming more than shifty, he was wrongheaded. In a company of infantry he would be morbidly jealous of his rights, would know inside and out every regulation that could be bent to his benefit, and that of his friends. Yet, he had been a sergeant under Enos. "Why did you come down to Lorient?" asked Ward.

"Why?" echoed Houston. "It's a place ships sail from, ain't

71

it? Sooner or later something's going to happen to that blockade. I'll be aboard the first ship to clear for home if I have to
build myself into the planks on the deck."

"You really want to get home?" asked Ward dubiously.

"Home? The lowest American mudflat'd look like the Kingdom of Heaven to me."

"Suppose I knew of a voyage — a very risky voyage — that
might at least get you started back to the army."

Houston's clawlike hands swept across the table, clutched at
Ward's cuff. "You know of such? You're not humming me?
Get me aboard the leakiest craft that ever put out and so help
me I'll clean your boots the rest of my life. I'll give you a
seven-year bond on me."

"I can't promise. I'll see what I can do." Ward laid two silver
pieces on the table. "Get yourself freshened up and be here at
sundown. But don't count on anything." He left Houston sitting sag-jawed at the grimy table, the money and the remains
of the food and wine untouched before him.

Ward regained the barge and sat back in the stern as the
crew pushed off. Had he encouraged Houston too much? The
voyage might end at Marseille or Brest, leaving Houston just
as badly off as before. Yet Tremarec had said that the Ministry
of Marine did not send a ship like the *Sauvage* after pilchards.
He looked far off to the south where the sinking sun was
touching the mouth of the harbor with gold and purple. Did
the sea run out there into a blind alley? No. That harbor must
be the beginning of a long passage that led straight to his country, his army — and to Faith. He shivered a little as he thought
of the letters that he had so hopefully sent out from Passy to
faraway Valley Forge in Pennsylvania. What if none had
reached her? She would only know that he had been captured.
Usually, capture meant the British hulks in the North and East
Rivers or the foul pens in the old Sugar House on Liberty

Street. And, in far too many cases, hulks and House meant a hasty burial in the flats below Wall Street.

The breeze across the harbor freshened and Ward sat up straighter. As surely as he *knew* that the *Sauvage* would take him home, so he knew that Faith would be waiting, confident that one day or another Ward would come riding along the road by Fatland Ford.

The barge sculled smoothly on, weaving past high sterns, brushing under weed-hung cables to the low, jaunty hull of the *Sauvage.* "Where's the Captain?" he asked the guard as he swarmed up the gangway.

"Over there on the island," answered the man, pointing toward the rocky island with its stone buildings.

Ward looked toward the stone wharf where several longboats were moored, then at the gray-white walls of the fort, the half-buried magazine. As he looked, a cannon gushed smoke and a dull boom rolled over the harbor. By the wharf, drums beat and a column of men worked, antlike, toward the longboats. On the *Sauvage,* a watchman's rattle brayed and a detail of seamen began levering the cover from the forward hatch. On the island, drums sounded louder. One longboat pushed out, another, until five were strung out between the stone wharf and the ship. Oars dipped and flashed, the drums throbbed and boomed nearer and nearer.

In the stern of the last barge Ward saw Tremarec and beside him an official whose gold braid caught the sun. In Tremarec's boat, as in all the others, Royal Marines with fixed bayonets sat by the oarsmen.

A short, thick boom was run out from the *Sauvage,* a net of stout rope dangling from it. The first longboat swung alongside. The marines shifted as the net fell and the sailors began piling stubby, oblong boxes that seemed immensely heavy for their size, into the net. In perfect order the other longboats

73

swung alongside, some of them waiting for the first to unload, the others bringing up by a boom aft. Tremarec vaulted onto the deck, followed more slowly by the braided official. "This way, *Monsieur le Commandant*," Tremarec motioned, and smiled pleasantly at Ward as he strode by. The two officers made their way forward and Ward saw their heads vanish down the hatch.

The unloading went on smoothly, machinelike in its precision while the minutes went by as though marked off by the clack of the capstan and the creak of ropes. Tremarec and the official reappeared and made their way quickly to the aft cabins, two clerks with great sheafs of paper following them. A sturdy sailboat from the chandler's came alongside with Ward's purchases and for a few moments he was busy checking over what was slung onto the deck. Linen clothes, wide-brimmed hats of soft straw, light shirts and underwear, kegs of pickles, frails of figs, small casks of raisins, table wines, rum and a few bottles of brandy.

Ward called a pair of cabin boys, told them what to stow below and what to leave in the cabin that had been hastily pointed out to him as he had left the ship earlier. As the boys scurried about, Ward surveyed his lodgings for the first time. The quarter-deck, he saw, had been extended some ten feet along the port and starboard bulwarks, so the whole structure resembled a stump-armed "U." The extension that formed Ward's cabin housed a sixteen-pounder, secure in its rope breeching. There was a built-in bunk at the right of the thick-barreled gun, a set of drawers on the left, flush with the side-boards. By edging past the gun, he could just squeeze into his bunk and he found that he could open the drawers by leaning across the barrel. Beyond the muzzle of the piece was a tight-closed gunport.

When he returned to the deck, he found that barges and

port officials had gone, but there was a message that the Captain wished to see Monsieur Gratwick in his cabin.

Ward found the big Breton seated once again behind his paper-strewn table. "And your trip ashore was profitable, I trust," began Tremarec.

"Your recommendations were most helpful. It may be that I have been able to render you a small service in return. I've found at least one man to make up your crew-shortage."

"One more man? But I find that magnificent. Tell me, Monsieur, did you organize a press-gang such as our English neighbors use?"

Ward laughed. "No, a willing recruit, an American who has seen some service on a privateer." He gave directions for finding the somewhat dubious Mr. Houston and Tremarec at once sent a petty officer ashore with a note to Houston from Ward.

Then the Breton faced Ward. "We sail with the dawn tide." He sat back in his chair, placed his finger tips together in a gesture that somehow reminded Ward of Franklin. "Here is the story," Tremarec began. "In a northern arsenal there was a great store of military equipment — dragoon helmets, sabers, muskets, bayonets, flints, powder. It was made available to our mutual friend in Passy after much difficult negotiation, since there were, and are, many at court who do not wish your country well. It had to be done without their knowledge."

"I see. And all this time I am still at Passy?" asked Ward.

"Yes. But as soon as the last link is forged, you leave for Rouen."

"But why the secrecy?" Ward asked.

The Breton looked surprised. "Why? Had you left openly for Rouen, you could well have been followed by agents of those who oppose all aid to America, since they knew you to be in the Doctor's confidence. Once there, secrecy did not matter. Your presence in Rouen, where there are probably no agents anyway, would not attract attention, since you might have a hundred innocent reasons for being there. Your departure, of course, was a different matter."

"I begin to understand. I would only draw attention while moving, not while stopping," said Ward.

"So far as Rouen is concerned, yes."

"But why did I wait there so long? Why didn't I go right to a port?"

Tremarec placed his elbows on the table. "Consider, my friend. In my story, you are still at Rouen. The weapons are yours, but you have no ship. Now, had not a ship materialized, you would have returned at once to Passy. But, the ship was found — my ship. At a northern port, it loads the cargo and sails, by short stages, to Lorient. In the meantime, you move from one town to another. Without knowing it, you are housed by people intimately concerned in the whole scheme."

Ward frowned. "But why didn't I come straight to Lorient?"

"Ah, for a very profound reason. Our cargo of arms was complete. But it did not make up our full loading. For arms and clothing alone, we would not risk the loss of a ship like the *Sauvage,* you understand. Secretly and with much difficulty, the matter of the full cargo was arranged. If it had not been arranged, you would no doubt at this time be with the Doctor at Passy."

"You took on more cargo here? Yes. I begin to see now. The little boxes and their Marine guard, the presence of a high port official."

Tremarec nodded. "Gold, my friend."

Ward began to laugh. "In brief, my passage money. I tell you, Captain, even though I am a mere landsman, I can see that it would be most desirable to own shares in a ship that requires so much gold to transport one inconspicuous American."

"It might be an investment of the most profitable," answered

Tremarec blandly. "But do not say 'mere landsman,' for such may enjoy many of the greater moments of life which a wandering seaman must miss. Two years ago, I am at sea when my daughter Mirabelle makes her first communion. And now the formal betrothal of my eldest son Alcide to the daughter of neighbor de Croizet will find me far from land. Madame Tremarec must witness these family peaks without me."

After sundown Ward leaned his elbows on the low bulwarks between two sixteen-pounders and looked out toward the ocean, toward that path that must lead to America, to Fatland Ford. A few fishing boats shimmered ghostly and unreal as they worked into port. There was a hail at the gangway and Ward turned to see Houston being brought aboard by a petty officer. Enos's former sergeant had somehow been able to find clean clothes and he had shaved. There was a real spring in his step as he crossed the deck and his eyes turned like Ward's south to the open ocean and the sea-lanes that led out and out to the west and home.

V

The High Seas

SLEEP WAS DIFFICULT that night. Hour after hour the deck outside Ward's cabin echoed to the clump of boots and the jolt and jar of barrels and cases. Tackle creaked and wailed, whistles shrilled as water-casks were slung aboard. Then the night was filled with a babel of grunts and bleatings, the squawk of poultry and bewildered lowings as livestock were herded into the pens beyond the foremast. At last he managed to shut out the din and fell into a deep sleep.

His cabin was still dark when a cautious hand shook his shoulder. The tumult on deck had ebbed noticeably, but booms and ropes still creaked. "What is it? Are we sailing?" he asked, peering uncertainly at Tremarec's steward who stood in the doorway.

"Not yet, Monsieur. The Captain will be obliged if Monsieur will come to his cabin."

In the dark, Ward fumbled into his clothes as best he could, buckling his shoes and settling his neckcloth while he wondered what the Breton could want. Was it that a last-minute change in orders would take him from the *Sauvage* and set him down once more on a French road bound for Passy? He hurried down the passageway.

Three people sat at the table with Tremarec. Deborah Dale sprang up with a cry of surprise. Mrs. Lathrop stiffened, and Ward saw her hands go tense on the edge of the table. Paul

Dale, beyond her, jerked backward in his chair and Ward read sudden, deep anger and astonishment in his eyes.

Pushing the gray crimson-lined hood from her hair, Deborah ran to Ward. "You! Oh, *you* can do something about this. It's the stupidest thing I ever heard of!"

Ward drew a deep breath. "Well! This is a surprise, Deborah." He turned to the others. "Mrs. Lathrop, your servant. Good evening, Paul."

The lamp beat strongly on Mrs. Lathrop's handsome lined face as she said in a crisp voice, "Do you mind telling this gentleman precisely who we are?" She looked acidly at Tremarec. "In most circles our word should be enough."

"I regret the necessity of my insistence, Madame. But now Monsieur Gratwick has unconsciously identified all of you." He looked at Ward and tapped some papers at his side. "The orders from Monsieur de Sartine lacked a description, you understand, the omission of some clerk. Lacking identification of the bearers I could hardly honor the Minister's orders. But as we talk, Mademoiselle mentions our Benjamin Franklin, and I think at once of you, who may have seen our guests at Passy."

Ward answered, "Of course I've seen them at Passy and at their own house. There's no mistake."

"But there *is* a mistake — " began Deborah, sitting down again.

Paul's expression tightened, and Mrs. Lathrop said "Hush!" in a low tone.

Ward passed his hand over his hair. "Will someone tell me what this is about? There's no change in our orders, Captain? De Sartine isn't putting us in the graving dock?"

"No change," said Tremarec. "Save that we have three more passengers, now that you have vouched for them."

Paul leaned across the table. "Without that vouching — what then?"

"What then?" Tremarec smiled pleasantly. "I should have been obliged to set you ashore."

Deborah turned quickly. "You would have? There would still have been time to end all this?"

Mrs. Lathrop rose. "We may spare you a family argument, Captain. Will you show us to our quarters?"

Paul followed her. "We've talked this all over, Sis. You'll end by thanking us."

"The state cabins, then, since the Minister so specified," said Tremarec. "This way, Madame."

He led the way, Mrs. Lathrop and Paul following. At the door, Paul paused. "Ah — really a very nice surprise to see you on board, Ward. Had no idea, you know — " His footsteps echoed on down the passage. Deborah remained seated, her head bowed.

Ward stood looking down at her. "Hadn't you better tell me something about this?"

She said in a low voice, "Ward, you've got to help me. I don't want to go to the Sugar Islands. I want to go back to Paris." Her eyes were dark with anger and exasperation. "They never told me a word till the last minute. Cousin Sue even had my trunks packed without my knowing it."

"What about the Sugar Islands?"

"That's where we're going. To Fort-Royal in Martinique."

"And you don't want to?"

Deborah's lips quivered. "Of course not. I want to stay in Paris. It'll be different when there's peace again, and I can really go home. But this — " She bent her head. "No, Ward. I don't want to go."

"All right," Ward said. "I'll speak to Tremarec. I'm sure he doesn't want to take an unwilling passenger. We'll get you rowed ashore. It's pretty late, but you could find our agent, James Moylan. His wife would look after you. After that — I don't know. You could go to Passy and stay with Franklin's Scotch friends, the Alexanders."

She gathered her cloak. "Let's go now. Right away." Then she sank back wearily. "It wouldn't help. I haven't a sou. Not one."

"But you've got what your father's been sending you. Mrs. Lathrop told me so."

"I haven't got it," said Deborah dully. "He's been sending it all right, first to Amsterdam and then to Hamburg. Paul's been looking after it for me. I gave him some kind of a paper — a power, they called it."

"You mean he's been using up your money?" asked Ward sharply.

She faced him, eyes alight with indignation. "He hasn't done anything of the sort. He's been in Spain and the Low Countries, and you know how clever he is. Why, he's turned my money over four or five times. He showed me the figures. Of course, he's made a lot for himself, but *this* was for me."

"He's made money for you but won't let you have it."

She stamped her foot. "Will you please stop criticizing Paul. He thinks he's doing the right thing for me. Now he's found a chance to make heaps and stacks of money for us all and to do it he has to go, we all have to go, to the Sugar Islands. Monsieur de Beaumarchais is in it somehow. Cousin Sue is terribly enthusiastic."

"I don't see why you all have to go."

"Why, to sign things. Paul explained it all and *Oh!* I do wish he hadn't. What do we want more money for? And why do we have to go to the ends of the world to get it? There was all we needed in Paris. Oh, Ward, I was so happy there. And now!" Her hands suddenly caught at his worn lapels. "Go and see Paul now. There's still time. Tell him how silly it all is, how

81

angry I am with him. Make him change his mind. Paul thinks a lot of you, and he'd listen where he wouldn't to me. Do it, Ward, and I'll never forget it as long as I live."

She was distractingly pretty as she looked up at him. "I'll do what I can," he said. "Wait here."

Ward entered the carved elegance of the port cabin. Under Tremarec's orders a big bed had been clamped to the floor. One or two heavy trunks stood against one wall, and a sailor was just staggering into the women's quarters with another. Paul finished unknotting a lacy neckcloth. "Good of you to look in."

"I'm afraid it's pretty late."

"Nonsense. I'm all keyed up. Off at last, and it was the devil's own time arranging passage. I told old de Sartine we'd take a fishing boat if that was all he had." He looked about the cabin appreciatively. "Nothing very fishlike about this, is there? Sorry Sis is so dead against this. I suppose she's dropped a hint or two."

"Yes," answered Ward. "Frankly, she asked me to act as her ambassador. It's no business of mine, of course, Paul, but couldn't some other way have been found?"

"Family matter," said Paul shortly.

"I quite agree it's none of my business," said Ward, "but she's pretty upset. From the captain's chronometer, I'd say there were a good two hours before we sail. She's devoted to you, but this might be the beginning of a deep rift between you. Then there's another thing. Tremarec strikes me as a first-rate seaman. This craft must have amazing speed built into her. As a gunner, I can tell you that she's well armed, and I like the looks of the crew. But a single British frigate could probably blow us all out of the water. Paul, this could be a damned dangerous voyage."

Through the door, Mrs. Lathrop spoke crisply. "Our minds

are quite made up. Deborah's acting like a headstrong, spoiled baby."

Paul winked at Ward. "We're not going to change, Cousin Sue. Don't worry. Look here, Ward, I appreciate your concern. And you know how fond I am of Deborah, always have been. It was a real blow to me when she took this attitude. But she'll get over it. It's for her own good."

"I hope you're sure of that, Paul."

"If I weren't, I shouldn't stir a foot. I've been in a dozen ventures since I began running about Europe, and they all have turned out well — more than well. This is the biggest of all — and the surest."

"In wartime?" asked Ward. "With the British controlling the seas?"

Paul gave him a friendly smile. "You've been a fighter, Ward. I've been out of it, and I tell you frankly that I envy your record. But I have learned something about commerce and the most important thing I've learned is that gold flows anywhere. I have an agent in England. Through him I could be in touch with Boston or Amsterdam or Madrid, any country that is now at war with England. My agent in Amsterdam can do business for me in Liverpool. And so it goes. Now from Martinique — But I'm on matters that are better left untouched. I only say this. My operations shouldn't take long. We'll wind up sharply. After that, Sis can live where she pleases. She'll be an heiress in her own right, regardless of what may happen to Father's affairs in America. Six months — a year at the most."

"And you've told her all this?"

"Over and over. You know, Ward, maybe you could help smooth things over. When you go back, give her the gist of what I've told you. Coming from you it might have just the authority she needs."

"Mm," said Ward dubiously.

83

"Really, I'd appreciate it if you would. And another thing. Just between us. This may wind up even sooner than I think. Will you do something for me?"

"Delighted, if it's in my power," said Ward.

"Then see that I am taken into our army. God knows what's ahead of us, but I'd like to feel that I'd contributed at least something."

"You can count on me," said Ward. "I'll talk to Deborah."

"Then tell her for Heaven's sake to come to bed," called Mrs. Lathrop. "Good night, young man."

As Ward entered the captain's office, Deborah rose quickly. "What did he say?"

"I'm sorry, Deborah," said Ward. "Paul's convinced that he's making you — all of you — secure for life. Don't forget, Deborah, that the Paris merchants and traders, the bigger ones, think a lot of his judgment. I've heard talk in the salons. Really, I'm afraid you've no choice, as things are. It won't be so bad. Fort-Royal is a colonial capital after all. There's bound to be good society there, and you'll have entree to it. Tremarec can tell you all about it."

Deborah bounced to her feet. "All for the best! Stuff! And society! Pickaninnies in a swamp!"

"Even if it is as bad as all that, it won't be for long. Paul said so. Maybe as little as a year."

Deborah flushed. "As *little* as a year?" She suddenly gathered her cloak about her, glided to the door and slipped the key from the inner side. Before Ward could move, she was across the threshold, the door slammed and the key clicked.

He sprang after her, shook the heavy latch. Then he shrugged. She could come to no harm with the deck crowded with sailors, with petty officers everywhere and Tremarec surveying the whole scene from the quarter-deck. He dropped into the nearest chair and mopped his forehead.

In a few moments the key turned and Deborah sailed in, head up and looking straight ahead of her. Without speaking to him, she crossed the cabin, picked up a small cloth-covered bag from a dark corner.

"Here," cried Ward. "Where are you going?"

"Ashore," answered Deborah loftily.

"Not while I'm on board. Besides, you haven't any money."

"Please, Ward. I'm going to Mr. Moylan, as you yourself suggested. I don't need money. I gave one of my rings to a sailor, and he's going to row me ashore without the Captain knowing. Mr. Moylan will sell the others for me!" Deborah hitched her chin higher. "And no one's going to stop me."

Ward reached for her, then his arms dropped. There was a gentle creak of timbers. The deck rose slowly, gently under their feet, fell away, rose again. Far earlier than Ward had reckoned, the *Sauvage* was under way.

"Too bad, Deborah," said Ward gently. "But you never could have got ashore, you know."

Speechless, she sat down, still clutching the little bag. There was silence in the cabin.

Through three bright days and three nights when the roll of the waves gave back the shattered reflections of the stars, *Le Sauvage Royal* scudded on a general westerly course. At least it seemed westerly to Ward, for day broke gold and apple green and blue over the stern, and the last flare was red and black and blue beyond the lift and dip of the bowsprit. Since leaving Lorient there had been no sign of their three unexpected passengers. Had it not been for occasional glimpses of cabin boys disappearing under the quarter-deck with covered trays or trundling empty trunks out of it, Ward could have supposed that they had slid ashore at the last moment.

Forward of the luxurious state cabins, the ship seemed to him

85

like a floating fortress awaiting a siege. Watches aloft and on deck were doubled. The gun-crews were never far from the nine- and sixteen-pounders that crouched in their rope breachings behind the low bulwarks. Slow matches burned night and day in buckets of sand close by each piece. Officers and petty officers succeeded each other on the quarter-deck, but Ward never looked up there without seeing Tremarec, legs braced and hands behind his back, dominating the brains and heart of the ship, nor did he ever hear the Breton's unmistakable tread coming down the steps from his post. Knowing something himself of the strain of unbroken vigils, Ward was surprised always to find the captain immaculate as ever, powdered, shaven, braid and buttons gleaming, calling down a greeting as though the ship were peacefully working up the Seine. Ward never ventured to the quarter-deck. The ship was running through dangerous seas, and he would only be a landsman among highly skilled professional seamen.

He took his meals in the senior officers' mess, a narrow compartment below the main deck where the ceiling was even lower than that of his cabin and which he entered through a bewildering maze of thick uprights that helped support the upper works. The mess was dark and unventilated, and the swinging lamp above the plank table soon burned blue after being lighted.

None the less, the food was good and arrived in great wooden bowls and trenchers not too cooled after its trip from the galley far forward. His companions were Tremarec's two senior officers, Bretons like the Captain. The elder, Keratry, was a big, explosive man with a loud voice that somehow sank to a low, commanding tone when on duty. The second, Gaos, was almost dwarfish and slipped quietly into the mess, ate rapidly without speaking and slipped out as silently as he had come. The third permanent member was the surgeon, Brotier, a lean, stooped man yellowed by tropical suns and fevers, relics of service in the

86

old India Company. Brotier was well-read and inclined to look down on his fellow officers whose world began at the high-tide mark, and ended there. At times he made Ward uneasy for he took pleasure in voicing antimonarchical opinions, backed by copious quotations and allusions, which sent Keratry into storms of roaring disagreement. These scenes always ended with Keratry, his every counterargument reduced to shreds, stamping from the mess while Brotier smiled sardonically into his winecup.

On the fourth day Ward, hunched in his cabin, finally discarded the worn brown coat that had almost become a uniform for him at Passy and put on the clothes that he had bought at Lorient. The coat was good, serviceable dark blue sea-cloth with solid brass buttons, the breeches white and well cut and the stockings white again, of a fine, light wool. He smoothed the deep, turned back cuffs and clapped on a cocked hat that had a gold braid about the brim. If the cuffs and the revers of the coat had only been red, he would be virtually in uniform again. The notion increased his feeling of well-being as he mechanically settled the chain of the Doctor's packet about his waist. It couldn't be too long now. Each forward lunge of the bow, each bulge of the gold-brown sails took him farther and farther along his journey.

He ducked out of his cabin and stepped into the full early morning sunlight on deck. The *Sauvage* was thrusting along through deep-blue waters, and a brisk wind was edging each wave with a lace of sheerest white. Ward raised his eyebrows. At mess Keratry had told him that the wind still blew from the same quarter. Yet now he felt its steady pressure behind his right ear, not quartering across his face as it had before, and the shadows of the masts with their endless stretches of sail fell toward the bow, not across the bulwarks. The course had been altered, and Tremarec was now pointing the *Sauvage* south.

Hands behind his back, he began his routine walk up the deck, striking out as though he were paralleling the course of a gun-team. Groups of sailors were holystoning the deck. Others were mysteriously busy with great coils of rope. On a hatchway, the sail-maker sat cross-legged and ran his great needle through soft sailcloth. Some of the sailors spoke to him as he passed. By the foremast he came upon James Houston kneeling as he pushed a holystone along the deck. The ex-sergeant was wearing a ragged blue jersey and stiff-looking breeches rolled to the knees. His hands were blistered, and the sun had turned his face and neck crimson. Ward said, "Good morning."

Houston spat on the deck. "Pretty soft berth you got for yourself, Gratwick," he grunted out of the corner of his mouth.

"You got what you wanted, didn't you?" asked Ward.

Houston straightened wearily, hands on the small of his back. "I didn't ask for that son of a bitch of a bos'n." He began pushing the stone again. "Never mind. Give me time, and I'll berth soft as you. Maybe softer."

Ward passed on, frowning. He had not expected gratitude from Houston for getting him out of France, but it was rather hard to be blamed for the conditions of the voyage. He edged past the pens that had been run up well forward. Small pink pigs scuffled and squealed about a trough where a bearded sailor was pouring slops. A few sows fussed and shoved among them. Beyond, sheep bleated, and he leaned over the fence to scratch the throat of a very small lamb whose wobbly legs had difficulty coping with the gentle roll of the ship.

Up by the port cathead, beyond the cackle of the innumerable hens, Ward leaned on the bulwarks and looked down at the cut-water. Through the bluest water that he had ever seen, the sharp bow was thrusting and thrusting, catching up the waves and tossing them back along the slim flanks of the *Sauvage* with a soft grinding sound that died away aft in an endless fading chuckle. Each day he had come there, looking out beyond the blunt point of the jib boom toward the curving line of the horizon. Someday he would stand there and see that line blurred by a dark mass, and his journey would be nearly over. He would land at some unspecified port, and the army would be close by. He could see the sentries in their hunting shirts and broken hats at a road junction. Then there would be the gun-park, rows and rows of trim field pieces and the picketed horses champing at their hay beyond. The vast bulk of Henry Knox, chief of all the gunners, would appear and men would come running from tents or brush shelters. Caleb Blair would be hurling genial insults at him, Bill Leverett, taciturn and dependable, would growl out a greeting that meant almost as much as Caleb's. There would be Chandler Gray — no, not Chan — he had fallen in that vague scuffle in the snow beyond Kingsbridge, and Bill Brady would be missing and —

He shook off the picture of the camp. Wherever it was, he knew that the Commander would grant him leave unless an action were imminent. Somehow or other he would make his way to the banks of the Schuylkill and somehow word would have reached Faith. She would be standing just inside the white picket fence about the fieldstone house whose roof would have been miraculously repaired. Her soft golden hair would be uncovered and she would look up at him with those hazel eyes and her smile would follow. In his mind he could see her take a few steps forward and her hands would reach out to him. She would —

Memory and hope became too keen. He left the bow and walked briskly aft, touching the cascabel of each nine or sixteen as he went. Halfway down the eighty-odd feet of deck, he stopped. Standing in the entrance under the quarter-deck was Deborah, a fluttering green cloak about her and the sun bright on her black hair. Her eyes were narrowed to the glare of the sun, and it was obvious that she did not see him, or at least recognize him, as her head turned slowly from right to left and back again.

"Damned if I ever saw her hair unpowdered," he thought. "So black it's almost blue."

He settled his new neckcloth and resumed his walk. Then Deborah saw him and began to smile, eyes still puckered up by the sun.

The spontaneity of that smile touched Ward. It was all very well for him to be filled with eager impatience and anticipation. The *Sauvage* was taking him exactly where he wanted to go, but it bore Deborah to an unwanted exile in a strange place and among strange people. "She's got the makings of a good little soldier," he thought as he took off his hat.

Her eyes sparkled as she sketched a mock curtsy. "What a wonderful day, Ward. Do take me for a walk."

Ward glanced up at the quarter-deck. For the first time he failed to see Tremarec, alert by the aft railing. The man at the wheel looked easy and relaxed, and Keratry, the only officer in sight, was crouched by the longboat trying to hammer out a light for his pipe. The *Sauvage* must have sailed out of the zone of imminent danger.

He offered Deborah his arm. "I met a lamb and some pink pigs up forward. I'd like to introduce them to you."

She answered gravely, *"Enchantée, Monsieur.* It was thoughtful of you to send those notes in to us. Cousin Sue and Paul appreciated them, too. I'd have come out before only — well, I just didn't feel like it."

"I'm glad you've come now."

She tossed her head. "I still don't like things any more than I did, but what's there to do about it? Besides — " her smile shone again — "it's really fun, in some ways. Everything's so new and we're going to new places and the ship's so clean. My,

90

you should have seen the one we came out on in '75!" She wrinkled her tilted nose in memory of past squalor. "But here our cabin really might be in Paris and we've got a gallery that hangs out over the water and the ship's cat and two kittens have moved in with us. Ouch! I nearly tripped over that rope. And all these cannons! I don't see why we have to have them."

"They are in the way, aren't they?" said Ward, thinking of the long sixteen that crowded his cabin. He did not think it worth while to tell her that twice, in the earlier stages of the voyage, strange masts had been sighted. Then the guns had been manned, loaded and their muzzles run through the open gunports while other sailors scrambled aloft to set more sail.

Deborah cried out delightedly, "Oh, the pigs!" They had come abreast of the pens, and she was bending over the low partition. "They look as if they were made of pink silk. And is this the lamb you told me about?" She steadied the tottering mite which rolled soft eyes at her and licked her hand.

She gave a reluctant farewell pat to the lamb, and Ward moved forward with her. "Are Paul and Mrs. Lathrop coming out today?" he asked.

"I think so. Oh, do look at the little birds out there in the spray, little brown birds. Yes, she and Paul'll be out. They've been in his cabin going over papers and sealing things up and writing ever since the first day out. I've had to sign two or three papers."

There was a hail from the quarter-deck, and Ward looked up to see Paul Dale, elegant yet somehow seamanlike in dark blue, leaning on the rail. "Hello, you two," he called. Ward helped Deborah up the steep companionway.

"We had a wonderful walk, Paul, way up to the bow and back, and they've got some darling little pigs and a lamb. Do sailors always have pets like those? I thought it was parrots and monkeys and things."

Paul pinched her cheek and winked at Ward. "Too cold up here for parrots. Wait till we get farther south. These ships run around everywhere."

"Like Ward," said Deborah. She turned to him. "Do you know we waited hours for you at the Comtesse d'Houdetot's that time after the Doctor's party? We'd be waiting yet if Sue hadn't sent a footman back to the Petit Manoir. The Doctor made excuses for you, but we never saw you again. Where were you all that time up to our meeting at Lorient? You've never told us."

"Didn't I?"

"Isn't this a good time to stop being mysterious?" she asked. "You always did act mysterious about what you did for Doctor Franklin."

"Mysterious? I suppose I did."

"Where were you?" persisted Deborah.

"Here and there," answered Ward. "The Doctor knows people all over France, and his gout makes it hard for him to travel. Sometimes he sends me in his place. I was just on a trip like that when he sent me word of a ship that might take me on. That's how you found me at Lorient."

"An odd place to reach from Paris," said Paul, eying the bulge of the sails high above him.

"Quite. But you know what travel is in France."

"Don't I!" exclaimed Paul. "Sometimes you start east to go west. Looping back and forth."

"I looped," said Ward. "From here to there. One funny thing, Paul. I could have sworn that I saw you one night in Rouen. You and a man named Jabish Frost."

Paul craned his neck still more as though trying to follow the spidery lines of the stays that ran to the main topgallant mast. "Amazing how they can keep track of all the ropes and things on a ship." The pressure of his collar made his voice sound thin and strained. "Rouen? Never been there. I know Frost by sight. Odd sort of a stick, but they say he's uncommon sharp."

Deborah tugged at his collar. "Your head'll stay back like that, Paul. You're getting red as a turkey's wattles."

Paul lowered his chin and rubbed his cheeks. "Getting red, was I? All this tackle fascinates me without making me want to know about it. I'm going to get permission to climb up to one of those platforms. Then I'll wonder why I took the trouble. Were you in Rouen, Ward? Lovely old town, they say."

"Just passing through before I headed south."

"Oh, the Rouen-Evreux-Mayenne-Rennes route?" asked Paul.

"For someone who's never been in Rouen, Mr. Dale, you're pretty glib with the roads south," Deborah remarked.

"Why not, Sis?" laughed Paul. "Part of my business has been to know how to get from here to there. I've never been in Besançon, for example, but I could draw a map of the best way to get from there to Verdun where also I've never been."

"Didn't I tell you he was clever, Ward?" cried Deborah. "Heavens, how this wind blows us about. Do you know your coat is all wrinkled in back. Here, let me smooth it out." She gave a lusty dab at his back. "What on earth have you got tucked in there? It's a bulge, not a wrinkle."

Ward straightened up quickly, gave a furtive tug to the flat chain about his waist. Franklin's packet must have worked around past the small of his back until it showed through the blue cloth. "Thanks, Deborah. That's where I keep some mementos of France that I'm taking home with me."

"Smooth it out more," commanded Deborah. "Lord, between Paul trying to strangle himself with his neckcloth and you bulging like a bullfrog I'm sure I don't know how I'll ever manage to keep you two in order. What sort of mementos?"

"Little pictures of Louis XVI, stamped on discs of yellow

93

metal, Deborah. Not many of them, but I'd rather like to keep them," said Ward.

Paul grinned at him. "Turn them over to me. I'll guarantee to give back four for one."

Deborah nodded. "He would, too."

"These are just minnows, Paul. They'd be lost among your whales. Hello. There's Mrs. Lathrop down on deck." He called a greeting to her, waving his hat as she came out below the break. She looked handsome in her gray cloak with its soft blue lining, or pretty, rather than handsome, Ward thought. The noon sun seemed to soften rather than to accentuate the few lines on her face, and her teeth flashed in a quick smile as she answered him.

Deborah cried, "Do come and join us, Cousin Sue. It's lovely up here."

Mrs. Lathrop shook her head. "Later. But you've got to come to dinner now. It's ready to be served. You too, Mr. Gratwick. Please join us."

Deborah went carefully down the companionway, Paul's steadying hand on her shoulder. Ward followed, dropping the last two feet. As Paul reached the deck he said, "What do you think, Cousin Sue! Ward was sure that he saw me in Rouen not long ago."

Mrs. Lathrop was about to lead the way in, but she stopped, looking back over her shoulder, a hand on each side of the doorway. "In Rouen? What a mistake!" she cried, then bit her lip.

"I found afterward that it was not he at all but a most respectable burgher of that town," said Ward.

"Nice to be taken for someone respectable, anyway," laughed Paul. "Lead the way, Cousin Sue. After you, Sis."

V I

"My People"

A FEW DAYS LATER Ward emerged from his cabin, yawning and
stretching in an overcast dawn. The sharp bow of the *Sauvage*
was still pitching on a southerly course, lurching a little to port
under a steady quartering wind that brought a fine drizzle humming against the rain-darkened sails and drifting in an almost
invisible spray across the deck. He looked up at the glistening
masts whose noticeable rake seemed to add to the impression of
speed. Not that the *Sauvage* needed to create any illusions. The
night before he had stood with Deborah, Paul and Tremarec on
the quarter-deck while the log was heaved astern. When the
whirring reel had run its length and the chip was finally hauled
in, the Breton, chronometer in hand, had announced calmly,
"Eleven knots. *Pas mal*." Decidely *pas mal,* Ward had thought,
remembering the British transport that had wallowed at between
five and six knots. Of course, eleven had meant almost perfect
sailing conditions, but even now he reckoned that they must be
making eight or nine, and each dip of the bowsprit measured off
a few more yards conquered from the stubborn distance home.

Ward was about to go below for early coffee when the door
of the cabin across the deck from his swung open and a sailor
scuttled out with a bucket and a swab. Forward, another sailor
made his way aft, carrying a sea-bag over his shoulder. After
him the carpenter's mate marched majestically with a basket of
tools in his hand. The two squeezed into the cabin and presently
a sound of hammering and sawing reached Ward. Ward hailed

the sailor with the swab and bucket. *"Holà,* LeBon! We expect to take on a new passenger, then?"

"Who may say?" LeBon plodded off along the deck, bending to the slight list.

Then from the forward hatch another figure showed, ghostly in the thickening drizzle. In a new suit of bottle-green that didn't fit him too well and with a worn cocked hat on the back of his head, James Houston strolled nonchalantly aft, while Junot, toughest of the petty officers, glared helplessly after him.

Houston waved airily at Ward. "Morning, Ward. We're in for some wet weather, I guess." He carelessly swung open the cabin door and snapped in bad but fluent French, "You two, have your fingers all turned into toes? One novice would have finished the job in half the time." He sauntered over to Ward. "God, what a crew of shambling, fumbling goats!"

"What's it all about?" asked Ward.

Houston's shrug was super-Gallic. "Oh, nothing much."

"All right. Be mysterious," laughed Ward. "Well, I'm going below for coffee. See you later, maybe."

Houston showed brownish, irregular teeth. "Didn't I tell you I'd berth soft as you, if not softer?"

"You did."

Houston said quickly, "Well, I've *got* me a good berth. And I'm not forgetting who put me where I could take it. If it hadn't been for you I'd still be running along the water front with my shoes worn through. I'll never be able to pay you back for the chance you gave me, but by God I'm going to try." He nodded briskly, held out his hand.

Ward shook it, was surprised by the firmness of the grip. "Good luck to you."

"God damn it, why don't you give me the satisfaction of asking what's happened?" said Houston grimly.

"I'm asking."

Houston edged nearer. "It's Mr. Dale. Mr. Paul Dale. I'm secretary to him. Him and that Mrs. Lathrop." He jerked a scarred thumb at the opposite cabin. "They're building me a folding desk in there."

"You certainly moved fast. How did you manage all this?"

Houston winked. "I'd spotted young Dale strutting about the deck. I took care to be where he'd see me, let him hear me talk." He nodded wisely. "He took the bait. Asked the Captain about me. Had me brought to his cabin and we talked for half an hour. He fixed things up, and I'm off the crew-list and on the Dale payroll. The Dales aren't losing anything, either. I write a good hand, and I can cipher and keep books. Likewise keep my mouth shut."

"Don't underrate Paul Dale, Jim," cautioned Ward.

Houston laughed shortly. "I got him sized up all right. He's going a long way, I tell you, and I'm going to be right with him. Well, looks as if my boudoir across the way was about finished. See you later." He ducked through the low door of his cabin.

Ward watched the door close. "The cards have certainly begun to run for him," he thought. "Maybe it's about time." Yet somehow the idea of Jim Houston being closely associated with the Dales and Mrs. Lathrop, even as a clerk, made him uneasy.

He went down the steep companionway and pushed open the door of the senior officers' mess where the lamp burned blue. Brotier, lean face in his hands, was lazily baiting Keratry. "And so, *mon petit* Keratry, to insure that his cubs enjoyed the fruits of his skull-cracking, the tribal chief forced the priests to invoke the aid of the forest gods, forced them to proclaim him and his progeny divine. So today that is how your fat, stupid Louis rules."

Huge Keratry roared, as Ward entered, *"Non!* That is not,

cannot be true. Here, my good Gratveek! Tell me how to answer this species of blasphemous, sacrilegious shark!"

Brotier smiled wickedly. "By all means, tell him, you who fight to strangle one king and who will surely end by setting up another of your own, blessed by your priests. Ah, I tell you it will happen so, for man is born not only a poltroon but fatbrained into the bargain. You will only change the style of your fetters. You will not free yourselves."

"Then I hope you'll be the first French ambassador to our court," said Ward. "Pass the coffee, please."

More days passed, and again Ward sat with Deborah, Mrs. Lathrop and Paul under an awning that had been rigged for them on the quarter-deck. The watch had just been changed and Tremarec had turned command over to Gaos. Down on the main deck, the door of Houston's cabin was open, and Ward could see him, crouched comfortably over the folding desk just forward of the nine-pounder, writing busily.

"How does he suit you, Paul?" asked Ward.

Paul smiled. "For the present, very well. He has an excellent incentive. He knows that if he doesn't please, back he goes below to his ropes and his holystones. I'll probably keep him on when we get to Martinique, if his work holds up. He's deft and he's close-mouthed."

Mrs. Lathrop nodded. "I was telling Deborah just last night that we may be able to make something more than a clerk out of him."

"No doubt you could," said Ward. He was always surprised when Mrs. Lathrop spoke like the head of some firm of merchants. With her delicate features and soft eyes, her completely feminine air, she seemed better fitted to be planning a ball.

"We'll watch Houston," said Paul.

Ward laughed. "Just how are you going to, Paul? He wants

to get back to the army. And you want a berth in it, too, when you finish up whatever your business is."

"True enough," answered Paul. "But the war won't last forever. I might need a reliable agent in the Indies." He rubbed his chin thoughtfully. "Maybe I'd make it worth his while to forget the army and stay in the Indies while you and I go north."

Deborah looked inquiringly at Ward.

"Yes, Paul and I are going on to win the war," he said banteringly.

"What a dreadful thought!" Deborah shuddered then turned to Ward. "I should think you'd had enough of wars and things."

"The war's still going on," said Ward.

Mrs. Lathrop sighed. "It shouldn't have started in the first place. People just lost their heads."

"But why?" asked Deborah. "Why did you start fighting, Ward?"

Ward shoved his hands into his jacket pockets. "People will give you different reasons. Most on the other side were either against any change or felt that to oppose the Crown was blasphemy. I guess what turned most of my people was that we'd been used to governing ourselves for about a hundred and fifty years and didn't want to stop."

"But Ward," Mrs. Lathrop broke in, opening and shutting her fragile fan. "There's government everywhere. What difference does it make who does it? Life goes on. There's plenty of trade. People live well."

"That's what I always come back to," said Paul. "There must have been some other way."

"A lot of ways were tried," said Ward. "But from the end of the French wars, everything the Crown did seemed to turn us into nothing but a lot of trading posts instead of free colonies. The Crown was taking over more power all the time, trying to appoint nearly all the officials and paying no attention to local conditions or ideas. In many cases they sent people out from England, mediocre hacks at the best. If native-born men were appointed, then they looked to the Crown for support and favor, not to the rest of us."

"But things went on just the same, didn't they?" persisted Mrs. Lathrop.

"No. Take Massachusetts. All power was passing into the hands of two families, the Hutchinsons and the Olivers, thence to their friends, some of whom were none too savory. You see what that meant? In a few years the State would have been run by a very small group, answerable only to the Crown. There'd have been the Squire in his big house on the hill with the rest of us touching our forelocks most respectfully."

"But that always happens," objected Paul. "Ability rises to the top and stays there."

"In this case, preference, not ability, Paul," answered Ward. "Let's use a touch of fantasy and assume that by unfathomable wisdom and immense gift of leadership, I become a great power in central Massachusetts. Can I do anything for the people? Not at all. The real power, from the office of hog-reeve up, will lie in the hands of those who look to the Crown alone. I'll be called a demagogue, a rascal, an unpleasant turbulent fellow and probably in the pay of the Papists."

"But you'd rise right along with the Crown people," said Mrs. Lathrop.

"So long as I was careful to please London and not my own people, I might go reasonably far. But I'd always be subordinate to some hack sent out from England to pay a political debt."

Paul frowned. "I've heard people say, though, that it's really a rising of the poor against the well-to-do and the rich."

"What!" cried Ward. "A sort of peasant's revolt? Nothing of the sort. You'll find big land-holders against the Crown as well as for it. And you'll find small farmers and cobblers and laborers staying by the King while others fight against him. You'll find brothers, from any walk in life, on opposite sides, depending on their convictions. And it takes pretty deep conviction to make splits like that."

Paul rose, looking at his watch. "I ought to have been able to reason that out. Come along, Cousin Sue. Houston must be through with what I dictated this morning. Let's go below and look at it."

When they had gone, Ward glanced at Deborah. "Have I answered any of your questions?"

"It all sounds like the talk we used to hear at Doctor Franklin's. All about government."

"But that's what it *is* about. The way men think they ought to live."

"But you could have been a Crown man."

"Not I. I don't want to touch my forelock to anyone and hence I don't want people touching theirs to me. Does that sound too simple? It's just an idea, but the war's being fought for one."

"People don't go to war for ideas. I've heard enough talk in Paris to know that. They go on account of forts or boundaries or cities and who's to be on a throne."

"You can defend an idea just as well as you can one of Vauban's forts," observed Ward. "You've been so far from it, and you left so young. If you'd been there — "

"What would I have seen?" asked Deborah quickly.

"Nothing, I hope. But you would have heard, you would have known." Ward closed his eyes for a moment, and the bitter years flowed through his mind. "You *could* have seen people, through all the New England States and New York answering the call to equip those men who had to be raised so hurriedly in '77 when Burgoyne was coming south. You'd have seen people who owned five blankets giving four to the army, people who owned two blankets giving one and people who had only one cutting it in half."

Deborah looked doubtful. "Who made them give all that up?"

"Just that idea I was talking about," answered Ward. "You could have seen soldiers living in huts in the snow, not able to go out and forage because they didn't have clothes, let alone shoes, and a sick list of one out of two and rations once a day, if that. Some of them quit and went home, but not many. That idea again."

"But that wasn't fighting, was it?"

"It was for those who were strong enough and had enough clothes. They went out and raided the British and Hessian posts. They didn't lose very often either. Sometimes the strongest of the raiders had to carry the weaker ones back to the camp. It was at a place called Valley Forge."

"And they could have all gone home if they'd wanted to?"

"I suppose so."

"Ward! All winter like that? What did they have to look forward to?"

"The spring — and more fighting — and their idea."

"Go on. Tell me more."

"It'd just be repetition," said Ward. "Sometimes they couldn't fight, didn't have anything to fight with. I remember, in '76, when we were retreating through the Jerseys —"

"But that's my country!" interrupted Deborah.

"You were well out of it. The British were pressing us, and if they'd caught up with us just once — well, it would have been all over for us, for the country. Our horses were dying. A lot of our men didn't have shoes. Powder and shot were scarce and so were rations. Well, the British nearly caught us once because a column was slow in breaking camp. Some volunteers took four cannon to hold off the British. The rest of the column hurried on. We could look back and see the gunners going through their drill on the sky line."

"And you all got away?"

"Not all. You see, those gunners didn't have a crumb of powder. They just stood there with their empty guns. Of course, the British eventually found out that they *were* empty, but by that time the bulk of the army was out of reach."

"And the men with the guns caught up with the rest?"

"Not that I saw," said Ward dryly.

"You mean the gunners just stood there, pretending that they were going to shoot and knowing that they couldn't?"

"It was a gamble, of course," said Ward. "Wish I knew what happened to them."

Deborah watched the gold-brown swell of the sails above her. "I saw a lot of paintings of battles in Paris. You know, in the palaces and châteaux. They were all white uniforms and blue uniforms and red uniforms and horses prancing and bombs bursting. They fascinated me."

"I know the kind you mean," said Ward. "There was a big one at the de Chaumont's, and I'll bet the artist had never seen a battle. The colors in that painting are fine, but just the same—"

Deborah sat up abruptly. "I know now that those paintings are unreal. You've shown me. Those men in the snow! While you've been talking, I've been saying over and over to myself, 'And those are *my* people!'"

Ward looked quickly at her. "You see that now? *Your* people."

She nodded slowly. "I'm just beginning to see that. They are my people. Do you remember, way back in Passy, you told me never to forget that I was American? At the time I thought it was rather an odd thing to say. Now I understand—a little. If Father hadn't sent me to France, I could have stayed there, been part of it, though I suppose there wouldn't have been much that

103

I could have done. The other night you were talking with Paul about the army at Morristown. Why, I know Morristown almost as well as I know Paris, but it seemed to me that you were talking about a strange place. Now I see that *I* was strange, not Morristown. And that other name — Valley Forge. It has such a pretty sound."

"It isn't pretty — or wasn't when we were there. I saw men drop dead —" Ward made a sudden gesture. "But all that's nothing for you to hear about."

"Was it so horrible? It must have been, from your expression," said Deborah. "I suppose you'd never want to go there again."

"That's where you're wrong, young lady. I want very much to go there, just as soon as I've found the army again."

Deborah raised her eyebrows. "Back to Valley Forge? H'm. Is she pretty, Ward?"

"To me — and to most other people. You'd like her, Deb. Her father's a surgeon who was lamed in the French wars. When the army settled along the Schuylkill that winter, Doctor Kortright went about among the troops, helping out the army surgeons. Faith came with him. The first time I ever saw her, she was making shirts for the soldiers, she and Lady Washington and Nat Greene's wife and Henry Knox's. Then she used to find out from her father about the men in the hospitals. She'd cook up little dishes for them. I don't know where she got the food to do it, but I've a good idea." He paused.

"Why didn't you ever tell me about her before?" asked Deborah. "My — doing all that and for our soldiers. How did she get them food? Did she buy it for them? Paul says money's always scarce during a war."

"There was nothing to buy," answered Ward. "She must have made all that up out of what she and the Doctor had — and that was mighty little."

104

"Faith," said Deborah slowly. "Faith Kortright. I think I can almost see her, from what you've told me."

"Another one of your people, Deb."

"I'd like to think that she'd own me for one of hers." She got up quickly. "Take me for a walk on the deck, Ward. You've given me so much to think about."

The next dawn broke in an explosion of colors such as Ward had never imagined possible. Dazzled, he stared at the new day, leaned over to see the rainbows burning about the cut-water, straightened up to watch the bands of ruby and flame and apple-green that shifted on the horizon. He looked about for someone with whom to share this dawn marvel and was delighted to see Tremarec strolling unconcernedly forward, arms behind his back. "Come join me, Captain," Ward called. "It's something really — hi! Look at that off to the southwest! Is it a bird? There's another. One to the right and one to the left. Miles apart, I'd say."

Tremarec, with an indulgent smile for a landman's fancy, came up beside him. "You see what, my friend?"

"Way off there!" Ward watched the two silvery brown patches that shimmered where blue met blue. They glowed, faded, reappeared. "Can they be sails, Captain?"

His question was drowned by Tremarec's deep shout. *"Holà! Les signaleurs.* You aloft there! Where are your eyes?" His shouts were taken up by petty officers who sent the topmen swarming up the rigging. High overhead fresh sailcloth fluttered, swelled as it caught the breeze.

"Sails?" asked Ward again.

"Sails," answered Tremarec. "English sails. There's no mistaking them. Now that we have seen them in time, thanks to you, I incline to welcome them in a spirit of professional pride. Two Englishmen on the far horizon who approach each other and who, I should judge, should meet at right angles to our course."

"Then we're to engage two enemy ships at once? I've been shot at enough on land not to relish the idea of being shot at at sea."

Tremarec raised a soothing hand. "But I did not say that we engage. No, my friend. You are about to witness a little of the speed of which I boasted to you when you first joined me. We shall carry every inch of sail possible. I promise you that we shall run most neatly between the two Goddams, neatly and safely. You see, I know my ship." As the Captain spoke, the *Sauvage* gave a smooth lunge ahead as though an unseen hand had pushed at its stern. The breeze beat stronger in Ward's face, and he felt an exultant lift to his spirits as though in answer to the new life that the ship had taken on. Tremarec watched the sails for a moment, then excused himself, making his way aft no doubt to visit his wrath on the lookout who had left it to a landsman far below on the deck to sight the hostile sails.

All through the brisk morning, the *Sauvage* drove on. To Ward's unpracticed eye, the English ships seemed to be in exactly the same position as when first sighted, but from comments from Keratry and Gaos he gathered that the *Sauvage* was more than living up to her reputation for speed and that all went well.

In the afternoon, Ward climbed to the quarter-deck where Deborah and Mrs. Lathrop were installed under their awning. "Like flying, isn't it?" Deborah called. "The Captain was here a few minutes ago, and he says we'll end by going much faster than this."

"If he says so, we'll leave the waves and really fly through the air. Where's Paul?"

Deborah wrinkled her nose. "Oh, below with that nasty Houston, writing and dictating and writing."

"It's all for us, Deborah," said Mrs. Lathrop. "You know, he'll be very pleased if we do make the Sugar Islands in good time. This is — " She held up her hand, frowning. "Why — we aren't really going fast now. I declare, we've almost stopped."

Ward looked aloft. The clouds of sailcloth were hanging loosely against the towering raked masts, giving an occasional swell and flap. Astern, the great white flag with its sprinkling of gold lilies drooped limply, its folds flapping halfheartedly from time to time like the tail of a weary horse. Ward looked toward the horizon where the sea stretched away with scarcely a ripple to scar its intense blue surface.

"What's happened?" asked Deborah.

"Becalmed," answered Ward tersely.

On the horizon, port and starboard, the two points of light still showed. At least, he thought, the calm had struck them, too. Or had it? He tried to line one of the strangers up with the foremast, staring intently, but the slow sway of the great wooden column prevented him from taking a bearing. Time would tell.

VII

The Tube

THAT NIGHT Ward tossed and turned in his stifling cubicle in the motionless *Sauvage,* sweat stinging his eyes and turning his bedding into a sodden mass. Close to midnight he got up, wrapped his straw mattress in a fresh sheet and padded out onto the deck.

The sailors who were off duty lay sprawled about the foremast and from the pens beyond came unhappy grunts and bleatings. He stopped by the water-breaker at the mainmast and filled a dipper. A subtly heavy odor rose from it. He sluiced the water into the scuppers, carefully wiped the dipper with his clean sheet and filled again. The odor was still there. With a grimace he gulped down a couple of tepid mouthfuls. The water was bound to go bad sooner or later, but it was a pity that it had to happen during this lull.

He mounted to the quarter-deck where Tremarec stood, motionless as his ship, by the useless wheel. "Evening, Captain," said Ward as he spread his mattress and sheet. "I thought it might be a little cooler up here."

"It will not be," said the Breton. "But you will expect it to be and the thought will refresh you a little."

"Christ, it's hotter up here than in my kennel." Ward recognized Jim Houston's voice from the other side of the deck.

Ward lay down by the starboard rail. The deck felt very hard through the thin mattress and he became aware of mingled smells that rose slowly, almost visibly from the ship: the clean, pungent reek of pitch softening between the planks, a heavier, noxious smell that came up from the deepest recesses, the rank stench from the animal pens forward. The smells must have been with the ship right along, but he had barely noticed them in the favoring winds that had prevailed from Lorient south and then west. "How long is this apt to last, Captain?" he asked, wiping his forehead.

"Who may say? A few hours. A few days. A few weeks."

"A few weeks?"

"And why not, my friend? It is not so likely here, but I have seen it in the Indian Ocean and was not amused by it."

"Your crew'd die or go mad," growled Houston.

"True, Mr. Houston," said Tremarec smoothly. "Some die. Some go mad. But in the end, one manages somehow. One reaches port — save only the weak in spirit."

Gaos had sidled up onto the deck. Tremarec exchanged a few words with him, bade Ward and Houston a courteous good night and went below. Houston spat over the rail. "Superior son of a bitch, isn't he?" he muttered.

"Not in my log. He'd be a damned good man to have at your elbow in a scuffle."

"You can have him," grumbled Houston. "God's truth, but it's hot."

"Cheer up," said Ward. "Think of Deborah and Mrs. Lathrop, battened down there in the cabins. Anyway, there may be a breeze by morning."

"There will not be a breeze by morning," said the mournful Gaos. "On the word of a Breton, no breeze."

Gaos was right. The sun came up, coppery and sullen, and its early rays struck along a lifeless sea. The *Sauvage* wallowed slowly back and forth in answer to the nearly imperceptible motion of the water, its swift, sleek lines and towering sails useless. On the far horizon, the two strange sails held their positions, snared by the same dead calm.

In the fearful heat below deck, Ward tried to eat, but everything tasted soggy, heavy and a little foul as though tainted by the water in the breaker. It was no better on deck. The sun climbed and climbed and he watched the pitch begin to bubble between the smooth planks.

The sailors lolled in the scuppers or rigged up bits of canvas against the broiling rays. Gaos and Keratry, the latter dripping with sweat, took their turns on the quarter-deck, though there were no orders to give, no essential work to supervise. Tremarec alone seemed unmoved. He went about the ship with the assured air of a man who has seen so much that he is not merely ready to accept anything but quite prepared to cope with it. Ward watched him speaking with quiet cheerfulness to the sailors, setting tasks for them which might occupy mind and hand without exhausting the body.

Sundown brought no relief. There was a slight lift in spirits when the surgeon Brotier mixed vinegar with the drinking water, partly to guard against scurvy. At a first gulp, the acid seemed to cleanse the water, but soon the heavy, foul aftertaste crept into the throats of the drinkers. The crew fell back on its coarse red wine which only heated the blood while failing to cool the throat.

Through the night Ward could hear the voices of the sailors. At first they sang, in a desultory minor about *"Les Jeunes Filles de Camaret,"* about the husband who had gone to the Iceland fisheries. The songs died away, were replaced by mutterings in French and Breton. Ward did not like the tone. The rumor had spread through the ship that the Captain himself had announced that the calm would last a good ten days and probably more. Ward was quite sure that Tremarec had made no such pronouncement. Sailors were just like soldiers, clinging frantically to the most fantastic of rumors, embroidering them, elaborating on them, until they became a part of an unshakable credo.

The next day was even worse. The ship lay sullenly, sails limp, in a trough of its own sewage and garbage, the stench mingling with the reek of the holds and the bilges. About noon a cabin boy brought Ward a rather damp little note. "Did our people have this, as well as snow and ice? D." Drying his hands as best he could, Ward scrawled, "Yes. It was worse than this at Monmouth. Don't worry. The breeze will come. W." and sent it back. There was really no need for her to reply, but he was somehow cheered when the boy brought back another blurred line, "If they stood it, I can try. I'm still marching."

The hot night closed in. Fights broke out among the crew, and Brotier had to dress two knife-wounds. Later, in the stifling messroom, Brotier accepted a glass of brandy from Gaos, then remarked acidly that his colleague must have been keeping live fish in the glass to judge from the smears and the smell. The silent Gaos lunged at the surgeon with a drawn knife and when Ward caught his wrist, Keratry struck at him for interfering. Luckily the surgeon began to laugh at himself as well as the others and the scuffle died away as quickly as it had begun.

In the morning Tremarec launched two boats and Ward stood in the bow of the *Sauvage* watching them. Each was joined to the ship by a long cable that lay sometimes partly submerged, sometimes pulled taut. Out on the brassy water, oars beat and churned futily while the barebacked sailors dipped, bent, straightened in their killing struggle against the dead weight of the ship. There were passages that looked easier when the *Sauvage* slid forward a little and the oar blades cut smoothly into the water. Then the momentum died and the savage battle began all over again.

It was bad enough on deck, but Ward felt uneasy qualms as he thought of the sailors out there a cable-length beyond the bow. He tried to picture himself among them, the sun burning down on head, neck and shoulders while blistered hands drove an oar through dead water, each muscle and nerve cracking until the *Sauvage* reluctantly yielded to the combined tugs of the two boats and hunched forward, only to come to a stop again. The bos'ns out there must have their hands full trying to keep the crews to their work.

The task seemed cruel, but it was probably ordered to give the men something to do, and also to draw the ship at least a little beyond the patch where carrion-fish played in the stinking refuse.

Deborah came and stood quietly beside him. "I wonder," she said thoughtfully, "how long it will be before we are on our way again — back to our own people!"

Ward looked curiously at her. "So now you think of them that way?"

"Of course," she cried. "Because of all the things you have told me."

"You must have heard a lot more than that in France from LaFayette and Fleury and duPlessis."

She made an impatient gesture. "It never seemed to have anything to do with me until you spoke that time of retreating through the Jerseys. Then I could begin to see because that was my state. Then you told me why they were fighting in the Jerseys and Pennsylvania, and how they didn't give up. You told me about wives and mothers coming to your columns when you were retreating and giving out bread and coffee and pork, and how they kept crying, 'Where's my Jack?' or 'Isn't Darby with the guns?' and when they got no answer they kept on giving."

Ward smiled at her. "Don't you see, Deb, as soon as you think of them as 'your people,' you belong to them as much as they to you. You're one of them."

She shook her head. "It's one thing to admire them. It's another to *be* like them. I don't know whether I could ever do what they've done. Take Faith — I never could have gone into the typhus huts at Valley Forge the way she did. I know I couldn't have."

"How do you know?" asked Ward. "I'll bet a Spanish-milled dollar against a torn Continental note that she'd have said the same thing before she really had to face up to it."

"Do you really think so?" She leaned on the bulwarks, looking down into the water. "Oh, I can see a fish. It's all silver and it's swimming right up to us."

Ward saw a slim, silvery blur rising, rising. He gave a muffled exclamation. A landing net lay in the scuppers beside him. He caught it up, dipped the long pole overboard, poised, waited, then gave a sudden scoop. "There's your fish, Deb," he said, lips compressed.

In the dripping net lay a hollow tube of light metal, capped at one end. Deborah looked on, while Ward fished it out. "A hollow tube of very light metal. I guess that someone put, well, let's say, a few musket-balls in this, capped it and heaved it over. The weight rested on the lower cap, worked it off and fell clear through. Enough air was left in the tube to float it right to the surface."

"Ward! It's just like the tube we found in the hollow tree at Passy!"

"Just what I thought when I saw it bobbing up toward us. They're common enough, though. People use them to protect papers from the damp." He slanted it toward the light. Crudely stamped or scratched on the smooth surface he could make out some letters. His fingers kept playing over the lower end. "It's certainly very like the one that we found, as hundreds of others are. But the Doctor didn't want us to say anything about the first one. Let's keep on following his advice."

"But talking about it couldn't hurt anyone way out here, Ward," protested Deborah.

"It was hard to see how talking could have hurt anyone in Passy." Ward slipped the tube into his pocket.

She looked suspiciously at him. "Do you know — I'm just beginning to remember — it struck me at the time that you didn't think much of the Doctor's theory."

Ward hesitated, then said slowly, "This is just between us?"

She nodded.

"Well, then," Ward went on, "let's not go into what I thought of the billet-doux. But I had a letter — some time later — from the Doctor in which he took pains to tell me that the hollow tree had been cut down."

"What was it all about, Ward?" she asked, perplexed.

"I don't know. But we're in a war. A lot of people would give a great deal to know just what the Doctor plans there at Passy — for that war. He's been terribly important in it. He has got us money, arms, the best powder in the world. He got us von Steuben who made an army out of us. He got us our alliance with France and Spain and Holland," said Ward.

"I never guessed he had done all that!" said Deborah. "Do you know, Ward, it seems even hotter." They stood watching as the two tired boatloads of rowers pulled wearily on.

That night, Ward carefully wedged the tube with its long, deep dent and Jabish Frost's name on the shelf just inside the door. He would have to talk to someone about his find, probably Tremarec, but first he wanted to reason things out. Someone on board the ship had tried to jettison the very tube that he had found in the hollow tree beyond the Château de Chaumont. But why try to destroy such a harmless-appearing object? Someone must suspect that to some eyes on board the tube would not appear harmless. Whose eyes? Obviously those of one Ward Gratwick. Someone knew that he had seen it at Passy, someone

114

feared that he might have had time to examine it for distinguishing marks. In the morning, in the bright sunlight, he would go over the metal, inch by inch.

Later, Ward was awakened by a sudden lurch that banged him against the side of his cabin. Outside he could hear the thud of bare feet, the shouting of orders. Strong gusts of cool air were darting in past the crevices of the gun-port cover and the deck beneath the sixteen-pounder was lifting and giving in regular rhythm as the *Sauvage,* all sails set, greeted the end of the calm.

He yawned, sniffed the cool air blissfully, slept again. There was full sunlight on his face when he woke. The cabin door was open. Two men were hammering at his makeshift walls with mauls and a third sailor was shaking him gently.

"There is no haste, Monsieur," he said. "But perhaps Monsieur would care to descend and take coffee with the officers." As he spoke, the forward wall of the cabin fell away, fell with a clatter to the deck. "Action?" asked Ward, swinging his feet over the side.

"Perhaps," answered the sailor, as the port wall and doorframe were removed and stacked neatly with the other partitions. Dodging about the breech of the gun, eluding jab of crowbar and swing of maul, Ward managed to dress, first mechanically settling the chained packet about his waist. There was no stepping out on deck. He was on deck. The last trace of his cabin was being carried below and the crew of the gun swarmed about the piece, testing the breeching, knocking up the gun-port.

All up and down the long, narrow deck the scene was being repeated. Houston's cabin was gone, like his. By each piece, nets of shot were stacked, limp cartridges in their flannel wrappings lay ready and slow matches burned in their sand-tubs. Details of men ran about, strewing the deck with sand. Aft, Tremarec and Keratry stood easily by the man at the wheel.

115

Forward, far across the dawn-bright sea with its curls of white rollers, the two strange sails still glimmered. Both seemed harmless, impersonal. The clearing for action was probably precautionary since no orders had yet been issued to send the passengers below. First a leisurely cup of coffee and then he would talk to Tremarec about the tube.

The tube! He started to feel in his pockets, then remembered the shelf where he had wedged it the night before. He plunged in among the round shot and cartridges that covered what had been the floor of his cabin. There was no sign of the tube. He thought it might have been dislodged and slithered forward along the troughlike hollow that ran from the bow to the quarter-deck. But the whole length was empty and freshly sluiced with seawater.

With a last look he started for the after-hatch, nearly colliding with Deborah as he ducked around the mainmast. There was clear color in her cheeks and her dark eyes sparkled. "I called to you. Didn't you hear me?"

Ward glanced about. The nearest sailor was ten feet away, reeving a rope through a cascabel ring. "Deborah — the tube. They knocked down my cabin before I was up. I can't find it."

Her eyes were serious. "But we've got to find it."

"I know. They've got the partitions stacked forward of the officers' mess. I'm going down to have a look. Come along."

The officers' mess was empty and Ward reached in, unhooked the lantern and started forward, Deborah close behind him. He hurried her past the cramped cubbyhole where the petty officers messed. Brotier was in there, humming to himself as he carefully laid out his surgical instruments on the scarred tabletop by the light of a guttering candle.

At the next bay, Ward found the stacked partitions and doors of the temporary cabins. "What a mess! Can't be helped. Mind holding the lantern, Deb?"

Deborah stood patiently while he cleared the pile down to deck level. "Anything yet, Ward?" she asked in a low tone.

He stood up wearily, taking care not to knock his head against the low beams. "Nothing."

Section by section he replaced the frames, giving a last careful heave to the piece that had Houston's desk built into it. With a final shove he settled the frame.

When they reached the sun-bathed deck, Tremarec was calmly watching the far horizon. Forward, the two strange ships had become almost invisible, a pair of barely seen bright flecks where sea and sky met.

Normal routine was resumed on deck, and save for the guns jutting through the open gun-ports, the piles of ammunition beside each heavy cartridge and the two sails on the horizon, the day seemed like any other. Sometimes the sharp bow pointed due west as though stabbing toward the starboard ship. Again, the *Sauvage* heeled sharply, almost at right angles to its former course, and drove south, paralleling, so far as Ward could guess, the course of the port ship. Twice in the afternoon the horizon was empty and Ward chuckled at the thought of Tremarec outwitting and outsailing the strangers. Each time another change of course brought the two sails up over the horizon again. Yet it seemed to him that the three dots on the sea were edging closer and closer together.

Paul strolled out onto the deck. "Can you make any sense out of this, Ward?" he asked in amused perplexity, as the bow swung slowly west and then almost north.

"No. Damned if I see how Tremarec can find anything to go by."

"Just what I was thinking." He passed his hand over his sleek black hair. "I've been meaning all along to thank you for a favor."

"Thank me for what?" asked Ward, surprised.

117

"That man Houston. He tells me that you got him on board. He makes a very good clerk. Orderly, and writes damned good hand. I can dictate pages and pages to him, and he never makes a mistake. And he can draw off a mighty good abstract of a long paper."

"Glad he suits," said Ward. "He's had a pretty rough time and it's not all his fault."

"He suits as a clerk," said Paul. "His personality's another thing. He's not the sort you are glad to have around after hours, of course."

"You merchant princes!" laughed Ward. "You can afford to be finicky."

Paul went on more seriously, "Oh, I'm nowhere near being a prince yet. But some day —" he smoothed his hair again. "You and I'll have to have a talk before this cruise ends, a talk about what you're going to do after the war."

"Back to Marlboro, I suppose," said Ward. "It'll be a lifetime work straightening matters out when the peace comes."

"No doubt of that," agreed Paul. "I remember what you were telling Deb and me the other night. You know, about your wanting to build houses, and the way you wanted to build them. You've a very sound idea there. Suppose I want to build a really fine house in the Jerseys. Why should I badger an architect into transplanting a château from the Loire to the banks of the Hackensack? I've seen pictures of lovely houses in the Cotswolds in England, but they wouldn't belong in the Watchung Mountains."

He began to question Ward. Suppose there was a great push to the west after the war. People would need houses, of course. Take Marlboro, for example. Where would the timber come from? Was cheap labor plentiful? How about roads? Could you float timber from here to there? What sort of stone could be easily obtained? Where were the brickyards, the sawmills? Ward was surprised at the way Paul's mind broke down a problem into its essential parts.

"That's the way we'd have to go about it," Paul concluded. "I'm just taking your Marlboro as an instance. It isn't very far west, but you'd have an influx from the coast beyond any doubt. And if we begin thinking of western New Jersey or Pennsylvania or even out into the Ohio country, that's the way we'd have to approach things. Well, I'm off for an hour or so with Houston. Look into my cabin about six and we'll talk more over a bit of brandy." With a graceful wave of his hand, he strolled off.

Ward yawned, stretched. The fresh air and the sun were making him sleepy and he thought longingly of his bunk, now stacked below with the cabin walls. With a resigned shrug he stretched out at the foot of the foremast, pulled his hat over his eyes and dropped off into a deep sleep as he used to nap during short halts on the march.

He was awakened by shouts of alarm, running feet. Sailors were pointing at him and Paul Dale was bending over him, pale, and, Ward thought, rather shaken. "What's the matter?" asked Ward.

Paul's voice was unsteady. "By God, that was close! I'd just come on deck and saw the flash and — "

Ward blinked. "What flash?"

Just then a swarthy, wizened sailor dropped to the deck from the mast, was pounced on by two of his fellows and dragged forward.

Paul shouted, "Don't you see?"

Ward looked down at the foot of the mast. A marlinspike was embedded in the hard plank, less than a hand's breadth from where his head had been resting. He jumped as though the spike had been a coiled snake, then touched it gingerly with his foot. The metal quivered but stayed upright.

"It'd have cracked your skull like a teacup," said Paul hoarsely.

The wizened sailor stammered, "But yes, I knew that the lanyard was frayed. *Vraiment,* I had intended to replace it this morning and said as much to Jules, a good sailor. But there was the call for action. Time lacked. Since then — " His thin shoulders hunched up about his ears.

Ward tugged the marlinspike loose from the deck. The lanyard which had held it about the man's neck was frayed through, rotten. It was easy to see how a sudden move aloft had parted the last thread, sent the spike hurtling to the deck. "Not his fault," said Ward to a petty officer. "As a favor to me, don't prefer charges."

"As Monsieur wishes," said the petty officer with a malevolent glance at the sailor.

The group broke up, leaving Paul and Ward together. Paul ran a silk handkerchief over his forehead. "How the devil can you take it so calmly, Ward?"

Ward shrugged. "It was probably worse for you, seeing it, than for me waking up after it was all over."

"I suppose so. You must have had many closer calls than that, though how they could have been much closer is beyond me. Join us for brandy in half an hour? Good." Paul wove off toward the quarter-deck.

VIII

Action!

THE SEA GREW ROUGHER as the sun dropped under the western rim. By the time Ward spread his blankets on the floor of the officers' mess, the hull of the *Sauvage* was shaking and thundering to the blows of the faintly glowing waves, and the lantern above his head creaked and complained as it swung with each roll. He settled himself on the hard boards, thinking over the good talk that had accompanied the brandy and then the dinner in the state cabin. The way Deborah and Mrs. Lathrop made him talk about America and the war was flattering. Deborah in particular had listened with bright eyes and slightly parted lips. Paul, too, had asked searching questions and yet, recalling the evening, it seemed to Ward that Paul had been restless, almost nervous, looking often at his watch.

Ward shifted in the cramped space, wishing that he had had the foresight to bring his mattress into the mess. His shoulders and hips began to ache as he lay listening to the beat of the waves. Yet he must have slept, for the lantern was burning low when the sounds of quick footsteps and excited voices woke him.

A dark-lantern flared suddenly through the open mess door. Mrs. Lathrop, a shawl over her head, stood clutching at a deep red dressing gown. Behind her, dark hair in disarray, was Deborah, whose slippered feet showed under a blue silken hem. Beyond her, Paul, fully dressed, held the lantern high.

"Ward!" Deborah cried. "He sent us down here. He's furious about something."

Ward was now fully awake. "Tremarec sent you below, did he? Probably just a precaution. Here, Mrs. Lathrop, wrap this blanket around you and stretch out on that bench if you can."

Mrs. Lathrop huddled the blanket about her and half lay, half sat on the narrow seat.

"Now tell me what happened, Deb," Ward said.

"I don't know. We were all asleep. Someone, Mr. Gaos I think, pounded at our door and told us all to come here below. He wouldn't even give us time to dress. Then we saw Paul."

Paul was squatting by the door, biting at a fingernail. He nodded. "I hadn't gone to bed. I followed the girls out. All Gaos told me was to hurry."

"As if we weren't hurrying," said Mrs. Lathrop sharply. "I called up to Mr. Tremarec — of course I couldn't see him in the dark — but he just shouted that it was his order. Nothing more."

For Tremarec to have answered so curtly could only mean that something serious had happened, Ward reflected. He said, "It must be the rough weather. He always takes over navigation when things are difficult."

"But it's not very rough," said Mrs. Lathrop.

"Well, then, the blow may have sprung a mast. Isn't that what they call it? Or carried away some rigging."

Deborah looked earnestly at Ward. "He wouldn't have sent us below for that, Ward. You know he wouldn't."

"Why not, Deb? A falling mast could do a lot of damage."

Deborah's chin went up. "You were telling us tonight about that Molly woman. The one who served a cannon at Monmouth. Maybe Sue and I wouldn't know how to serve a gun like Molly, but at least we can try to face things the way she did. What's the matter? Are you afraid we won't measure up?"

Ward met her dark eyes. He knew that she was struggling against fear, as he himself had always struggled when his guns were in action. She was winning her battle. She knew fear, but it would not master her. He looked at Mrs. Lathrop, then at Paul. The latter seemed the most upset. Yet Ward had an odd impression that Paul was gripped by intense uncertainty rather than actual physical fear, as though he were waiting for something to happen. Ward nodded encouragingly at him. "Is Houston above decks?"

Paul shook his head. "Berthing forward with the crew. Don't ask me why. A liking for low company's one of the things I don't care for about him."

Muffled but distinct a gun thudded somewhere off beyond the wooden walls of the *Sauvage*. A sick, shrinking feeling clutched at Ward's heart. A dull, whining noise grew louder, became a sudden, jarring crash above. Deborah turned to Ward. Her voice was quite steady. "It's begun?"

"I think so." Ward braced himself. Another thud sounded a little nearer, the dull whine again, smashing sounds that shook the timbers, high-pitched cries that rose, then stopped abruptly.

Paul huddled his knees in his arms. "Any idea how things are going up there, Ward?" he asked.

Ward shook his head, trying to translate what he knew of land warfare into terms of the sea. He knew that the *Sauvage* had taken two solid hits. He was sure that so far Tremarec had not replied. The cannonading broke out again, and the timbers shook more violently. That last shot, he guessed, had hit fairly close to the water line. On deck the *Sauvage's* gun-crews would be standing by, waiting for the command to fire. Why didn't it come?

He bent suddenly, fastened the buckles of his shoes. "See you later," he called as he ran out.

He pried up the hatch cover and stepped out, slamming it back into place. As he straightened up, the night flared in a blaze of red-orange. Timbers smashed somewhere forward, and he had a hideous glimpse of bodies being pitched and hurled

123

about up by the bow-chaser. A stinging, whining noise filled his ears, and a six-foot length of wood, sharp and swift as a lance, drilled past his shoulder to shatter against the mainmast.

Convulsively he ducked back of the mast, breath coming fast. He was as used as a man can be to the churning whine of round-shot, the hot hiss of grape. He could judge the dart and lunge of a ball that ricocheted crazily over broken ground. But the deadly, flying wood splinters were a new hazard to him. The red-orange again. He could just make out the English ship about a hundred yards off across the water. It was nearly broadside to the *Sauvage,* whose main batteries were useless. In the bow, as the last flash died, he saw men struggling to man the little bow-chaser, the only gun that could be brought to bear. The English guns flared again, and no one moved in the bow of the *Sauvage.* Crouching, Ward stared hard into the night. Where was the second enemy ship? Another flash of gunfire lit up a wide stretch of tossing water and failed to touch the lift of another mast, the curve of another hull. Somehow, Tremarec had shaken off one of the attackers, which probably rolled and pitched miles away over the dark wastes.

From the quarter-deck he heard Tremarec's voice, strong, dominating the din of the night. The *Sauvage* heeled slowly to port, straightened, heeled again. Ward's eyes were becoming accustomed to the ebb and flow of light. Port and starboard, the gun-crews stood to their pieces, seemingly heedless of men who lay quietly on the deck or writhed slowly out of the way. "I'd better get out of here," he thought shakily. "Just in the way. Isn't my kind of fighting."

The Englishman was now on the starboard side, its eerily shimmering sails mounting high into the night sky. Dullish flares showed in her rigging, and Ward threw back his head as the familiar whine of a musket ball, several balls, linked him a little with this strange, reeling world of masts and decks. By the nearest nine-pounder a man yelped and spun away from the piece, clutching his shoulder.

The two ships drew apart, then began slowly to close again. Braced against the mainmast, Ward shouted in alarm. The *Sauvage* seemed to be pointing her bowsprit directly at the Englishman's and the foes drove on toward each other through the night. He saw enemy sails high over his head, and musket balls hummed to the deck about him. Then he heard Tremarec shout once more, and the *Sauvage* sheered off slightly to port. There was the whole flank of the English, and Tremarec was yelling, *"Voici le beau moment!"* The night world exploded in light and thunder, and Ward was thrown to the deck, eyes and nose filled with stinging smoke. As the Englishman shot past, Ward could see ragged holes in the black planking with its orange-yellow stripe along the line of the gun-ports. He found himself cheering. His voice died away as two of the *Sauvage's* guns collapsed on shattered carriages, men crumpled in ghastly attitudes on the deck, in the scuppers.

The *Sauvage* and the Englishman had rushed past each other, and for a moment the night was still, save for the din of the wind and the sea — and thick, broken noises that rose piteously from the deck. He jumped to the hatch cover, pried at it. It had been foolhardy and worse to come on deck.

Hands on the heavy cover, he crouched, incredulous. The sails of the *Sauvage* began to flap, and her bow wove to port and then to starboard. Panting, he stared aft. There were shouts, and the sound of running feet on the quarter-deck. A *contre-maître* sprang down, followed by a squad of sailors, pushed Ward roughly aside, wrenched up the cover and dropped into the depths below, his men after him. He knelt, frozen, as he realized the sense of scraps of talk that he had heard. The rudder ropes had jammed — or so men hoped. If not, the rudder itself was hopelessly damaged. Somewhere off there in the dark, the English ship was circling, ready to plunge along on a new course that would leave the *Sauvage* entirely at her mercy.

Ward lost all sense of time. Half a minute might have passed. or half an hour. The *Sauvage* still rolled helpless in the trough of the sea. Then Ward saw a faint glimmer far aft as though the dreaded sails had been touched by starlight. First they were a vague blur, now seen, now lost. Then they hardened, took form, bore down on the *Sauvage* in silent menace.

Ward felt utterly alone on the battered deck, felt that the on-rushing ship was poised to strike at him and at no one else. The Englishman seemed to be carrying less sail than before, and soon Ward could make out the masts themselves. Then they seemed to hover over him. The enemy guns were silent, but bright whiffs of flame shot out from the yards and flat reports sounded faintly.

Ward's head cleared. Musketry from the fighting-tops of the Englishman, firing while still far out of range! Somehow the familiar sound took panic from him and gave him back to the *Sauvage*. As clearly as though he had shared in the planning, he guessed the Englishman's purpose. The enemy, disregarding the light stern-chaser on the quarter-deck, would close its bow against the rudderless stern quarter of the *Sauvage,* blasting it with its forward guns while boarding parties swarmed over the low bulwarks of the drifting ship.

The *Sauvage* remained silent, lying wounded in the water. Then suddenly the ship quivered under his feet, seemed to leap forward. The sails no longer flapped, but bulged taut to the push of the wind. The ship heeled to starboard, cutting through the water in a great shallow curve. All about the deck men were shouting from the depths of their lungs. The repair crew scrambled up from below, and Ward could hear Tremarec's booming, "Well done!" The rudder ropes had been repaired.

Now the *Sauvage* would have no trouble outrunning the Englishman. Sharp orders snapped from the quarter-deck, were repeated along the twin rows of cannon. Something in the air brought Ward to his feet, sent him to the bulwarks. The course of the *Sauvage,* if held, would infallibly cross the enemy bow, rendering the Englishman's main batteries useless while Tremarec's starboard pieces could rake the whole length of his deck.

For a while the two ships raced on, relative positions unchanged. Then Ward realized he was seeing less and less of the enemy hull, more and more of the rounding of the bow. The English guns began to flame, and the night was barred with silvery columns of water that shot up between the ships. "They're getting jumpy! Firing far too soon!" he cried.

A hand caught at his shoulder, pulled him away from the bulwark. A petty officer yelled in his ear, "Noncombatants below. By order of the Captain!"

Ward shook his head obstinately. He braced himself against the mast, eyes always to starboard.

Then he swung his arms above his head, yelling. The gap between the ships was narrowing, and the Englishman was heeled so far over that his port guns seemed to be pointing straight to the stars. The forward pieces of the *Sauvage* roared, and splinters flew from the enemy bow. Gaos appeared from the darkness shouting to the two gunners nearest Ward, *"À vous les mâts!* Take care of their masts, you!"

The *Sauvage* was cutting closer and closer toward the Englishman's bow. Ward's head hammered with the din of the *Sauvage's* guns, and his vision blurred from the flashes that alternately brought the other ship close, then wrapped it in utter darkness. A flash close by, and he could see men clinging to the fighting-tops of the enemy, could even make out the lines that ran from mast and bowsprit to the deck. The flat chatter of musketry broke out again. He jumped as something burned his neck and shoulder.

There was a sharp crash just as the nearest gun captain gave the command to fire. Grapeshot rattled and smacked along the deck, and Ward stood staring as men tumbled and writhed by the pieces just in front of him. The dying flashes showed the English masts still riding high above the tinted smoke.

He leaped forward to the breech of the nearest gun. A man staggered against him, swore, then shouted, *"Allons! Les mâts!"*

"Is it loaded?" yelled Ward.

"Bar shot. My leg! It bends like a dead cod. I have the slow match."

Ward crouched by the breech, old skills returning to his fingers as he fumbled in the dark. He swore happily as he found that the piece had an elevating screw instead of the hard-to-manage quoins. He slowly elevated the muzzle, delicately as a watchmaker, holding his breath as he brought the muzzle to bear on the half-seen ship across the water.

The wounded man huddled beside him, one leg stretched out at an awkward angle. The spark at the end of the slow match glowed dusky red. Ward saw the hand move toward the breech, brushed it aside. "Not yet!" He started as a piece farther up the deck blasted out. In the flare, he saw the foremast of the Englishman shake slightly, then steady itself. "At best, a graze," growled his companion.

"N'importe!" snapped Ward, hands still on the little wheel of the elevating screw. The *Sauvage* was rolling slightly to starboard. Tense, he watched the muzzle dip and dip until he was sighting into the dark glitter of the sea. The roll ended, and a slow rise began. Eyes along the barrel, he crouched, then snatched the slow match from the wounded man, slapped it across the vent. Fire spurted from the breech as Ward sprang clear. The piece roared and backed into its breeching, its solid wheels pounding on the deck.

Ward raised himself unconsciously on his toes. The wounded

sailor caught him about the waist, tried to struggle to his feet. Without looking away from the target, Ward flung an arm about the man, held him up. Another piece thundered, and in the flare the two men saw the British foremast bend gracefully forward in a flutter of sail cloth, recover, dip to port, hesitate.

There was a ripping sound across the water. Wood and sailcloth gave a hideous lurch, and a final round from the *Sauvage* lit up a trailing welter of mast and sail that dragged deep in the water, lit up agonized forms that pitched, still clutching their useless muskets, from the cross-trees to sea or deck.

"Your shot did that," said a deep voice behind Ward.

Ward turned quickly, easing the sailor to the breech of the gun as he did so. Tremarec stood there, hatless, powder-smeared but calm.

"Mine — or another's. What difference?" panted Ward.

Tremarec's big hand fell on Ward's shoulder. "So long as the shot came from the *Sauvage,* it does not matter which piece, *hein?* You begin to think like a sailor, *mon ami.*"

Something in the tone of the Breton's voice sent a glow through Ward, cancelling the strain and shock and fatigue of the engagement. "Not a sailor yet, perhaps," he said. "But I can see this. You've disabled the Englishman. All you've got to do now is circle or tack or come about or whatever you call it, and finish him off."

"You see that, do you?" Tremarec's teeth glinted in the dark. "But your idea is most sound."

"Good. I'll stay by this piece, then."

"It will not be necessary. The idea, as I said, is sound, but I do not follow it."

"But you've got him!" cried Ward.

Tremarec shook his head. "My mission is not to sink English ships. It is to run from one port to another. *Tout simple.* And remember — two ships we saw. One is gone, but one remains and that one may be joined by others." He made an angry gesture. "But for two accidents, we should have sailed by this unfortunate Mister Goddam in the dark."

"Two?" asked Ward. "I heard about the rudder ropes. The other?"

Tremarec lowered his voice. "Someone showed a light at our bows, long before we engaged. That gave the Englishman our position. It was cleverly done, with a dark-lantern that shone only out to sea."

Ward felt cold creep over him, but tried to argue away the Breton's thought. "You're only guessing," he muttered.

"Say, rather, reasoning," answered Tremarec grimly. "The Englishman knew just what course to set. And — a dark-lantern was found in the bow during the action and brought to me. It was badly dented as though the owner had thought to throw it overboard, only to have it strike some obstruction — the bulwarks, perhaps."

"But it can't be," said Ward obstinately. "Whoever signaled was on our ship. He would have gone down with it."

"Put yourself in his place, *mon ami*. He knows the Englishman will recognize us for what we are — a merchant brig. That should mean light armament and heavy cargo. The Englishman strikes quickly in the dark. He disables us, but does *not* wish to sink us. He comes alongside, puts a boarding party onto our decks. *Voilà.* He has a probably rich prize, little damaged. Few of our crew are dead — as our enemy plans his attack. Our crew is mustered on deck, including our man of the dark-lantern. He lets it be known to the British captain that the light was not accidental. He will then be signed on as a member of the British crew and will share in the prize-money, along with which, he will undoubtedly be given a handsome reward. It has happened before."

"No!" exclaimed Ward. "It's too fantastic. Your own crew!"

"Yes — composed of good Bretons, in large part. But also there are Germans, Poles, Spaniards and men of no country. Now I return to the quarter-deck, where there will be reports of damage and of casualties. You have perhaps forgotten that there are other passengers? I commend them to you." He sprang up to the quarter-deck.

Ward was vaguely aware that someone behind him was tending to the wounded sailor who had stood to the gun with him. Then he turned and raced toward the after hatch, pried it up and clattered down the companionway.

The door of the messroom was ajar, but no light showed through it. He shouted, "Deborah! Mrs. Lathrop! Where are you?"

An unsteady voice answered him. "Ward, are we sinking? Get us out of here!"

He plunged into the messroom, rapping his shins against the end of a bench. From the darkness, Paul Dale spoke quite calmly. "All over, is it?"

"Yes. But where — "

"I thought so. No more firing, ship moving under us. Lord, Sue, haven't I been telling you all along there wasn't any danger?"

Ward turned toward the sound of his voice. "Go on deck, if you think there hasn't been any danger."

Paul gave a rather airy laugh, but there was a tremor to it that told Ward that Paul had not been quite so oblivious to the fight as he pretended. "That's just the crew. Got a tinderbox with you? Blasted light went out. The concussion of the guns, I suppose."

Ward heard a deep sigh, and Mrs. Lathrop spoke more evenly. "So it's all over. We're not going to sink?"

"No!" shouted Ward. "And *where's* Deborah?"

"Deb's all right," answered Paul. "Coolest of the lot, she was. Maybe the cleverest. She said the ship was much thicker forward in that cubbyhole beyond here, so she went there. She'll be back in a minute, now that things are quiet. How about that tinder-box?"

Ward groped for the swinging lantern, unhooked it and set it on the table. With unsteady hands he hammered out a light, saw the wick catch. "Thanks," said Paul, reaching for the lantern.

Without glancing at him, Ward snapped, "Later!" caught up the lantern and made his way forward through the maze of up-rights. The door of the petty officers' mess was open, and he thrust the lantern inside. One sailor lay motionless on the rough table, his head nearly severed by a shot. On the floor, propped as though trying to rise, another sailor sprawled.

Ward peered wildly forward. The lantern light struck on the bulkhead that divided the *Sauvage* amidships. Right and left were neat stacks of cargo, built-in lockers, and he lowered his lantern. Blood. More blood, A weaving trail that led on to the bulkhead, that ran past him into the messroom where the two dead sailors lay.

Head bent to avoid the threatening beams, Ward hurried on, found where the blood began. Then he saw the cracks that marked a door cut into the bulkhead, became horribly aware of a thin, keening sound that rose and fell beyond the barrier of planks. Lantern still high, he butted the door open and stood transfixed at the high threshold.

He was looking into a sort of bay, luridly lit by several swing-ing lanterns, that ran the width of the ship, a section of the thick foremast reaching from deck to ceiling. Just at his left, two men, one with a bandaged head, were holding down a shrieking sailor while a third smeared hot pitch on the raw stump of an arm that ended just above the elbow. Another casualty lay almost at Ward's feet, a lean, bearded man whose body from breastbone to waist was a mass of bloody rags. Even as Ward stared in horror, the man arched his whole body so that only heels and shoulders touched the deck. Bright blood gushed out over his beard. He shuddered once, was still.

Ward wiped his forehead with a shaky hand. Then he saw Brotier, naked to the waist, calmly laying open the shoulder of a sailor who lay face down. The surgeon's hands moved with a sort of contemptuous skill, and he kept grumbling in an impersonal way over the stifled moans of his patient. Brotier straightened, tugged hard at a jagged splinter of wood that lay wedged under the tanned skin, jerked it free and tossed it away.

Something moved in the deep shadows beyond the foremast, and Ward cried out in shocked amazement as Deborah swayed toward him. Her gay blue dressing gown was rumpled and marked with sinister stains. There was blood on her bare forearms, blood on her hands that clutched a basin heaped with stained bandages.

Quickly Ward stepped over a prostrate man and took the basin from her, set it on the deck. She said, "Thank you, Ward," in a faint voice, then stumbled against him. He caught her about the shoulders, steadying her. Her head fell back, and her dark-lashed eyes closed. Deborah! She had floated daintily across the smooth lawns of Passy; she had presided over fragile Sèvres-ware in the salon in the rue Neuve des Petits Champs; she had laughed and flirted with elegant young officers of the Guards — and now —

"Steady, Deb," he said. "You're all right." Then raising his voice he snapped, "Brotier! What the devil do you mean by letting her come in here?"

Without looking up, Brotier answered calmly. "I do not let her. I merely find her at my elbow when I move in here from the petty officers' mess. *Voyez,* she hands me my knives, smoothes out lint. She holds Trudeau's hand while I remove his leg. So why should I ask questions of her?"

Still leaning against Ward, Deborah whispered, "Tell him I've

133

got to go. I hate myself for going — but everything swims around me. My hands shake. I might hurt one of these men."

Ward glanced quickly at Brotier, who nodded, an unusually warm gleam in his sardonic eye. "Come on, Deb," Ward said gently. "You saw Brotier through the worst of it." He guided her through the door.

"Faith didn't stop at Valley Forge. She went into the typhus huts, didn't she?"

"Never you worry about Faith. She'd be proud of you — two real soldiers together."

Ward beckoned to a passing sailor, handed him the lantern and told him to lead the way. Then, Deborah's hand on his arm, he followed. "A real soldier, Deb. Paul'll be mighty proud of you." He called, "Paul! Here we are. Coming aboard."

Paul's voice, quite steady now, came to him. "That's our lantern," he said to the sailor. "Set it in here. That you, Ward? What have you and Deb been doing? You found her, I suppose."

The sailor limped off, and Ward saw light flood the messroom as Paul slung the lantern on its hook. Ward kept his voice low. "I found her. She's here. She's all right."

Mrs. Lathrop, ghastly white under the lantern, pressed her hands to her cheeks, staring. Then she cried sharply, "Where did you find her? What's happened? Call Brotier!"

Deborah's eyes blinked in the unhealthy glow of the lantern, and she passed a hand over her forehead. "I'll be all right," she said.

Paul caught her to him. "Tell us, Sis. What happened? Where were you?"

Deborah only shook her head, a hollow look in her eyes. Ward said, "She was helping Brotier."

"Helping Brotier, the surgeon? Are you out of your mind?"

"I thought I was when I saw her there."

"Is that true?" asked Mrs. Lathrop, beyond astonishment.

134

Deborah nodded miserably, and Ward went on. "There were a lot of wounded men up there. She stood by helping — "

Mrs. Lathrop leaned across the table. "Deborah, dear, *what* made you do it?"

Head turned away, Deborah said, "Ward."

Paul faced Ward angrily. "Damn it, if this was your doing — "

"It wasn't." Deborah's voice was muffled. "He told me how our women at home had looked after the wounded at a massacre — "

Ward nodded. "At Paoli. It was necessary there. But — "

Deborah went on. "When I left here, I went to the petty officers' mess. There were dead men there already. I wanted to come back here. Then I heard someone through the bulkhead farther along. I thought it was a cat crying. I went to see, and pushed a door open. It was awful — "

"I know," said Ward. "Don't try to live it over."

"But I thought of the massacre and our women, and I thought if I were *really* one of them I could do what they did. Dr. Brotier saw me and began handing me things and telling me what to do and I tried to help him and follow what he said and then — " she paused, dropped her eyes — "and then Ward came in. I just couldn't go on any more. He brought me here." She straightened her shoulders. "Ward — I think I'm better now. I can go back now — really I can."

Ward frowned at her. "You stay right where you are. Didn't Brotier dismiss you, with thanks? You did your share and more."

Paul sat weakly back with a long, low whistle. "And that's my sister," he said at last. Mrs. Lathrop only stared in admiration that was tinged with perplexity and perhaps disapproval.

"With all those men — "she said. "I wonder what Dr. Franklin would say about it."

"Franklin?" exclaimed Ward. "I know just what he'd say. He told me once that what we needed to win this war was men greatly in earnest. If Deb hasn't qualified for the 'greatly in earnest' part, I don't know anyone in our armies who has."

Paul shook his head. "Deb, you're making me feel the way Ward makes me feel sometimes. I ought to have been there with you."

Ward glanced at Deborah, saw that color was once more coming into her cheeks. Then the light fell across her blood-stained arms, and he sprang up. "And another thing we ought all to have been doing! I'm going to scout the galley and see if there's hot water for Deb. Then I'll go aft and see what your cabins are like. Mrs. Lathrop, a word with you first."

A firm hand under her elbow, he lifted her to her feet, guided her through the door. In a low voice he said, "If you so much as hint to her that what she did was not quite ladylike, something that a well-bred young girl shouldn't have done, I'll curse you from the topmast to the keel of this ship."

Mrs. Lathrop's head went back. "I'll thank you to attend — " She broke off, seemed to be studying Ward in the uncertain light. "I'm beginning to see why Dr. Franklin liked you. No, Deborah will never hear a word of criticism from me."

Paul's shadow blocked the door of the messroom. "Look here, Ward, I'll go to the galley. You see about the cabins. I want to go forward anyway. I've no idea where my man Houston was during the fight."

"Working." Houston's thick voice came from the shadows, and he materialized into the faint glow, more thickly smeared with blood than Deborah had been.

"Hit?" asked Ward quickly.

"Not me. They chased me down into the stinking bilges when the action started. I got sick of the reek down there and came up and helped with the wounded."

"With the wounded?" echoed Paul. "It seems to me you should have looked after my sister."

136

"Miss Deborah?" Houston sounded surprised. "Why, when she was with you?"

Ward interposed. "She left, and went forward to help Brotier. Do you mean to say you didn't see her?"

Houston cleared his throat. "Oh — Brotier. I didn't say I was amidships with him. That damned splinter of ice is too grand to pay any attention to a clerk. They brought some of the men into the forecastle. One of the hands, Prunier, was running things up forward there. He used to be a surgeon's mate on an East Indiaman. He and I finally got things in fair order so I came aft to report to you, Mr. Dale."

"Well, I don't see what else you could have done," said Paul slowly.

"Did the only thing I could," answered Houston.

Paul looked at him coldly. "That is for your employer to say, rather than yourself. Ward, I think I'll go aft to the cabins instead of forward. Houston, you go with Mr. Gratwick. Get yourself cleaned up. See if there's anything you can do for the ladies. Then report to me in the cabin."

Forward, they found that the galley smokestack had been shot away, but the cook had kept a low fire going and had been sending buckets of hot water to Brotier. Ward commandeered a bucket for Deborah while Houston swabbed off his hands and arms.

Ward and Houston regained the deck where the night was clamorous with the sound of hammering and a muffled, metallic clanking that went on in a deadly rhythm. Paul stood waiting by the break of the quarter-deck. "The after cabins weren't touched, though there's some broken glass in the gallery. I'll take the bucket."

"How's Deborah?" asked Ward.

"Amazing. Picked up a lot."

"My respects to her, Paul."

Paul smiled. "I'll tender them. Houston, come to my cabin in about an hour. Some of our papers got pitched about, and I'll want you to right them." He paused, listening. "What the devil's that eternal clink-clank?"

"Can't you guess?" asked Ward. "Pumps."

"The ship's leaking?"

"Can't be a bad leak or you'd hear Tremarec giving orders. We must have taken at least one round at or below the water line."

Paul's voice was hoarse. "You mean we're just butting on through the night, shipping water all the time? Damn, that's dangerous."

"Not until Tremarec says it is. A lot better than to have had a mast shot away, or our rudder. In that case, you and I would be answering questions put to us by some beef-faced British skipper."

Behind Ward, Houston murmured, "Maybe that wouldn't have been so hard."

"When I want comment from you, I'll call for it," said Paul angrily. "Good night, Ward."

Ward turned on his heel as the door slammed and walked along the deck. Houston was a few feet ahead of him ambling on, head down, as though brooding over Paul's unnecessary rebuke. Then, to Ward's amazement, he caught a suppressed chuckle as though Mr. James Houston, one-time sergeant under Colonel Roger Enos, had thought of something most amusing.

The deck was alive with repair parties, with gun-crews swabbing out their places, and Ward was jostled at every turn. He went aft again, dropped down the hatch and entered the mess-room where the lantern still burned sullenly.

He thought of his own near-panic on deck, the nerve-shaking effect of a new kind of war in a new element. Only the chance of serving a piece, of wrapping himself in routine gunnery had finally steadied him. He recalled the thudding crash of shot striking the hull, and his hands were moist and unsteady again.

He reached into a locker, tugged a brandy bottle from its rack and poured four fingers into a glass and drank. The brandy warmed him, slowly banished remembered fears. Houston, a landsman like himself, had played his part, tending wounded under a kind of fire that was new to him. The experience must have bolstered him, giving him fresh assurance in the face of Paul Dale's bitter displeasure. Ward's nerves relaxed, and his eyes grew heavy. Below, the pumps clanked on.

I X

The Sealed Packet

THE FOLLOWING DAY the *Sauvage* drove on west, her sharp prow with its carved and gilded figurehead cutting diagonally across the troughs of the ever growing waves.

Ward walked cautiously along the slanting deck. He looked at the sails above, listened to the endless plaints of the pumps below. Whatever water the ship was taking in, the pumps were apparently able to handle, for it maintained a fine rate of speed. The deck was noisy with the sound of saw and hammer, as sailors replaced broken timbers along the bulwarks and closed up the gaping rents one by one.

The day wore on to the sound of the pumps and the high singing of the wind through the rigging. Ward ate well at noon, then rearranged his possessions in his restored cabin and returned to the deck.

Since his own share in the fight, he was aware of a feeling that now he was part of this ship and it part of him. He rejoiced in the crash of the bow into the deep-falling hollows in the blue waters. He began to understand how men could spend their lives beating across whole oceans in fair weather and foul, could come to love long months out of sight of land.

In the late afternoon he made his way to the very peak of the bow, the catheads jutting right and left just behind him. The sun was dropping into the west in a riot of apple-green and bronze and turquoise and scarlet. Flying fish skimmed away from the cut-water in flashes of sun-touched silver to vanish in the creaming tops of the waves ahead.

Clinging fast to a taut stay, Ward stepped onto a jutting block to avoid the swirl of water that eddied about his feet. The *Sauvage* heeled far to port and he looked nearly straight down into a hissing swirl of gold-blue foam. The ship righted itself, heeled far to starboard. There was a giddy exhilaration about it that reminded him oddly of coasting down those long, steep ridges that sloped west from Marlboro toward Shrewsbury and Worcester, flying on with the powdery snow beating at his face and the white fields zipping past him.

Suddenly there was a plunge. His feet slipped from the block, swung wildly in the air. Something cracked across his knuckles and his grip on the stay broke. He fell into the swirling water, banging against solid, half-submerged objects. The water fell away for an instant, then broke harder about him and he turned head over heels. He tried to shout, but the sea choked his words. He caught at something hard, gripped for an instant, then lost it. He flung out an arm and his fingers closed tight on something wet and muscular. His other hand clawed, felt a tough shoulder under soaked woolen cloth.

The whole world heaved up under him and for an instant he found himself, horror-struck and gasping, his legs over the port bulwark. With a frantic heave he tugged at what he was holding and rolled back onto the deck, just as the *Sauvage* hovered on an even keel. His hands were locked on the shoulders of a drenched seaman who half lay, half crouched on the deck.

Ward reached out, caught hold of a heavy ring in the deck. Coughing and gasping, he managed to say, "You saved my life."

In the dim light he could see that the man was trembling. Ward said again, "You saved my life. In another second, I'd have been overboard. What's your name? Whose watch are you in?"

The sailor, trembling harder, rose unsteadily, tried to run aft. A rope about his waist checked him, and sent him tumbling to the deck. Ward was on his feet at once. He worked beyond the most dangerous part of the bow, lifted the man, who began to curse and struggle. "God damn it, I'm just trying to thank you," cried Ward, his voice hoarse with sea-water. "Wait a minute. I'll cut the rope." He whipped out a dripping knife, slashed until the strands parted. "So you saw I might lose my footing, lashing yourself fast so we both wouldn't go over? Lucky thing for me. No need for you to have the tremors. I'm the one to do that." He kept a tight grip on the man's shirt. "Now what's your name?"

"Doriot," was the shaky answer.

Ward, bracing his feet, pushed Doriot gently toward the fore-castle hatch. "Below, then, and get dry clothes. Understand? I'll report to the Captain what you did for me. Believe me, you will not lose by this action."

Ward could hear the man's teeth chatter as he croaked, *"Oui, Monsieur,"* and scuttled below decks.

Knees unsteady as full realization of his miraculous escape struck, Ward went to his cabin, towelled himself vigorously and got into fresh clothes. As he was adjusting the chained packet there was a knock at his door and the familiar voice of Tremarec's steward told him that the Captain expected him at once in his cabin.

Ward found Tremarec seated at his neat table, a packet resting on a spread-out chart before him. The Breton's strong, dark features lit up with a pleasant smile. "Ah, our *maître-pointeur!* You and the demoiselle — I may say particularly the demoiselle — have become transfigured in the eyes of our crew. Already they compare her to Jeanne Hachette who saved Beauvais from the Burgundians three hundred years ago, save that la Hachette struck down where our demoiselle healed."

"Don't compare me with the demoiselle. I just resumed my old trade."

Tremarec nodded gravely. "Whereas she turned to an utterly new one. However, you are still *maître-pointeur*. One thing about the fight still puzzles me. Tell me, *mon ami,* is it an American custom, perhaps derived from your redskins, to smear oneself with the blood of wounded men? A primitive idea, perhaps, that one gains strength and heart thereby?"

"Smearing yourself with wounded men's blood?" exclaimed Ward. "Never heard of such a thing. What put that into your head?"

Tremarec spread out his hands. "What else than that my good Gaos came upon your Monsieur Houston, who had been well secreted during the fight, daubing wet and bloody bandages along his arms. He even picked up a severed foot and rubbed it on his shirt."

Ward could not doubt the truth of what Tremarec had just told him, since Gaos would not have invented it. Then Houston had been playing a grisly sham, appearing at the last moment, looking like a butcher, and saying that he had been tending the wounded.

"Well?"

"Nothing I ever heard of before and nothing that I can explain," said Ward.

"Never mind." Tremarec tapped the packet. "Now let us return to our muttons. According to my reckonings, we are on the exact spot where my orders, received at Lorient, call on me to open this. They further call for your presence. Will you — " He glanced at Ward. "*Tiens.* Your hair is wet. I interrupt you at your bath with my message?"

"Not at all. An accident which I wish to report to you later. The packet?"

"*Bon.* Now you see me open it." His strong brown fingers

broke the seals and unfolded four thick sheets of paper covered with copperplate writing. "H'm — the Ministry of Marine — de Sartine — consult if need be with Monsieur de Bouillé, Governor of Martinique — " he looked up — "but this needs no explanations. What next? Be guided by any instructions of his — may send picket-boat to intercept — set new course if need be. Ah, now I see. Fort-Royal at Martinique may *not* be our first port of call, but why you need be troubled to watch me read these seaman's instructions, I do not understand."

Ward shook his head. "A witness might be required. Could that be it?"

"*Incroyable!*" said Tremarec. "Now further — ah — this may explain a little." He handed the second sheet to Ward, whose heart gave a leap as he saw Franklin's familiar handwriting.

The letter was dated at Passy a few days before Ward's arrival at Lorient. He read eagerly, with rising excitement.

MY DEAR YOUNG FRIEND:
May I hope that the bit of jewelry which I insisted on fastening about your waist has not proved too galling. At least, I may tell you now, as you read this, long weeks after I have written it, that it may be removed and the packet opened in the presence of Captain Tremarec. In the packet you will find another letter of general instructions to yourself and a second package, heavily sealed. This last, in modification of the general instructions, you will deliver according to where you may be able to land.

Should you be able to pass into Chesapeake Bay, a decision that will lie with Captain Tremarec, you will deliver it in person to the Marquis de LaFayette, who is operating south of the Potomac. Should your destination be Philadelphia, then to the President of the Congress, the Honorable Thomas McKean. Should Boston be your port, you may hand them over to the Honorable John Hancock, Governor of Massachusetts, enjoining him that they be sent at once to His Excellency General George Washington, wherever he may be.

Lest you think that I have involved you in a stupid game of blindman's buff — we had a truly gay romp over this game at

Madame Brillon's last night — let me say that secrecy in this whole matter has been so essential that I have feared to trust the least details to any save the immediate principals. But at this distance I may tell you that the papers which you carry deal with the most important part of your cargo, its origin, the obligations which it entails and the names of those therein concerned and the channels employed.

You may be sure that whoever receives the papers and the cargo will not be insensible to the part that you have played in their delivery, and none can be more sensible of that part than

Your affectionate friend,
BENJAMIN FRANKLIN

Ward got up quickly, stripped off his coat, began unbuttoning his shirt.

"May I use that knife of yours?" he asked. "Thanks." He ripped open a little leather pouch that was attached to the chain about his waist, drew out a minute key. Then he worked the little padlock, which he had kept carefully oiled, to the front, slipped the key into it. The tumblers gave and the padlock flew open. Careless of the rasping, Ward stripped the chain from his waist and held it up, Franklin's oiled silk packet swinging from it.

"Lord, but I'm glad to get rid of that thing. Now watch, Captain, since the Doctor's letter is like your orders in that it specifies another shall be present at the opening." He seated himself, handed the packet to Tremarec. "Will you look at the seals and see if they are in order?"

Tremarec turned it over in his hands, holding the red wax squares carefully up to the light. "All in order, in my opinion." He gave it to Ward.

Ward slid the knife blade under each seal that swedged down the edges. They broke with a sharp, ripping sound and little flakes of red fell onto the chart. The oiled material crackled stiffly under Ward's fingers, folded back to show an inner cov-

145

ering of linen. "Take care," breathed Tremarec anxiously as Ward slit the tough thread.

Ward's hands shook as he unwrapped the linen. "Ha! Here we are and — God Almighty!"

The thick pack of paper stirred, its edges curled slowly, then the sheets flapped back along the creases showing spotless, unmarked surfaces. Ward cried, "It's another wrapping. It's got to be," and peeled off sheet after sheet until the very last lay like a half-opened book on the table.

Ward slumped on his chair. "Blank. Every last damned one of them!"

Tremarec clutched at the mass, caught it up. "But they cannot be blank. No! It is not possible!" He thumped the table. "I say it is not possible. I — Ha! I have it. Your Doctor Franklin, he is a scientist, one of the greatest. Chemicals he knows as I know the vintages of France. This will be in a secret ink. Heat or the juice of a lemon will unlock all this as you unlocked your padlock."

Ward shook his head dully. "No. I worked with him. I know his methods. He never used secret ink to my knowledge."

Tremarec snatched up a sheet. "Nor did you know of this voyage, or of this cargo. See — thus shall we bring out the writing." He held one sheet, a second, a third close to the lamp until brownish spots appeared on them, but no trace of writing was revealed. Tremarec produced two small, dried lemons from a locker and smeared the juice diagonally across sheet after sheet.

When the last had been tested, Tremarec carefully wiped his hands on a fine handkerchief, strolled to the port and tossed the remains of the lemons into the sea. Then he seated himself across from Ward. "*Voyons,* my friend. We are faced with two possibilities. The first is that our good Doctor played an impish prank on you. And on me. But such was never his way. So it ceases to be a possibility. The second is that someone, somehow,

146

has been able to detach that chain from you without your knowing it and substitute this false packet. This last I believe to be true. Let me add," he went on hastily, "in no way does this reflect on you who have been under my eye since Le Havre."

Ward rubbed a hand across his face in a baffled gesture. "But I wore the chain. If you're right, the packet was taken from me."

"Let us consider the matter."

Ward took heart from Tremarec's calm manner. He picked up the sheets and examined them. "The whole reverse of the outer sheet is stained, Captain. That could come through the linen from the oiled wrapping. Therefore, the substitution was made quite a long time ago. Perhaps several weeks."

Tremarec nodded in approval. "Unquestionably. Unless — " he raised a finger — "unless this blank packet was prepared a long time ago, in anticipation of taking the place of the true one."

"That's too fantastic. Who'd know about it far enough in advance? And who'd take the trouble?"

"Ah, *mon ami,* you do not know the infinity of elaborate intrigue that goes on."

"Maybe, but let's get back to my part — as messenger."

"Our messenger," agreed Tremarec. "Let us put it that he is a heavy sleeper. And the sleep may be the deeper when he has been watching the stars fade in company of our good Gaos or Keratry and a bottle or two of cognac. Or discussing the state of the Colonies — your pardon, the States — with Monsieur Paul after the ladies had retired."

"I should have been more careful," said Ward ruefully.

"Short of swallowing chain and packet each night and pulling them up each morning, I do not see what else you could have done."

"Thank you for putting it that way. But what can we do now?"

Tremarec shrugged. "Develop the eye of the eagle by day and of the cat by night. That is all, and it may not serve us, since the answer may not lie on the *Sauvage*. The case is odd, you conceive. As master, I hope that my ship is not involved."

"Guess that's all we can do, just watch," said Ward. "There are other odd things that have happened though. I meant to tell you about this one in particular, but the action drove it out of my mind." He told of the finding of the metal tube in the hollow tree at Passy, of the reappearance of what he believed to be that selfsame tube in mid-Atlantic, of its disappearance from his cabin.

Tremarec's face was impassive, but the veins in his forehead swelled a little. "*Tiens!* You say Jabish Frost. I have met him. He was associated with Beaumarchais and some of his underlings in the Hortalez affair. But such tubes are common enough, with or without names stamped on them. And you missed it when your cabin was dismantled? No doubt it fell into the scuppers and was picked up by some sailor. He might wish to store coin or keepsake in it. Nonetheless, I shall have the ship searched, most quietly."

"Then there was the marlinspike that stuck in the deck less than a foot from my head when I was napping at the base of a mast."

"And why not? Masts are high. Sailors are not always sure-fingered. I myself have seen dozens of escapes like yours, and never an accident."

"You were close to seeing one then," said Ward. "Luck did turn for me tonight, though. That's why my hair is still wet. I was up in the bows and a wave would have carried me over if one of your men hadn't lashed himself fast to something and hauled me back."

"One of my men? Then he must not only have moved quickly, but thought quickly, since he was able to lash himself and rescue you in so short a time. His name?"

"Doriot."

148

"Ah, yes. One who was signed on at Lorient. I will summon him. Such devotion should not pass unrewarded."

Ward rose. "I tried to thank him, but he ducked below. Well, this has been a damned odd talk. The packet. The tube. The marlinspike. The wave."

"Do not take the packet too much to heart. There is one possibility which comes to my mind. The pages *may* be covered with writing in invisible ink after all, with the key lying in the hands of those who may receive the papers. Wait now. I make the packet up all over again." With surprising deftness he folded, wrapped and sealed the packet, attached it to the chain again.

Ward locked it about his waist. "Hoped I was free of the damned thing," he grumbled. "Still you may be right about the ink. We'll go through with it."

"That is wise," said Tremarec. "And it may not be for long. In three days' time, perhaps two, we shall sight the peaks of Mt. Vauclain on Martinique. Once there, Monsieur de Bouillé may have direct word for us from your country. Good night and a good rest."

Late that night Ward was awakened by a petty officer. Standing at attention in the doorway, the man said in a mechanical voice. "By order of Captain Tremarec, I repeat to you the following *extrait du loch* — "

"Extract from the log! What do you mean?"

The toneless voice went on. "At six bells in the dogwatch, the seaman Doriot, under orders to report to the quarter-deck at the expiration of his watch, was carried overboard by a wave and lost. *C'est tout*, Monsieur."

"Doriot lost overboard?" cried Ward. "Here — wait a minute."

"There is nothing to add." The petty officer vanished into the night closing the door behind him.

So Doriot would never receive Ward's thanks or the commendation of his captain! Poor devil. Ward lay there, looking up at the low ceiling, until sunlight began to creep through the cracks in his door.

The next morning Ward was leaning against the carriage of the piece next his cabin, watching the swish and heave of the deep blue water as it slid past the starboard side of the *Sauvage*. A light step sounded behind him and he turned quickly. Deborah stood by the breech of the gun, smiling at him from the shade of her wide hat that was tied under her chin by a broad blue ribbon. "Welcome on deck again!" he called. "Sure you're all right?"

"Of course." Her smile faded and deep concern showed in her dark eyes. "But I've been worried about you. The steward told me about your nearly being carried overboard." She shivered.

He gave a short laugh. "I'm going to stay square amidships from now on. But look here, you're sure you took no fever from being with Brotier?"

"Fever? Of course not. Oh, Ward, I can never forget those men. They were — oh, excuse me." A slight roll of the ship made her lose her balance a little and with a backward step she brushed against a sailor who squatted near the bulwarks, busy splicing a rope. He mumbled an apology for his presence and hitched away a few feet.

Ward glanced carelessly at him, then took a longer look. That same sailor seemed always close at hand, hammering, scraping at a plank or sloshing water about. He made a mental note to speak to Tremarec about it.

Then he dismissed the matter as Paul came on deck. "Hello, Paul. Come join us," he called.

Paul, quite pale, nodded casually to Ward. Then he held out an embroidered bag that Ward had seen many times swinging from Deborah's slim arm. Paul spoke easily, but Ward thought he could detect a harsh undertone. "I know you didn't mean to leave this lying about, Sis."

Deborah caught at the bag and slipped it onto her arm. "Oh, I am sorry, Paul. Especially when you asked — "

Paul cut in quickly. "It's just that things can be tossed about and lost. I know it's one of your favorite kickshaws."

It seemed to Ward that Paul was making a strange to-do about his sister's fripperies. Deborah patted Paul's cheek. "I'll keep it with me all the time. Thanks for bringing it to me. Now when you go back to the cabin, please tell Sue — "

Paul shook his head. "I'm not going back for a while yet. Houston's copying out some stuff for me and I don't want to stay cooped up on a day like this." He stiffened, wheeled around to face forward. Ward, turning to look, heard a long-drawn hail from the foremast.

"What's he yelling?" asked Paul, tilting his head forward.

"The same as our 'Sail-ho!'" answered Ward. "Look here, Deborah, if Tremarec begins to clear for action, you're going below and you're going to stay there if Paul and I have to hold you down. Wait! Here he comes. Captain! Captain Tremarec! Are you sending us below?"

Tremarec paused, touching his hat to Deborah. "Ah, I think not. Our lookout reports a French sail closing on us. A dispatch boat. I warned you that we neared Martinique." He nodded at Ward. "In view of what we read the other night, surely you are not surprised."

"I see," said Ward, recalling the brief reference to a picket-boat in the papers Tremarec had opened.

Deborah smiled at Tremarec. "Couldn't we all be mysterious with you and Ward?"

Tremarec bowed. "Your pardon. I should not speak in riddles. Our orders mentioned we might be met by such a ship."

"What will she do? Escort us into Fort-Royal?" asked Paul.

"Hardly. But we may learn of the state of the sea, the presence of hostile shipping in these waters, which anchorage we shall use at the Fort, what we need by way of supplies and repair," answered the Breton. "The usual dull commonplaces of seafaring folk, Mademoiselle. With your permission, I shall mount the foremast. Our newcomer may be flying signal flags."

Ward caught up with him as he walked forward. "Just one question, Captain. Is it customary to arm your sailors when action is not threatened?" He indicated the man splicing rope.

Tremarec looked coolly at him. "Ah, so you noticed it?"

"How could I help it? It's a very small pistol, but the butt bulges under his blue sash. Everywhere I go and whatever I do there he is. And I'm damned certain that he slept on deck just outside my door last night."

"Yes. I judged it advisable. I trust you do not find it irksome."

"*You* told him to hang around me?"

"As I said. You see, *mon ami,* there have been near-accidents on board. Another time there might not be the obliging Doriot to pull you to safety. Another time a marlinspike might fall fatally close. The lives and properties of all my passengers are in my charge. So I take precautions. You must trust the sailor Moen, who comes from my own estate in Morbihan." He gave Ward's shoulder a light tap, then started nimbly up the shrouds, a closed telescope jutting from his pocket.

Ward walked slowly back to where Deborah and Paul were staring out to sea, trying to pick up the distant glimmer of a sail.

A light padding and tapping caught his ear and he looked back over his shoulder. The sailor Moen was listlessly moving barefoot along the deck, pausing by each gun to tap the iron rings sunk in the deck with a copper-headed hammer. The tassel of his red stocking-cap dangled over his forehead almost on a level with his eyebrows, giving him a vacuous, cross-eyed look.

*　　　　　*　　　　　*

That afternoon the dispatch boat *Fantasque* rocked idly less than a cable-length from the *Sauvage*. She was a slim craft with little freeboard and two stumpy masts. The longboat which had brought an elegant and gold-braided young officer to the *Sauvage* lay along the port side. Two of Tremarec's boats were made fast to the *Fantasque* and Ward could see the crew rigging a boom from the foremast.

Mrs. Lathrop and Deborah joined Ward on the deck. He greeted them, handed Deborah up onto the barrel of a sixteen-pounder and opened Mrs. Lathrop's parasol for her.

The crew of the *Fantasque,* mostly big, competent Negroes, were slinging squat casks over the side and into the *Sauvage's* boats. "That looks like good Martinique water," Ward said. "Fresh vegetables and fruits in those crates, I'd say."

Mrs. Lathrop nodded, then looked toward the quarter-deck. "Hello, here's our glittering guest taking his leave. I wonder what he had to say to our captain."

The elegant young officer walked quickly along the deck, threw a surprised glance at Deborah and Mrs. Lathrop, touched his hat with a quick, *"Serviteur, Madame, Mademoiselle,"* and swung himself over the side into his longboat.

Deborah, embroidered bag over her arm, fanned herself as she watched the glint of oars that swept the *Fantasque's* officer to his ship. "Listen, you can hear the *Fantasque's* crew singing as they lower those kegs. And here comes our first boat back. Heavens! What's that!"

All three turned toward the quarter-deck as a high-pitched voice sounded from within. Unconsciously Ward glanced at the omnipresent Moen, stolidly polishing a brass powder-measure nearby, but the sunburned Breton worked on unconcernedly. The voice rose higher. Mrs. Lathrop turned white. "That's Paul's voice."

Deborah dropped from the piece, her eyes troubled.

"Wait here," said Ward quickly. "I'll see what's happened." He started for the door that led under the quarter-deck. A brisk click of heels sounded in his ears and Deborah caught up with him.

He stepped aside to let her go through the door, followed after her. Out of the corner of his eye he saw Moen sauntering after them.

The door of Tremarec's cabin stood open and Paul was thumping his fist on the Captain's table. His face was the color of putty. The usually impeccable fall of lace at his throat was disarranged. He was storming at Tremarec, waving papers in his face. The Captain sat opposite, listening with a rather weary courtesy.

Paul's voice cracked as he shook his papers again. "But *this* is from de Sartine. And *this* is from de Fontanelle and this is from Vergennes himself. By God, if you cross them, you'll find the seas so hot they'll melt every nail in your planks."

"I have my orders, much as I regret them," said Tremarec evenly.

Paul shouted, "Orders from a damned little bedizened popinjay in a fishing smack. What'll they say in Paris when they hear you've disobeyed orders from the Ministry of Marine, from the Foreign Minister? Vergennes's letter has even got the King's endorsement on it. You're wrecking my plans, you're wrecking the plans of other people who are so powerful that they can break you like that!" He snatched up a pencil from the table, snapped it in two, and hurled the pieces away.

Deborah sailed across the cabin, her head high and her eyes flashing. "Captain Tremarec, what are you doing to my brother?"

Paul whirled on Deborah. "You keep out of this. You, too, Gratwick. Out of here, both of you. I don't want you listening. I'm going to fight this through and this damned freshwater sailor will find himself without his papers if he doesn't show a little sense."

"What is it, Captain?" asked Deborah in a low, clear voice.

Tremarec bowed. "Perhaps, Mademoiselle, it would be best to follow the suggestion of *Monsieur votre frère.*"

Deborah's head went still farther back. "He's my brother and if you're talking to him you're talking to me." She bit her lip, went on more calmly. "Please excuse me for coming in like this. But really, you must listen to Paul. He's always been so right."

Tremarec drew up a chair for Deborah as Ward stepped into the cabin. "Look, Deb, wouldn't it be better if you and I left them to finish their talk?"

Paul threw himself into another chair. "You'll hear about it soon enough anyway." He pointed a trembling finger. "That man refuses to take us to Martinique. Here's my passage guaranteed by King Louis himself, by de Sartine, by Vergennes, by Fontanelle."

Ward looked questioningly at Tremarec. "We're not going to Fort-Royal?"

Tremarec started to speak, but Paul was on his feet again. "That's what *he* thinks. And why? Because a little braided clerk in a bumboat comes alongside and tells him not to."

Ward said quietly to Tremarec, "The dispatch boat brought new orders from the Governor?"

"As I have been trying to explain. Now that we are close to Martinique, I pass under the orders of its governor. That is normal procedure. The Governor now sets a new course for me. I have no choice."

"Oh, but couldn't you just put in to Fort-Royal long enough for us to get off?" asked Deborah.

"Such is not possible," replied Tremarec. "Believe me, I regret the derangement of your plans."

"You are making a big mistake and you'll pay for it," said

Paul coldly. "Another thing, Captain. How about your cargo? I don't pretend to know what it is, but I can make a good guess that a ship like your doesn't take off secretly from Lorient with just a load of knitting needles. And I can guess that it was supposed to be landed at Fort-Royal. How are you going to explain that to the Ministry?"

"Explain?" The Breton shrugged. "It is not I who explain. The Ministry sends me out, bound for Martinique, but, as I pointed out, I pass under the orders of the Governor, once in these waters. He says I shall not enter Fort-Royal."

Ward looked at Paul who sat back in his chair, chin on his chest. "Tremarec's right, any way you look at it, Paul."

"He can't be," muttered Paul. Suddenly he sat upright. "Here's the solution, Captain! Whatever your cargo is, it's needed at Fort-Royal. Transfer it to the *Fantasque*. You give me letters to the Governor and I sail with the dispatch boat to Fort-Royal as a sort of supercargo." He slapped the table, color returning to his face. "That'll solve everything. Come on Sis. Get hold of Sue. Collect your things and we'll move over to the *Fantasque*. Ward, would you mind finding Houston and sending him to me? Tell him to hurry."

The Captain shook his head. "It seems my fate to disappoint you always. Unfortunately, the *Fantasque* does not return to Fort-Royal. It does not even return to Martinique."

"God blast it!" exploded Paul. "It begins to look as though you, or someone, were trying to thwart me!"

"Paul!" said Deborah firmly. Then she turned to Tremarec. "Just one thing I'd like to ask. If this was supposed to be a secret voyage, how was the *Fantasque* waiting for us so neatly?"

The Breton answered courteously. "That is what I have been trying to explain to Monsieur. It was known that a ship like the *Sauvage might* be sent to Fort-Royal at about this time. The

Fantasque had been watching for such a ship and any others flying our flag that might be sighted."

"And things have been happening that make it advisable for you to avoid Martinique?" broke in Ward.

"Yes," answered the Captain. "Some weeks ago, our Admiral de Grasse was at Martinique with a strong fleet. He beat the Englishman, Hood. Then de Grasse was sent to a destination which need not concern us. However, the rest of Hood's fleet, a strong force, is in these waters, though rather to the south as last reported. His ships cruise widely, looking for just such morsels as the *Sauvage* and its cargo. That is why our orders are changed, and why the *Fantasque,* its mission ended, goes to safer places."

"There, Paul," said Deborah. "I know you're disappointed, but you must see that the Captain can't do anything else. Heavens, do you want to hear cannon balls smashing into the hull again? I know I don't. And don't forget about Ward, either. He's an escaped prisoner, so far as the British are concerned. You wouldn't want to see him taken again."

"No. No. To be sure," said Paul absently. Then he straightened up. "Captain, if it was known that a ship like this *might* come to Fort-Royal, wouldn't that knowledge be pretty general?"

Tremarec sighed. "Possibly not. But probably it would be. People are stupid, people are indiscreet, people are venal."

"Then," Paul went on eagerly, "wouldn't the change in orders be known?"

The Captain raised his hands, dropped them to the table. "Again, possibly no, but probably yes."

Paul's face set in intense, swift thought. He muttered, "Of course, of course. That would be — " He leaned across the narrow table. "Where do we head now, Captain?"

"For the moment, only toward a point on the map, toward a given latitude and longitude. Then I shall open a letter from the Governor which I trust will be more specific."

"Which direction do we sail?" asked Ward eagerly.

"That I may not tell you," replied Tremarec. "And now, Mademoiselle, Messieurs, with your permission, I shall confer here with my officers."

Paul left the cabin quickly, his face set like a mask. Deborah followed, more slowly, Ward at her side. "Poor Paul," she said. "He does go at things so hard. But he'll be his old self in just a few minutes. You wait and see."

The *Sauvage* stirred, gathered momentum. In a wide, graceful curve the bow swung southeast, east, hesitated, curved on, settled on a northerly course.

Ward watched Deborah out of the corner of his eye as he thought of the scene in the cabin. He had seen a new side of Paul, a side that suggested ruthlessness, an immense obsession with his own plans, an urge to ride over anything or anybody that stood in his way. He began to wonder a little, trying to picture Paul in the American milieu. He was strongly and unpleasantly reminded of men who took quick commissions in the army and then suddenly dropped out of the combat zones, of merchants and owners of privateers bent on profit even to the extent of trading with the enemy. Of course, Paul would do nothing like that, but —

Deborah cried out at his elbow. "Look, Ward. We're going north. That means home!"

He thought of the army, of Faith, of the broad yellow house in the Marlboro ridges with his father and mother under the fanlighted door. All that waited for him. And for Deborah? Her father would be there, of course, but from hints dropped by Mrs. Lathrop, Ward had gathered that the elder Dale's interest in his son and daughter had grown more perfunctory with the passing years. Of course, Mrs. Lathrop and Paul would be with her — those two — but Paul?

"Yes, home for all of us, Deb," he said. But he was thinking, "Here's a new friend and a little job for you, Faith."

The *Sauvage* dipped and lunged on, steady wind in her sails.

X

The Fleets of France

FOR DAYS the bowsprit of the *Sauvage* glided on over wind-ruffled seas, bearing more and more to the northwest. Then, in a blaze of color, a low black line appeared on the horizon, slowly thickened, climbed higher and higher in an ominous tangle of mountains, the mountains of Haiti. Tremarec finally dropped anchor at the narrow mouth of a harbor to wait for the morning tide to carry him between the half-seen forts to the bay beyond. Ward saw with surprise the Captain's barge launched. Paul and Jim Houston dropped into it, each clutching flat parcels wrapped in canvas. Keratry asked Ward if he would like to go ashore with the others. The prospect of solid land under his feet was tempting, but then Ward thought of landing in a strange port in the dark with no place to go. He decided to wait until morning.

It was well on toward noon when he finally sprang onto the quay of Cap Haitien and set out to explore the capital of this tropical French colony. He had hoped that Deborah would come with him, but Mrs. Lathrop complained of a slight fever, and the girl had stayed to keep her company.

Through the blanketlike heat, Ward wandered idly along the water front, sniffing the hot land breeze and the unaccustomed scents that came from the warehouses. There was raw coffee, keen and penetrating, and the rich blandness of the roasted beans. There was the silky scent of stored cacao, the tang of steeping logwood and the almost musky smell of honey.

Little gray donkeys, shepherded by Negroes, trotted phil-
osophically under flapping loads of tanned hides. Bullocks and
horses strained between the shafts of low wagons that creaked
under their baulks of logwood. A few trim carriages bowled
smoothly past him with rather sallow-looking Frenchmen staring haughtily from the shaded back seats. White-clad soldiers
with the facings of the Gâtinais, Agenais or Touraine regiments
marched smartly out toward the Royal Battery under the guid-
ance of competent-looking sergeants or, in twos and threes,
lounged out of wineshops, or chaffered with black vendors for
fruits, honey or white rum.

Ward turned into a wide street lined with low buildings of
fine stone-work and walked toward the deep tangle of green
that seemed to mark the end of French dominion and the beginning of the jungle. Beyond, the land swept up to a range of
mountains toward which the sun was just beginning to dip. He
worked back toward the center of the city, found a cool, dim
cavern of an inn where he lunched on native beef, tough and
stringy, fresh-ground coffee and a succession of fruits few of
which he could even name.

As he sipped his brandy, he thought of the great map that
Tremarec had shown him over morning coffee, a vast sheet on
which he could read that he was nearly a thousand miles closer
home than had the ship made Martinique, far to the south.
No ships were heading north from Cap Haitien, at least for a
few days, Tremarec told him. That would give him time to
write a long letter to Faith, to be taken by the first north-bound
vessel. The Captain hinted that a prolonged stay in this port of
Haiti was more than likely, but he did not suggest where his
ship might go, once the anchor was raised. Uncertainty again.
Sailing blindfold instead of riding blindfold. The pattern did not
seem to change for Ward. At any rate, here was a chance to get
a letter off to Faith. And, as added consolation, he had been

able to get ashore without the eternal, haunting presence of the sailor Moen.

His brandy finished, he resumed his walk, keeping to the shady side of a wide street that skirted the sleepy walls of some great merchant's gardens. Then the street ended abruptly in a twisting dirt path that died away a hundred yards ahead in a waste of rank growth and mud-walled huts. He was about to turn and retrace his way toward the water front when he saw that, deeper inland, the jungle did not stretch away unbroken. Here and there, like the châteaux that dotted the woodlands west of Passy, solid white houses shone in emerald-green clearings, their long drives sweeping up past smaller houses that clustered in miniature villages. He could see a carriage rolling up to one of the big houses.

"Planters' estates," he thought. "At least, I can get a look at them from the outside." He swung back down the street, and struck into another broad thoroughfare that ran at right angles to it. This street seemed to be given over to merchants' counting houses. He noted the names on the signs that hung out from creaky iron brackets. Simoes et LaPlante; Pajol Fils; Coelho y do Valle; Baer und Norgaard, Frenchmen or foreigners who had taken French citizenship in order to trade.

The street ran along the shoulder of a hill so steep that Ward found himself looking down into the second stories of the buildings on his right. The signs continued to indicate an amicable mixture of races and nations. Pentheroudakis e Zonta. He stopped to chuckle over the uncompromising Scotch of Clackmannan linked with the romantic Galarmendi.

A hand drew aside the slatted blind that masked a broad window, and the sun streamed full into the room beyond. He saw Paul Dale, seated at a broad mahogany table with his back to the street. Across from Paul was a squat, swarthy man who might be Galarmendi. Beyond Galarmendi sat a thin, spare man, bony-faced and with iron-gray hair neatly dressed. He was speaking to Paul. The strongly accented French came faint but clear to Ward in the hush of the side street, though the words themselves were lost on him. The precise, creaky voice sounded oddly familiar.

Then memory flooded into Ward's mind. He saw again the quay along the bend of the Seine, a ferry poling from the far side and a thin, spare, plainly dressed man speaking to him in a creaky voice, addressing him as Captain Gratwick. As though to complete the cycle of memory, the man, with a contemptuous gesture, pitched a shining metal tube across the table toward Paul. Paul, his back still toward the street, sprang to his feet, rapped sharply on the table, and without speaking, shoved a sheaf of papers toward Jabish Frost.

Shaking off the shock of recognition, of seeing Jabish Frost, supposedly far off in Paris or Angers, of seeing the tube reappear in Cap Haitien, Ward hurried out of eyeshot of the window. At the corner, he paused, glanced down toward the harbor. The *Sauvage* lay at anchor a quarter of a mile offshore. He must tell Tremarec what he had seen. The presence of Jabish Frost might mean little to the Captain, but the tube, tossed scornfully out onto the table — did the tube mean anything? Was it the one that he had fished out of the sea, the same one he and Deborah had found in the hollow tree at Passy?

He hurried through the growing heat and down to the quays where he hailed a skiff and had himself rowed out to the *Sauvage*. As he clambered over the bulwarks, he wondered if Deborah knew of Paul's errand ashore. He called to a steward only to be told that the ladies had gone ashore after all. Ashore! Could it be that Paul intended to leave the *Sauvage* for good, condemning Deborah to an indefinite stay in this unwholesome port? He questioned the steward further and was relieved to learn that none of them had taken more than the lightest of hand-luggage ashore. Their trunks and other belongings were in the state cabins and nothing had been brought up from the hold. His mind easier, he sought out Tremarec and told him of the scene at Clackmannan y Galarmendi.

When Ward had finished, the Captain said calmly, "An odd meeting, my friend. And yet, why not? It was common rumor that the affairs of Monsieur Frost in France were at an end. He is a trader. What more natural than that he appear in a more fertile field? And the firm of the Scot and the Spaniard is just where he might be met."

"But how could he have come here ahead of us?" asked Ward.

"Why not? We do not know when he left France. He could have shipped under a neutral flag and come directly here. Our own course was not of the most direct, nor the least interrupted," observed Tremarec.

"But the tube?"

"One of many thousands, as you yourself must have noted."

"Just the same — Oh, well. It's all sheer speculation," said Ward, frowning. "Now, what are we going to do about the voyage?"

"I have called on the Governor. For the moment, we lie here. It will, at least, give us a chance to provision and make repairs."

"And your cargo?" asked Ward.

"Who knows? It may be that one of your own ships will put in here. In that case, she might take the cargo — and yourself."

"I shouldn't like to leave the *Sauvage*," observed Ward.

"Thank you. But it might be necessary." Tremarec smoothed his hair, well-powdered for his recent call on the Governor. "I wish, my friend, that those who deal in official papers — and in men's lives — would talk more freely to those whose course is set by those papers. At least, one may use one's eyes and deduce. You have seen French troops ashore?"

"Yes. The Agenais, Gâtinais, and Touraine regiments."

164

"Of course. Your soldier's eye would see them." He leaned across the table. "But I, my friend, have seen more than that. I have seen their requisitions for rations. Not more than a squad or two of those regiments remains."

"Only a few squads?" cried Ward. "Where are the others?"

"And where is the Duc de Saint Simon, who commands the whole group? They were here. They are gone. No one at Government House will admit it." Tremarec lowered his voice. "Another thing. I find the naval stores very low. Why? Again, they will not admit it, but I am sure that de Grasse's whole fleet has been here, drawn on the warehouses and sailed off."

Ward was on his feet in an instant. "For America!"

"Gently, my friend. The ocean is broad and holds many destinations. There was whispered talk of a joint French-Spanish coup against the English in Florida."

"In Florida? That won't help us."

"To those in the higher seats, the matter may appear differently," said Tremarec. "It would involve Spain still more in your war, might produce more supplies, more gold for you. I do not know."

"No," said Ward. "One French soldier ashore in the northern States, one louis d'or in Philadelphia would be worth ten expeditions like that."

"I do not say no," remarked Tremarec. His manner changed suddenly. "But I do know that if de Grasse has gone north, then — " he paused.

"Then what?"

"Then it may be that we must follow, my friend. We must follow, in the full knowledge that there are no more French ships in the southern seas, that Hood and his British ships of the line must in all logic follow de Grasse." He gave a cold smile. "It will be an interesting race, if I am right. Does the *Sauvage* find itself closing on the rear of de Grasse or find the

British van closing about it? On that note of optimism, I bid you good night."

Ward crossed the deck to his cabin, his mind a whirl. He found the sailor Moen squatting by his cabin door. As he returned Ward's greeting, he muttered that a boat from shore had brought a letter. It was on Monsieur's blankets.

Ward broke the seals, held the sheet to the light.

DEAR WARD:

I've had about all I can stand of the merchant-crown-prince. I've found a good berth ashore, so the *Sauvage* won't see me again. I've not given up my idea of coming back to the army. Maybe I'll see you when we kick the last damned lobster-back off the continent. In a few months I'll have made enough to start out again and I guess the war'll wait for me.

I haven't forgotten what I owe you. You'll be repaid for helping me out. That our debt be settled is the unchanging wish of,

Your obedient servant,

JAMES HOUSTON

Ward reread the brief note. Then he folded it and stowed it away. He could hardly blame Houston for freeing himself from Paul's highhanded badgering. "Anyhow, I've done my part," Ward reflected. "I got him out of France. If he wants to spend the rest of his life in this steamy port, that's his business."

He dropped a folding shelf over his bunk, brought out pen, ink and paper and began to write. ". . . and trust that this, if an American ship can take it, will not precede me by very much. But Faith dearest, I have the strongest hope that before too long you'll see me riding along from Fatland Ford. Later, if the gods are good, I shall have the pleasure of presenting to you a most sound, competent Breton gentleman who has steered me to you all the way from Lorient in France. You will like him on any account and, I hope, a little on mine. As for my fellow passengers, it may be that you will meet them. I'm almost sure that

166

you will meet one of them, a young American girl who hardly knows America and who quite possibly will need your help."

He read over the last lines of his letter. He wondered if the mention of the young American girl, a fellow passenger on a long voyage, might disturb Faith. With a smile he shook his head and picked up his pen again.

Three nights later the *Sauvage* echoed to the slam of hammers and the screech of saws as the crew, aided by gangs from the shipyards, made good the last of the damage inflicted by the British ship in faraway midocean. Tackle and ropes whined and heavy casks slammed to the deck or were lowered into the hold. Through the din, Ward slept fitfully.

He woke with a start when bare feet thumped past his door on the run. He called to Moen, asking what was happening.

Moen said that Madame, Mademoiselle and Monsieur had returned. Monsieur had brought heavy cases which the crew now hurried themselves to bring on board, a waste of time, *alors,* since so much real work remained to be done.

Ward curled up again under his thin blanket. Outside the din rose to new heights, but he slept soundly through it.

He was up by sunrise the next morning for a breakfast of tropical fruits and coffee. He ate alone, since Keratry was on duty and the surgeon and Gaos were sleeping off the effects of hours ashore among the delights of Cap Haitien. Ward waved away the steward's offer of more coffee and ran onto the deck. The sun was catching the tops of the emerald mountains that shut in the port and the white buildings that flowed down to the water front were just beginning to glow, pinkish and bluish in the slanting rays. A few cable-lengths beyond the *Sauvage,* a low, fast-looking brig lay, the neutral colors of Denmark at the peak, the *Skagen* emblazoned on her stern.

Ward looked over his shoulder just as Paul, in immaculate white linens, stepped onto the deck. He carried a sheet of paper in his hand and he was scowling. Swiftly he strode over to Ward, fluttering the paper. "God damn it, Gratwick, do you know anything about this?" He flapped the paper. "It's Houston! I pulled that bastard up from the bilges and gave him his chance. Now he's gone. Left me. And this letter! No one can insult me like this without paying for it! What do you know about it? You recommended him to me."

"Steady," answered Ward. "I brought him on board as a common sailor. The first thing I knew about his working for you was when he moved into that cabin across the way."

"Well, if it hadn't been for you, he wouldn't have been on board." Paul paced up and down the deck, rattling the letter.

Ward shrugged. "Look here, Paul, I'm sorry if he slipped his cable on you. True, I brought him on board, but you brought him up from the forecastle."

Paul faced Ward and a new, hard look came into his eye. "Yes," he said thickly. "Yes. And I got Tremarec to assign him to me. In fact, I hired him. Now I discharge him and what's his status?" He crumpled up the letter, smacked his hands together. "I've got it. He's a crew member again. He's deserted the *Sauvage,* not me, and he comes under French maritime law and usage." His eyes snapped. "Just a runaway sailor. Tremarec'll send a shore party looking for him. I'll see to it that the Governor helps, orders the garrison to join in. We'll see Master Houston back on board. I doubt if the crew and the petty officers will welcome him, but that's no concern of mine." He glanced quickly at Ward. "And his going is news to you?"

"Not exactly. He left a note for me, thanking me for helping him get this far. He hinted that he'd run into luck ashore, would get on to America later."

"H'm," said Paul. "Never mind. We've got all we need so far as he's concerned."

"And how about Deborah and Mrs. Lathrop?" asked Ward.

Paul rubbed his fingers along his jaw. "Ah, they're all right. Deb didn't seem to like the town very much. Can't see why. It's really a sort of tropical Paris when you get to know it." He dropped his voice a little. "And there's nothing dead about it, either. I thought missing Martinique and putting in here was going to play hob with my plans, but it's worked out very well. I had some pretty heavy trade commitments, but Clackmannan took them off my hands and I actually turned a better penny than I'd hoped. I got a few more ventures started. So here we are on the *Sauvage*. In confidence, I can tell you that the Governor thinks we're bound for the coast of the Americas and I've an idea that our ponderous Captain thinks so too, though he's said nothing."

"And you don't share that belief?" asked Ward.

"I?" said Paul, raising his eyebrows. "I'm only a merchant. But I do know that sometimes influences are at work that change the minds even of Governors. But I don't *know* anything." He gave Ward's shoulder a friendly tap. "I'll go see Tremarec now about a shore party to arrest Houston. We'll bring him back with drums beating and bugles blowing while he reflects on his error of judgment."

Left alone, Ward eyed the Danish brig nearby. Perhaps the skipper was bound for an American port. As a neutral he could sail with fair assurance and with a West Indian cargo could slip into Newport and dispose of his goods at fabulous prices. Perhaps along with the goods he would send Ward's letter ashore.

He heard an uncertain tread on the deck and turned to see Brotier, heavy-eyed and pale from his shore leave, coming toward him. The surgeon's bleary eyes blinked stiffly. "So Monsieur Dale cries to heaven, and to our Captain, that a boat must be sent ashore to bring back Monsieur Houston. A not very clever man, the latter. Who but a fool would leave the *Sauvage* for the uncertainties of life in that fever-hole yonder? Did he perhaps go to seek a more powerful sleeping potion?"

"Sleeping potion?" asked Ward.

Brotier nodded, then winced as though the motion were painful. "As I said. Long ago on the voyage he came to me complaining that sleep eluded him. I brewed him a draught that I had learned in the East India seas, which pleased him. Again he came to me, just before we met the British ship and again I obliged him, but told him that next time I should decline since a prolonged use of my brew leads to bad habits. La-la. No doubt he found some obliging black who dabbles in West India drugs."

"Let's hope he finds what he wants," said Ward.

Brotier smiled sardonically. "May we all find what we seek, first knowing just what it is. The knowing is often more difficult than the finding."

"What a philosophical mood you're in this morning! It's from mixing too much Voltaire with too much Cap Haitien rum."

"I do not say no," observed Brotier. "But in the case of our Mr. Houston, he puzzles me. I tell you this, my friend. Not a night has passed on the voyage that I have not walked by his cabin and — note this — not a night has passed that I have not heard him snoring enough to shake the deepest timbers of the *Sauvage*. What does such a man need of a potion?"

"To experiment with," said Ward. "To sell to the crew to mix with their rather weak ration wine. Give me time and I'll think of a dozen more reasons. He might have — " His hands suddenly smacked down in the bulwarks, and he cried out, "No, No. Not yet!" The *Skagen,* sails set, was making for the harbor mouth.

"You appear distressed," observed Brotier dryly. "I prescribe a draught of brandy."

Ward turned from the rail. "It's just — " The letter to Faith still lay in his cabin instead of in the pouch of the Danish master.

Well, it couldn't be helped and anyhow he did not even know where the *Skagen* might be heading. Curaçao and Surinam might see her before she turned north again.

The Danish brig had been hours gone, and still the *Sauvage* lay in the harbor of Cap Haitien. Slow days dragged by. Then, in a hot dusk, sails were set, the anchors raised and the ship slipped through the narrow jaws of the harbor. The next morning found Haiti a dull blur on the horizon and the *Sauvage* drove on north through cobalt seas that were combed with ivory. The sun beat down on the quarter-deck where Ward sat with Deborah and Mrs. Lathrop. Paul was lounging nearby, while the sailor Moen worked sullenly within earshot.

"What's the first thing we'll see when we reach America, Ward?" asked Deborah.

Ward grinned at her. "Americans," he said.

She flipped her embroidered bag at him. "All right, be clever. But what next?"

Mrs. Lathrop calmly plying a fine needle, smiled to herself. "You're reasonably sure you're really going to America?"

Ward nodded good-humoredly. "Where else, so long as the bowsprit points north?"

Paul, his soft straw hat over his eyes, murmured, "We could always swing west and make for the Spaniards in Louisiana."

"Paul! We wouldn't do that, would we? Of course not. Just the same, I did wonder what was happening when we put about so suddenly last night," said Deborah.

"Maybe Tremarec had an idea of yielding to Paul's pleas and putting back to Cap Haitien for another look for Jim Houston," suggested Ward softly.

"He could have done worse," said Paul. "Just the same, that wharf-rat hasn't heard the last of me. The Governor'll still be looking for him and so will Clackmannan."

Ward sat back in his chair. "Let the tropics take Houston,

171

Paul." He glanced aft. "That's funny. There's that Danish brig, the *Skagen,* still hanging on our heels. We overtook her easily enough and now we can't seem to lose her."

Paul squinted at the Dane. "Wonder where she's been. She left harbor long before we did."

"Probably around the island to Port-au-Prince," ventured Ward. "Maybe heading north to the Bermudas now. That's the advantage of being a neutral in time of war. She can go where she pleases. Anyway, she's nothing for us to worry about."

"Oh, I wasn't worrying," said Paul. "What's that noise?"

Ward bent his head toward the deck, then frowned, a shiver of apprehension creeping over him. The pumps again! He glanced quickly at Deborah, then said, "Just the usual commotion below. Some mechanical contraption. We hear it because the hatches aren't battened down."

Deborah moved impatiently. "I wish they'd stop it. Oh, look! Way, way off astern! Can you see them? What are they? More Danes?"

Just over the horizon two sets of sails winked in the sun, right and left of the *Skagen.* Ward decided there was no point in repeating the fears Tremarec had expressed to him, that the *Sauvage* might be sailing between the rear of de Grasse and the van of an English fleet.

Paul joined Ward at the rail and stared aft with him. For an instant his face showed an intense, almost joyful eagerness. Then he recovered himself. "By Jove, Ward. Suppose they are English, those new fellows. What a laugh we'll have. Tremarec will let them come a little closer, then clap on more sail and leave them playing span-farthing. I'd give a hundred pounds to see the look on the fat British skipper's face when we really start to move."

"We ought to have no trouble," said Ward, still listening to the beat of the pumps. "Anyway, one of them is bound to stop the *Skagen* and at least look at his credentials." The sailor Moen caught Ward's eye, pointed to the planks that formed the roof of Tremarec's cabin. "Now?" Ward formed the word silently. The sailor nodded. "I might just see if they can tell us anything below," Ward said as he dropped to the main deck and made his way forward.

He found Tremarec leaning back in his chair and gazing at the ceiling with a half-benevolent, half-sardonic smile. "Sit down, my friend," said the Breton. "I have been indulging in a most interesting discussion with our good Brotier."

Ward drew up a chair. "A pastime which I find to be often irritating and always stimulating."

"Precisely," agreed Tremarec. "In this case we were speaking first of the desire of the departed Mr. Houston for opium. From there we turned to your acquired fondness for the rather powerful curry dishes that have been served on board. You follow me, of course?"

"At a vast distance," said Ward frowning. "Go on.'

"You do not see? All opium mixtures have a distinctive flavor. This flavor can be disguised, so far as Brotier is aware, solely by curry. So we have an explanation for the substitution of your papers which is at least possible and very simple."

"My papers!" cried Ward.

"As I said. The good Houston manages somehow to include a heavy dose of opium in one or more of the curry dishes which you have eaten. You then sleep heavily, possibly aided by the brandy which you and our Brotier have been in the habit of consuming. While you lie in a drugged sleep, the papers are taken from you and a dummy set put in their place. You agree it is possible?"

"Possible? Maybe. It's — no, no! Utterly impossible! Houston's turned out to be a slippery character, but he couldn't have known that I had these or any other papers."

"It distresses me that I disagree with you, my friend," observed Tremarec. "You were seen talking to Houston in Lorient. Between that time and his arrival on board, he is told that you have those papers and that he may earn a large sum by obtaining them."

"No one but the Doctor and I knew that they existed," said Ward obstinately.

Tremarec raised a cautioning hand. "Have I not told you again and again that very important people and groups of people were interested in this voyage, and not benevolently interested? Must I remind you once more that you, new to the scene, cannot understand the exquisite delicacy and scope of European intrigue, that one in important surroundings may not so much as plant a cabbage without that planting being known in half the chancelleries in Europe?"

"It's hard to grasp," said Ward. "Then I suppose we've got to assume that Houston, if your theory is correct, knows just where to take those papers, how to sell them. Damn and blast. The only hope is that by the time they are bought, the normal passage of events will make them worthless."

"A not unreasonable hope," observed Tremarec.

"In the meantime," said Ward, "do you still have to keep our destination a secret?"

"For the time being, yes."

"I suppose that your lookouts have told you long before this that we're not sailing alone."

"The Dane?" asked Tremarec innocently.

"With a distant escort of at least two," said Ward.

"Ah, so you have noted them. Yes. They have been reported. There is no doubt but they are English. You have heard the pumps, of course. Our repairs at Cap Haitien were, to speak leniently, bungled. The *Sauvage* makes water. Not dangerously, but enough to reduce our speed to a point which might not be safe."

"I'll trust in your seamanship," said Ward. "In any event, you have the *Skagen* astern of you. They'll stop to search her and you'll gain a good many miles."

"The *Skagen*," repeated Tremarec. "Ah, yes. That Dane. My friend, I may tell you that I do not relish her presence."

"Why not? She's a neutral," said Ward.

"Perhaps that is why. You will perceive that a neutral enjoys many advantages, not the least of which is leaning to whichever side promises the most profit."

For the next two days, Ward spent most of the daylight hours on the quarter-deck staring aft, while below the pumps clanked drearily on. It seemed to him that the battle against flooding was being won, for the *Sauvage* moved more lightly through the blue seas. And yet no matter how favorable the winds and sea-currents the *Skagen* was always a mile or so astern and the British sails looked larger, more distinct.

On one clear evening, all four passengers stayed on deck till the last light had faded and the *Sauvage* pressed on through a seemingly empty sea. The water was phosphorescent and a weird greenish light flickered along the boiling wake. Bright streaks, just below the surface, marked the passage of fish.

Ward leaned over the rail. "Look at that fish go, Deb. A huge one, maybe a shark. Tremarec says they're thick in these waters."

"And a falling star," cried Deborah. "See it off there? Now it's gone — no, there it is again."

Paul laughed. "Star nothing. It's a light in the stern of the *Skagen*. She must have veered to the west long enough for us to see it. Now she's straightened out again."

Ward turned from the rail. "Oh, my God! A light on the *Skagen*?"

"Why not? You wouldn't deny them a light, would you?"

Ward shook his head silently. The light in the stern of the Dane must be in clear view of the British ships, giving them a fixed point toward which to set a course. He left the rail, murmuring something about seeing the Captain.

The Breton looked around pleasantly as Ward came up.

"Captain, the *Skagen's* showing a light astern."

"Ah," said Tremarec. "Yes, I see. A most convenient beacon for our friends, the Goddams. In the morning, I shall signal the Dane to heave to long enough for me to make a most polite request."

A little after sunrise, Ward emerged from his cabin. The stern-chaser of the *Sauvage* had fired twice and he could see that the course was radically altered so that the *Sauvage* was broadside to the Dane. Bright colors blossomed from the fore-peak as the morning breeze shook out a chain of signal flags. The *Sauvage* swung again, heading nearly south, then curved east across the course of the Dane, the sailors furling the sheets aloft.

Ward watched the distance lessening, saw answering flags from the *Skagen*. Instead of stopping, the Dane veered off to the east and great bursts of yellow showed aloft as more sails were unfurled.

Ward turned to see Tremarec coming down the ladder, very grave, shutting a telescope in a series of little clacks. "What did he say to your signal, Captain?" Ward called.

"My signal, it was of the clearest. I was not amused by his reply."

"Did he refuse to stop?"

"No. His flags read, 'Signal not understood.' His action you saw."

"You're going after him?" Ward asked.

"That would give me great pleasure. The fellow needs a slight lesson in maritime courtesy. But I have already wasted more time and miles than we can properly afford. No, my friend, we continue our old course."

"H'm," said Ward. "Did it ever occur to you, Captain, that the Dane and the senior British skipper might not be entirely strangers?"

Tremarec shrugged. "Who may say? When seamen foregather in a friendly tavern, many things may happen. A friendship may be formed over a bottle of rum, with nationality forgotten." He touched his hat to Ward and strode forward.

All through the day, Ward restlessly watched the ugly, familiar pattern form again. The *Skagen* was a mile astern of the *Sauvage* and, right and left of the Dane, the two Englishmen showed clear against a glassy sky. The attempt to extinguish the Dane's lights had been costly. The pursuing ships were much closer, and Ward could make out the yellow bands, two to each ship, that marked the gun-decks. Seventy-fours, perhaps, or even more heavily armed, far too much metal for the few nine- and sixteen-pounders of the *Sauvage*. When dusk finally came, less than four miles separated the *Sauvage* from the rearmost British ship. Tremarec and his officers efficiently prepared the ship for the action which must come with the dawn.

Ward tried to think. He had gradually lost all fear for himself. Tremarec, he was sure, would fight so long as he could work a gun and in that fight what would happen would happen. But the bales of clothing below, the cases of muskets and sabers for the army, *his* army, the powdercasks deep in the hold and, even more important, those heavy little chests of gold louis in their lead wrappings!

Hour after hour he paced up and down, at one moment convinced that the Breton, like a sensible man, would strike his colors when the British closed in, sure the next moment that every iron tube on the *Sauvage* would blast out. The night seemed endless and grew increasingly dank as the hours wore on. Then a hand fell lightly on his shoulder and he heard Tremarec's voice. "A respite, my friend," said the Breton.

"Respite?"

"We are running into dense fog and through safe waters. It may be that we may shake off the Goddams."

When dawn at last came, the sun was blanketed by the heavy overcast and the mantling fog. The air was dank, heavy and Ward found himself breathing through his mouth.

He went below for coffee and biscuits. Keratry was there in the mess, red of eye and unsteady of hand through want of sleep. He cursed the dirty fog that made an honest sailor grope through the seas like a blind man. Ward agreed tersely, laced his coffee with brandy and crumbled biscuit into it. From above, footsteps and voices came to him, oddly muffled.

Then somewhere, far astern it seemed to him, a gun thudded flatly, was answered by a second, a third. "What in God's name is that?" he said hoarsely.

Keratry shrugged. "Signal guns. The Goddams and the Dane give their positions, one to the other."

Ward poured himself more coffee and brandy. "Sounds to me as though they were pretty far astern."

Keratry gulped more steaming coffee. "I do not agree, Monsieur. The fog tricks the ear as well as the eye. In my opinion, the three ships are sailing along nearly abreast. We may only hope that we shall not march with them."

"We're not firing signal guns?" asked Ward.

Keratry wagged his head. "Ah, I believe you, we do not fire. Our Tremarec is courteous, but not to the point of informing our neighbors just where we are." He pushed his cup aside and rose. "Now I go to relieve our Gaos."

Ward followed him to the white world above where vision was limited to a few yards of plank and a few yards of water. High above him, unseen sails rustled and dripped. A small, cloaked figure, head muffled in a pointed hood, appeared aft of the hatch.

Ward called quickly, "Deb! Be careful. The hatch is open."

"I can see all right," she answered and seemed to step to him through a dense curtain.

They went cautiously forward, stepping over coils of rope, across rammer-staffs. A dark line ran up and up, became the foremast and at last they saw the root of the bowsprit, the great triangle of sailcloth that was the jib. Below, the sea rolled, oily and sluggish.

Deborah shivered. "It's weird. We might be sailing right off the rim of the world. What's that?" She started as a series of flat thuds sounded astern.

"Nothing to worry about," answered Ward reassuringly. "Those ships behind us don't want to run into each other."

"But couldn't they run into us? I don't see why Mr. Tremarec doesn't fire." She peered into the fog. "It's just like — Ward! Another gun *and it came from dead ahead of us!* There are more ships out there, waiting for us!"

Ward winced. "No! There can't be! You must have heard the jib cracking or something heavy falling below decks under us."

Her voice trailed off to a whisper. "It was a shot and it came from in front."

Ahead and off to starboard, another gun sounded. There was no use trying to deceive himself.

"What does it mean, Ward?"

"Hard to say. We'll — we'll just have to wait and see. Anyhow, sound does odd things in a fog." He listened intently. There were more shots ahead. Behind, the sea seemed to lie silent and empty under its cottony pall. Either the British ships had managed somehow to work ahead of the *Sauvage,* or others of their fleet had been attracted by the sound of firing and were closing in, answering.

The thick morning wore on, punctuated by occasional dull thuds. Suddenly Deborah's voice broke the silence. "I see it!"

There was no need for her to point. Off the port bow, a darkish blur showed, like a ripe plum packed in wool. Soon Ward could make out a rather clumsy hull, the suggestion of masts and sails. He tapped his foot impatiently on the deck. "All right so far. Just a slow merchantman. Blast all, why aren't any colors showing?"

Deborah shook his arm. "The bow. I can see it. There's a sort of rope running straight out from it, going right into the fog."

"Towline!" snapped Ward. "But the other end of it, the other end —" His words were drowned in a volley of yells from the crew.

Deborah cried. "The fog's lifting! The sun!"

Almost as though it had freed itself from some physical obstacle, the *Sauvage* lunged forward into bright sunlight. Its bow cut deep into blue water and its sails lifted to a clear blue sky. And right and left and as far ahead as Ward and Deborah could see, the ocean was dotted with the soft gold of sails. The wallowing merchantman was being towed by a black-hulled seventy-four. Ward grew dizzy trying to take in the whole expanse of sail-dotted sea. Wherever he looked his eyes picked out the white flag and the gold lilies of France. On the nearer ships a line of fluttering black rippled above the white coats as French soldiers waved their hats in answer to the cheers from the *Sauvage*. More and more ships, frigates, deadly-looking ships of the line.

Shaken by the depth of his relief, Ward said, "It's all right. Deb, we've run smack into de Grasse's main fleet and his trans-ports."

He leaned on the bulwark watching the clouds of white-coated infantrymen on the transports, trying to count the warships, losing track and beginning all over again. "Where do you suppose they're all going?" asked Deborah, looking up at Ward.

He shook his head, emotion choking back his words. At last he managed to say, "North — to join our people. They *must* be."

She threw back the hood of her cloak. "To our people," she whispered.

The great fleet plunged on. Far aft, by the break of the quarter-deck, Paul Dale stood in the open door. His face was like parchment as he stared at the forest of masts.

During the bright morning, the *Sauvage* pressed on through groves of gold-brown sailcloth that thrust up from the blue of the ocean. Ward stayed in the bow, with Deborah silent beside him. His fingers drummed on the broad rail as he read off to himself the names that gleamed on the counters — *Andromaque, Glorieux, Triton, Conquérant.* He was aware of Deborah's glance. "Oh, what is that ahead of us, just to port?" she asked. "Can you read the name? There's something high above the carving on the stern. There — something Paris — *La* — *La Ville de Paris.*"

Ward saw sails that towered up incredibly, a mammoth hull whose stern showed a wealth of gilding, row after row of bright glass casement, more gilding and carving and, along the starboard side, tiers of gun-ports that seemed to reach from the water's edge up and up to the main deck. "My God! What a ship!" he exclaimed.

"*Assez coquet,*" said a deep voice behind them. They turned to see Tremarec, elegant in sleek blue cloth and fresh gold lace. "Yes," the Breton went on, "Pretty enough. A neat craft." He spoke with elaborate casualness but Ward read deep pride in his eyes as he watched the great ship. Tremarec flicked invisible dust from his cuff. "A nice conceit of the good people of Paris. They subscribed their sous and their louis d'or to build her. One hundred and twenty guns and a rate of speed that one could hardly call contemptible."

The *Sauvage* was losing headway. Pipes twittered amidships. Tremarec carelessly drew on a pair of stiff new gloves, raised his hand to his gold-braided hat and bowed. "I go across now to pay my respects to our de Grasse. It may be that I shall have news for you when I return."

They watched the longboat, manned by an immaculate crew, pull across the intervening water. The *Ville de Paris* was now only a cable-length away, and its starboard rail was lined with men. "The Governor at Cap Haitien must have told him to place himself under de Grasse's orders if we caught up with him," Ward said to Deborah.

"Oh dear," she said, "I do hope nothing will happen to upset Paul's plans. Come on, let's go find him."

She turned to go aft, then stopped. "Ward! Look! Just beyond the *Foudroyant* and weaving away from us! It's — "

"You're right — the *Skagen*."

The *Skagen* bore farther to port, then was lost behind a high-sterned merchantman. Ward shrugged. "There she goes."

The *Skagen* had now cleared the merchantman and was working on a starboard tack that brought her nearly bows-on to the *Sauvage*.

Ward watched the Dane, now less than a quarter of a mile away. "Maybe the skipper wants to apologize to us for sheering away from our signal. Now she's straightening out, running about parallel to us." He turned toward a petty officer who was studying the flotilla through a small glass. *"S'il vous plaît,"* Ward said quickly. "Your glass. Just for an instant." He took the brass-bound tube, focused it and then swung it toward the *Skagen*. For some seconds he stood motionless. Then he handed it back and returned to Deborah with a half-anxious, half-puzzled look on his face.

182

"What was that all about, Ward?" she asked.

His eyes shifted away from her. "Nothing. I'm not sure. I got the glass on her too late, but I think the man standing by the starboard rail — " he paused. "Blast all, I'm sure it was Jim Houston."

"What?" cried Deborah. "On the *Skagen?* It couldn't have been."

"That's what I say. Anyway — come to think of it, it's Tremarec's business and Paul's. We'll tell Tremarec when he comes back. It'll be easy enough for de Grasse to halt the *Skagen* and search her."

"I suppose so," said Deborah slowly, eyes on the *Ville de Paris* that had worked ahead of the *Sauvage* by several lengths. Then she turned to Ward. "You don't have to report this, do you?"

"I don't really have to, I guess. Why?"

"Well — I never liked Mr. Houston and of course he shouldn't have left Paul without a word. But just the same, if that were he and they brought him back, it wouldn't be pleasant for him, would it?"

Ward's jaw tightened. Maritime law would have to take its course, but not before Houston had answered some very searching questions about opium and curry and a pack of sealed papers. Deborah said pleadingly, "It wouldn't help anyone to drag him back here as a runaway seaman, would it?"

"There might be more to it than that. Anyway — Hi! It's out of our hands now. The *Skagen's* closing on the *Ville de Paris,* breaking out signal flags. Now they're dropping a boat over the side. The Dane's going to have a word with de Grasse and he'll have to allow a search." He glanced at the girl beside him. "Just the same, Deb, I like your standing up for Houston."

It was midafternoon before Tremarec's gig crept back over the rolling water. Ward and Deborah leaned over the rail and waved to him. He flourished his braided hat in reply, obviously in high good humor. Then he pointed to the man who sat near him in the stern sheets, a tall, bearded man in rough sea-clothes and with a telescope thrust through the red sash at his waist.

Tremarec swung lightly onto the deck. The stranger, a bony, awkward-looking man, followed nimbly as a squirrel.

"What news for us, Captain?" asked Ward.

Tremarec bowed to Deborah. "I answer many question merely by introducing Monsieur Jonas White, pilot of the Chesapeake Bay."

Ward gave a shout. "A pilot — Chesapeake Bay — " He shook White's hand warmly. "Very glad to see you. I'm American, too."

The pilot's hard hand barely returned the pressure. "Be you?" he said dully. His eyes swept up to the high foremast, dropped to Deborah. His whiskers parted long enough to let out the words, "High Moses! A gal!" Then he grunted to Tremarec, "Let's look."

Tremarec indicated the quarter-deck. "There you will find my first officer, Monsieur Keratry, a good seaman."

"Time'll tell," said Mr. White. "Good-by all." He clumped aft.

Deborah began to laugh. "Where did you find such a chatter-box, Captain?"

"Where but on the *Ville de Paris*. Ah, I tell you, many like him were sent down from the north to await de Grasse at Cap Haitien. This matter has been well thought out, my friends, and has involved months of letters many of which show the hand of the Philosopher of Passy."

"Dr. Franklin?" cried Deborah. "Then we are going to America, just as Ward said?"

Tremarec looked surprised. "Did I say to America? I assure you, I *know* no more than you. But, like you, I may reason that Chesapeake pilots are not sent us to guide the fleet into the rivers of Senegal."

"You didn't get any further orders from de Grasse?" asked Ward.

"Of the most explicit," said Tremarec. "They were, 'Conform to my signals.'"

"If I were a sailor, I'd like to know a lot more than that," said Deborah firmly. "For instance, I'd like to know what's over the horizon."

Tremarec smiled. "Empty blue waters, Mademoiselle. Since leaving Cap Haitien, de Grasse has sighted five British sail. And five British sail he has captured. He has learned that the northern British fleet is anchored off New York."

"Wait a minute," put in Ward. "How about the *Skagen?* Remember that he showed lights and refused to answer your signals."

"All of which the master, who rejoices in the sonorous name of Ek, explained to me on the *Ville de Paris.* He is a peaceful man, a fearful man. He showed his lights each night lest the British mistake him for a Yankee trader. He avoided meeting us for fear we sought to plunder him. Now he wishes nothing better than to bury himself in our flotilla. He even asked that I inspect his ship, which I did with the permission of de Grasse."

Ward and Deborah exchanged quick glances. "Did you see anything suspicious?" he asked.

"His cargo is as peaceful as himself. His officers and crew, work-a-day mariners. Now I go to listen to the verbose Monsieur White."

When he had left, Deborah turned to Ward. "Well, I am relieved that you were wrong about Mr. Houston being on the *Skagen.*"

Ward frowned. "I told you I wasn't sure. Anyhow, Tremarec's been on board so that settles it." He instinctively stepped away from Deborah as heels clicked on the deck behind him. Then he called, "Good afternoon, Mrs. Lathrop. Isn't this a wonderful sight?"

Mrs. Lathrop, pale and drawn-looking, flicked a rubbery smile at him. "Quite wonderful. Deborah, your brother isn't feeling at all well. In fact, he's lying down. He'd really like it if you went and sat with him for a while."

"Paul wants me?" Deborah, deep concern on her face, gathered up her cloak, swung her embroidered bag more securely on her wrist. "Of course I'll go to him. What is it? Has that fever he had last year come back to him?"

"No. Just the long voyage. Run along."

"This very minute. I'll see you later, Ward." She hurried aft.

Mrs. Lathrop was watching the dip and heave of the endless masts about her. "Where are all these ships going?" she asked.

"I wish I could tell you. North — that's all I know."

"Hasn't the Captain told you?"

"Nothing except that he's to conform to de Grasse's signals."

Mrs. Lathrop bit her lip and frowned. "Were we supposed to meet them?"

"Again, I don't know. Why? Don't you like such a grand escort?"

She shook her head and the lines of her face showed more clearly. "No. They're warships. They'll attract other warships — enemy ones. We were better off sailing peacefully by ourselves."

"You think so? Remember that when we were alone, *we* attracted warships and were very lucky to get clear of them."

She leaned on the bulwarks, chin in hand. "Where's that ship from Cap Haitien?"

"The *Skagen*? Oh, she's over there somewhere beyond the *Ville de Paris*. Tremarec says she's going to sail right along with the convoy."

She turned from the railing. "Maybe you're right, Ward.

Maybe this is better for all of us." She smiled pleasantly and left him.

The next sunrise found Ward in the bows, reveling in the spread of sail that stretched from horizon to horizon. The *Sauvage,* under scant sail had slowed her pace to that of the other ships. Suddenly a shout came from the quarter-deck. As Ward turned he saw the *Sauvage* alive with sailors who swarmed up the rigging. Sail after sail shivered, spread, caught the quartering wind while square flags sent their glowing answers to the *Ville de Paris.* The *Sauvage* dipped and dipped, rose, dipped again, lanced forward as though a restraining bond had been cut.

A frigate was passed, a sloop, another frigate and at last the *Sauvage* broke away from the main fleet, gaining speed each moment as though eager to be first to sight that mass of land that lay somewhere over the western rim of the sea.

Ward hailed Paul Dale who was making his way along the deck. "Feeling better, Paul?"

"Better? Oh, yes, Jove, this is a surprise, isn't it? We seem to be walking away from all this." He gestured toward the fading sails to the south. "So we'll sail right home alone, eh? Not tied to de Grasse's leading-strings?" He rubbed his hands. "Couldn't be better. Right up Chesapeake Bay."

"How do you know that?" asked Ward.

"Why, Deb told me about the Maryland pilot. Guess I'll have some breakfast. See you later."

Ward stayed by the bulwarks, looking ahead on a sea that was empty save for one hovering sail far off to starboard. In a few days, the lookouts would be shouting "Land!" from the tops. Land! If his hopes were fulfilled that land would be covered with roads that, in his mind, all led from the coast straight to Valley Forge and the Fatland Ford where Faith waited.

187

And what else? While armies moved slowly, news was often slower.

So far as was known, Rochambeau and his French were still at Newport. Washington and the main American army lay above the island of Manhattan. That much for the north. In the far south, Nathanael Greene seemed to be losing battles so successfully that the British held little outside the city of Charleston in South Carolina. In Virginia, Lord Cornwallis apparently had set himself up quite solidly on the Yorktown Peninsula that jutted out into Chesapeake Bay. Blocking his possible exit from the peninsula, too strong to be brushed aside and too weak to take the offensive were the Marquis de LaFayette and Anthony Wayne. Wayne had brought his Pennsylvanians with him. As to the Marquis, his men were largely picked light infantry from New England.

Yet, troops clustered here and there up and down a vast continent seemed to promise no concerted offensive. What could Rochambeau do at Newport? Washington did not have the strength to take New York. The troops in Virginia could at best be considered a detachment. And even if they were reinforced, there was nothing to prevent Cornwallis from embarking his troops and sailing to New York or south to Charleston. Nothing — except de Grasse's huge flotilla which now could block off Cornwallis's sea route.

"That must be it," he thought. If LaFayette and Wayne could hold the landward exit while de Grasse held the sea, Cornwallis would be trapped. But to land the French regiments from the transports would only be reinforcing a detachment. Surely the great fleet would be wasted on such a minor campaign. He shook his head. "No, we must be going on north. Washington and Rochambeau *must* be stewing up something against New York. That's where the war'll be won, not in Virginia swamps."

*   *   *

At first it looked like a star, low and steady on the horizon. Little by little its color changed, became a murky orange. Ward studied it through a telescope from the quarter-deck, carefully running out the sections of the brass-bound glass.

"Looks like a star — with corners," he said.

Paul, lounging by the rail, asked sharply, "What do you mean by corners?"

"Corners. Angles. Like — say, a door or a big window. It's —" He shut the glass with a snap. "We're home!"

"Home?"

He opened the glass again, handed it to Deborah. "Look for yourself. That's a house of some kind."

While Deborah held the glass to her eye, Ward carefully adjusted the focus. "That's it — don't move it any more. I do see it — a window, two windows. That's what they must be." She began to hop up and down. "There — one light's gone — no, it's showing again. Ward! That's America — those two points of light!"

Ward laughed softly. "Those are the lights we've been steering for ever since we cleared Lorient. Look, Paul, can you see the land? We're coming into a sort of narrow harbor." He turned to Jonas White who stood alert at the wheel, his head moving from side to side as though picking landmarks out of the night to guide him. "Hi! Mr. White! Where are we?"

"Virginny."

"I'd guessed that. But what port are we coming to?"

"Ain't." Mr. White was emphatic.

Paul left the rail. "Look here, my man," he said sharply. "We're *somewhere,* aren't we?"

"Likely." Jonas White crouched a little, then straightened up and gave a sparing nod to Gaos. Gaos barked a command and was answered from high in the rigging. Sailcloth rattled and Ward could hear men scrambling nimbly about the yards. Far

189

forward a rumbling and a clanking filled the still air, followed by two heavy splashes that sent columns of white water about the bow. Then the night was still. The pilot said curtly, "Time to move," and clattered down the ladder to the main deck.

Ward looked down at the black water astern. The last ripples were dying under the counter and the deck was steady under his feet.

Paul said impatiently, "Are there any big ports along here?"

"I'm not sure," answered Ward. "Once there was talk that my lot might go to the Carolinas with Lincoln and I looked over some maps. I think it's mostly shoal and sandbar from the mouth of the Chesapeake, which must be well north of us, until you come to Wilmington. But I'm guessing."

"That's all we've been doing — just guessing," said Paul irritably. "There's something funny about all this. Come on, Deb. I'm going below and see if Tremarec knows why we've anchored in this mosquito swamp."

He helped Deborah down the ladder, Ward following more slowly. He could hear Paul calling in the dark, "Captain! Captain Tremarec. *Un moment, s'il vous plaît!*"

"He's not here," said a dry voice and Brotier emerged from the shadows.

Ward, one foot on the deck, looked to port. The night was broken by rhythmic, muffled splashes and he thought he could make out a long-boat gliding easily to an unseen landing.

"But what the devil's he going ashore for?" Paul burst out.

Brotier shrugged. "A surgeon may not question a captain. He embarked himself in the longboat with the pilot."

Paul caught Deborah's arm. "Come on, Sis. We're wasting time. Maybe Tremarec spoke to Sue before he left."

When they had gone, Ward went to his cabin and stretched out on his bunk, his lightest blanket over him. He dozed fitfully, odd noises wakening him from time to time. Once he was sure that a smaller boat had been launched and rowed away into the night. Later he heard footsteps on the deck, recognized Tremarec's voice, the grudging accents of Jonas White and two or three strange voices that spoke in English. He started to dress and go to the Captain's cabin for news. Then he realized that if Tremarec had wanted him, he would have sent word. The ship was quiet once more and Ward dropped into a heavy sleep.

X I

Jabish Frost

WHEN WARD STEPPED OUT ON DECK the next morning the sun was high. He saw that the ship was in a narrow inlet shut in by sand hills. At the far end a road twisted out of sight inland toward greener-looking country, and the roof of a fair-sized house showed over the tree-tops. He heard a hail to starboard. A boat was putting out from the beach in front of one of the huts. He could see Tremarec erect in the stern while a fisherman sculled along, his oars making bright ripples in the water. The Breton came nimbly over the side and the fisherman worked back to shore.

Ward waved. "You look like a pirate captain who's just buried his treasure ashore."

Tremarec laughed. *"Quand même,* I have brought treasure of a sort from shore where I most unexpectedly spent the night." He drew out a sheet of paper and handed it to Ward. Ward's eyes widened as he looked at the strong, black script and the English words that stood out from the paper.

Afloat: 2 British frigates in the York River, by Yorktown. Sundry supply ships whose armament does not seem weighty.

Ashore: Cornwallis fortifies Yorktown, though none too diligently. Some forces at Gloucester Point across said York River where works also are raised but slowly. He hath in all some 7000 men.

The Marquis lyeth with his Yankees nr. the White House on the Pamunkey River which floweth into sd. York.

Anthony Wayne with the Pennsyla. Line, may be found on the

south bank of the James, nrly. across from Mr. Harrison's Landing on the north bank. Of Patriot troops, there is a total of about 5000. Some of these have experience; all have empty bellies.

"How reliable is this news, and how up to date?" Ward asked.

"I was impressed by the judgment of Squire Trimble who wrote this for me last night at his house yonder on the inland road. A courier from the interior rode up while we talked."

Ward ran over the intelligence in his mind. "There really isn't enough to go on. Wayne and LaFayette are probably strong enough to block Cornwallis if he tries to come up the peninsula. Wayne moves north and the Marquis south. But Cornwallis is fortifying at Yorktown, so he doesn't intend to march out. And we are not strong enough to attack him at Yorktown behind his earthworks."

"Ah," said Tremarec, nodding. "Milor Cornwallis does not move from Yorktown. It is obvious that he waits for something. Place yourself in the mind of Cornwallis and tell me what that is."

"H'm," said Ward. "Waiting near the tip of, say, a forty-mile peninsula, with water on three sides — the York, the James and Chesapeake Bay." He frayed out a bit of rope and tossed it overboard. "He can be waiting for — transports to bring reinforcements so he can cut through Wayne and LaFayette, or transports to take him north."

"*Parfaitement,*" said Tremarec. "But Milor Cornwallis is not aware of the approach of de Grasse's fleet. Even so, there remains a way of escape and he must learn of it quite soon."

"What?" cried Ward. "He'll have a way out even when de Grasse comes?"

Tremarec sighed. "As we learned last night, Wayne is under orders to quit this theater at once, to march south and join your Greene in the Carolinas."

"My God. That will leave LaFayette here with only fifteen

hundred men at the most." Ward looked long at the sandhills that shut in the inlet. "So we close our books on the Virginia campaign and start in all over again somewhere else."

Tremarec laid a hand on his shoulder. "I regret that it is I who bring you such news."

"It's the sort of news we've been getting ever since the war started. Give up in one place, try another. Over and over." Chin in hand, he leaned on the bulwarks. "Wayne finds a stalemate here, so why waste his men? He's a magnificent combat man and those Pennsylvania troops with the bucktails in their hats are as good as we've got. So we clean out the Carolinas and then move *both* Wayne and Greene north to join Washington!"

Tremarec looked at him soberly. "Still more do I understand the words of our friend Franklin. 'Men greatly in earnest.' And in the meantime there is our own mission."

"There's that," agreed Ward. "What are you going to do?"

"I sail under set orders and those I must carry out, even if we unload our supplies and other matters in Wayne's empty camp," said Tremarec. "There may be some great plan of which I am a very small part. My friends ashore have couriers on their way to the Marquis, telling him of the *Sauvage* and its cargo."

"Orders, yes," agreed Ward gloomily. "You can't go beyond them. So what do we do now? Unload here? You'd have an eighty- or ninety-mile haul, I'd say. I don't know anything about Virginia roads, but in most parts of the country it'd take you weeks to complete your job."

Tremarec shook his head. "Not here. We lie over by day and sail by night, always finding some blind little cove like this."

"And then?"

"Around Cape Henry and up the James."

"The James!" Ward's voice rose in protest. "With the British holding the tip of the York peninsula?"

"Why not? We sail by night and without lights. Milor Cornwallis, so I am told, confines himself to the York River shore. We shall find, Monsieur White assures me, a good anchorage near the landing of one Monsieur Harrison."

"I don't like it. Damned if I do," said Ward. "The Marquis himself may be gone and Cornwallis will be all over the peninsula. Don't forget he has two frigates. Oh, I know they're well up the York, but frigates can move as well as armies."

"Yes," said Tremarec calmly. "He has two frigates. And we have our orders." He touched his hat. "We sail at sundown. Until then — " His footsteps died away across the deck.

Ward went below for a hurried breakfast of coffee, burned bread and thick Cap Haitien honey. When he returned, he found Deborah standing below the quarter-deck, clad in a deep blue traveling dress. The embroidered bag dangled from one wrist. "There you are," she called. "I was afraid you might have slipped away ahead of us. When do we land?"

"Land?" asked Ward. "We don't. This is just a stop. We'll probably have others like it."

"What a funny way to travel. But when we've stopped stopping, where shall we be?"

"Lying very close to our army — or a part of it." He spoke with more confidence than he felt.

A slight frown appeared on her forehead. "Ward, if we land where you think, will it be far from Faith?"

"Rather, I'm afraid," said Ward gravely.

"Then it'll take you quite a while to go to her. Do you think that I'll be able to see her soon?"

Ward sighed. "No telling when I'll be able to go north."

"But she's waiting for you."

"I know. So's the army. That's got to come first. She knows. But at least I'll be able to start a letter on its way to her. Then I'll have to get to work."

At sundown the *Sauvage* had spread its sails once more and

worked out of the inlet under the skilled hands of Jonas White, and a curious pattern of navigation began. By night the *Sauvage* worked north, but before each sunrise dropped anchor in some sheltered inlet or shallow saucer of a bay. Then the course seemed west and White grudgingly identified an anchorage as somewhere near Lynnhaven. At last, under black, dripping skies, the ship worked into a broad river.

Thunder and lightning joined with the rain and Ward caught glimpses of low, distant banks. Slowly, slowly the Sauvage slid on, now veering sharply to the north shore, now trending toward the south as White followed an invisible channel. Ward heard the thud of boots and was just able to make out Tremarec dropping to the main deck, followed by Jonas White. The *Sauvage* had stopped.

Ward ran beside Tremarec to the low bulwarks and looked to port. The south bank of the James was hidden in the pouring night. He could barely make out a lighter patch of water where the current rippled against unseen banks.

"We have arrived," said Tremarec. "You have seen armies before, my friend. Can you find me one in this blackness of seven hells?"

Ward shook his head. "There ought to be at least a faint glow reflected by the clouds. Campfires show, even in flat land like this, from over ten miles away." He stared shoreward. At last he said wearily, "No troops here, Captain." He was sick at heart.

"Is that the *Royal Sauvage?*" The voice from the river came with stunning unexpectedness.

Ward's ears strained for the echo of that voice while a sudden tingling ran over his scalp and back.

Tremarec, cupping his hands, shouted, "Who hails the *Sauvage Royal?*"

There was a muffled splash of oars in the darkness and the

same voice roared again, "God damn it, *I* ask the questions on this river. Name yourself!"

Ward brought a hand down hard on the Breton's shoulder as he leaned out and shouted, "*Le Sauvage Royal,* Captain Tremarec. Come aboard, General Wayne."

Wayne's voice thundered again. "Who the devil's that up there? Your ship's supposed to be French. Speak up smart. There are shore batteries covering you. Who sent you here?"

Tremarec leaned forward. "Who but the Squire Trimble, *Monsieur le Général?*"

"I'm coming aboard." Oars slopped closer and closer. Ward saw a hand clamp on the bulwarks. Then in a wild flutter of dripping cape a big man vaulted lightly on board. Tremarec bowed to the vague figure. "Yves Toutant Tremarec, master of *Le Sauvage Royal,* sailing under orders of Monsieur de Sartine, Minister of Marine," he said formally.

The other stood to attention as though on parade. "Anthony Wayne, Brigadier General, Continental Line, under orders of Major General the Marquis de LaFayette." Then something of his drill-ground manner left him. "Who's that with you? Who called my name?"

"Ward Gratwick, sir. Lieutenant, Continental Artillery."

Wayne looked in Ward's direction. "Gratwick — seems to me I've heard — yes! I've got you now — Monmouth, Germantown, Barren Hill. You used some of your gunners as a covering party at Stony Point. Always getting yourself smashed up. How the devil'd you get here? A prisoner, weren't you?" A cascade of water fell from the folds of his tall Kevenhuller hat. "God blast this. It's raining enough to drown all the snakes in Prince George County and it's black as a paring from the devil's hoof. Let's go in."

Tremarec led the way to his cabin, Wayne clanking after him, sword and spurs jangling. Ward followed, feeling very junior.

197

He was careful to enter the cabin last, to draw up a chair for Wayne, remembering his love of military punctilio. Wayne seated himself at the table, wiping his face with a huge silk handkerchief, and Ward looked at him curiously. The Pennsylvanian, with his finely cut features, was as handsome as ever. There was an impression of energy, of dashing restlessness in his bright eyes, in the set of his head, an impression that was underscored by the cut of his fine blue coat with its high white collar, in the white leather breeches and shining boots whose perfection seemed somehow enhanced by splashes of mud.

Tremarec brought out brandy and Wayne chuckled with delight. "Your health, Captain. Yours too, Gratwick. Jove, this is prime. Better than anything the Marquis has." He set down his glass, eyes closed as he savored the aftertaste. Then he was alert again, the glass forgotten. "I had word from Trimble, Captain. What have you for the army?"

Tremarec, who had been watching Wayne through narrowed eyes, answered, "For you?"

Wayne shook his powdered head. "I said for the army."

Tremarec's eyes became normal and he smiled. "Ah, yes. For the army. The list — it is a long one. We may save time if you glance at this." From a drawer he pulled out a thick sheaf of papers, handed it to Wayne.

The General frowned. "Mean you want me to read all this? The devil, man, just tell me — this is all clerk's work and —"

He began to leaf rather irritably through the papers. Little by little, irritation turned to wonder. His lips stirred as though reading to himself, going down one sheet slowly, then flipping the pages off onto the table with a hasty glance. His reddish eyebrows lifted higher and Ward caught a mutter, "Item — twelve bales infantry coats, not dyed — item — seven bales breeches ditto — item — twenty-two cases muskets — item — one hundred ten barrels powder — "

Wayne pushed back from the table, stared at Tremarec, then at Ward. His big hands shot out, caught the sheets and sent them flying in a wild whirl over his head. He sprang to his feet, caught Tremarec's hand in his, shook hands with Ward, slammed his Kevenhuller to the floor, snatched it up again. "Muskets!" he roared. "Powder! Clothes and shoes for the boys! Beef! Biscuits! Coffee! Rum! The damnedest, most undisciplined, mutinous lot of riffraff that my State ever spawned. They're a disgrace and an outrage, Captain! Gratwick remembers 'em. Good for nothing. By the powers of hell, I'll line 'em up in the rain and I'll stuff 'em with beef and biscuit and rum until they can't stand. I'll fit every last skrimshanker among 'em like a major general. Do you know how they dress now, Captain? Most are down to a blanket and a breechclout and I'll have to show 'em how to put their shoes on. And do you know how they've been eating? A whole mess fighting over the carcass of a half-starved rabbit." He slapped his hands together. "Come on. Let's get it ashore. God above, you don't know what it'll mean to those murdering vagabonds." He paused, out of breath.

Then his face was grave. "If you knew how they'd been marching and living and fighting. God love 'em, troops never stood up to what they've faced, never before. That may not tell you much, Captain, but Gratwick knows what I mean." He gathered the strewn papers from the floor, shuffled them together. "You know, I really believe the Marquis and I can open the ball against Cornwallis now. It's punishing work making starving, naked men fight." He dropped the papers to the table, flapped his hand on them. "And even so, we gave Cornwallis a damn warm time at Green Spring back in July. Now we'll really have at him. Only — " he slapped the papers again — "he seems to be digging himself a hole at Yorktown and we can't get him out of it without a siege train." He looked appealingly at Tremarec. "You haven't a gun or two to spare us, have you?

Just enough to hammer down a few redoubts? To blast out a demilune here and there? They'd have the best of care. Turn 'em right back to you when the siege is over."

Tremarec shook his head. "My armament is light. To my regret, it would not help you."

Wayne looked deeply disappointed. Then his face cleared. "We're not strong enough for a siege, anyway. But we'll keep Cornwallis's snub nose back of his earthworks, damned if we won't."

Ward spoke diffidently. "You're talking about this theater and no other, sir. Does that mean you're not going south to join Greene?"

Wayne made a disparaging gesture. "Oh, that! I was under orders to go. Had just about broken camp, though how those weedy devils of mine could have marched to the Santee is beyond me. Anyhow, the Marquis squawked like a flock of hens with a fox in the coop. I'm staying. How about unloading, Captain?"

"I think daylight is better, if you can guarantee that our friend Milor Cornwallis will not interfere."

"Daylight, then. As for Cornwallis, forget about him. My boys'll claw the weasand out of any red-coated bastard who shows himself on the north bank." He turned to Ward. "Now how about you? You'll join us, of course?"

Ward nodded. "I was hoping for a command, sir."

Wayne guffawed. "A command, eh? I suppose you want a brigade — or will a regiment do?"

"Just a pair of grasshoppers, sir," said Ward smiling.

Tremarec looked puzzled. "Grasshoppers?"

"Light field guns, Captain," answered Ward.

Wayne nodded approvingly. "We can do that much for you, Gratwick. I only mentioned the brigade because so blasted many people when they rejoin the army after being wounded or prisoner feel they ought to have my berth or Nat Greene's

200

or von Steuben's. Well, I better have my oafs row me ashore. Just let me have one more look at that cargo-list. Does me even more good than the brandy, and that's saying something."

Ward glanced at Tremarec, who smiled blandly. "There is still more cargo, General."

"Here? On board? Fine." Wayne ruffled through the sheets.

"Not on board, but on the high seas," said Tremarec. "Our Admiral de Grasse works north with many ships of the line. Also transports, wherein will be found the regiments of Agenais, Gâtinais and Touraine, not to mention some hundred dragoons, half a hundred gunners and some artillery."

Ward jumped to his feet. "They are coming here?"

Tremarec bowed. "It is now permitted that I tell you that much."

"God Almighty," said Wayne quietly.

Ward glanced curiously at him. The news of food and clothes and arms for his men had set him off like a skyrocket. This later and more important intelligence he received with his mind and not his emotions.

"God Almighty," said the general again. He went on in a low, thoughtful voice. "If this force is constituted like Rochambeau's at Newport, that means, say three thousand men."

Tremarec nodded. "That is as I tally it."

"And siege guns?"

"A few."

Wayne sat for a few moments, chin sunk. Then he looked up. "We still won't be enough to prod Cornwallis out from behind his works. Three thousand men. Say twenty-five hundred seasoned men between the Marquis and myself. No. We're still weaker than Cornwallis, though I'd meet him in the open field on those terms. But a siege, no."

"We've attacked with worse odds than that, General," said Ward.

"Not in a siege. The attacker ought to be about four to the defender's one. That's what both Knox and Greene are always preaching, and they know book-fighting as well as the field." Wayne riffled the pages of the cargo list. "Well, something will come of this. At least, we can keep the damned garrison in Yorktown like a periwinkle in its shell. Or maybe we can go north. If Rochambeau'll join Washington and we join the two of them, we ought to have a good shot at New York."

"And Rochambeau?" asked Tremarec quickly.

"Still enjoying the Newport scenery, so far as I know," said Wayne. "Oh, I'm not criticizing him. No doubt there are excellent reasons." He rose with a clank and a clatter. "I'll have working parties on the bank by dawn and all the flat-bottomed boats you need."

Ward looked quickly at Tremarec. Arms, clothing, food, drink had been mentioned. But there was more to the cargo than that. Guarded boats had rowed out from that rocky island in the harbor of Lorient, bringing small, heavy boxes to the *Sauvage*. Perhaps Wayne did not have sufficient rank to receive the gold. Or it might be consigned to some definite person, such as the Marquis. The Marquis — it seemed to Ward that a curtain had suddenly rolled back in his mind.

He was on his feet in an instant. His journey was over, his goal had been reached. He must leave the ship with Anthony Wayne, fit himself into that army, which really lay under the command of the Marquis. LaFayette might or might not be entitled to receive the *Sauvage's* gold, but there was no question about the little packet still fastened to its chain. Ward winced inwardly as he thought of presenting the papers to the Marquis, of seeing him open them, find them blank and demand an explanation. But delivery had to be made and the consequences faced. He cleared his throat. "With your permission, General, I'll go ashore with you."

Wayne clapped him on the shoulder. "That's the spirit. Want to get back into harness as soon as you can, eh?"

"That's why I left Passy, sir. But first of all, I must beg your good offices to see that I get to the Marquis as soon as possible," Ward went on.

"Bon!" said Tremarec, with a nod of quiet approval.

"The Marquis?" Wayne looked surprised. "No need of that. I command here in his name. If you've got word for him, it ought to go to him through me."

Tremarec interposed gravely. "General, I assure you the young man has no choice. The Marquis he must see."

"Damned irregular," muttered Wayne. Then he caught Tremarec's glance and his manner changed. "I'm sure you know best, Gratwick. To the Marquis, then. I'll get you a mount and a guide as soon as reveille beats in the morning. Captain, I'm immensely grateful to you. Come along, Gratwick, I'll do what I can for you ashore."

"I've got one very particular favor to ask, General," said Ward quickly. "I'm anxious to start some letters north. I'm — "

Wayne interrupted him, smiling. "Of course you are. By luck, a post'll go out at dawn and we'll see that your scribblings are included. When we get to camp, use my tent if you like to add a more recent line or two." He winked at Tremarec. "She'll be glad to know."

Ward darted out to his cabin, caught up the growing pack of letters for Faith and stowed them under his waterproof cloak and rejoined Wayne and the Breton at the bulwarks.

Tremarec handed him a small packet. "For the Marquis. You do not mind taking it for me? *Merci.* I hold your cabin for you and shall inform the other passengers of your departure. *Au 'voir.*"

There was a last handshake and Ward dropped into the waiting skiff after Wayne.

The general made room for Ward in the stern of the boat and the two gaunt oarsmen pushed off.

Soon the boat swung broadside, its thwarts scraping greasily along a muddy bank. Wayne sprang ashore. "All right, boys. You're through for the night. Get under cover. But make sure you're raring and stamping by dawn tomorrow." He walked away from the bank, shouting, "Chesbro! Bring on my animal! Come on, Gratwick."

From a half-seen shed a few yards inland a drenched man appeared, leading a horse. Wayne caught the bridle. "No need for you to splash clear back to camp. Bed down in that hut. Report to the officer in charge of the unloading details tomorrow."

The man repeated, "Unloading?"

"What I said. The ship out there is bulging with rations." He mounted. "Sorry there isn't another beast about, Gratwick. Catch hold of the halter-shank and keep up with me. It's not too far."

The general started out at a bouncy trot, Ward clinging to the neatly braided rope by the horse's neck. The path that Wayne followed was a horrible pudding of mud mixed with small stinging pebbles. Each plop of the hooves sent showers into his face, about his shoulders.

Wayne called down to him, "Getting on all right, Gratwick?"

"Fine!" spluttered Ward.

Wayne laughed. "You'd get less of a shower if I slowed down, but I figure you'd rather get there early and drenched, than later and half-drenched."

Ward wiped his face with his free arm. "God above, don't mind me, General. This is American soil. You can drag me at the tail of your horse for all I care." He trotted on, heedless of near-stumbles that threatened to pitch him into mud holes. He could feel his heart pounding from more than the exertion of the run as his mind hammered and hammered at the thought, "This is home! I'm home!"

Then something moved in the darkness and a twangy voice barked, "Halt! Who goes there?"

Wayne shouted, "Brigadier General Wayne, Continental Army."

"Advance, General Wayne, and be recognized."

The horse started slowly forward and Ward found himself squaring his shoulders, stepping out briskly as the well-remembered formula echoed in his ears. A lantern glowed, showed a group of four men, then swung onto Wayne. The twangy voice said, "Pass, General."

Wayne nodded to the picket. "That's right, boys. Don't take anything for granted. Come on, Gratwick."

As he passed, Ward eyed the men of the picket. The lantern showed sodden, shapeless hats, tattered coats, hunting shirts that were glazed with grease, leather leggings, bare shins, broken shoes, poorly cobbled moccasins. But two of the men had bright bayonets. All the muskets looked well-tended and their locks were carefully wrapped in rags against the wet. Ward muttered, "Still there. They're still there."

"Who's there?" asked Wayne.

"Just thinking," said Ward, his words broken up by the rhythm of his gait. "Don't know the names of the men that made up your picket. But I know the kind of men. Rags. Hollow bellies. Pinched faces. Never could last another month. About to quit. Go home, Scatter. But they don't." He paused, then went on. "Hard to put in words just what I mean."

Wayne cleared his throat loudly. "Know just what you mean. You told the story when you said, 'They're still here.' Here's camp."

Ward could make out a few tents, some black blotches that were cleverly woven boughs, a few topped with bits of sailcloth.

As Wayne halted his horse, Ward dropped the haltershank and breathed deeply. Even without the sullen light of the embers, he could see the camp in its last detail, a typical camp of the Continental Army. Men would be asleep under those woven shelters, tattered blankets or deerskins pulled about them. In the driest parts of the shelters, worn shoes would stand, carefully filled with warm wood-ash. Those men who had moccasins would have them under their blankets next their skins. Muskets would be propped close at hand, the locks well-wrapped and carefully whittled wooden plugs hammered into the muzzles.

Wayne shouted, "Fullerton! Captain Fullerton!"

From the biggest tent a man emerged, settling a battered cocked hat on his head. "Present, sir."

The air crackled with orders. "Send an orderly for my horse. Rout out all the field officers. Have them report to my tent at once. Send for the commander of the boat-guards. Tell my orderly to bring hot water and towels to my tent. Then get a horse and a guide for Mr. Gratwick. He's to go at once to the Marquis. Come along, Gratwick."

The camp began to buzz before Ward and the general reached the tent. Drums were snapping out the odd staccato call for field and company officers. Fires sprang up and lanterns went bobbing through the mist. A gaunt orderly in an old British coat dyed a muddy purplish-brown hung a lantern under the marquee outside Wayne's quarters, hastily set a battered basin of hot water on a bench and handed him a flimsy towel.

Wayne nodded at Ward as he sat down at a scarred field desk. "Get the mud off. Your horse ought to be ready any minute. Here — what's this you're giving me? Oh, those letters you talked about. I'll shove them in the mail pouch myself. It's — Sorry! Couldn't help seeing the address. That's not Kortright's daughter, is it? The one who pitched in at Valley Forge?"

"The same one. The other letters go on to my people in Marlboro," said Ward.

Wayne nodded affably. "The little Kortright girl. That must have been you that I saw with her so often around the camp. Of course, a gunner-officer. That was the winter of '77-78. This is '81 and you're still writing her?" He looked shrewdly at Ward. "By God, you're a lucky young man. She'll get these letters if I have to take them myself."

"Thank you, sir!" mumbled Ward through a mask of very thin lather. "But you don't need to tell me I'm lucky. I knew it long ago. There. Most of the mud's off."

"And here's your mount and your guide. Good night, Gratwick, and good luck," said Wayne.

As Ward left the tent, Wayne's officers were streaming past him in the dark and he caught familiar names, Colonel Stewart, Colonel Butler, Colonel Febiger . . .

His guide called grumpily, "Let's git. It's a wearyin' way."

The wet night stretched endlessly ahead as Ward followed his guide north from the horse-ferry. At the top of a short, steep hill the guide swung his horse about. "Far's I go. Ride straight on. The Marquis's pickets will be yapping at you soon enough." Without waiting for Ward's thanks, the man cantered off to the south.

Ward let his mount pick its way down the slope. Then a man in a brass helmet with a stiff horsehair crest, glided onto the road, musket held across his worn blue coat. Ward dismounted and gave his name and his unit quickly, adding, "For the Marquis from General Wayne. This paper'll vouch for me."

The sentry took the sheet and looked at it. As he handed it back to Ward he said tersely, "Pass."

Ward looked curiously at the man. Two years before, his type could hardly have existed. Now, clothed by LaFayette, trained by Baron von Steuben, he stood, alert and workmanlike on a

Virginia trail, sure of himself and at home in his assignment. "Where are you from?" asked Ward.

The sentry answered briefly, "General Muhlenberg's brigade, Colonel Gimat's battalion." His mouth closed with a snap and he stood aside.

Half an hour later Ward sighted the huts and tents of the Marquis's army stretched along the Pamunkey, flanking the solid White House and the landing that bore its name. Sentries, trim and military as the one he had met on the trail, passed him to the house where a young Pennsylvania captain shook his head in answer to Ward's eager query. The Marquis and some of his staff had ridden out the night before. They were headed, the captain thought, for Fredericksburg on the Potomac, but no one knew exactly. Oh, yes. Couriers were sent after him at regular intervals, but knew nothing of the party's destination beyond the spot where the Marquis had been overtaken. "Something big's blowing up," said the captain confidentially. "Just what, no one knows except maybe the Marquis. No. I can't send you along with the next courier. That's orders. Better wait here. He can't be gone more than three or four days. I'll see to your horse and your rations."

All through that day and into the next, Ward fretted the hours away. Normally, he would have enjoyed himself, for LaFayette's men made him more than welcome and he found uncounted old friends among the companies along the Pamunkey and much to wonder at. LaFayette's little army impressed him. There was the sentry's own brigade, under the orders of Peter Muhlenberg, a Virginian and a Palatinate German parson. And his battalion of men from Massachusetts, Connecticut and Rhode Island, led by the Frenchman Gimat, who had saved the Marquis's life at Brandywine close to Ward's own guns so long ago. Francis Barber of New Jersey commanded companies from his own State mixed with New Yorkers, New Hampshiremen. As Ward looked along the tree-hung banks of the Pamunkey, he knew with ever-increasing elation that he was not merely seeing a conglomerate of state levies, but a fusing of states into a nation, the birth of an American army.

But his anxiety to see the Marquis gnawed at him. He wanted to get rid of the chained packet even though he knew that he ran a chance of meeting severe reprimand if the papers turned out to be worthless substitutions.

In the late afternoon he rode east out of the camp. Topping a low hill that sloped into wooded country, he saw a patrol of mounted musketeers riding toward him. As they neared him he hailed the stocky sergeant in charge. "Been down Yorktown way?"

The sergeant halted and saluted. "Right up to the works, sir. Quiet as burned-out taproom."

"No sign of new troops landed there?"

"Not's we could see. Did talk to a townsman, out cuttin' hay beyond the works. He says a ship come in last week, first they've had in a sight. Say she's a trader and ain't British. Had a funny name painted bigger'n hell on whatever they call a ship's behind. Sounded like one of them rivers in Maine territory. What was it, now?"

"The Penobscot?" Ward prompted.

"No. 'Tain't that."

"The Androscoggin?"

"Sounded something like that."

Ward felt a sudden chill of apprehension. "Not the *Skagen?*"

"That's it, sir," said the sergeant frowning judicially. He saluted again and clanked off toward camp with his men.

The *Skagen* anchored off Yorktown! But why not? The Danish skipper might have sprung a leak, lost a mast and headed blindly for the nearest land. Or he might have been picked up by a British frigate and brought in for questioning. The ship

was neutral and could have been cleared by the shore authorities quickly. And once up the York River the skipper might
have found a profitable market for his cargo, whatever it was,
with the British Commissary. Last week, the sergeant had said.
Well, the *Skagen,* sailing a straight course, could have outrun
the *Sauvage,* which had sought shelter each night along the
coast.

When Ward returned to camp, the sentries about the White
House told him that there had been no word from the Marquis.
Still brooding over the presence of the *Skagen* off Yorktown and
filled with an uneasiness which he could not define, he wandered off toward the lines of one of Vose's companies. A Pennsylvania officer hailed him. "What's up?" Ward asked. "Wayne
coming to the Pamunkey?"

The captain shook his head. Wayne had broken camp and
moved his force some miles down the James opposite James
Island and the ruins of Jamestown. Yes, the *Sauvage* had been
unloaded and Wayne was holding the supplies pending instructions from the Marquis. Wayne had called for militia from
around Petersburg to act as guard for the ship.

Ward rode on, aware of a growing feeling of apprehension.
The Petersburg militia might or might not be dependable. But
Wayne, despite his reputation for headlong action, was a careful
man, and so was Tremarec. The *Sauvage* had a good crew and
full armament and anyway the whole attention of the British
command seemed focused on the York River side of the peninsula. Even if Cornwallis ranged wider, he would hardly risk
losses to take a brig whose cargo was now ashore. Or was it?
So far as Ward knew, Tremarec had never mentioned to Wayne
the boxes of gold that had been brought on board at Lorient.
"None of my business," thought Ward. "Any more than the
Skagen is." Then, with an abrupt gesture that canceled his
highly logical thought, he turned his horse and started south.

Darkness fell and he let the horse pick its own way. When at last he rode out onto the north bank of the James, he tried to remember just where the horse-ferry was where he and his guide had crossed. In a sudden decision he turned his horse downstream. He knew that the river widened as it ran toward the Chesapeake and that would mean boat-landings and the chance of an abandoned skiff or flatboat.

All at once his horse shied. Voices shouted in the night and there were men all about him, men and the faint glint of musket barrels. Hands reached up from the dark and caught at his bridle. He gripped the nearest wrist, twisted hard. Then he loosed his hold. The man was shouting to him.

"The French ship, Mister! Know where she is? We're pure lost."

Ward dropped to the ground. "Who's asking that?"

A babble thinned to a single voice and the man nearest Ward spoke. "We were sent from near Petersburg. Supposed to guard a ship. Are you from hereabouts? Heard of any such?"

Ward froze in alarm. "From Petersburg? You're the guard for the *Sauvage?*"

"Sounds like that. Set out in plenty time, we did. Come dark we met the overseer from Rand's place and he told us to hit the north bank, not the south. The ship, in his telling, was near to Harrison's Landing."

"Near Harrison's?" echoed Ward. "You mean she's been moved?"

The man spat. "Not to my figgering. Mister, they ain't so much as a log raft to the creek."

Ward spoke sharply. "Who did you say changed your orders?"

"Like I told you. Rand's overseer."

Another man growled, "Hell, that warn't Rand's overseer as spoke to us."

Ward leaned wearily against his horse and addressed the

spokesman of the militia. "No harm done. You had your orders in the first place to come to the south bank."

"Right. Treloar's Creek it was," said someone.

"Then on the way someone rode up in the dark and told you to go to the north bank instead? Well, no one can blame you for that."

The spokesman grunted. "Sure as hell can't. Well, we kind of got fooled. Let's get home, boys."

"Hold on," said Ward. "You've still got your orders, haven't you? The job's not done. I'm Lieutenant Gratwick of the Continental Artillery. Show me how to get to the south bank and I'll take you to the ship."

"Pretty late," grumbled an unseen man.

"That won't matter," urged Ward. "For one thing, I'll guarantee you'll get the best rations and plenty of rum from the ship. And I'll write a letter to your local commander saying that you did your job like soldiers. No need to speak about the change in orders."

He could feel an air of uncertainty about him. Then one man spoke resignedly. "Well, don't mind if I do. But if the rum and rations ain't like you said, I'm high-tailing it home."

"They'll be there," said Ward quickly, sensing a change in the group. "Now how do we cross?"

A stocky man led the way downstream. Ward followed with the others. In a few minutes they turned down the bank and Ward could make out a broad scow and a skiff rocking gently on the water. "Who's in command here?" asked Ward.

A man stepped forward. "I am. James Munro, militia lieutenant."

"How many of you?"

"Thirty-two," answered Munro.

Ward peered down at the scow and the skiff. "We'll never get them all into these boats, not on one trip. Now here's what we better do — " he hesitated, remembering militia touchiness in other parts of the country — "that is, here's what I'd do in your place."

"Don't bother to tread easy," said Munro. "You're senior. The boys'll do what you tell 'em."

"Then you and I and two others go in that skiff," Ward went on. "The scow won't take more than fifteen. Count out your best men. Leave the rest on this bank under a good man and we'll get them on a second trip. One man can take my horse and cross higher up the river. He'll join us later on the south bank. Does that sound all right?"

"Does to me," said Munro tersely. He turned to the men who stood about the bank, rattled off a string of names.

As Ward watched the men tumble into the boats, he was sure that few of this militia group had seen service, but Munro handled them efficiently enough. Then he followed Ward into the skiff where two men waited, resting on their oars. "Cast off," he said. "The scow'll conform to our moves."

The skiff slid smoothly out into the stream, slanting westward to make up for the current. Ward touched Munro's arm. "Better drop back and tell the scow to maintain silence. The *Sauvage* might let off a blast or two at us before she knew who we were."

"Done that when we loaded. You at the oars, try not to splash so much."

The south shore showed vaguely through the dark. "There's Treloar's Creek," Munro said. "And I'm telling you, there's no ship in it."

"You're sure? Maybe she's deeper in."

"Not without jamming her keel into mud and rocks."

Ward set his teeth. "Look here, Lieutenant. You know this river. If you were a skipper and found the creek didn't suit, where would you go?"

"All I figure is the skipper wouldn't have gone upstream. So he must have gone down." Munro moved his head back and forth as though trying to question the night. "Let's scout. First off, got to keep together." He waved his hand, a whitish blur in the night, and the scow crept up close. Munro tossed a painter to it and Ward heard a dull scuffling as it was made fast. Then the two boats started downstream, keeping fairly close to the shore.

Ward crouched in the stern, scanning the sky for a glimpse of the *Sauvage's* masts. Suddenly lights showed some twenty yards off to the right. There lay the *Sauvage*, partially screened by a point where pine trees towered.

"Hold your oars, boys," said Munro in an undertone, as he waved to the scow astern. "All right, Lieutenant. You hail. We'll move when the ship answers."

Ward took a deep breath, then slowly expelled it. The broad gallery of the *Sauvage* was in front of him and lights burned in the state cabins. On the gallery a man stood leaning against the rail and Ward thought his back was toward the river. He could make out a musket standing against the rail. As he watched, the man threw back his head, drank from a bottle then tossed it into the river.

Munro whispered, "Something wrong?"

"Yes." Ward's hands began to shake and his blood felt like ice in his veins. He put his mouth close to Munro's ear. "Row under the gallery. Hold the scow here. For Christ's sake, no noise."

"That bad?" whispered Munro.

"Worse. Get me under that gallery."

Munro hauled close to the scow, whispered to a man in the bow. Then he motioned to his own rowers and the skiff glided on, a single stroke of the oars carrying it smoothly.

Ward looked up. The man was quite visible now and Ward

knew at once that he was no member of Tremarec's crew. He reached up, caught the rail. The man swayed, looked back over his shoulder. "That you, Jem?"

Ward, his temples pounding, answered hoarsely, "Aye!" He gave a push, swung himself onto the gallery. The man lurched about, but Ward glided behind him, clamped a forearm against his throat, caught the man's right arm with his other hand and twisted it back while he drove his knee into the other's spine. His victim wrenched and struggled but Ward's hold, an old Indian trick which he had learned from one of Dan Morgan's riflemen, was paralyzing. With a sudden heave, Ward swung the man's feet over the rail, saw hands reaching up from below to help. There was no need to talk. Munro and his men would keep the prisoner secure and silent.

He stood alone on the gallery, breathing hard. Then he stepped into Paul's cabin. The place was a shambles. Trunks spilled their contents onto the soft carpeting, papers were everywhere, drifting in the light breeze. He went to the door that led to Deborah's cabin and peered hastily in, only to be met by the same confusion of yawning trunks and overturned chairs.

With a last swift glance he returned to the gallery, beckoned out into the night. There was no need of an answer. Munro and his men would know what to do. Then he picked up the guard's musket, kicked off his shoes and moved silently into the corridor that ran forward to Tremarec's cabin.

The door leading to the deck was closed, but that of the office was partly ajar and he could look through the crack between hinges and wood.

Tremarec sat facing him, an expression of quizzical amusement on his face. Deborah was in the armchair at his right. Her eyes were angry and her mouth set. If Paul and Mrs. Lathrop were present, they were out of his line of vision. The man who sat facing the Captain was thin and spare and his iron-gray hair was neatly dressed. As the head turned a little, Ward could see hard cheek bones and long jaw. "Really, you're being obstinate, Captain," said Jabish Frost.

Tremarec smiled pleasantly, indulgently. "It is you who are being obstinate, Monsieur. You must surely realize that, had I such a cargo, I could scarcely hand it over to you. And you do not follow out my most reasonable suggestion that you take your men and search below for that cargo."

Frost flapped his hand gently on the table and Ward saw a brace of pistols in easy reach. "My method, Captain, is much simpler and quieter. Those of your crew still aboard, are neatly held below decks by my friends. If we venture among them there will be bloodshed, a fact which I am sure you deplore as much as I. No, no. A simple word from you and the decks will be cleared and in half an hour I and my men will be gone. I shall have the boxes and you will have a clear conscience, since you obviously yield to *force majeure.*"

There was a subdued scuffling aft and Ward slipped back toward the gallery. Munro and his men were climbing with a minimum of noise into Paul's cabin. They were a nondescript lot, but Ward liked their looks as they stood quietly under the lamp, unmilitary but steady-eyed and responsible. Munro was revealed as wiry and small with a tanned, lean-jawed face. He dragged one leg as he stepped forward and his left hand was replaced by a polished hook. Munro raised his eyebrows in question.

"The ship's been taken," whispered Ward. "Most of the gang seem to be forward. Have four men climb to the quarter-deck from the gallery. When I signal, bring the rest straight ahead to the deck. Fire high and then rush. Let me have your pistol."

Munro handed Ward the weapon. Ward gave his musket to the nearest man and glided into the corridor again. The scene in the office had not changed. Frost was saying " — a long time

216

in planning. We knew everything that that sham-Quaker Franklin did, wrote or said, nearly everything he thought."

Tremarec inclined his head. "Most astute, Monsieur."

Frost gave a dry laugh. "We knew you were to sail a long time before you did. We took steps. You were lucky to escape the two British frigates that were watching for you. You were lucky that your orders did not send you to Martinique. There, Captain, your cargo would have been lifted in the full light of legality and de Bouillé himself would have been powerless to prevent it. But as things have worked out, I have no complaints. While Governor Nelson might not quite recognize the Virginia militia that came to guard you, in my eyes they've done their job very well. Now for the last time, Captain, do I get your cargo peacefully or must there be bloodshed?"

Tremarec placed his finger tips together. "Your summation is admirable. My answer is — no cargo, no bloodshed."

Ward saw Frost start in his chair. "Don't be a fool, Captain. Now I'll have to call my men in to wind up this business. If unfortunate incidents occur, the blame is yours." He pushed back from the table.

Ward signaled to Munro, who started forward, followed by the men who had not climbed to the quarter-deck. Then Ward glided into the cabin, caught Frost by the shoulders and jammed him unceremoniously back into the chair. "Just a moment, Mr. Frost. The conversation's not over."

The effect of his entrance was startling. Frost sank into his chair with a strangled cry. Deborah sprang to her feet and with a single sweep sent Frost's pistols clattering across within Tremarec's reach. Almost out of the lamplight Mrs. Lathrop cried out brokenly, one hand to her throat. In a corner Paul, shaken and dishevelled, stared in stunned silence, his arms bound behind him. Tremarec did not move, but continued to survey the scene with bland approval.

217

There was a spatter of musketry outside. "Watch Frost, Captain," Ward called as he ran out onto the deck. He heard the thud of feet, a series of heavy splashes and flounderings. Munro appeared out of the confusion. "Ship's yours. They jumped at the first shot. What next?"

"Pry up the hatches and release the crew. Post guard. Make sure no one swims back here or is hiding. This is sheer piracy and treason. Tell your men they've done a good night's work, but keep them alert. Report to the cabin when you've got things tidy."

Deborah was cutting Paul's bonds when Ward returned. Mrs. Lathrop, very pale, was sniffing at a jeweled vinaigrette. Tremarec, still seated easily, had one big hand firmly clamped on Jabish Frost's collar.

Paul, free of the cords, chafed his arms. He strode across the cabin, fists clenched. "Frost, I don't know how the devil you got here from Paris, but I'll see you hang for this."

Ward checked him. "Let him alone, Paul." He looked keenly at Frost. The gaunt man's face was pasty and he kept moistening his lips with his tongue while his eyes darted this way and that. Ward said, "What is your idea of Frost's disposal, Captain?"

Tremarec chuckled. "Ah, yes. It is I who am the aggrieved party, *n'est-ce pas?* Since it is my ship that he attempted to take over." He took a firmer grip on Frost, crossed his legs comfortably. "Let me set the stage for our friend Gratwick, who did not appear until the final act."

The door swung wide and Lieutenant Munro entered. Ward introduced the Virginian. "He brought his men to the *Sauvage,* after finding boats for them. His men were meant to guard you, Captain. On the way, the party received orders which they thought bona fide, to go to the north bank." He turned to

Munro. "The gentleman whom the Captain is holding is probably responsible for your wanderings."

"Like to talk to him later," said Munro.

Tremarec nodded in approval. "All may have that chance, Lieutenant. But to return to my muttons, which I now see concern you as well as the others. When your General Wayne receives my cargo, I come to this anchorage. Most of my crew I send ashore since they have been long at sea. Their camp, to avoid the swamps, is farther from here than might be thought advisable, but I must keep them on dry ground. And besides I am to have militia men to guard me. They come aboard and presently this gentleman — " he looked almost benevolently at Frost — "joins them. The rest you may guess. My ghost of a crew they drive below decks. They secure my passengers. Then Monsieur Frost, in a most courteous way, suggests that I turn over that part of my cargo which General Wayne did not receive, and which you, Gratwick, *mon ami,* saw loaded at Lorient."

"But how the devil could he have known about it?"

"Come, come," said Tremarec indulgently. "Have I not pointed out to you that to say a thing is secret is to say that it is known? But, *mon bon* Monsieur Frost, your intelligence slept at Cap Haitien."

"Never been in the place," mumbled Frost. Ward suppressed a start, kept himself from looking at Frost. And why didn't Paul speak up?

Tremarec went on. "Let us say, then, that someone slept. For listen, my astute Monsieur Frost, and you others. When our de Grasse, at Martinique, had his orders to sail north, he found the coffers of Fort-Royal empty, as were his own. At Cap Haitien, he anchored, was met by other elements of his force who brought him iron and powder but no gold. Our admiral is a man of action. With the aid of authorities ashore, he manages to obtain heavy loans from Spanish bankers, French planters. He loads the gold. He sails. Many wonder what will happen to their money. Then into the harbor of Cap Haitien, there sails *Le Sauvage Royal* and the carefully planned drama of Monsieur Frost becomes *opéra bouffe*. My cargo from Lorient goes ashore quite openly, which is often the surest secrecy, the notes on the royal treasury which our de Grasse issued are taken up and canceled. Spanish banker and French planter are paid in full while de Grasse sails north with plenty of gold for the armies of your Washington and our Rochambeau. *Cher* Monsieur Frost, you are quite welcome to the dust and the dead rats which now occupy the specie-well where the gold used to repose."

Frost's jaw quivered. "You lie! Nothing came ashore at Cap Haitien."

Tremarec's eyes darkened. He answered easily enough, "You are hasty, Monsieur Frost, in applying such a term to a gentleman, especially when your knowledge must rely on hearsay, not having been at Cap Haitien yourself."

Paul said hoarsely, hands gripping the edge of the table, "Why didn't you tell us before — I mean when Frost first boarded the ship?"

"A reasonable question," said the Breton. "I was not sure of the effect that such a statement might have on the rather violent-looking gentlemen who accompanied Monsieur Frost — or on himself. They might have become angry and acted with less restraint than one could wish."

"But, Captain," put in Deborah, "they'd have found out sooner or later."

"True," said Tremarec. "But for one thing, the specie-well of a ship is not easy to locate, especially for landsmen. For another — " he glanced at his watch — "within half an hour our good Keratry should appear with a large party to relieve those men who have stood watch up to now. At the first hail he would have known something was amiss and would have taken steps accordingly, though those steps could hardly have been more deft and silent than those of our friends Gratwick and Munro." He turned to Ward. "A question, if I may. You came to the ship in the dark. How did you know all was not in order?"

"I was uneasy when I heard that the *Skagen* was lying off Yorktown and I can't tell you just why."

Paul started. "The *Skagen*? What's wrong with her putting in? She's neutral."

"I can't tell you why I felt uneasy."

"Go on," murmured Tremarec.

"I started down here and met Munro and his men. I was pretty sure something was wrong when I heard his story. But the real clincher, Captain, is a tribute to your discipline. I saw a man, obviously on watch, on the gallery. He had his back to the river and was drinking out of a bottle. You would never have a watch on the gallery. A watch of yours would be facing the river and would not be tilting a bottle of rum. Therefore, you were no longer in command, therefore something had happened. By the way, Munro, what about that man?"

"Tied in the scow. Guarded. He didn't seem much interested in what was going on," answered Munro.

"And now for Frost," said Ward coldly.

"Gently," said Tremarec. "There is the matter of law. While not on the high seas, this surely comes under the laws of piracy. As captain I am sole judge."

Frost's hands worked as though trying to free themselves from invisible cords. "I'll bargain with you. I know plans against both the French and the colonists. I know people, their names, what they're trying to do, what they *will* do if you're not warned. I'll tell you all the people who were in this, some fine American patriots in Paris, some high-nosed nobles at the court, merchants in Martinique who'd scuttle a whole French fleet to turn a couple of louis d'or. I'll tell you who sends word to Sir Henry Clinton in New York, men who are preaching the simple Republican virtues while they make a fortune through treachery."

Tremarec sighed. "My heart goes out to you, Monsieur Frost, that fate has forced you to know such unsavory men." He turned to Ward and Munro. "One of you speaks for the Continental Army, the other for the State of Virginia. How would you answer our fastidious friend here?"

Munro, his weatherbeaten face flushed, was glowering at Frost. "Talk!" he said. Ward nodded.

Frost mopped perspiration from his face. "Then it's my freedom for what I tell you. That's a bargain. Only I won't make you depend on what I say. I've got papers here — " he plunged his hand inside his coat, then sprang to his feet so quickly that he broke Tremarec's hold. "Gone! They're gone. My last chance." He began to whimper. "Had them all here. Wait. Give me a minute to think. Oh, you'll know everything. Look! My coat's ripped — the whole pocket torn out." He turned to Paul, jaw quivering and tears trickling along his nose. "You'll bear me out. There was a scuffle in your cabin. There was. For God's sake, say so."

"There was," said Paul grimly. "I laid one of your men out and I wish to Christ it had been you."

Frost waved his hands futilely. "You see, you see! It's the truth. I felt my coat rip. You believe me. You've got to. The papers must have fallen there in the cabin."

"The cabin's paved with papers," said Ward shortly.

"I know. I know. Let me go and look. Oh, with a guard, of course." His voice broke and he scuffed his arm across his eyes. "A guard, ten guards. I've got to have those papers. I'll show you that Nova Scotia stuff — those people in Connecticut — that group in London and Paris. It's all there. I won't have to say a word, once you see what's there. A sealed parcel. I'll know it at once."

"What do you say, Captain?" asked Ward.

"I say that I am a little nauseated," replied Tremarec calmly. "But I see no reason why you shouldn't accompany him to the cabin." He picked up one of Frost's pistols. "Take this, *mon ami*. It is primed, as you may see, but not cocked."

Ward took the weapon and gestured to Frost. "Come on. And be careful how you step."

Frost turned an agonized face to Ward. "Thank you, sir, thank you. I'll justify myself, never fear."

Ward prodded him out of the cabin with the muzzle of the pistol.

Paul shouted, "Wait a minute. I'm not going to have him going through my papers while he hunts for his." He hurried out after Ward, Deborah following.

In Paul's cabin Frost dropped to his hands and knees, began mumbling to himself as he felt in the debris on the floor.

"For God's sake, look at this!" shouted Paul. "All these dossiers loose. It'll take me weeks to get them in order again. God damn you and your clumsy oafs, Frost. I've a mind to call off the bargain."

Frost wailed abjectly. "No, Mr. Dale, no. Just a packet. Brown paper wrapping — red sealing wax — it ought to show up plain as plain —"

Suddenly Frost lashed out with both legs, tripping Paul and sending him heavily against Ward's knees. Then the bony man shot forward, caught the edge of the gallery rail and vanished into the night. A second later there was a heavy splash.

Paul yelled, "That slippery bastard. Get him."

Ward ran out onto the narrow gallery. He could just make out a floundering, faint ripples spreading. He raised his pistol, pulled the trigger. The pan flashed but no explosion followed. The pistol had been primed, but not loaded. The muffled splashing and floundering continued faint but still audible. Ward said, "He's still swimming."

Tremarec appeared at the door. "So he got away? I do not feel like weeping. I have a distaste for hanging."

"Damned if I have!" cried Paul. "Land some men, search the banks. He can't have gone far!"

Deborah said softly, "Paul, Paul. Forget it. He failed."

"That is most wise," said Tremarec. "Now we have nothing to do but tidy up the ship."

Munro said from the doorway. "One thing missing, Captain."

"And what might that be?"

Behind Munro Ward saw three or four militiamen. The tallest, leaning over his commander's shoulder said huskily, "Like we was told. Rations and rum. Then some more rum."

XII

The Allies

ON THE *Sauvage* watches were doubled while Munro stationed some of his militia ashore, some on the main deck. A judicious issue of rum and rations made it reasonably certain that the more independent-minded would not drift away to their farms.

While Paul wearily sorted out his papers and Tremarec went forward to inspect the crew, Ward took Deborah and Mrs. Lathrop to the office where wine and brandy were set out beside a platter of biscuits. Mrs. Lathrop sipped diluted brandy grudgingly between snorts of indignation. "Such disgraceful proceedings. I think we all — that is, you and I and Paul, Deborah — ought to have damages from the Captain. Letting himself be surprised like that!"

Ward looked curiously at her. Her words had been angry, but her tone and expression struck him as being reflective as though she were spreading her rather acid protests across her true thoughts like a fan.

Her eyes met his and her expression tightened as though she feared that he might be reading a mental process of hers that she wanted to hide. She recovered herself and went on more energetically. "And as for that Frost person! How did the Captain let himself be taken in by that little nobody!"

"H'm," said Ward. "I don't think I'd call him exactly a nobody!"

"Always has been, always will be," said Mrs. Lathrop, as she crumbled a hard biscuit.

Deborah sat up. "Why, Sue, I didn't know that you'd seen him before, that you knew him."

"Of course, I never really knew him, but he was hanging around Paris in the old days. Nasty little unsuccessful pettifogging merchant! Paul helped him out a few times a couple of years ago, but I can assure you he never set foot in the rue Neuve des Petits Champs."

Deborah turned to Ward. "What on earth did you do after you went away with that general? We heard about it from Mr. Tremarec."

"Went to Wayne's camp and then he thought I'd better go right to the Marquis."

"Did you see him?"

"No. I'd still be waiting for him if I hadn't had that premonition I'd better get back here."

Mrs. Lathrop said quickly, "Then you saw the army? What is it like?"

"Like?" Ward was surprised. It was a question that Deborah might have asked, but Mrs. Lathrop — "Well, it's still small and it's still ragged and it's still tough, and still greatly in earnest."

"Did they seem to have guns enough and powder and cannons?" asked Mrs. Lathrop. "Never mind. That's nothing that a woman would understand, I suppose, but you must be sure to tell Paul all about it in the morning. He'll be so interested."

"It'll have to be very early morning, Mrs. Lathrop," said Ward. "I'm going to get a little sleep and then start back for the Marquis again. Once I see him I'll know better what I'm going to do — what we're all going to do."

"And what, pray, has the Marquis de LaFayette got to say about what we do?" asked Mrs. Lathrop coldly.

He smiled at her. "All of us, including this very fine ship, are riding on the tides of war. The Marquis may know whether they are ebbing or flowing."

"Utter nonsense," said Mrs. Lathrop. "And just what will you do when you've seen the great Frenchman?"

Tremarec entered the cabin as she spoke. "*Chère* Madame, and you, Mademoiselle, you will be well advised if you arrange to be present at that moment."

Mrs. Lathrop bit her lip. "I do not see the need for two women to wade through the swamps to see a runaway Marquis."

Tremarec was smiling, but Ward thought that there was both anxiety and anger behind his smile. "The *Sauvage* will lie here for some days, even weeks," he explained. "A pessimist might say that if things go badly she might lie here forever. While heavy British frigates can hardly come this far up the James, they can easily keep us from coming down to the open sea. But I digress. Just now I talk with that taciturn but most thoughtful young man, Munro. In the zone of your armies there are fine houses, now waiting for a tenant. The owners, he says, are with the troops or living in Yorktown under the protection of the British."

"And we could move into one of them?" asked Deborah.

"Such would be my advice," answered Tremarec. "Get together such things of yours as pack-horses may carry. The rest you may leave in my care. Then tomorrow you ride north with a guide and our young friend here."

Deborah rose in a graceful swirl of skirts. "I'll be ready in no time." She ran out of the cabin, Mrs. Lathrop following more slowly.

Tremarec picked up some papers that lay on the table, ran a careful eye over them. "Puzzling," he muttered. "Most puzzling."

"Anything I can help on?" asked Ward.

Tremarec glanced at his papers again. "This, my friend, is the very devil. I find that a good dozen of my men left the ship along with Monsieur Frost's."

"No!" cried Ward. "As prisoners?"

"Of their own will." Tremarec sighed. "I believe that our late guest did not boast idly when he said that many knew of this voyage before I did."

Ward stared. "But how could he have tampered with them?"

"How indeed?" said Tremarec calmly. "Perhaps at Cap Haitien. Now you better get ready for tomorrow. I shall have you roused early."

An unhealthy pre-dawn mist was rising from the banks of the James as Ward came out of his cabin, his belongings neatly packed in a sea-bag. A watch was being relieved and he could make out dim forms floating about the deck. Ashore some of Munro's men were starting a fire and the flames showed through the thick haze like a single coal. Someone moved below the quarter-deck. Then Deborah called, "Ward! Ward! Where are you?" There was deep anxiety in her voice.

He came quickly to her, found her fully dressed and in a light cloak. "Here I am, Deb. What's the matter?"

"It's Paul. Oh, Ward, whatever has happened?"

"Paul?"

"He's gone, gone without a word."

The river mist gave an alarming pallor to her cheeks. "Don't worry," Ward said. "He's probably ashore, talking with Munro about the pack-horses."

"Can't you understand, Ward? He's gone. His portfolios are missing. Most of his clothes, his shaving things. One of his trunks is all roped up, but it's empty. I lifted an end of it."

"If he didn't leave any word, then he's just being forehanded. Getting his decks cleared. He'll pop over the rail at any minute,

228

chaffing you for not being ready. He probably didn't want to wake you when he left. Have you asked Mrs. Lathrop?"

"Of course. And all she says is that Paul knows what he's doing," said Deborah, her lip quivering.

"Well, doesn't that strike you as reasonable?" asked Ward soothingly.

"No. We talked last night. He was going to call us and then help us decide on what we were going to take. I'm frightened. I'm so afraid that that dreadful Jabish Frost somehow got word onto the ship and tricked Paul into going ashore."

"After Frost tied him up!" cried Ward. "Not Paul. He's too clever!"

She looked a little cheered, then her face fell again. "But this isn't like him."

"Wait here. I'll be back in a few minutes," said Ward.

He went below and talked with the petty officers, roused a few grumpy sailors from their sleep, questioned a squad of Munro's men who had just come on board for rations. Then he returned to Deborah. "It's all right, Deb," he said. "Paul went ashore with a lot of things sometime after the dogwatch. He went in the longboat. It's all entered in the log."

"Ashore?" cried Deborah. "With his things?"

"Why not? He'd been ashore while I was away, hadn't he?"

"Ye-es. A few times. Just for a walk, he said."

"Then he knows a little about the country around here. He got a pack-horse from Munro and a guide. He said he wanted to look at some of the empty houses we'd heard about. So you see, it's all right."

Deborah looked a little relieved. "I suppose so. But Frost's men may get him."

"He must be sure there's no chance of that or he wouldn't have started."

229

She twisted her hands. "But we don't know *what* house he's chosen."

"Remember the guide. He'll send him back. If not, we'll see Paul himself at the Marquis's headquarters. That'll be the center of everything."

"You're sure of all this?"

"Of course. Now better get your things together and have some breakfast. We want to start as soon as we can. It's very likely we'll meet Paul on the trail."

Deborah looked searchingly at him. Then apparently satisfied, she said, "All right. Can I have an hour?"

"And a half. Run along now."

Less than an hour later, Paul's guide had returned to the ship, chuckling over two easily earned gold pieces. He had seen Paul to the horse-ferry far upstream and across the north bank. There Paul had given him the gold and a receipt for the two horses and ridden off into the mist.

Now Ward turned over and over in his mind the question of whether or not to tell Deborah. Tremarec appeared on deck, complacently wearing a magnificent new gold-braided coat which he explained was in honor of the call he would soon make on the Marquis. Ward told him of Paul and the guide, of his perplexity about sharing the news with Deborah.

"*Ça!*" murmured the Breton. "My friend, your expression tells me that you do not wish the young lady to know just now. I find that wise. Let her seek her brother on the trail. It may even be that she will find him there. Ah — now she appears with Madame."

"Ready?" asked Ward, coming forward to meet them.

"Has there been any word from Paul?" cried Deborah, disregarding his question.

"Oh, stop fussing about him," said Mrs. Lathrop, stepping aside to let two sailors, loaded with small trunks and bags, come onto the deck. "Paul wouldn't like it at all if he knew you were stewing like this."

"After all, he's my brother," said Deborah, rather sharply. "There's nothing from him, Ward?"

"Nothing, but it's all right. Now if you're ready — "

"But I'm not. Ward, I can't find my embroidered bag anywhere and he told me to be so careful of that, to keep it with me at all times. I've looked everywhere."

"It'll be safe on board, Deb."

"But it's the first thing Paul will ask me for," protested Deborah.

"Ah, the bag," put in Tremarec. "Wait. Did it not vanish when our charming guests were here? I am a dull seaman with only an eye for wind and weather, but I did not see it in your hands when you were brought into my cabin."

Deborah colored. "No. You didn't. You see, when I first heard the shouting, I thought of the bag and hung it where it couldn't be seen. But I had it."

"A most farsighted young lady," said Tremarec softly. "With your permission we will search the cabin again."

The Captain, Ward and Deborah returned to the cabin, but an inch-by-inch search revealed no trace of it. "At least I shall have cabin and gallery sealed in your absence," said Tremarec. "In the meantime, the sun will soon be climbing. May I now wish you *au revoir* as I look forward to seeing you again in the camp of the Marquis?"

The brick cottage, obviously the overseer's house of the burned mansion back in the oak grove, was occupied by a picket of New Hampshire and New Jersey men from Francis Barber's command. The ensign in charge, a ruddy-cheeked boy from Paramus, quickly cleared his men out. The ladies were more than welcome.

Mrs. Lathrop looked about her disapprovingly. "The first house we came to was better than this," she said.

"But this is much closer to Williamsburg," Ward pointed out. "The Marquis is moving his whole force down there, the ensign says."

Mrs. Lathrop sniffed. "Being near the army's no advantage, to my way of thinking."

"Of course it is," cried Deborah. "That's where Paul will head, straight to headquarters. Come up onto the porch, Sue. The men will unload our horses."

"And we'll see everyone who comes by," said Ward. "We're just below Cole's Ferry and anyone coming down the Chickahominy will pass right under our windows."

While the trunks and valises were being unloaded, Mrs. Lathrop sank onto a rustic chair on the porch. "Please yourselves,'" she said dryly. "As for me, I'm going to sit right here until that boy sends those blacks who go with the place. He said they'd be glad enough to have work and all I'll have to do is feed them. I must say, Ward, that I don't think much of your all-conquering army, if those men are a sample. Why, some of them wore moccasins instead of shoes and all their coats were faded and in need of darning, not to mention cleaning. Their helmets! All dull and dented. They looked like quay-side beggars."

"Sue!" cried Deborah, eyes bright. "They're *our* people. Paul would be proud of them. Don't forget he wants to serve with those very men." Her color faded. "But where *can* Paul be? No one seems to have heard of him and this is the Five Oaks cottage and Mr. Munro said that was where Paul was heading."

Ward smiled reassuringly. "He'll turn up. I'm going to ride down to the Marquis's camp and I'll surely pick up his trail there."

232

Deborah got up quickly. "I'll ride with you. I've just got to find out about him."

"Go ahead, then. But don't blame me if Paul comes here while you're away and then rides off again," observed Mrs. Lathrop.

"He'll stay. Look over the house while we're gone and be sure you pick out a good room for Paul. Bring up the horses, Ward. Good-by, Sue."

There were camps to the right and left of the Richmond Road as Ward and Deborah neared Williamsburg. He surveyed them professionally. "I tell you, Deb, the Marquis must have started this move right after I left the Pamunkey."

"How can you know?" she asked, head turning from side to side, as the ends of the road showed new neat lines of tents or brush shelters.

"By the amount of digging they've done. By the way that crowd over there — must be some of Barber's New Jerseymen — have woven boughs together. And see beyond the little pond? Some of Vose's companies. Those cook-fires were lighted last night, to judge from the ashes and burned spots about them."

She looked about her. "Just seeing all this makes what you told me on the ship so much more real. The men all look so gaunt and their clothes are so old. And they've been living like this, year after year."

"And next year and the year after," said Ward. It was useless to try to make her see that these camps in the sunny meadows were close to luxury compared to some that he had known, that the men looked hungry, not starved, that their clothes were still solid enough to be patched. Huts sinking into knee-deep, icy mud, raw red elbows and knees sticking out through patches over patches, a handful of moldy flour for a day's ration — such things had to be experienced. They could not be described.

233

Deborah cried suddenly, "Oh, what's this ahead of us?"

Far in front, half-seen through the twisted trunks of apple trees, rose-pink brick glowed softly. High in the sky, two finger-like towers hovered white and shimmering in the hazy, sunlit air.

"Williamsburg. Must be," said Ward.

A guard halted them, listened impassively to Ward's account of himself, then stepped aside. The Marquis had a tent pitched north of the Richmond Road, he explained. He wasn't one to have a roof over his head when his men were under brush and canvas. Ward and the young lady were to keep right on going. They couldn't miss the Marquis. Just watch for a guard of dragoons in a field to the left.

Two big men in blue sat under the fly of the tent beyond the dragoon guard. "Well, here's a surprise, Deb," cried Ward. "That's General Wayne with the Marquis. He must have ridden up from the other side of the James. It's all right. Go right ahead. They've seen us. There, they're getting up."

The Marquis de LaFayette had changed little in appearance, Ward thought, since he had last seen him along the Hudson. He looked even younger than his twenty-four years and his face still seemed unformed. Yet his manner had matured to match the two stars on his epaulets. He deferred courteously to the older Wayne, who had ridden up from his new camp along the James, but there was no waiving of rank. LaFayette was in command in the Virginia theater.

Yet the Marquis struck Ward as being oddly distrait. Twice he rose from his camp chair to stare up the road that led north to the Pamunkey. He fretted with his watch and once asked Wayne to verify the time. When Ward began his story, the Marquis listened closely, but Ward had the feeling that, mentally, the young Frenchman was looking past him to the northern fields.

When the account was ended, the Marquis replaced his watch for the third or fourth time. "A most interesting story. I regret that I missed you at the White House. Colonel Gimat told me of you and I recalled you as the officer who brought the cattle into camp at Morristown that winter. *Baste!* It was worse than Valley Forge, wasn't it? Then I remembered your two pieces at Germantown and before that — "

Ward reddened with pleasure as the Marquis brought up other memories of him. Just the same, it was hardly remarkable that the Marquis recalled him. It had always been a small army and many served in it for limited periods. A man who had been in since nearly the beginning would be remembered for that, if nothing else.

"So now we must regularize your position as lieutenant with the army, Lieutenant," concluded the Marquis.

Wayne interrupted, "We've only got those four grasshoppers but Gratwick could help Stacy with them."

LaFayette turned a warm smile on him. "The very thing, General. Like you I had thought of Stacy and, also like you, of the troublesome question of seniority. What a pity that we may not replace Stacy, who has done so well. And yet he would be uncomfortable having a man of Mr. Gratwick's service as his subordinate."

"Oh — seniority," said Wayne hastily. "Of course. Wouldn't do at all."

"Then I shall consult with General Muhlenberg. Something will be arranged."

"Anything Pete Muhlenberg wants to do will suit me, General," said Wayne. "Now about Miss Dale's brother. We'll alert the mounted patrols." He gave a semi-paternal pat to Deborah's hand. "Bless you, it's easy enough to get lost about here but we'll fling the men out like a shad-net and bring him to you before sundown." He rose reluctantly. "If you've no more need of me, General, I'm off for the James again." He bowed deeply to Deborah, saluted the Marquis and clanked out of the tent with a friendly nod to Ward.

The Marquis's watch was in his hand again and his eyes strayed to the west. "I shall order an escort for Mademoiselle, who on no account is to be concerned about her brother. And you, Mr. Gratwick, had better stay close to headquarters. Colonel Gimat will see to you." He strode to the entrance of the tent.

"If the General can spare me a few moments," began Ward.

"Eh? *Quoi?*" He returned to his chair. "A moment? But certainly."

Ward worried the little key out of his pocket, felt for the padlocked chain about his waist. He dreaded the moment when he must give the Marquis the pack of blank papers, but it seemed a little easier with Deborah there. He pressed the key till he heard a faint click, then whipped out packet and chain, the links twirled and twisting snakelike. "From Doctor Franklin, General," he said.

"Ah!" cried the Marquis. "And how is the good Doctor?" He broke the seals. "This may tell us much. France is so far and we hear important things slowly." The papers crackled and Ward's mouth went dry. In another moment the young General would be staring at blank pages. Unless — unless —

There was a sudden exclamation from the other side of the field-table and the Marquis's face had nothing boyish or unformed about it. He said in a low, harsh tone, "This is a joke, then? I fear, Mr. Gratwick, that it is very ill-timed." Sheet after sheet rattled to the table.

Ward felt the blood draining from his face. Then he heard a low exclamation of distress from Deborah. "You have, perhaps, some explanation of this, Lieutenant?" asked LaFayette coldly.

"Only this," said Ward, handing him Tremarec's letter.

LaFayette accepted it grudgingly, opened it. "And this is another prank? If so, you would be well advised to keep it to yourself. H'm — Tremarec? He is unknown to me — he — " His voice died away and he began to read.

Deborah said, "Ward!" in a choked voice. She rose, murmuring, *"Monsieur le Marquis —* your tent — for an instant." She scurried into the main shelter, drew the flaps after her.

"I have read this," the Marquis said, rather less severely. "If this Yves Toutant Tremarec is a man of credence, a somewhat different light is thrown on matters. Nonetheless, Monsieur, you must surely be aware that a messenger carrying secret documents is responsible for them, at all costs."

"Parfaitement, Monsieur le Marquis," said Ward, his mind half on the General's words, half on the ripping sounds that came from the inner tent.

"I think, then," the Marquis went on, "that the matter must be dismissed as unfortunate. More charitable we cannot be. It is all very well for de Grasse to disembark three thousand seasick men *en passant.* A help, but no more, unless we know more. The true papers might have been the whole key." He looked at his watch again, peered past Ward to the western road. "So. We may only forget about this — "

The tent-flaps parted and Deborah came out. "I had this," she said in an odd, thin voice as she laid a packet of papers on the table.

Ward cried, "Deb!"

"Que diable!" exclaimed the Marquis. "It is identical with the first." He ripped open the seals, laid out a sheaf of papers covered with firm script, exclaiming, "Ah, but these are the true gems! Nothing of de Grasse, but plans, such plans for next year. New sources of money. New agents. Old agents of whom to beware. And the imbecile expedition against Nova Scotia is dead. A ruse to free the force now waiting at Brest. Enough men to take the island of Manhattan. And this, sealed, for His Ex-

cellency! Ha! I laugh at Milor Cornwallis who thinks himself so snug in Yorktown. May he stay there and enjoy himself. There is bigger game afoot. Next year!" He bowed to Deborah. "So you were the true messenger. I do not need to ask how you came by these."

"I — I had them," said Deborah faintly.

"But of course. Ah, that old fox of Passy. You were of his household, Mr. Gratwick, a man whom ill-minded people would watch. The false papers he entrusts to you, the true ones to Mademoiselle, whose services must be mentioned in dispatches to His Excellency."

"Please," said Deborah.

The Marquis glanced at her, then at Ward. "Ah, it is I who am stupid!" he cried. "You two will wish a word alone. That leaps to the eye. I shall be within call." He bowed and left the tent.

Ward looked at Deborah, speechless. She stood across the camptable from him, eyes on the ground. At last he managed to say, "Deb — where did you get them?"

Without looking up she shook her head. "I had them. Please don't ask me anything more."

He stepped closer. "The embroidered bag! You were afraid of losing it, so you sewed the papers into your dress. Deb, I'm not blaming you. I just want to know." Suspicion swelled into certainty. "And the bag is gone! Whoever took it must have suffered a terrible shock when he — they found the papers missing. Did you tell anyone you'd moved them?"

She turned her back. "Please don't ask me anything more, Ward. The Marquis has the papers. Isn't that enough?"

"But this is important, Deb. If Paul — "

She turned on him, eyes blazing. "Leave Paul out of this. Yes, he did give me the papers and I did move them from the bag because he told me they were important. But *he* didn't know what they were. He thought they had to do with business. Someone duped him, tried to make him look like — "

Ward set his jaw. "But the blank papers were substituted while we were on the *Sauvage*. They must have been."

She stamped her foot. "Don't you dare even think that my brother could have anything to do with it. He's just as good a patriot as you. Doesn't he want to give up everything and join the army? No! Someone tricked him into this and anyway, the Marquis has the papers. Why, when Paul learns what was really in that bag, he'll be so furious. Ward, how *can* you — you just don't know what you're saying!"

"Who could have tricked him, in the middle of the ocean?" said Ward stubbornly.

"I just won't listen to any more," cried Deborah, small fists clenched. "How do I know who tricked him? It — yes, it must have been that dreadful Mr. Houston who left the ship at Cap Haitien! He was always writing things for Paul, making up little bundles of papers. Of course. He could have done it. He must have."

Ward shook his head. "I picked Houston up on the water front at Lorient. He couldn't have known about the papers."

Her voice was tight with anger. "I tell you, I will *not* — " her manner changed and her eyes filled. "Oh, Ward, even with this long voyage, you haven't come to know Paul, his steadfastness, his fineness. Do say you agree with me — that he *couldn't* have known what it was that he gave me."

"I — I can't — well, I mean I'd want to hear his side of this."

She faced him, a hopeless look in her eyes. "You believe my brother is a traitor!" Then she turned and ran out of the tent to the Marquis.

Ward saw the Marquis motion, and four dragoons rode up, leading Deborah's horse. The Marquis helped her into the saddle, bowed deeply, the soft sunlight glinting on his powdered hair.

Then the horsemen cantered off up the Richmond road, Deborah in their midst.

He saw the droop of Deborah's head, the unwonted sag of her shoulders. She had had a great shock. She would want to think things out alone. She would not want to talk with him now, would see him only as an outsider bringing hideous charges, at least by implication, against her beloved brother. As for Paul —

Little rings of memory began to link themselves into a chain in Ward's mind. He now was sure he *had* seen Paul and Jabish Frost in the rain at Rouen. There never had been any doubt about the meeting in the offices of Clackmannan y Galarmendi at Cap Haitien. (And why had not Paul spoken up when Frost denied having been in that port?) The tube that he and Deborah had seen at Passy had reappeared in an Atlantic calm, had vanished from Ward's possessions and reappeared in Frost's hands at Cap Haitien.

On the voyage, there had been the incident of the marlinspike, the near-drowning from which the seaman Doriot had snatched him. (Or had Doriot, well-secured by ropes, tried to push him over the rail and into the sea? The same night, the sea had stopped Doriot's mouth forever.) Nothing was conclusive. Marlinspike and wave could have been accidents.

After leaving Cap Haitien — his frown deepened. That was where James Houston had deserted. Houston, who had mixed with the crew, who had wheedled opium from the surgeon Brotier. Could there have been a tie between Frost and Houston? Hardly, since Ward knew that the chance to sail on the *Sauvage* came as an unexpected windfall to Houston. And how would Frost or Houston have benefited by Ward's disappearance? Would that have made the looting of the *Sauvage* any easier or safer?

He recalled the scene in the cabin, with Frost quietly boasting about far-reaching plans. Regardless of earlier meetings he had treated Paul contemptuously and certainly the latter had given no sign of being involved with him. Yes, and Paul was the only one to be bound. Any tie between them must have been snapped at Cap Haitien, and snapped violently. Nothing linked Paul with the taking of the *Sauvage,* with Frost's machinations. Nothing. And another thing — Paul had been furious at Houston's desertion. Yet — how did Deborah come to have Franklin's packet?

He rubbed his hands over his eyes. As soon as he began building a logical sequence, the next fact that he marshalled nullified what had gone before. It was like one of the Doctor's experiments where one liquid poured over a bit of metal caused a great hissing and smoking that was instantly killed when a second liquid was added.

At last a single thought crystallized in his mind. Paul's anger at Houston, Frost's contemptuous disregard for Paul must exonerate the latter. As to the papers, there was surely an explanation that Paul could and would give.

One arm still resting on the saddle, Ward stared somberly across the fields at the square U of the College of William and Mary whose mellow brick and harmonious lines basked in the September sunshine. He would give Deborah time to recover from the shock of his suspicions of her brother. Then he would ride up to the brick house by the Chickahominy.

What could come of such a visit? Paul would clear himself. He repeated the thought to himself with waning conviction. Paul could not clear himself. And that led directly to Mrs. Lathrop. Houston had spoken of the way she worked with Paul. Worked on what? She must have known and known thoroughly what was afoot. And if she knew? No. None of this could touch Deborah, no matter how the others were implicated. He knew that as surely as he knew the unshakable integrity of the Commander-in-Chief. For her sake he would have to make the trip to the Ferry.

Recalled abruptly to the present and to the army, Ward looked about him. Off-duty dragoons were running their horses. The Marquis stood on a hillock at some distance from his tents, looking south through a brass telescope. Light infantrymen and militiamen ran pelting toward the Jamestown Road, yelling and waving their hats.

Ward leaped on his horse and made for higher ground to the west that commanded the route from the river. There was white on the road, solid white broken by splashes of bright color and the gleam of brass and steel. Now he could make out a group of horsemen riding on toward Williamsburg and behind them came massed fifes and drums. A thick hedge of bayonets followed the squeal of the fifes and the throbbing boom-boom-boom of the drums. Men were yelling all about Ward and he found himself shouting with them. This explained Wayne's sudden move down the James, accounted for LaFayette's preoccupied fumbling with his watch. The Duc de St. Simon had landed his regiments near Jamestown and now the Touraine, the Agenais and the Gâtinais were marching up the Yorktown peninsula to close ranks with LaFayette's lean files.

Under the roar of the drums Ward could catch the steady crunch of marching feet and an unbroken rumble. Guns, heavy guns were being trundled up the Jamestown road.

Ward looked toward the rear. Gunners were rolling light field pieces out of the west end of the town and an ammunition wagon jolted after them, ready to fire a salute of welcome to St. Simon's men. On the hillock, the Marquis was mounted, sitting poised in the saddle as though ready to gallop down to meet his oncoming countrymen. He made a sweeping gesture to the cannoneers below, then, to Ward's amazement, swung his horse about and raced off along a tracklike road that led north and away from town and marching column.

Surely the Marquis must have seen the advance as clearly as

he himself had. Then why — Driven by an unreasoning impulse, Ward turned his mount and tore across the fields and onto the track of the speeding Marquis who rode on alone.

Bending low in the saddle, Ward saw the Marquis head down a long, gentle slope toward an empty skyline. Over the crest, a few hundred yards away, a knot of riders came on at an easy trot. In the lead, growing more distinct with each spat of hooves, rode a big man. His cloak blew back as the river-wind met him, rolled back to show blue and buff. Far ahead LaFayette had reached the group and vaulted from the saddle. The man in blue and buff dismounted in a flurry of blue cape, threw an arm about the Frenchman's shoulder like a father greeting a long-absent son.

The fields about Ward were full of yelling men. A light-infantryman caught Ward's stirrup, let himself be towed along in great, sweeping strides. He was waving his helmet and roaring, "It's him, it's him!" Ward reined in and the light-infantryman let go of the stirrup, went stumbling on. A red-faced man rode past Ward shouting, "That's Rochambeau with him. Saw him at Newport last year!"

Sitting his motionless horse, Ward stared. Washington in Virginia! It was incredible. Yet there he was, walking arm in arm with the Marquis while a shorter, stocky man in blue and gold kept pace at his other elbow. Washington *and* Rochambeau in Virginia! That could only mean that the Newport French and the cream of the American army were not far behind, were to join LaFayette and Wayne and St. Simon.

So this was why the Marquis had fumbled with his watch, listening a little abstractedly while he had talked with Ward and Deborah.

Washington, Rochambeau and the Marquis came on, bridles over their arms. Behind them followed aides and orderlies. Back in Williamsburg, the light American field-pieces began to slam

243

out salutes. The three commanders were abreast of Ward and over a sea of heads and shoulders he caught quick glimpses of them: Washington, his usual stern intensity softened by a smile as he listened to the Marquis, and Rochambeau, dark and heavy-featured, nodding in grave approval at Washington's terse comments.

He found himself carried on with the press, over the rolling fields to a hillock below which the Marquis's tents were pitched. Down in the rose-brick of the town, the American guns were still barking out, masking tile and shingle with yellowish-white billows of smoke. Along the Richmond road, LaFayette's light infantry was drawn up in rigid lines. Down the Jamestown route, St. Simon's French had halted. The last salute blasted out. The irregular white masses of French tautened, became a solid column. Fifes yelled and drums boomed as the leading files stepped out toward the town, wheeled and headed for the broad fields west of the college. Along the blue, brown and gray lines of the light infantry, commands snapped out. The companies swung into column, countermarched and struck out toward the open meadows where the first of the French were debouching.

A sudden hush fell over town and sunlit fields. Ward was seized with a weird sense of unreality, as though he were looking at the world before him through thick, clear glass, a transparent barrier that cut him off from any contact with that world. There were the buildings of the College of William and Mary. There was the long, straight stretch of the main street with its neat, bow-fronted shops, green shutters clear against white wood walls, graceful arched doorways in their rose-red settings. The slender aspiring towers of the Court House, of the distant Governor's Palace, seemed to draw away from him as though he were looking at them through the wrong end of a telescope.

The few sounds came muted to him through his invisible barrier. He heard the pad of feet as townspeople ran through the streets toward the fields where the two armies were forming. Somewhere in the distance an axle trailed a thin splinter of sound. A dog ran barking past the college, almost within stone's throw of Ward, but its voice came to him faint and disembodied, like a noise heard in a Massachusetts blizzard.

He passed his hand over his eyes, found that his palm was moist and his fingers unsteady. He was startled to find that he sat his horse in a dense group of people — men off duty, orderlies, citizens and their wives and daughters. Like him, they were dazed, as though not taking in the significance of what they saw. The last slow eddy of bright bayonets and cocked hats died away. The Army of the United States had taken its place at the left of the Army of France. Ward could see Washington clearly now, turning his mount by the far right of the French. The Commander's hat swept off in a wide gesture. Behind him, tall LaFayette and stocky Rochambeau, another figure in white and gold who must be St. Simon, uncovered, followed the Commander along the French lines.

The drums slammed on, accentuating the stiff silence of the ranks. Then an ensign on the flank of the Agenais whipped off his hat, spun it aloft on the point of his sword. Like a flutter of dark wings, a cloud of hats followed, lifted high on bayonet points, on swords, on bright *espontons*. The French were cheering and the crashing sound swept on, was taken up by Barber's men, by Gimat's, by Vose's. Ward saw the Commander's head bow as though he were struggling against emotion. Then it went proudly back and he rode on through the shouting that swelled and swelled under the swaying canopy of high-raised felt.

A spatter of shouts rose from the hillock, then died away. All about Ward men had uncovered, as he himself had uncovered. Here and there people dropped to their knees, eyes fixed on the field below.

The Commander and his generals were riding off toward the

open court of the college. The drums changed their tempo, rattled out brusque, staccato commands and taut lines melted, eddied, became columns that flowed smartly out of the meadows. On the hillock, men and women drifted slowly toward the town.

Ward shook himself, gathered his reins. In another day, two days, a place would be found for him in those ranks. In the meantime, he must find Deborah. And in all probability Paul would be at the brick cottage, ready to solve, one way or another, the mystery of the packets. Again, a chilling thought gripped Ward. *Could* Paul solve it? He turned his horse toward the Richmond road, then halted.

Someone was calling his name. "Hi there! Gratwick! You are Gratwick, aren't you?" A short man in a blue jacket with incredibly faded artillery facings and a battered captain's knot on his shoulder was riding up from behind.

Ward raised his hand to his hat. "Ward Gratwick, Captain. At your service."

The captain's broad face split in a tight grin. "You're to go to James Island at once. I'm Captain John Crosby. You're on the rolls and under my orders. Go down to James Island and help out with the off-loading of the rest of the French guns. Then wait there until General Knox's barkers come in."

"Very good, sir," said Ward. "The French guns and —hold on — what did you say about Knox's?"

"They'll float down presently. Good God, man, where have you been? Don't you know that our men and the French are coming down the Chesapeake in French transports? Things have been happening pretty fast around here, but I'd have supposed that you'd heard about de Grasse. He scuppered the British fleet off the Virginia Capes. Chesapeake's safe as a mill-pond. Stir that animal of yours, now. Straight down the Jamestown road until you come to the river. Report to the Vicomte d'Esterel."

246

Ward rode off across the trampled grass toward the river road, pushing Deborah and Paul out of his mind. The army reclaimed his thoughts, dulled his concern. He was back where he belonged, part of the fabric into which the lives of thousands like him had been woven since 1775. Of course, Crosby had not spoken literally. There would not have been time for the name of Ward Gratwick to be regularly inscribed on the rolls. The Marquis must have flung a brief word to the gunner captain, telling him to put Ward to work at once.

He looked back over his shoulder. Williamsburg was hidden from him by the green rolling ground, but against the sky he saw a little column of men swinging along, probably a guard detail being posted. The right-hand file wore white. The men on the left were in dull blue with a hunting-shirt showing drably here and there. At the head of the column, a French officer, probably a very junior ensign, matched strides with a stocky American officer. France and America were mounting together on a Virginia peninsula.

It seemed to Ward that he could almost see another man leading the column on, an old man in a long loose coat with white hair showing beneath a pushed-back fur cap, with a patriarchal apple-wood staff tapping American soil beside the Quaker-like shoes — another man greatly in earnest, Benjamin Franklin.

By sunlight, by starlight and torch, low-hulled merchantmen and wallowing barges crawled up the James to moor by the trampled banks. Ropes and tackle creaked as heavy-wheeled guns were slung out of deep holds. Wooden ramps echoed as panting men rolled lighter cannon from barges. Ward threw himself into the work, directing gangs of big Negroes and interpreting for French gunners who knew the swamps of the West Indies and of Senegal.

As he plunged deeper into his work, his world narrowed to

the river, the field-pieces that would cover infantry in action and the squat, gape-mouthed mortars that could blast Cornwallis out of Yorktown. But two questions hung in the back of his mind. How far north was Wayne's post-rider with his letters to Faith and to his family in Marlboro? And, underlying that, the mystery of the packet in Deborah's possession nagged at him.

During a midnight thunderstorm, while Ward was struggling with a bronze gun that had skidded into mud and water, a huge, fat man materialized, a lean, silent Frenchman at his elbow. Ward, plastered to the collar with mud, was fleetingly pleased that General Henry Knox remembered him, that he took some pains to present him to his dripping companion, General d'Aboville, chief of the French artillery. Of course, it was good to hear Henry Knox's "Smartly done, Gratwick" and d'Aboville's crisp *"C'est tout à fait bien!"* But it was better still to see the gun standing on firm ground while sodden gunners dropped its lunette over the limber-pintle.

When the last unwieldy coehorn on its thick platform was ashore, there were more lights on the river and Ward heard the plunging splash of anchors, the creak of thole-pins. Bonfires sprang up along the shore, threw their dancing lights out onto the current to pick out loaded barges. Every muscle aching, raw knuckles smarting, Ward watched the slow procession of troops as they landed. He heard men shouting hoarsely. *"Royal Deux-ponts! Rassemblement ici! Soissonais! . . . Légion de Lauzun . . .* First New York! Head in here! . . . Third Maryland . . . *Bourbonnais! Rassemblement!"*

Under the night rain the river bank was swarming thicker with men. Ward was pushed aside, jostled, engulfed in a tide of men in dripping fur busbies. They carried carbines and eight-foot lances as they flowed over the broken ground in a compact, disciplined mass. To Ward's questions they answered courteously in a tongue that he had never heard before and he caught names that sounded like Dombrowski and Wyzanski and Mladnick.

At last a pale, watery dawn broke over the James. The hosts of the night resolved themselves into scattered groups of men. More men waited to disembark.

Ward wandered inland along a muddy path, wondering vaguely what his next assignment would be. There seemed to be no coherent chain of command linking him to the allied armies.

From a field beyond the path someone hooted derisively, "Ho-ho-ho! Look at the soldier!"

Ward turned to see, perched on the trail of a limbered piece, a gnome-faced little man in faded blue and red rocking back and forth, jeering and slapping his knee. Ward shouted, "Caleb! Where the hell did you drop from?" The twisting paths of war had thrown him and Caleb Blair together many times in the past. Ward liked Caleb, had deep respect for his wiry courage, hard competence and unwavering loyalty.

Caleb jabbed at Ward's ribs. "There I was, all snug at head-quarters and Henry Knox told me to come down here and fish you out of the river. I damn near fainted when I heard your name. We were all sure you were on a prison hulk or in the Sugar House on Liberty Street."

"Never mind! Do you know anything about Faith? Have you had word from her?"

"Of course I have. I was going to tell you about her. She's — "

Ward shook him. "Is she all right? Has she got any idea of what happened to me?"

"I'm telling you," snapped Caleb. "She's fine. When we lay over near Philadelphia on the way down here, I rode up to the Forge. She hadn't heard from you, of course, but she's a mighty smart girl. She's figured out that you're the kind of lucky clunk that'll get his head taken off by a cannon ball and then grow a new one, just as good as ever. She's — "

"Never mind about that. How's she been living? Has she been getting enough to eat?"

Caleb eyed him sadly. "You're the most romantic bastard I ever saw. Here I'm telling you about Faith and all you can ask is, how have her rations been?"

"Why not? She didn't fare so well that winter at the Forge, or that time we were at Morristown. You know that as well as I do. And she was always giving stuff away to the hospitals."

"She's fine, I told you. Crops have been good and the country's been quiet. Later on I'll tell you every word she said and how she looked and everything. Just now I've got a job for you."

"*You've* got a job for *me!* You, a damned ensign — hey! Wait. Let me have a look at you." Ward held him out at arms' length. "Let me see that shoulder knot. By God I knew the army was in bad shape but I didn't know they'd reached the point of making you a lieutenant." He let Caleb go, slapping him on the shoulder. "Damnation, but it's good to see you again. Where are the rest of the boys? Where are Alden and Carey and Bates?"

"Back up the Hudson," grinned Caleb. "They only picked the best to come down here."

"The best skrimshankers!" Ward amended. "What were you saying about Henry Knox?"

"Oh, Henry just wanted me to do a favor for you."

Ward laughed. "Keep it. The last one you did for me was when you offered to look after my horse for a few minutes. Then I walked fifteen miles in the rain and didn't see you or the beast for forty-eight hours."

"You needed the exercise," Caleb retorted. He picked up a haversack from the trail. "Let's get going."

"Us?"

"That's what I said. It's the favor Henry and I decided to do for you. You and I are named for special service. You're to do the heaving and I'm to do the thinking. We're going to the far side of the York River where I'm to deliver you either to Governor Thomas Nelson of Virginia or General George Weedon, likewise of Virginia."

"Across the York?" cried Ward. "Away from the army?"

"Nelson and Weedon have some very patchy militia there. Likewise two very small guns and no one to man them. They're for us and we'll have to train the gun crews."

"You mean we're to be school ma'ams for a bunch of militia? Are you serious?"

"Henry is. You see, there are other people at Gloucester Point. Some first-rate Tory levies. Some British Marines. Earthworks. Heavy guns from the fleet. Simcoe's there. And they say Tarleton and his British cavalry are coming over to join him."

"And we're supposed to hold off that crowd with raw militia and two toy guns?" asked Ward.

"In addition to such other duties as the Commander-in-Chief may from time to time prescribe. Got a horse?"

"I've got a mount of sorts in that picket line. So we hit across the York?" He brightened. "Well, that's not so bad. We'll have to go up and cross the Pamunkey. There's a call I want to make at Cole's Ferry. You can hold my horse while I'm inside. No doubt the servants will bring you some refreshment."

"I'm honored, sir. But we do not cross the Pamunkey. We take a ferry right across the York." He took off his hat reverently. "Signed, Henry Knox, Brigadier General, Continental Artillery."

"That's all right. We go up the Pamunkey first."

Caleb shook his head. "Time's pressing."

"This won't take long. There are some people up there I've got to see. There's quite a snarl to straighten out and in a way it affects the army. Cornwallis won't run away."

"No, but some of our allies will. You knew about de Grasse's fleet coming in and bringing St. Simon's troops, I suppose."

"I ought to. I sailed right through that fleet."

251

"You don't say. My, you soldiers lead such adventurous lives. You must tell me of your experiences some day."

"Later on, when you've grown up. What were you saying about the allies not waiting?"

"Just that. De Grasse is under orders to get back to the West Indies pretty soon, taking St. Simon's men with him. It's no rumor."

If the allied armies squabbled and delayed, as they had at Savannah, de Grasse and his three thousand men would sail off to the Indies, leaving the seas open to His Majesty's fleets. Ward hunched his shoulders doggedly. "All right, Caleb. Let's get on with the war."

At the end of the second day of drilling the militia men as gunners, Caleb and Ward sprawled exhausted on straw mattresses in a hut near the Severn.

"Will you let go of that rum bottle long enough for me to get a drink?" grumbled Ward good-naturedly. He raised himself on one elbow and mixed rum and water in a bark cup. "Look here, Caleb, this school business isn't going too badly. Think you could take care of all the shining morning faces for tomorrow?"

Caleb retrieved the rum bottle, carefully corked it. "Never, by God sir, never! I'm adamant."

"Maybe you're adamant, but I'm senior."

"There's rank asserting itself," murmured Caleb. "It always corrupts. I'll do all the work and you'll get all the credit, plus a captaincy. All right. I'll preside over our Select Seminary for Young Gentlemen. Why?

"I want to get up to Cole's Ferry on the Pamunkey. A personal matter."

"What for?" Caleb looked searchingly at him. "What's this all about? Has it got anything to do with that girl who crossed

252

on the *Sauvage* with you, the one you were telling me about last night?"

"Yes. It's got a good deal to do with her."

Caleb's manner changed. "Do as you please. None of my business. I might remind you, though, that you sent a letter out to Faith last night. Did you tell her about this girl?"

"Don't be a damn fool. You ought to know me better than that. This is a pretty good sort of girl, but there isn't a heart-beat between us. That goes for her as well as for me. And of course I told Faith about her. This Deborah may be in for a pretty bad time here in America and I want Faith to look after her if things do turn out badly."

"All right, all right," said Caleb quickly. "But you might at least tell me about your great haste to see her. And you don't need to assure me that her little heart doesn't go all a-flutter at the thought of you. I wasn't thinking about *her*."

"Maybe you will think about her when you see her," said Ward. "Yes, I'd better tell you something about this whole business. Pay attention and try not to fidget."

He went on to tell Caleb of the day at Passy with Franklin and of the garden with the hollow tree, of the chained packet and the mysterious trip that ended aboard the *Sauvage* at Lorient. Odd things had happened on the voyage and at Cap Haitien — he talked on and Caleb's pipe went out as he sat up on his mattress.

Once Caleb broke in "You're not humming me, are you?"

Ward shook his head. "There's a lot more. I'm only giving you the framework. Remember the name Jabish Frost? Well, when I got back to the ship after my trip up to the White House — "

When Ward had finished, Caleb blew out his gaunt cheeks. "It's got to be true. You just haven't got the brains to think up anything like that. Never mind about the tubes and papers. The boys with all the gold braid get paid for seeing to such things. H'm. What a lovely lot of passengers! You're too close to all this to judge properly. That Houston — of course he tried to scupper you. Of course he drugged you. And as for Paul Dale — damn it, don't you see that he's right at the bottom of everything?"

"Way down on the bottom — out of sight, Caleb. Don't you remember my telling you that Jabish Frost had him tied up like a trussed fowl?"

"There's some reason for that. Maybe the two got into a brawl in Haiti. From your description, they weren't having any love-feast at that Scotch-Spanish firm." He scratched his blunt chin. "And you've not been near that girl for several days."

"I've been busy with the war."

"You get started there tomorrow. I'll see to the Select Seminary. The more I think of it the less I like the way things look. Yes, Deborah'll need help and she'll need it long before she sees Faith."

Early the next morning Ward was awakened by a faint thudding that drifted up from the south. Caleb was standing in the open doorway, listening. Ward joined him. Somewhere far off in the mist the allied artillery was opening up on the British works. No doubt the best gunnery that the continent had ever seen was being conducted off there in the dying night — while Ward Gratwick taught militia the nomenclature of a worn-out three-pounder!

Dull flickers of light fingered along the low-lying clouds. More guns, closer, joined in the muted clamor.

Caleb grunted, "There go the British, answering."

"Not much volume," said Ward. "Too early to tell yet, but I'd say that d'Aboville and Knox were smothering Cornwallis's gunnery-man."

A louder explosion stirred the dead air about them. "Hey! Listen to that."

"Damn it, Caleb, I'm not going to leave you today. If Cornwallis finds he's catching too many bombs, what's to stop him from shipping his force across here and breaking into the interior?"

"Time, for one thing," answered Caleb. "I woke up long before you did, when the guns first started. A patrol had just come in from the Gloucester Point Lines. Everything quiet there and no traffic on the river. You better go. Didn't Weedon and Nelson both bless you when you asked? 'Of *course* we can spare you, my boy.' They only needed to add, 'Your absence won't be noted in the least.' "

"I'll be back by noon," Ward promised.

The sun was breaking through the cloud-tatters in the east as Ward tested the cinch that ran under his horse's shaggy barrel. Caleb eyed the animal sardonically, then wheeled suddenly, facing a strip of woods that blanketed the country to the west. The sun was working in between the trunks, touching them with gold and bringing out a glory of green among the dusty leaves. Just inside the trees, bright points were moving, growing sharper.

Caleb shouted, "Where in hell are the guards?" He snatched up a drum that someone had tossed carelessly on a nondescript pile of equipment and began banging his fist against it. The points of light came on. Then out of the woods rode a single line of horsemen in perfect skirmish order, stretching from far right to far left. They carried pennoned lances and tall white plumes jutted from their busbies. Ward snatched the drum from Caleb. "It's all right! I saw them on the James!"

The skirmish line moved in precise pattern, formed into column and wound on toward the camp. By Ward's elbow, Caleb was shouting, "But who are they?" Ward could only shake his head as the din increased. The lancers were close now

255

and he could see their sky-blue jackets elaborately piped with white, the baglike folds of black cloth that hung jauntily down the left side of each busby, the deep cuffs of bright yellow and rakish blue pelisses caught loosely about the shoulders. Ragged militiamen gaped at the glittering officers who paced at the flanks, crimson bags bright with gold braid and tassels against the glossy marten fur of their busbies. Their pelisses were white and gold and staring tigerskin covered their holsters and saddle-cloths.

Countless hoofs clopped on over the soft dirt road, and lance points glittered in the sunlight over the toss and ripple of red and white plumes. "God!" cried Caleb. "Never saw anything like this in my life. Where did they come from? Look at those faces! They're all like those aides we used to see with Pulaski and Kosciusko."

Ward remembered the names he had heard along the James when the lancers first landed — Dombrowski, Wyzanski, Wyrostek. Poles, of course, Poles in the service of France, riding down a country road in Virginia.

The last rank of lancers had gone by and after them rode a slim, almost unbelievably handsome man at the head of a gorgeous staff. A triple red and white plume of heron's feathers towered above his sleek busby, and arabesques of gold twined and twisted on the silky sky-blue of his jacket, along the tight raspberry-red breeches. A Virginia captain was nodding in admiring approval. "Know who he is?" said the Captain. "That's the big chief of them all, the Duke of Lauzun. That's Count Dillon with him. 'Beau' Dillon they call him. Supposed to be the handsomest man in the French army, next to the Duke. And here come the Irish boys. Dillon's the only man who can handle them."

Troop after blue troop, they rode by, heading for a distant hillock where Ward could see Weedon and Nelson waiting.

256

Caleb, almost voiceless with amazement, was tallying the files. "Four hundred fifty — two more troops coming out of the woods — another hundred — more coming — say six hundred in all."

"Wait," cried Ward. "This isn't all." The last of the cavalry had cleared the woods and a heavy column of foot choked the road. They came on with a rolling gait and the sun glistened on low glazed hats. "Marines!" Ward shouted. "French marines from de Grasse's fleet." He laughed excitedly. "They've put those poor devils of marine officers on horseback. There never was a sailor yet who could ride."

"There's one tar-breeches who can handle an animal. See him, riding wide of the column?" Caleb pointed.

The seaman came on, checking his mount from time to time, bending from the saddle as though asking questions. Ward recognized Tremarec and ran forward. The Captain flung up a gloved hand, then dismounted nimbly and strode toward Ward, bridle over his arm. The strong, well-remembered voice rang out. "Ah, friend Gratwick. I find you sooner than I expected. I am told at Williamsburg that you are here. So I march with these men from the fleet." Tremarec's dark face wore its usual expression of mild amusement, but Ward read real friendship in the steady eyes.

"I'd been wondering where you were, Captain. I'd been hoping for time to get across to the *Sauvage* before they shifted me over here but someone with more braid than I kept pouncing on me for a bit of work."

"But I find that quite natural," observed Tremarec. "One does not come down from one's post aloft when a storm is brewing, just to give the shake-hands to a friend."

"So the friend joins me aloft," said Ward, beckoning to Caleb, who ambled up, eyeing Tremarec curiously. Ward presented him to the Captain.

"Enchanté," said the Breton, surveying the little man with

approval. "I see that our friend Gratwick is more fortunate in his companions ashore than afloat, where he had to put up with a blundering merchant-captain and a *fainéant* American. I refer, of course, to masculine companions only."

Caleb glanced at Ward. "He's always done all right with the feminine ones. There's a doctor's daughter near Valley Forge, waiting for him to ride up the Schuylkill."

"Of her I have heard much. Our friend Gratwick is to be congratulated. But it is on account of one of the feminine companions of the voyage that I ride over here. There is news of her."

"Ride back to Cole's Ferry with me, Captain, and tell me about it," said Ward. "I've got leave. Besides, I've got some news to tell you. Have you seen her?"

"Not I," answered Tremarec. "That is one reason that I come here."

"Then you haven't heard about the Marquis and the papers?"

"Of the papers, not a word, though I hoped that my letter to the Marquis might have made your task easier."

"Better sit back and listen then," said Caleb dryly. "Go on, Ward."

The Breton's dark face was impassive as Ward told about the packet which Deborah had produced. At last he said, "Ah, the poor little one. I can imagine the scene. She sees the packets. She must believe and yet she cannot believe. Of course, she is shaken. Of course, she turns on you, because you share her belief." He laid a hand on Ward's shoulder. "All the same, there is no need for you to ride to the Ferry."

"Why not?" cried Ward. "Paul may be able to clear himself. Anyway, we've got to get the story."

"My friend, do you truly believe that Paul can clear himself? No, you only hope for her sake that he may. But I must tell you that Mademoiselle is not at the Ferry. She and Madame and

Monsieur now find themselves within the British lines. In fact, they are in Yorktown."

"Yorktown?" Ward's voice cracked with surprise. "Deborah in Yorktown? She'd *never* go there. Maybe six months ago she might have, not knowing what it meant. But now — "

Tremarec absently ran his hand over his horse's sleek muzzle. "My friend, I do not speculate. This is fact. I learned about it as I came through Williamsburg. I had ridden there in the happiness that I was to see an old friend again. I left in sadness that I must bring grave news to that friend."

"How did it happen?" asked Caleb, as Ward looked incredulous.

"Now listen well. Thus it happened," Tremarec began. Paul had appeared at the camp, three or perhaps four days ago. He had gone straight to Washington's headquarters. Valuable properties were at stake, American properties, and the key to their recovery lay on board the Danish *Skagen*. The matter could be simply adjusted, after which Paul would lay all his resources and his services at the feet of the American people and their armies. A flag of truce was arranged, documents written and a coach containing Paul, Mrs. Lathrop and Deborah had been duly passed through the lines. The parley that followed the flag of truce indicated that Cornwallis would place no difficulty in the return of the party, provided that all members permitted themselves to be blindfolded. After all, men of the sword concerned themselves little with men of the pen and the ledger.

Ward sat down on a stump by the roadside, his mouth tight. Many such things had happened in the past. He remembered escorting Quaker merchants to the British lines about Philadelphia. He himself had passed known Tories through the American pickets on the Hudson, silent, angry people on their way to see what might be salvaged from their confiscated estates.

He kicked at a bit of turf. "But damn it all, this was different, Captain. The Commander should have called everyone who had ever known Paul to headquarters for questioning."

Tremarec shrugged. "Such was the opinion of the Marquis. But I am told that my friend General Wayne may be easily swayed by a pretty face and Madame Lathrop is a most attractive woman. It was she who induced him to speak for Monsieur Paul."

"But Deborah would never have gone. Good God, Captain, you heard her talk often enough on the voyage. She was with us, she was of us."

"May I further point out," said Tremarec, "that she is also the devoted sister of Monsieur Paul. But there was more than that. She was assured by Monsieur her brother that you had been captured and that she might not only see you, but might even be useful in effecting your exchange. After that, she offered no objection."

Caleb jammed his shabby hat on the back of his head. "So that girl'll get to Yorktown, hoping to rescue Ward, and find nothing but a lot of simpering macaronis in red? I'm not beginning to like that brother of hers very much, Captain."

"I agree that it is hard to kindle any very bright flame of enthusiasm for him," observed Tremarec. "She does not find our friend in Yorktown. She does find the heavy shot of d'Aboville and your Knox pitching down among the houses."

Ward rose, brushing at a bit of raveling on his cuff. "H'm. I see. Paul's tricked her into going into the enemy lines. She's turned into too good an American to have that happen to her."

"Yes?" said Caleb quickly, as Ward paused.

"Why, I'll just have to get her out," Ward went on. "It'll take planning, but I'll manage somehow."

"*You* will manage?" asked Tremarec, raising his eyebrows. "You, then, discount the Lieutenant and myself?"

"We're all in on this," burst out Caleb. "Damn it, it can be done. First, there's a river to cross."

"I took note of tides and currents as I crossed the York," said the Breton. "It seemed advisable. The whole matter is, of course, utterly fantastic and absurd. In short, I do not see why it should not be accomplished. The river —"

The clear notes of a cavalry bugle sounded from the camp. The three men turned quickly. Weedon and Nelson were standing on the little hillock, surrounded by the glitter and dazzle of Lauzun and his staff. The Poles and the Irish were picketing their horses on the flats beyond it and the marines were stacking arms on their right. On the slope, a major in a brown coat with red facings was shouting through cupped hands. Others took up the call. Voices became clearer. "Pass the word for Lieutenants Gratwick and Blair! Pass the word —"

Tremarec shrugged. "The war overtakes us again. You permit that I accompany you? I wish to pay my respects to the governor of this province, as well as to the Duc de Lauzun and Count Dillon. Then, surmounting this interruption, we shall consider soberly our private and important measures."

Halfway up the hillock they were halted by the brown-coated major. Ward, as senior, identified himself and his companions. The major nodded curtly. "The Governor and the Duke want to see you. Stand by until they're ready," he said.

Caleb shoved his hands into his pockets. "Dukes and governors and generals and counts and a marquis or two," he muttered, "Ward, we're moving into rarefied air."

Someone called from the crest and the major made a brusque gesture. "Just me, sir?" asked Ward. "Very well." He strode off up the slope.

Caleb eyed the skyline. There was Ward, standing to attention before the darkly handsome Lauzun who alternately gestured with a light crop and smoothed out his slim, carefully tended mustache. The towering triple plumes above the Duke's sleek busby dipped and nodded as he talked. From time to time Caleb could see Ward give an almost imperceptible nod as though saying, "Very good, sir."

Caleb's mind jumped back to earlier talk. "That girl, now, Captain. Is she all Ward says she is?"

Tremarec smiled. "To judge from your tone, I should answer yes — and more."

Caleb frowned. "You know — that girl back near Valley Forge. She's pretty good, too."

"And you are concerned for her, my friend? You need not be. This is all *en camarade*. I say so, who have seen them together for many days. The heart does not enter into the matter. To him, she is a charming compatriot who has changed from a tight, self-centered little bud into an American citizen in full bloom. To her — well, one may say that he is the personification of the cause in which she has come utterly to believe. It may be, too, that she sees in him qualities which she would like to find in her brother, qualities which she tells herself, desperately perhaps, are truly there."

"How about the brother?" asked Caleb.

"There we may find difficulties, Monsieur. That she may come to doubt or even to mistrust him could easily send her more firmly on his side. She may cling to the illusion even in the face of her own knowledge."

"We're really going after her?"

"Who may doubt it? Our friend will go. Of that I am certain. That being the case, how may we hold back, we others?"

Caleb sighed. "You're right. He'll go. And of course we'll be with him. Only thing to do. Hi — they're turning him loose."

"And I note that our Lauzun appears pleased with him."

"Damn well ought to be," growled Caleb. "I've served with him before." As Ward came toward them he called jeeringly,

"What are you looking so relieved about? Did they tell you that you wouldn't have to fight any more?"

Ward grinned. "Almost as good as that." He turned to Tremarec. "Does the Duc de Choisy mean anything to you, Captain?"

"De Choisy?" exclaimed the Breton. "Ah, I believe you, it tells its own story. One does not forget his part in the siege of Cracow in Poland. What of him?"

"He's to be in command of all troops on the Gloucester side. If he knows about sieges, it sounds like a good choice." He turned to Caleb. "They gave me a job to do. You, too."

"Pah! Drilling more recruits, I suppose."

"We'll work with recruits, but it won't be drill. You see, the Duke's very anxious to meet Tarleton."

"Tarleton?" asked Tremarec. "I do not know the name. He is of this province?"

"Not of it, but, unfortunately in it," answered Ward. "He's in command of the British cavalry. As a cavalry commander, he's superb, Captain. But he is even more distinguished for killing for the sheer love of killing, for plundering and senseless burning. He was notorious in the Carolinas, and has become even more so in Virginia. They call him 'Bloody' Tarleton." He turned to Caleb. "A few days ago, some of his men captured Colonel Alec Scammell."

"Not the Scammell from Milford?" cried Caleb. "He's one of the best combat officers we've got."

"Was," said Ward shortly. "Tarleton's men shot him in the back after he'd surrendered."

"Ah," said Tremarec softly. "One sees why our Lauzun wishes to meet him."

"About Tarleton," Caleb said. "What does Lauzun want us to do? Bring the bastard over here and introduce him?"

"Pretty much like that. Nelson and Weedon have word that

Tarleton and his Legion were passed over to the Gloucester side. They must have been in some of those barges we saw leaving Yorktown. Rumor is that Tarleton's going to make a sweep inland, foraging. People know by now what one of his foraging raids usually means."

Caleb looked toward the picket-lines where the Poles and the Irish were busy grooming their mounts. "Maybe we can rewrite Tarleton's orders a little."

"And perhaps the amiable Monsieur Tarleton will then decide to indulge his hobbies in another area," said Tremarec.

"That's what Lauzun's afraid of. He feels it very likely that spies have already sent word of the arrival of the cavalry and the marines. Then Tarleton will probably make a short reconnaissance and retire behind the Gloucester works. So here's what we've got to do. Weedon was saying that a good many weeks ago, at a place called Green Spring, LaFayette and Wayne had a brush with Cornwallis. Cornwallis masked the bulk of his force and left a couple of field-pieces apparently unsupported. Wayne snapped at the bait, tried to rush the guns and Cornwallis hit him. Luckily, Wayne was able to shake loose, but it was a very close call."

"Oh-oh!" exclaimed Caleb. "I see!"

"Right," said Ward. "We're to take our two guns and put them in position along about the only route that Tarleton and his gang can take."

"Just us?"

"And crews picked from the best of the militia. We'll be concealed just enough so it won't look like a trap."

"M'm," mused Caleb. "You did nearly the same thing at Barren Hill in '78."

"Yes, but it didn't work then. This time it's got to. Tarleton's got to see us, charge us — and then Lauzun's men suddenly appear. What do you think of it, Captain?"

Tremarec rubbed his broad chin. "It is thus that in India the rajahs hunt the tiger," he said, eying Ward and Caleb speculatively. "A young goat is tethered beneath a tree in which are perched the hunters. The tiger scents the goat, pounces upon it only to be neatly riddled by shots from above. My friends, it appears to me that you, collectively, represent the goat. Let us hope that our Lauzun does not hold his fire too long."

Caleb dusted off his hands as though a task had been completed. "We'll manage somehow. When do we start?"

"That depends on Tarleton," answered Ward. "We're going to take up our position just before dawn tomorrow. Then we wait there until something happens."

"All tomorrow?" asked Caleb.

"And the next day and the next."

Tremarec raised his eyebrows. "And the young lady still finds herself in Yorktown?"

"Can't be helped," answered Ward. "The war comes first. But if you go back to camp, you'll probably find some rather odd people who are able to slip through the lines — or who are allowed to. One of them might take a note from you to her."

"That's it," said Caleb. "We'll finish off Tarleton. Then you get back here, Captain. I know where we can dig up a boat. We'll launch it well above the British lines and drift down. Once afloat, you'll be in command."

XIII

Final Curtain

Hours and days crept slowly by. On the low ridge to the east Ward and Caleb waited, content for the moment with their work. The effect of the gun-position was exactly what they wanted — light field-guns clumsily concealed. Wheel-tracks had been smoothed over, but not quite enough. Branches had been ripped from trees to mask the guns and the scars on the tree-trunks stood out boldly, telling their tale of work having been done. Fresh-turned earth was scattered along the forward slope, glaringly apparent against the green-brown of the turf.

On the dawn of the third day of waiting, Ward surveyed the ground toward hidden Gloucester. The open, rolling meadows, dotted with random clumps of trees, ended in the low ridge. Some two hundred yards from the copse that sheltered his gun, a sandy track slanted off toward the ridge and the works of Gloucester Point that lay far beyond it. To the right were thick scrubby woods with another lane weaving erratically among the boles to join the first track.

In the early hush, broken only by the chirp and twitter of waking birds and the muted voices of the gun-crew in the copse, he reviewed what was known and what might be deduced. Tarleton's foraging party had left the Gloucester sally-ports at three o'clock, according to scouts. He would travel fast, since all pickets along his possible routes had been called in by Lauzun. Before long, he would be returning, laden with plunder. Carts, escorted by infantry, by green-jacketed troopers of Tarleton's

British Legion, by red-coated dragoons, would wind on east toward the ridge and the safety of Gloucester Point, following that track that slanted off across the open meadows. Not even a raw commander would take the wood-road with its hazards of ambush.

Ward looked at another copse where Caleb's crew had produced a fine effect of inefficient concealment. The underbrush stirred and Caleb came sauntering across the turf, hat tilted over his eyes. "Hey, Goat!" he hailed. "You all tethered, ready for the tiger?"

"Can't tell till the tiger comes along, Junior Goat," said Ward.

Caleb surveyed the brightening landscape dourly. "Listen, Ward, couldn't we fire just *one* round?"

"Against orders. All we've got to do is act panicky." He threw back his head as a dull slam drifted in from the east. "The first gun of the day. Must be one of d'Aboville's big ones. Now they're all joining in. God, but I'd like to be handling a battery over there."

"Not I," said Caleb, screwing up his face. "I'm a *good* soldier. I always like what I'm doing."

The sun climbed and long shadows pointed west across the meadows. Suddenly Ward cocked his head. "Hi! what's that? Hear it?" He dropped to one knee, head thrust forward. "Wheels — a lot of them."

The thud of hoofs, the grind of wheels and an occasional clank of metal came faint but clear from the woods, swelled to a solid stream of sound that seemed to funnel out of the wood road to the right front.

"Back to your gun, Caleb. On the double," cried Ward. As he spoke a squad of horsemen in brass helmets and green jackets appeared as though they had ridden out from behind a curtain. They rode slowly toward the junction of the two lanes. Ward made a gesture of exasperation. "Hell and death. They didn't spot us. Get your men stirring — just enough to attract attention." Caleb was already sprinting across the bare hundred yards that separated the two masked guns.

The carts were rolling heavily out of the woods, laden with oat-sacks and hay, with country produce. Some twenty head of cattle. More horsemen, this time in scarlet jackets, with white plumes whipping from brass helmets. Long files of red-coated infantry guarding carts and cattle. Dragoons again —

Ward glanced back at the copse that sheltered his gun and his men, saw tense faces peering from between the trees.

An officer had ridden out of the woods at the head of a small staff. The metal of his helmet was buried in a mass of tossing plumes. The scarlet of his jacket was vivid as new-shed blood, his white leather breeches shone immaculate above glossy boots. Behind Ward, someone yelped, "That's the bloody bastard! Seen him before."

Tarleton reined in at the junction of the two ways, shading his eyes against the glare of the sun as he carefully scanned the terrain in front of him. Ward darted into the copse and set his men milling about. One of them, according to plan, broke from cover and raced off toward Caleb's piece.

Ward could see Tarleton stiffen, rise in his stirrups. His hand flew high over his helmet and he seemed to be shouting to a little bugler who rode close behind him. The call sailed high and clear through the morning air and the woods seemed to boil as more red dragoons poured out into the open, followed by squads of the green-jackets of Tarleton's Legion. The carts broke into a lumbering trot and most of the infantry guards formed ranks at the double on the right of the troopers.

Without looking behind him, Ward snapped, "Corporal! Get your men ready. They're going to charge, sure as hell. Let them see you, then break for the thick woods in the rear. The cavalry can't touch you there. Move, now!"

268

Ward shot a quick glance toward Caleb's copse. The crew over there was breaking into the open in a wild mass. Caleb appeared among them, waving his arms, brandishing a pistol as though trying to stop the flight. He was jostled aside and Ward lost sight of him.

Down in the meadows the cavalry formed. Dragoons and Legion were in a great half-moon, red in the center, green at both ends. The infantry formed at the far right flank, ready to support the horsemen if serious opposition developed. Tarleton's horse minced daintily out in the curve of the half-moon. Ward saw a blade glitter, the bugle sang out again. The red dragoons started at a walk while the green of the Legion broke into a smart trot, curving wide to take both guns from the flank.

Something crashed in the brush behind Ward. A hand fell on his shoulder and Caleb panted, "Got the boys off, all right."

Without looking around, Ward growled, "You're supposed to have gone with them."

"So were you," panted Caleb. "Get on your feet and hit for the woods. Those green boys are getting close."

Ward saw a squad working slowly up at his right, not fifty yards away. Suddenly their leader turned in his saddle, faced toward Tarleton, raised his saber, lowered it. The boy behind Tarleton sent a clear call ringing through the soft air and the whole glittering half-moon broke, moved more quickly but still at a walk.

Caleb tugged at Ward's elbow. "For God's sake hurry. I knew that damned Duke's watch would be slow!"

Ward started to break for the woods but it was too late. Four troopers were riding cautiously over the open ground between the copse and the woods, carbines resting easily across their forearms.

Ward tugged Caleb back into the undergrowth of the copse. "Stay quiet! They haven't seen us — " As he spoke, a series of flat reports echoed from the woods. The leading trooper dropped his carbine, folded his arms slowly across his chest and pitched sideways from the saddle. Two files behind him, another trooper gave a leap, fell heavily. The remaining horsemen whirled their mounts about and galloped off headlong toward the still distant main body.

Ward wiped his forehead. "Those damn gunners! They weren't supposed to stay this close."

"Lucky for us they stayed and used their carbines. Come on. Hurry!"

"Hold hard," cried Ward. "That patrol'll be back with more strength. We'll—here's the answer." He broke into the open, seized the nearer horse that was grazing peacefully by its dead master. "Get the other one. That's it. Up with you. Hi! Here they come! Follow me!" He swung into the saddle and spurred his horse as more Legion troopers appeared, skirting a dense thicket that masked the whole slope from Ward.

He tried to follow the high ground that ran between the two copses, but his mount kept heading away to the right, toward the hidden slope and Tarleton's cavalry. Suddenly more bugles sounded. The horse tossed its head, caught the bit in its teeth and shot off toward the meadows. Ward tugged at the reins, but his mount only strained the harder, its hoofs thudding into the turf.

There was open space before Ward. To his right, a solid wall of red and green moved on at a sharp trot. He wrenched at the reins again, hoping to keep a course that would cut across the great moving half-moon of men and horses, cut across while avoiding the outflung tips. If he could just make the empty ground off to his left front—

But there was no empty ground to the left front. Instead Ward saw a swift-moving wall of sky blue, topped with dancing plumes. Ward gave a great shout of relief, fought hard to keep

270

his horse's head turned toward safety. He saw pennons flutter, saw their bright colors dip. Over the pound of hoofs he could hear the troop-officers shouting, *"Pointez! Pointez!"* as the lances were leveled. Half blinded by the rush of air past him, he saw the red-breeched officers drop back among the lances, saw the lines close again.

Then the first troop was past him, hurtling on toward Tarleton's red and green arc. Ward's horse spun, nearly unseating him, closed in on the flank of the troop. Now the whole sweep of the meadows was before him and his eye caught scattered details like a series of swift pictures — the British infantry hurrying in fine order for the shelter of the woods; the British cavalry wheeling and twisting and re-forming to meet this new and deadly threat; the brilliant Tarleton passaging his horse and watching the maneuvers of his men with cool approval, barely bothering to glance at the onrush of Lauzun's lancers and the tight ranks of Irish chasseurs behind them; a new flash of color, a towering set of red and white heron's plumes above a fur busby and a voice shouting, "Tarleton! Where's Tarleton?"

Ward brought his horse about in a wide circle close to the woods from which Tarleton's column had emerged. The fight was behind him and the men with whom he had charged were reforming expertly.

Ward was carried about helplessly. The infantry had begun firing from the woods, carefully so as not to risk hitting their own troopers. Occasional riderless horses blundered across his path or cannoned into his mount, looming suddenly through the golden dust haze that rose over the meadows.

All at once Ward was in a clear space on the fringes of the fight and he drew rein for an instant, trying to collect himself. This was the first true cavalry action that he had ever seen and he felt out of his element. He could find no sure pattern in the swift dashes, the quick rallyings for another charge. He made off toward a troop of lancers that was re-forming a little way up the slope.

Then out of the tumult two men burst, two vivid, plumed men who rode nearly side by side, their blades playing like living fire. Lauzun's heron feathers sailed high above the dust, matching the toss and sway of Tarleton's darker crest. They broke, rode off in tight circles, closed again, the clang of their swords growing louder. They were close to Ward and even he could see that Lauzun was pressing the fight, driving Tarleton farther and farther from the melee, his sword darting and flicking as he sought an opening. Once they swirled so close that Ward could see Tarleton clearly, his almost girlishly handsome face set and his wide forehead gleaming with sweat.

Ward gripped his saber tighter, urged his horse forward. "Surrender, Colonel Tarleton!" he yelled.

Lauzun roared, "Do not interfere! I order you!"

Ward rocked in his saddle as a horse jarred against his. Chasseurs and dragoons were all about him. He parried a slashing blade with the pommel of his saber, broke clear, headed back again toward Lauzun and Tarleton. The Colonel was giving ground fast and his face was deadly pale. Ward saw Lauzun parry a rather shaky cut, then shoot out his own blade in lightning *riposte*.

Ward pulled up suddenly, staring as Lauzun stared. Tarleton was gone. Two horses lay on the ground, Tarleton's underneath, pinned by a dragoon's mount from whose side jutted the shattered shaft of a lance. The dragoon lay motionless on the ground a few yards away. Then red stirred in the tangle of horseflesh. With a dancer's grace, Tarleton pulled himself clear, sprang to his feet shouting, "This way, lads!" Two dragoons thundered up, closed in on him. He caught a stirrup leather of each horse and the dragoons swept him away between them, the Colonel's boots winking in giant strides.

Lauzun sat his horse, flushed and panting, his saber dangling from his wrist at the end of a braided gold and scarlet lanyard. "But he was mine." Lauzun's voice was shaky. "Up to that last second." He glared at Ward. "You saw it. I call on you as witness. An imbecile of a lancer knocked a dragoon's horse against Tarleton's. He was thrown to the ground, then spirited away." His clenched teeth showed under his carefully trimmed mustache.

"The whole Legion must have seen it, *Monsieur le Duc!*" said Ward. "Tarleton was giving ground fast."

Lauzun's color slowly became more normal. "Ah, well. The fortunes of war. But another time — *Sapristi*, but he has a pretty trick of the wrist, that one. You noted it? It recalls that of — " He looked keenly at Ward. "'Ah, but I know you. I must report that you did very well with your guns. Now I must see what my little rascals are up to." He stood in his stirrups, rapidly surveying the field. Tarleton's men, in considerable disorder, were milling about close by the woods. Lauzun nodded. "One more charge and we break them. I shall lead it in person. You, Monsieur, will oblige me by riding at my left. Thus together we — " He broke off, stared hard toward the east.

Ward followed his glance. The distant low ridge was crested with red, with heavy masses of British infantry that moved steadily on toward Tarleton's men. Lauzun struck the pommel of his saddle angrily. "The whole Gloucester garrison marches out. We are not strong enough to force conclusions with them." He raised his voice. *"Trompette. Trompette. Sound the rassemblement!"*

Ward straightened in his saddle, rubbing his forehead. "It's over. And — but what the devil happened to Caleb? Oh, well, he probably took the gunners back to camp."

Off to the left, Irish chasseurs were herding a string of prisoners in green coats and red. A surgeon and his aides were searching for wounded, while a black-clad farrier-sergeant was swinging a short, heavy mallet against the heads of disabled horses.

A clump of bushes beyond a huddle of dead dragoons stirred, crackled fiercely. A helmetless man in a green jacket lunged out, arms and legs thrashing. One foot was still deeply embedded in the thicket, then was awkwardly withdrawn. A small, wiry man in a torn blue jacket was clinging desperately to it. Ward urged his horse toward the bushes. "Hang on, Caleb. I'm coming!" he shouted. A file of lancers clattered after Ward, shouting with him as they unslung their lances.

The dragoon stumbled and Caleb bore him to the ground. "Got him, Ward! Lie still, damn you!"

Ward reached far from the saddle, caught the green collar and jerked the dragoon to his feet. Then he stopped. Without loosing his grip, he dropped to the ground, saying in a cold voice, "So you're in your true colors at last, Houston."

"You know him, Ward?" Caleb barked. "I've got a score to settle with him. After he surrendered he tried to pull a knife."

Houston's jaw sagged and his head slumped forward. Then his eyes flicked toward Ward and he gave a rusty laugh. "You came up about the right time, Ward. Now I'm on firm ground at last."

"Hope you like the ground in the prison-pen," said Ward.

"Come now, you're smarter than that, Ward. Why do you think I'm wearing this coat? Frost and that damned Paul left me stranded in Yorktown, after promising that I'd get home. What could I do? I signed up with Tarleton's Tories, figuring there'd be action and I'd get a chance to desert to my own side."

Caleb snapped, "What about that knife?"

Ward laid a hand on Caleb's arm. "Steady, Caleb. This is the Houston who left the *Sauvage* at Cap Haitien. Remember? We're going to make him do a lot of talking."

Houston smiled sourly. "Can't make me talk against my will. I'm a free-born American. I got my rights."

"You're going to answer a lot of questions," said Ward quietly.

"So you think."

"Well, if I'm wrong there's only one other thing to do. Caleb and you and I and these lancers will ride to the British lines under a flag of truce. We'll turn you back to Tarleton as a would-be deserter whom we don't want. And there'll be men from your troop who'll remember you skulked in action."

Houston looked shiftily at Ward. "The trouble with you is, you're soft-smart. A hard man like Tarleton'd try to make me talk and then send me back just the same. You're just mealy-mouthed enough to keep your word. All right. I'll talk. But you've got to see that I get with Massachusetts troops."

"We aren't bargaining," said Caleb tersely.

"Correct," said Ward. "Talk or go back to Tarleton. After that, the provost'll have to make up his mind about your status."

"I got your word?" asked Houston sullenly.

"You have. First of all, where's Miss Dale?"

"In the Stannard house in Yorktown, right under the bluffs by the river. Mrs. Lathrop and Paul are with her and is he in a stew! Cornwallis won't even see him. Frost's berthing on the *Skagen*."

"Could you draw a plan showing us just where the Stannard house is?"

"I'll draw it. What else?"

"What else?" echoed Ward. "You sound as if you think you're through. You've just begun."

Caleb broke in, "This is going to take time, I guess. Let's get on to our hut."

Ward signed to the lancers and one of them bound a thong

about Houston's right arm, slipped the free end through a ring on his saddle. Ward and Caleb mounted and the little group clattered off toward the Franco-American camp.

"I'll send word to Tremarec as soon as we get in," Ward said to Caleb. "He ought to be with us." Caleb nodded approvingly.

In the dim hut, Ward sat alert on the edge of his bunk. Caleb stood by the flimsy door, his back against it. By the rear wall Houston perched awkwardly on a stool, sipping at a mug of spruce-beer. Ward looked at his watch. "Come along, Houston, we've been talking nearly ten minutes and so far you haven't told us a thing."

Houston drank again. "You're asking about stuff that happened before I ever heard of the damned *Sauvage*."

Ward sighed wearily. "I know I'm talking about things that happened before you joined us. But you spent hours with Paul Dale, going over papers, taking dictation. You must have learned plenty."

Houston set down his mug. "All right. I learned plenty. I guessed more. It all starts a long time ago." He leaned forward, dropping his voice to a confidential half-whisper. "Of course you've guessed who was back of everything."

"I haven't guessed. You better tell me," said Ward.

At that moment the door shoved gently against Caleb's back and Tremarec entered, bowing calmly.

Ward rose quickly. "Good of you to come, Captain. We thought you might be interested in our guest. We've only just started talking."

Tremarec seated himself. "I came the instant your message reached me. Yes, your guest does interest me in many ways. His status is interesting. A prisoner of war and at the same time a deserter from a French ship. I feel that I have some small claim on him."

Houston rallied himself. "Try and enforce French law on an American on American soil!" he snarled.

Tremarec nodded affably. "I agree that there might be legal difficulties. Perhaps the question will not arise. Proceed, my dear Gratwick."

Ward jerked a thumb toward Houston. "Better start talking."

Slumped forward on his stool, Houston talked in a dull, heavy voice. It had all begun long ago, probably before he had reached France. Many people had been interested in stopping or diverting the shipment of arms and gold to America, some because they objected to helping a revolt against an established monarchy, others because they scented personal profit.

Paul and Jabish Frost had become leading spirits in the second category. It was a risky business. "Don't know but what they'd have quit if she hadn't kept prodding them," said Houston reflectively.

Ward said quickly, "Whom do you mean by 'she'?"

"She?" Houston looked surprised. "Lathrop, of course. She's the brains. Paul's smart enough and so's Frost, but she —" He wagged his head in reluctant admiration.

"I confess," said Tremarec, "that that point escaped me. Yes, on looking back, I believe that we may place credence in this. You do not mention the girl, I observe."

Houston made a dismissive gesture. "Forget about her. She was just there. Funny thing, though, Paul sets a world of store on her. She was to share equal on all profits, but she knew nothing about the plan."

"A further question," said Tremarec. "How did they manage to get aboard my ship? Also, why did they want to? They could have stayed in Paris, let others carry out the details and still profited."

Houston gave a sly grin. "Not them. You see, the merchant prince had been speculating. He was in on a lot of smuggling, in buying up army supplies, in Spanish dealings that I haven't figured out. He had something to do with the tax-farmers and with commerce between Holland and England. All of a sudden, things began to go wrong. He lost a mint of money. So did Frost and Mrs. Lathrop. The girl's money went, too. But they moved fast and before word got around, they realized what they could do. Frost sailed from a Portuguese port for Martinique, ready for the arrival of the *Sauvage*. Paul used his influence to get the Minister of Marine to frank him through to Lorient and the *Sauvage*." He looked at Tremarec. "If you had touched Martinique, your cargo would have been taken over and transferred to another ship."

"The *Skagen?*" asked Ward abruptly.

"You're learning fast," said Houston. "Oh, don't worry. The transfer would have been perfectly legal — so far as papers went. By the time people had begun to ask questions, the *Sauvage*'d have been on its way back to France. Those who planned the transfer would have been on board the *Skagen,* bound for — well, it doesn't matter now. Anyhow, that dispatch boat sent us to Cap Haitien, didn't it? Wasn't the plan ruined?" He chuckled to himself. "By God, no. As soon as your orders were changed, Frost shipped up to Cap Haitien in the *Skagen,* with a new plan of attack. He was waiting for us when we came in."

"Hold on a minute," said Caleb. "What would have happened to Frost and the others if the Martinique plan hadn't been changed?"

"With their share of the loot and the sale of the cargo, they'd have set up as West India traders. They'd have done well, too. The islands are full of their kind." He hunched his shoulders and stretched out his legs.

"But you have not told us how you suddenly appear on an American battlefield when all thought you a mere runaway seaman in Haiti," said Tremarec.

"Runaway be damned, I went ashore on the orders of the merchant prince," said Houston. He grinned at Ward. "Did you like that beautiful good-by letter I wrote you? Paul dictated that, along with the one I was supposed to have left with him. Then I came north on the *Skagen* with Frost to get things in order for your arrival here." He frowned. "Funny thing about Paul Dale. God, but he's suspicious. He sent me on the *Skagen* so's I could watch Frost and the same time he had Frost watching me. He was afraid we'd try something that'd leave him out."

Houston rose. "That's the whole story. Better take me to the provost now. I can prove that I was enlisted with Tarleton under duress. And I can prove I quit my troop as soon as action was joined, hoping to desert."

Ward looked at Houston. "You've just begun. Suppose you tell about the opium you got from Brotier."

Houston lowered his head. "Don't know what you're talking about," he muttered.

Ward gave a contemptuous grunt, then wrenched the door open. "Sergeant!" he called. "Got the white flag there? And the trumpeter to sound for a parley? We'll turn him over to Tarleton as a deserter."

Houston jumped from the stool. "God damn it, Ward, you've bust your word. I've told you what I know and — "

"Mount up!" shouted Ward to the lancers.

"No, no!" Houston's voice cracked. "I — I'll tell you — "

Ward signaled to the lancers to remain as they were and closed the door. "We were talking about opium and curry to start with."

Houston was trembling. "I had to do it, Ward. By God, you don't know Paul. Of course, he paid me for it, but if I'd refused, my life wouldn't have been worth a sou. Sure, I saw you got drugged and it wasn't just once. Then Paul and I took that packet off you and he hitched on one he had with him. I don't know where it came from. Don't look so damn mad. Hell, you'd have done the same thing in my place."

"That I am inclined to doubt," said Tremarec softly. "How about the marlinspike that fell from a mast? Likewise the narrow escape our friend had from drowning, when he was saved by poor Doriot?"

"Didn't have a thing to do with any of that," exclaimed Houston. "Paul sent me forward among the sailors to find a man who'd do a risky job. I found him and told him to see Paul. That's all. Then later when this man Doriot had failed twice I had to find another sailor to see that Doriot didn't talk. It wasn't hard. A good part of the crew was placed on the *Sauvage* by people interested in the cargo. See? *I* didn't have anything to do with that sort of thing, any more than I did with showing that light for British ships to spot. I just found the man to do it. Put yourself in my place and you'd have done the same thing, like I said before."

"Even to the point of smearing yourself with blood and pretending you'd been helping out with the wounded?" asked Ward with a grim smile. "Go on with the story. I want to know the why of the marlinspike and the near-drowning."

"It was that tube you fished up," explained Houston. "Paul put some papers in it — what they were I don't know — and told me to weight it with shot and drop it overboard. Guess the shot and the papers worked loose somehow and the tube came up. Then I had to get it out of your cabin. Paul said he'd heard you'd seen the tube being picked up near Franklin's and would recognize it and maybe link him up with the whole thing. At Cap Haitien, Frost told Paul he was a jiggety fool, that there were thousands of tubes like it in the world."

"There was no quarrel between Paul and Frost?" asked Ward.

"Oh, they didn't get along too well, but Lady Lathrop always smoothed things over."

"Then I am moved to inquire why Frost's men took the pains to bind the young gentleman so firmly when they boarded my ship," said Tremarec.

Houston winked at him. "All planned a long time ago. The gold is gone, Frost is gone. The merchant prince looks as innocent as hell, due to the tying. He'd have a good story for the high-and-mighty patriot generals and could maybe do a little business in their camp. *She* thought of that." He began to chuckle hoarsely. "God Almighty, I wish you could have seen Frost's face when he swam ashore. I was waiting with some pack-horses to cart the gold away and he stormed up, cursed me and then kicked every damn horse we had."

Ward cut in sharply. "All right. Anyone got any more questions?" Caleb and Tremarec shook their heads. "Then we'll have the lancers take this man to de Choisy's provost. I'll send word that he's to be carefully watched and kept where we can get him when we want him."

When the lancers had taken Houston away, Caleb shook himself like a wet dog. "What a yarn."

"Fantastic," Ward agreed.

"Not at all," observed Tremarec. "I, who speak to you now, I have knowledge of plots and counterplots that make the present tale seem like an everyday occurrence in some sleepy Breton town. Yet there is one character in this tale of ours whom we must further consider."

"The girl," said Caleb.

"We've got to reach her, get her away from those others," Ward said grimly.

Tremarec raised his eyebrows. "But she may wish to remain. We know the strong tie between her and the brother."

"At least we've got to give her the chance to get out. If she doesn't want to take it — well, we've done our part. Damn it, though, there's another thing. Houston said Paul had lost all her money. However she chooses, she's in a bad spot."

"Such was my first thought," observed Tremarec. "Then I recalled that in the camp of your Washington I met many officers. One was of New Jersey, and from him I inquired concerning the family, which I found to be well known. Not too pleasantly known in these time. The father of Mademoiselle has been embroiled with the Royalists to the extent of joining the British in New York. His properties have been confiscated by the patriots. I remarked to this officer that Mademoiselle was a profound patriot, whereat he assured me that, her status being proved, her father's estates will be made over to her."

Caleb stared at him. "That's true enough. It's happened time and again to my knowledge. But her father! Isn't the girl going to have anyone left?"

Tremarec looked gravely at him. "Yes, my friend. The country which she discovered for herself, with the help of our Gratwick, remains. It will mean much."

"Besides," added Ward, "I'm sure that she and her father were never very close. Beyond sending money, he doesn't seem to have paid much attention to her after she left home and she rarely mentioned him to me. But when she learns about Paul — " He shook his head dubiously.

"She must suspect something now," said Caleb. "Lord, that packet that Paul made her lug around. That ought to tell her a lot. She'll have guessed more at Yorktown, finding out that Paul duped her into going there. She'll have to hear the rest from us."

"We first having succeeded in finding her," said Tremarec. "You gentlemen have, I judge, both thought and talked about our plan which was interrupted by Lauzan's pretty action. You still regard it as possible."

"Tough, but possible," said Caleb.

"Not so very tough," argued Ward. "A landing by forty or fifty men would probably fail. But just us, drifting across in a skiff at night and getting ashore a bit below the spot where the British right touches the river — No, I'd say our chances were excellent. We know from spies that there are lots of refugees, hangers-on, men from disbanded Tory units drifting about the place. We'll be going in where no one will be watching."

"Maybe," said Caleb. "How about uniforms, though?"

"What'll the uniforms of disbanded Tories be like?" asked Ward. "Just about like ours. Anyhow, I've laid hold of an old gunner's jacket like yours, blue faced with red. The same colors that the Royal Artillery wears. As for the Captain, well, in his blue sea-cloth he could be from any ship. The main thing is to go about our business as though we didn't care whether we were questioned or not."

Tremarec nodded to Caleb. "Our friend speaks with logic. I, for one, agree with him. When shall we start?"

"Tonight," said Ward briskly. "The more I think of our chances, the better I like them. We'll meet here at sundown. I'll go get Houston to draw a plan to show us where this Stannard house is."

That night heavy clouds swept down over Virginia, carried by a high wind. Ward, Caleb and Tremarec stood on the banks of the York, staring bitterly at the waves that butted and lashed against the shore. Away to the left, half seen through curtains of rain, the fires of the British army on Gloucester Point cast a murky glow through the storm. "How about it?" asked Caleb, hurling a stone into the wild toss of the river.

Tremarec shook his head. *"Pas possible."*

A wet dawn broke and the York raged on. Far downstream Ward could see the tall masts of anchored ships rocking and dipping. A cloud of smoke hung over a bend in the river, an inky pall that Tremarec said must come from a burning vessel. The rain stopped and the wind slackened. Caleb went back to camp for rations. Ward and Tremarec, screened by bushes along the sloping bluffs, studied the river and the opposite bank. A dull mist still clung low, masking the houses of Yorktown, but land directly across showed up fairly well, and Tremarec began to orient himself.

"You observe, friend Gratwick," he said, "that the river is nearly the width of two of your miles here. Opposite us and a little upstream, the lines of the Duc de St. Simon touch the river, his most advanced post, a battery, being a half mile from the British. We shall wish to land well below him. Hence we shall cover at least three miles if we are to land at the upper edge of the town itself. Yes, it is a pretty problem of navigation."

"Risky?" asked Ward.

"I do not hold it so. Our true difficulties begin with the shore."

"I'll do the shivering afloat and you look after it ashore," laughed Ward. He looked up at the sky where the sun was trying to break through a film of dank cloud. "Weather's clearing. You know, Captain, there's one thing I don't understand. Firing stopped with the gale last night."

"Ah, you noted that, too?" said the Breton. "I confess I find it puzzling. Do both sides gather for a sudden rush, one upon the other?"

"Might be. Anyhow, the busier Cornwallis is, the less heed he'll pay to us."

Caleb returned with rum, bread and two cold roast fowl and the party breakfasted in the shelter of the skiff which lay on its side below the bluff. Caleb reported little news in camp. Patrols had come in telling of utter silence in the Gloucester works. Couriers were dashing in from the main army in a steady stream and there was an air of excitement about de Choisy's quarters.

"You did not, then, stay to probe this sense of excitement?" asked Tremarec.

"Why should I? Ward and I have got four-day leaves and why waste them hunting for headquarters gossip? If it's big news they'll send for us."

The day wore on, faded into night, and the river grew smooth. When the last of the fowl had been eaten, Tremarec turned to Ward. "You have selected the hour?"

"Caleb and I talked about it while you were asleep. We figure that the British change their guards on even hours — eight, ten, twelve and so on. Can you get us ashore, say at three o'clock? Any guard-posts we strike'll be at their least alert then. Caleb, have you heard a shot all days?"

Caleb shook his head. "Quiet as a boozing-ken on Sunday morning. It's creepy. I'd feel a lot happier if someone'd let off a coehorn every now and then. Wake me up when you're ready to start."

It must have been well past three o'clock, Ward reckoned, as he shoved his oars through the water with long, slow strokes, his eyes on Tremarec who sat erect in the stern. The passage had been far more difficult than any of them had anticipated. When they had first launched the skiff, the current caught it and bore it downstream. That had meant rowing back to shore again, finding a spot considerably higher upstream and starting again.

Ward's oars creaked on. All at once Caleb cried, "Steady!" Looking over his shoulder Ward saw him lunging with a long pole. He shipped his oars and the skiff came to a halt. Ward whispered, "What is it, Caleb?"

"Sort of a low wharf. Got my hands on it. I'll get out."

"No!" said Tremarec quickly. "A wharf gives off a hollow sound. Push ahead. There will be soft bank beyond it."

The skiff eased on, shivered slightly as its nose burrowed into a muddy bank. "Now ashore," said the Breton.

Ward joined Caleb on the shore, Tremarec following. "We must stay together," said Ward, still in an undertone. "Houston's chart should take us right to the Stannard house. If Deborah wants to come with us, we'll make for the skiff. If not, we'll just have to come back alone. Ready, you two?"

Tremarec laid a hand on Ward's cuff. "Much as I should like to be present when Mademoiselle joins us, it is better that someone stay with the skiff. It might drift away. Also, others might have ideas of leaving Yorktown. So I mount guard."

"I'll stay," said Caleb. "After all, she doesn't know me. She's sure to stick her head out of a window and if she sees people she knows and trusts, it'll be better."

"I mount guard," repeated Tremarec.

"Guess you're right," said Ward reluctantly. "But if daylight catches us here — though there's not much chance of that — back to the north bank you go. We'll hide somehow and meet you tomorrow night at the same place."

"Let the dawn concern itself with the dawn," said the Breton. "Good luck, my friends."

Caleb found the slippery path that followed the bank and took the lead. "Better grab my coattails," said Caleb. "God's ears, but it's dark. What time do you reckon it is?"

"Getting on toward four, I'm afraid."

They made their cautious way along the path, trying to pierce the thick cloak of the night. Ward began to worry as the path crept on, seemingly leading nowhere. If they had landed fairly close to the spot agreed on, they should be passing a tobacco warehouse on their right, marked clearly on Houston's chart.

All at once, Caleb dropped to the ground, a move which Ward followed with war-trained instinct. He worked up beside his companion, his heart suddenly jumping convulsively. He put out a tentative hand, felt turf rising in front of him, then the wicker-work of an earth-filled gabion. There was no need to say anything. Caleb could recognize a gun-position as well as he.

Caleb's face was close to his and he caught a faint whisper. "No sound in there. Going to have a look." Caleb slithered away in the dark. Ward crept after him, knew by instinct that the narrow opening of an embrasure was closing in on him. He put up one hand, touched the throat of a twenty-four pounder, bumped his shoulder against an iron-shod wheel.

From the darkness in front, Caleb spoke in a more natural voice. "Can't figure it, Ward. Not a soul here."

Ward pushed back his hat. "British position. No doubt of that. Then — then that means that Tremarec dumped us farther upstream than we figured. We must be at the extreme end of the British outer lines. But where is the gun-crew? Caleb, I don't like this."

"Me either. Look — maybe they've left this piece and maybe more farther inland, as bait to tempt St. Simon. Another ambush."

"Maybe. Anyhow, this is no place for us. Find the path again and keep going."

Caleb set out once more. Over his shoulder he muttered, "Still no firing! Only there's one hell of a big fire somewhere. See the glow on the clouds off there?"

Ward looked up. "Another ship, maybe, or some pile of stores." They made their slow way on. At the end of ten minutes, Ward saw that the distant glow was stronger. He caught Caleb by the shoulder. "Fire be damned. Caleb, that's dawn!"

"By God, you're right," Caleb said in a flat voice. "But we can't go back now. Those guns may be manned from dawn on. They've probably got infantry patrols out between the lines. What about the Captain?"

"Don't worry about Tremarec. He'll do the right thing."

287

"That's what I figured. Come on, then."

The path led down from high bluffs to the water front with its warehouses, wharves and heavy barges. Along the bluff, brick and wooden houses clung. More roofs showed on the high ground above. A British sergeant, a Welsh fusilier by his facings, came down an alley, followed by four soldiers with kettles. The detail stopped at a pump and filled the kettles.

Ward walked on as calmly as he could. Caleb was absently whistling "The British Grenadiers," hands shoved deep in his pockets. Two of the privates looked up as they passed, but showed no sign of interest. Safely beyond the pump, Caleb said, "Sad-looking bastards, weren't they? The sergeant looked as if he was going to bust out crying and the men were worse than that. Must be a punishment detail."

"Certainly didn't give a damn about us. Say, not a single guard at the wharves. There's the big warehouse Houston told us about. We turn right up the second lane to find the Stannard house."

Caleb glanced up a cobbled alley. "H'm, maybe we better wait a bit. Companies are falling in up there. Funny as hell. Not a bugle, not a drum-beat."

From a doorway on the right a captain of Highlanders cannoned out, jostled heavily against Ward, then hurried on, mumbling, "Later, later!" as though Ward had stopped to question him.

Caleb stared after him. "What's the matter with this damn town?"

Ward saw another street thick with red coats and shabby cocked hats. "They're massing for something. Can Cornwallis be planning to break out?"

"Maybe we'll know some day. Let's get to the Stannard house."

More and more townspeople were in the lower streets. "Caleb, we could have prowled Yorktown any day we wanted. The only hurdle would have been getting in," muttered Ward.

"And getting out. But you're right. No one's even looking at us. This must be where we turn."

"And that's the Stannard place. A garden to the right and what used to be a carriage shed behind it. Here we are. I'd better go up alone."

He ran up the scarred wooden steps and rapped on the door. While waiting for an answer to his summons, he looked out over a long stretch of the York. Masts jutting out of the water showed where ships had been sunk by mortar-fire or scuttled. Other craft lay at anchor, their decks lifeless.

Ward rapped again, then pushed at the door. It swung open, showing a long, narrow hall with rooms opening from either side. He was about to call out when he heard a familiar voice somewhere on the second floor. The words came muffled but distinct. "Paul! I told you I would *not* leave. Please go away. I said I didn't want to see you again and I meant it."

Ward beckoned to Caleb who ran lightly up the steps. "The brother must be here. This may be a job for two men."

"I was kind of hoping for that. What's the next step?"

Ward called, "Deborah! We've come for you. Never mind about Paul. We'll see to him."

There was silence. Then Deborah appeared at the head of the stairs, white-faced and staring. Then she came down the steps, her hands outstretched. "Ward! I thought you must be Paul! He was coming back for me. Please don't let them take me to the *Skagen*." She looked up at him, her eyes haunted. "Ward! I know everything now. My brother, Paul. He's still my brother, Ward, but I just can't go on with him."

Caleb, eyes on Deborah, said, "You don't have to, Miss Dale. We know about you. You're too good a soldier for us to let go."

Deborah turned to Caleb. "Thank you, Mr. — " Ward hastily

introduced Caleb, and Deborah went on. "And I know about you, Mr. Blair." Her expression darkened again. "Ward, I don't want to go to the *Skagen*. They're all there now, even that dreadful Mr. Frost. Paul will be here any minute now to get me."

"He's coming back soon? That won't do. Can you think of a place where we can hide until dark? Then we'll take you back with us."

Deborah's eyes widened. "Hide till dark? But we don't have to do that. Why can't we go right now?"

"But Paul might sort of point us out to some of the gentlemen in red," Caleb said. "They'd wonder how we got here. Let's move, anyway. You show us where."

Deborah looked amazed. "*He* point you out to the British? Haven't you — " She broke off. "Come with me." She led the way up the stairs and stopped by a broad window in the rear of the house.

Ward whistled. A good section of the Yorktown defense was spread out before him and the fields between the town and the inner works were thick with troops in red or green. The streets that he could see were choked with solid red columns, the same grenadiers and light infantry and line companies that he had faced again and again over the long war years. Men were moving into sight along the crests, pouring down toward the field where the British waited, men in faded blue coats, in hunting shirts, in old cocked hats, in wide country hats, in battered light-infantry helmets. They came on in orderly files, squads breaking off to enter half-seen gun-pits, to man empty trenches.

Ward tried to shout, but his throat tightened. Caleb croaked, "Off to the right! Look to the right." The scene was repeated, only the actors were trim in white uniforms. In the mid-distance the British stirred and Ward saw that their colors were cased, muffled in dull oil-cloth. Fifes began to squeal down in the streets and drums beat dirgelike as the waiting troops moved sullenly out to join their fellows in the flat lands.

On the far left of the defense, bright color flared and men swarmed about a flagstaff, driving it deeper and deeper in the earth of the works that had faced them for so many days. The whole scene blurred before Ward as he recognized the red and white stripes, the starred blue canton of his flag. There was an answering flutter from the far right as the white and gold of France caught the morning breezes.

Caleb was muttering brokenly. "My God, my God! Cornwallis has surrendered."

Eyes still straining toward the colors, Ward said brokenly, "First Burgoyne, now Cornwallis. Of course, the main British army is still at New York."

"They'll be next," said Caleb. "I hardly hoped to see a sight like this — but somehow I always knew I would. Look at our colors off there!"

Ward suddenly took Deborah's arm and turned from the window. "This is no place for us to be. Let's get out with the troops."

Deborah let Ward lead her out of the room. "You're right, Ward. Paul had better not find us here."

They went down the stairs and out into the street, Caleb closing in on Deborah's left. There would be a long wait, Ward reflected, and after that the defeated British army would file out somewhere beyond the works and lay down their arms.

Turning the corner off a street that ran upward from the river came two men. After them trailed a half-dozen tough-looking men from the water front.

Ward stepped quickly in front of Deborah as the two leaders stopped. Paul Dale looked coldly at Ward, while Jabish Frost seemed to be enjoying some private joke of his own.

"It's all over," said Ward. "You've lost, you two. Deborah's put herself under our protection."

Paul's face flushed. "This is no affair of yours, Gratwick. She's my sister. She's coming with us. Let's have no trouble."

Ward watched the dock-hands closing in behind Paul. Some of them carried short clubs and he caught the gleam of a knife or two. "No trouble," said Paul again.

Caleb, with Deborah on his arm, stepped up beside Ward. "Look behind you," he said to Paul, triumph in his voice.

Ward saw a big man in blue sea-cloth and white breeches climbing the hill behind Paul. After him came file after file of men in cocked hats and white coats, bayonets slanting up past their cockades.

Paul and Jabish Frost turned quickly. Frost gave a short yelp and scuttled off down an alley. Paul drew himself up, eying Tremarec coldly. "If you try to interfere with me, Captain —" he began.

Tremarec smiled pleasantly. "I? Such is not included in my powers. But I may not answer for the little white devils who follow me. I judge that you wish to persuade Mademoiselle to accompany you. Should you attempt force, I feel quite sure that they would show their resentment in a rather marked way."

Paul's face contracted in anger. Then he squared his shoulders, faced about and strode off down the hill, his head high. His toughs were nowhere to be seen.

The Breton bowed deeply to Deborah, whose eyes were following her brother, hurt and clouded. "I rejoice that I am in time, Mademoiselle, though I am sure that our young friends could have handled matters most competently. May I say that, so long as the *Sauvage* is in American waters, you must consider it your home?"

Deborah inclined her head silently.

"Not for long, though," said Ward. "The Commander will

see that Lady Washington looks after her at Mount Vernon. That is, if it suits you, Deb."

"Whatever you say, Ward." Deborah's eyes were still on the ground and her voice was low. "But they can't keep me forever. I heard about Father joining the Crown. I — I'll find some other place to go."

"It's been found for you," answered Ward. "We'll talk to General Wayne and he'll see you get up into Pennsylvania. After that — why, you'll find Faith waiting for you."

Deborah looked up at Ward wonderingly. "You'll send me to Faith — after — after all this?"

"Where else? You'll find she knows a lot about you and will welcome you back among your own people."

"Thank you, Ward. I'd like to go to Faith," said Deborah in a low tone.

"That's settled, then. The siege is over. Everything is over. Now we'd better see about arranging things for you. Do you feel like walking through to our lines, or shall I see about a horse for you?"

"I'd like to walk, Ward."

"Then Caleb will lead the way. Come along, Captain."

"But with pleasure," answered Tremarec. "Just one little instant — my little devils, you know. There is a matter in which you can assist me. If Mademoiselle and my friend Blair will proceed slowly, perhaps you and I shall overtake them."

Deborah and Caleb started off up the street that led inland. Ward turned to his companion. "You really need my help, Captain?" he asked.

Tremarec smiled. "I have ever found it valuable. It is well, though, that Mademoiselle get out of earshot. You see, at dawn I learned of the coming surrender, through seeing a party of the Agenais leave their works. Thinking you might be in difficulties in the town, I persuaded the officer in charge to have them accompany me. Irregular, if you wish, but after all, the siege was over."

"So that's how you happened to appear just when you did?"

"How else? I found the chart of Houston a little confusing, but it served. I also had a hope that somehow we might find Messieurs Frost and Dale who have much to answer for to me as master of the *Sauvage*."

"A pity they got away," said Ward. "Though of course you couldn't have taken Paul right under his sister's eyes."

"But of course not. Ah, she is brave, that little one. I watch her face and see her win her fight over despair. Nonetheless, I do not say that our two gentlemen have escaped us."

"You can hardly hope to catch them now. They'll be off for the *Skagen*."

Tremarec said soothingly, "Ah, but you do not understand, my friend. These are not the only troops in town. Look down at the foot of the hill and you will see white coats and more white coats. You see, I found that my good Keratry had come over to see friends among the Duc de St. Simon's troops. He saw me from the works and ran to join me. Since he knows both our Messieurs and blocks every way to the wharves, I feel sure —" He paused, then smiled. "Look down yonder."

There were many white coats along the street that paralleled the water front. The familiar form of Keratry appeared among them, peered up the hill, then raised a vast arm. Tremarec answered the signal. "Yes, friend Gratwick. We have them both. It will be as well if Mademoiselle imagines them safe on the *Skagen*. Now shall we follow? And as we go, Monsieur, permit me to congratulate you on the success of your General Washington and his admirable army."

A very few hours had passed since the seizure of Paul Dale and Jabish Frost, but it seemed to Ward that a great deal had

294

been accomplished concerning the immediate problems that affected him and his little group. The Commander, of course, had been inaccessible, but his aide, Major Tench Tilghman, had assured Ward and Tremarec that Lady Washington's reception of Deborah at Mount Vernon could be taken for granted. A hurried word with Wayne, anxious to be off with his Pennsylvanians to take part in the surrender formalities, had taken care of an escort straight to Valley Forge and Fatland Ford.

Out in the York River, the *Skagen* lay at anchor between two of de Grasse's frigates. No action was to be taken against Mrs. Lathrop, but the next day Paul and Frost would face a Franco-American board, with Houston available for further questioning.

Now, in the early afternoon, with Deborah at headquarters and Caleb recalled to his guns, Ward stood on a hillock with Tremarec, looking in silent awe at the plain that stretched between the old Allied works and those of the British.

There were the French, the wiry Agenais, the Bourbonnais, the Royal Deuxponts, the Saintonge and their fellows. There was the bright bristle of lance-points that marked the lines of Lauzun's Legion, the glittering sabers of Dillon's Irish troopers. Heavy and menacing, d'Aboville's field pieces and heavier guns formed a dark mass under a flutter of gold-strewn white silk. Ward could make out Rochambeau in his dark blue, the toss of Lauzun's towering heron plumes, d'Aboville and de Mauduit with their ordnance.

These he could study with admiration, with friendship. But when he looked across at the ranks that faced the French, his vision was dimmed and he shook as though with a fever-chill. Benjamin Lincoln from his own state and von Steuben from Germany, Hazen the Canadian and Clinton from New York — the roll-call ran on through Ward's mind. John Laurens of South Carolina, Wyllys of Connecticut, Vose from Massachusetts and

295

Gimat from France. The Marquis must be there off to the far left —

It was increasingly hard for him to see. He could only identify well-remembered figures from their position in the great formation. That must be Wayne, that blur of blue and white with Walter Stewart close behind him. Mordecai Gist could be that touch of brown and red far behind Wayne, Henry Knox off there with the American artillery. And right and left of those patches of color stretched the lean regiments. Ward did not have to look at them. All through his months in France he had had them in mind. Hundreds and hundreds of men in town clothes, in country clothes, in hunting clothes. Worn, patched uniforms that had been cobbled up at home, smuggled in from France or captured from the British and treated to muddy dyes. Now at last he saw them in victory.

Tremarec's hand fell on his shoulder. "*Mon ami,* it would be worth a great treasure to see this as you must be able to see it, to look out there through your eyes which have seen so much, which have watched for so long."

The past whirled through Ward's mind. There was blood on the snow at Trenton, at Valley Forge, at Morristown, marking the path of a barefoot army. There were empty beef-barrels and cartridge pouches and silent guns with snow on their trunnions. There was panic at Long Island and Manhattan and Brandywine, blundering at Germantown and Monmouth. There was treason up the Hudson and mutiny in New Jersey. There were mass defections and typhus and cholera and small-pox. There was hardly a month in the six long years when a sensible man might not have said, "It is over. There is no more hope."

Down on the plains the lines were stirring, straightening. Shrill music slipped out of the mutter of drums in the British lines and the sally-ports were suddenly choked with marching scarlet and white. The British fifes were shrilling out "The

World Turned Upside Down" and behind them came the army of Cornwallis to lay down its arms in utter defeat.

The drab, ragged files stood to attention, their arms in their hands, in last salute to their beaten enemy. Ward thought suddenly of Passy and how, in a few weeks the news would be received there. "Men greatly in earnest," the Doctor would say.

Soon the Allied armies would wheel about, start north for the final drama that must take place near New York. Ward would march with them, riding beside his clanking gun-teams and the road would take him past a fieldstone house near Fatland Ford —and Faith.

"My friend," said Tremarec softly, "I repeat that I envy you."

Without taking his eyes from the shifting panorama, Ward answered, "Why should you envy us? What has brought this all about? There was de Grasse's victory at sea that cut Cornwallis off from any help. Rochambeau and St. Simon gave the added strength that was needed for the final stroke. In a way, I can envy you, for didn't your country really give us the means?"

Over the growing din of the fifes and drums, Tremarec said, "It is generous of you to see it thus. But reflect, my friend, that there were many factors working toward this same end. Of those, none was greater than one man whom we know. Instead of envy, one for the other, we may feel deep pride, you and I, that we may call the old philosopher of Passy our friend."

XIV

Faith

ON A WARM AFTERNOON in mid-December, Faith and Ward paused before the wicket gate in the outer wall to look up at the pointed towers of the Château de Chaumont.

"Everything is just as you described it, Ward," she said. "I could find my way to the Petit Manoir from here without any trouble." Ward smiled at her as he held open the gate. Her golden hair was bright under her dark green bonnet with its light green lining, and her brown eyes, gold-flecked, were dancing with excitement. "Show me the hollow tree where you found the tube," she said.

"It was over there to the left. But the Doctor wrote me that it's been cut down. Now here's the sunken garden, and see, the pools have been drained for winter. Let's slip up onto the terrace and surprise the Doctor. He won't expect us so soon." Ward took a thick packet of papers from inside his red-lined coat and handed them to Faith. "You give him these dispatches, dear, and tell him that this lot, at least, hasn't been tampered with."

"Poor Deborah," Faith sighed, as she took the papers. "What a shock it must have been to her when she found out about Paul. She's a brave person, Ward."

Just as they came to the top of the terrace steps, a liveried servant threw open the double doors from the rear wing of the house. The cat Minette marched proudly out, sniffing delicately and with her tail at a triumphant angle. After her, apple-wood staff gripped firmly and fur cap on the back of his head, came Benjamin Franklin. His spectacles were pushed up on his forehead and he was looking about him benignly. Three women followed and a few men brought up the rear.

"There's Madame Helvetius, Faith, laughing with the Doctor. And that's Madame Brillon — see, that pretty, trim little woman. I don't know the girl, but there's d'Alembert in the plum-colored coat, and Lavoisier arguing with a little fat man I've never seen before. It — "

The Doctor saw them and tucking his staff under his arm, hurried forward, both hands outstretched. Ward slipped his arm about Faith's shoulders. "Doctor — " he began.

But Franklin had their hands in his and was looking earnestly into their eyes. He was smiling but it seemed to Ward that the smile was a little unsteady. "My dear, dear children. So you've come back to me at last! Faith, my dear, you are very welcome and even prettier than Ward told me. You heard me say that you had come back? But you have. You may be seeing Passy for the first time, but I assure you that the walls here are very familiar with the sound of your name. Not only during the days when our young man was easing an old man's labors, but many times afterwards."

Faith quickly leaned forward and kissed the Doctor's wrinkled cheek. "This is the moment that we've been waiting for, Doctor Franklin. Ward's just a monosyllabic Yankee — except when he's talking about you."

Franklin beamed and patted her hand. "I knew this was to be a very rare day. You know, when I woke up this morning, there wasn't a trace of my plaguey gout and I took that for an omen. But I didn't quite visualize this meeting. Your letter from Rouen was most vague. But you couldn't have made me happier, just materializing as you did. Now you and I and Minette have a great deal to talk over. Let me present you to my guests and then we'll retire to my office."

Half an hour later, Faith and Ward were seated in the study that Ward knew so well. The Doctor had slipped out of his snuff-brown coat and was luxuriating in a new dressing gown, far more vivid and frivolous than the one Ward remembered. He smiled across at Faith who was ensconced in a deep arm-chair. She met his eyes and he knew that she had fallen under Franklin's spell at the first meeting as he himself had done.

Cakes and wine were set out on the paper-littered table, cakes from Madame d'Houdetot and wine from Madame Helvetius, the Doctor observed as he filled a glass and a plate for Faith. "Now, my children, before I even think of opening these let-ters — " he tapped the packet that Ward had given him — "let me inform you that in my more than seventy-five years I have been often astonished, but never more than when I received your tidings from Rouen — and never more pleasantly. May I ask what happy events transported you here?"

Ward smiled. "The Marquis had me appointed American aide to Lauzun, sir."

"But the Duke has been back in Paris for some time. He and Deuxponts brought the news of the surrender."

"Exactly," said Ward. "You see, I had very pressing business to attend to along the Schuylkill. Also this packet for you had to be prepared. You will find word in it from the Congress and the Commander. So the Marquis granted me leave to follow the Duke on a later ship. The *Sauvage,* in fact, whose captain sends you his warmest greetings."

"My dear friend Tremarec!" Franklin beamed. "I must not grudge him the very happy time that he is now spending with his family in Brittany, but I trust that my pleasure in greeting him here will not be too long deferred." He sat back in his chair, the tips of his fingers together. "You two, here in Passy. Then our Breton. How simple are the inner workings of great events. And often, how happy. But I wander. There are other people of whom we must speak, if only briefly."

Ward nodded. "I know, sir. Word has surely reached you about Paul Dale and his cousin, as well as Jabish Frost."

"I have heard. And their fate?"

"Nothing was done about Mrs. Lathrop," Ward went on. "Paul and Frost were banished. I believe that all of them are now in Jamaica busy with their usual occupations."

"But the little girl. Is she with them? Ward, I do not like to think of that."

"Faith dear, I think that's your story," said Ward.

"Ward sent her to me, Doctor. You see, she found out what the others were up to. Whatever bonds there were, she broke of her own free will." The cat Minette jumped purring into Faith's lap and she stroked it absently. "Now she's staying with my father and his sister. Later, she'll go into Jersey to live with her father. Ward and I heard, just before we sailed, that her father had been given a full pardon by the Congress. It seems that his Toryism was a pretense. We were so happy for Deborah."

Franklin looked gravely at her. "Yes, I can see that she was lucky to have a friend like you."

"She would have managed anyway," said Faith firmly. "She's rallied superbly and beaux were beginning to swarm about her before we left."

Franklin's smile seemed to warm the little room. "May our little Deborah for the rest of her life be as fortunate in her friends as she was with you two. Now let us consider the case of Lieutenant and Mrs. Ward Gratwick. What lies ahead of you?"

"We're to sail for home in January, I believe. Such things are easier now than when you sent me on my tour of France, Doctor."

Franklin sighed. "I never sent anyone out into the dark less willingly than I sent you. Nor was my mind any easier when I learned who your fellow passengers on the *Sauvage* were. Ugly rumors about Paul cropped up in Paris not long after you sailed. But to the future. You return to America. What then?"

"There'll be the spring campaign to get ready for. I'm to work directly under General Knox."

"H'm," said the Doctor, his eyes going from Ward to Faith. "Now really it seems to me, Faith, that Ward's done more than his share of fighting, seen more danger than any one man should." Faith's eyes were on the floor, but Ward thought that he caught a hint of twinkle back of the Doctor's spectacles. Franklin went on. "Now I have certain powers. There is no reason why I may not attach our young friend here to my person. Work, important work, remains to be done here."

"But, sir —" Ward broke in.

Franklin held up his hand. "Gently, gently, my young friend. One thing in marriage that you must learn is that you have to think for two, not merely for one. Faith, my dear, would you like to stay here at Passy with Ward, help him fight another kind of war for our country?"

Faith bent over the cat Minette, stroking its soft fur. Then she met Franklin's gaze. "Any woman would like to know that her husband is safe, Doctor, safe but also at ease in his mind. He wouldn't be at ease here, thinking of Henry Knox and the guns. I — I'm very proud indeed that you want Ward to be with you. But until there's peace we belong at home."

"There is often bigger work to be done for our country than on the battlefields," said Franklin in a low voice, and again Ward thought that he caught a glint of humor in his eyes.

"Faith's quite right," said Ward. "You've paid me a tremendous compliment, but home's where I belong."

Suddenly Franklin began to chuckle. "Man proposeth, Fate disposeth, if I may alter an old saw. My dear young friends, I regret greatly that it is I who have to overrule your wishes." He looked keenly at Ward. "You are not going back to the war. Wait — hear me out!" He smoothed back his long white hair. "Something has happened that will shake us profoundly, us and the whole world with us. Something we have dreamed about, hoped for, prayed for." He laid a hand on Ward's shoulder. "You are not going back to the war — because soon there will be no war to go back to."

Ward started to his feet. Faith had already risen and moved around the table to him. Franklin went on. "I've been in touch with London. His Majesty's Government is ready to sue for peace. Commissioners will be appointed. I am to represent the United States of America at the peace conference. I shall stand in great need of a discreet, competent secretary, preferably a quite newly married one." He gave a hand to Ward and Faith as he had at the first meeting on the terrace. "You and I, Faith, will never again have to wait and wonder when we hear of battles. They are over — for our country."

"Would you like to stay, Faith?" asked Ward.

"Of course I should — if you do," answered Faith quickly.

"Then that's settled!" cried the Doctor, his gravity vanishing in a sudden beam. "Now let us join our guests. Madame Brillon has composed a March of Victory to go with the Insurgents' March she wrote when we took Burgoyne. I shall accompany her on the armonica. A hymn to a victory that was not won *against* anything, but won *for* something, for our beliefs and our convictions. Would you mind handing me my stick, Ward. Thank you. Faith, will you take my arm? As Americans in true fact, let us go out among our well-wishers."

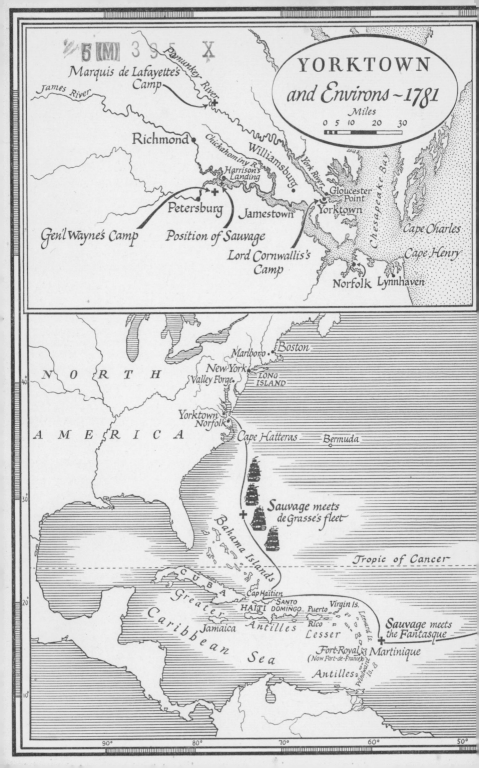

YORKTOWN
and Environs ~ 1781

Miles

0 5 10   20   30

Marquis de Lafayette's
Camp

James River

Pamunkey River

Williamsburg

Richmond

Chickahominy R.

Harrison's
Landing

York River

Gloucester
Point

Petersburg

Jamestown

Yorktown

Gen'l Wayne's Camp

Position of Sauvage

Chesapeake Bay

Cape Charles

Lord Cornwallis's
Camp

Cape Henry

Norfolk   Lynnhaven

N O R T H

Marlboro   Boston

New York
Valley Forge

LONG
ISLAND

A M E R I C A

Yorktown
Norfolk

Cape Hatteras

Bermuda

Sauvage meets
de Grasse's fleet

Tropic of Cancer

Bahama Islands

CUBA

Cap Haitien

Greater

HAITI

SANTO
DOMINGO

Puerto
Rico

Virgin Is.

Jamaica

Antilles

Lesser

Leeward Is.

Sauvage meets
the Fantasque

Caribbean

Fort-Royal
(Now Fort-de-France)

Martinique

Sea

Antilles

Windward Is.